Ben Pastor was born in Italy and lived for thirty years in the United States, working as a university professor in Illinois, Ohio and Vermont, before returning to her native country. *The Venus of Salò* is the eighth in the Martin Bora series published by Bitter Lemon Press and follows on from the success of *The Night of Shooting Stars*, *The Horseman's Song*, *The Road to Ithaca*, *Tin Sky*, *A Dark Song of Blood*, *Liar Moon* and *Lumen*. She is the author of other novels including the highly acclaimed *The Water Thief* and *The Fire Waker*, and is considered one of the most talented writers in the field of historical fiction. In 2008 she won the Premio Zaragoza for best historical fiction, and in 2018 she was awarded the prestigious Premio Internazionale di Letteratura Ennio Flaiano.

THE VENUS OF SALÒ

Ben Pastor

BITTER LEMON PRESS
LONDON

BITTER LEMON PRESS

First published in the United Kingdom in 2024 by
Bitter Lemon Press, 47 Wilmington Square, London WC1X OET
www.bitterlemonpress.com

Copyright © 2006, 2022 by Ben Pastor

This edition published in agreement with Piergiorgio
Nicolazzini Literary Agency (PNLA)

The moral rights of Ben Pastor have been asserted in accordance
with the Copyright, Designs and Patents Act 1988

A CIP record for this book is available from the British Library

ISBN 978–1–916725–06–5
eBook USC ISBN 978–1–916725–07–2
eBook RoW ISBN 978–1–916725–08–9

Typeset by Tetragon, London

Printed and bound in Great Britain
by the CPI Group (UK) Ltd, Croydon, CRO 4YY

MAIN CHARACTERS

GERMANS

Martin-Heinz von Bora, Colonel in the German army
Lübbe-Braun, Bora's second-in-command
Antonius Sohl, Lieutenant General in the German army
Klaus-Etzel Lipsky, Major in the German army, Sohl's aide
Herbert Kappler, Lieutenant Colonel in the SS
Egon Sutor, Kappler's adjutant
Eugen Dollmann, Colonel in the SS
Jacob Mengs, Gestapo agent
Albert Kesselring, Field Marshal in the German army
Karl Wolff, General in the SS
Zachariae, Mussolini's private physician

ITALIANS

Giovanni Pozzi, textile industrialist
Anna Maria "Annie" Tedesco, his daughter
Walter Vittori, Pozzi's brother-in-law
Rodolfo Graziani, Commander-in-Chief of the Italian Republican Army
Emilio Denzo di Galliano, Graziani's aide
Gaetano De Rosa, Captain of the Republican National Guard
Cesare Vismara, Inspector in the Italian Police
Passaggeri, Inspector in the Italian Police
Moses Conforti, antiquarian and photographer

Bianca Spagnoli, former music teacher
Marla Bruni, soprano
Fiorina Gariboldi, Marla Bruni's maid
Miriam Romanò, seamstress
Xavier Cristomorto, freelance partisan leader
Vittorio and **Italo,** partisan leaders, moderate faction
J.V. Borghese, Commander, X MAS (10th Marine Infantry
    Division)

GLOSSARY

Abwehr: The Third Reich's military counter-espionage service

Albergo: Italian for "hotel"

Animo: Italian for "Have courage!"

Atarot: In the Jewish tradition, crown-shaped embellishments for the Torah scroll

Ausserkommando SS Mailand: SS Foreign Command, Milan

Bandengebiet: German for "bandit territory"

Bedenken Sie es: German for "Mind yourself"

Besamim: Tower-shaped spice and perfume boxes, in Jewish tradition

Brigadenführer: SS military rank, equivalent to the rank of army major

Casa del Fascio: Italian for "Fascist centre"

Commissario: Italian for "police inspector"

Daven: In Judaism, the back-and-forth motion of the torso during prayer

Drei Hundert Rosen: "Three Hundred Roses", a popular German song

Durchgangslager: A transit camp for inmates and undesirables

Einsatzgruppen: Special SS units created to eliminate Jews, gypsies and political opponents in the occupied territories

Ganz genau: German for "good enough"

Generalleutnant: Lieutenant general, in German army and air force

Gnädige Frau: German for "kind lady"

Hauptsturmführer: SS military rank, equivalent to the rank of army captain

Kripo: Contraction of "Kriminalpolizei", the German criminal police

Luftwaffe: The German air force

Malachim ha-Maveth: Angels of Death, in the Jewish tradition

Obergruppenführer: A high rank in the SS, second only to Heinrich Himmler's rank of Reichsführer

Obersturmbannführer: SS military rank, equivalent to the rank of army lieutenant colonel

Organization Todt: German civil and military engineering organization

Permesso: Italian for "May I…"

Pinkas: A ledger listing the principal events in a Jewish community

Platzkommandant: German title for the commander of a given area

Radiosender: German radio station

Reichsmarshall: Marshal of the Reich, the rank given to Hermann Göring

Reichsprotektor: Nazi governor of the Bohemia-Moravia protectorate in Czechoslovakia

Rimmonim: Silver finials decorating the staffs around which the Torah parchment is rolled

SD: Short for "Sicherheitsdienst", the SS Secret Service

Shekinah: In Judaism, the spirit and actual presence of God

Shivviti: In Judaism, a small case containing a prayer scroll from the Psalms

Sipo: Contraction of "Sicherheitspolizei", the Internal Security Police of the Third Reich

Si vergogni: Italian for "You should be ashamed of yourself!"

Soldatensender: German army radio

Spielcasino: German army entertainment hall

Standartenführer: Paramilitary rank in various Nazi organizations, equivalent to the rank of army colonel

Via, via: Italian for "Go, go!"

Wehrmacht: Official name of the German army, 1935–46

Venus smiles not in a house of tears.

SHAKESPEARE, *Romeo and Juliet*

1

960TH GERMAN GRENADIER REGIMENT HQ NEAR
MT CASSIO, SATURDAY, 14 OCTOBER 1944

The voice spoke Russian. It cut through the dark, slicing it
like paper, and the shreds were not to mend again. Martin
Bora did not want to open his eyes, did not want to know
whether it was night or not, whether this was Russia or not. As
with voices in dreams, the sounds seemed to be inside him –
inside the dark within – not travelling to him from elsewhere.
Surely, if he stretched, he'd feel the jagged top of the wall
and mud cleaving to his boots, but he didn't. Instead, he lay
there on his back. He did not recall lying on his back when
the Russian dogs smelled him and strained furiously at the
leash.

There was no wall, no mud. And the voice was harsh, but
no longer speaking Russian.

Darkness broke.

Bora opened his eyes. The blinding glare of a torch filled
them, causing him to blink; no place in his skull was safe
from it. He recoiled from the brightness without averting
his face.

"Get up," the voice said.

Something told him it was useless to seek the handgun at
his bedside. Elbows propped on the mattress, Bora tried to
make sense of things, much as one stumbles through spider
webs, becoming tangled in their gummy wraiths. "What happened, what is it?"

The flood of light waved aside, just enough for him to discern civilian clothes, a baggy overcoat. A hefty man, middle-aged, a beefy jaw unhinging to speak.

"Gestapo. Get up, Colonel von Bora."

Bora stiffened across his shoulders. He was not awake enough to rally his wits, but enough to taste fear. Dog-tired, exhaustion overwhelmed him in bed despite the ever-present pain in his mutilated left wrist; he took penicillin and what not for it, but the injections hurt and he could not say they helped. So he stared into the glare, befuddled, resisting the temptation to ask, "What is the charge?" – a phrase that was second nature to all of them in those years. Instead, as he freed his legs from the quilts, he repeated, "What happened?"

The man said nothing. When Bora went to stand up and reach for his uniform across the chair, another figure flung his riding breeches at him from the dark.

"Get dressed."

Many times, he'd wondered what he would feel at a moment like this. The truth was that formless panic took over everything else. *This **has** to be Russia,* he made himself think. *Had better be.* Red Army voices from the past were still inside him, speaking not so differently from the man before him. He heeded all of them, automatically.

The whiteness of his underwear exposed him, lean and briefly vulnerable: at once, he began to cover it up with the field grey of the uniform. He slipped into his breeches, laced them with one hand and was halfway through buckling his prosthesis when the army shirt flew at him. He donned that, too, pressured into fitting himself.

The glare stayed on him; that invisible someone else was now rummaging in his dresser. Bora heard the army footlocker slam shut. The shaft of light moved up as he stood buttoning his tunic. The army cap came his way, and he put it on.

"What about my men?"

They shoved him forward, walked him through the dim silence of the small requisitioned house. "They know you're leaving. Your things are packed."

No sentry stood at his post by the front door. What appeared to be an unmarked, civilian car waited with the engine running. Under a sad drizzle, Bora was let into the back seat. The burly man sat down beside him; the other placed his footlocker in the trunk, and the car took off. Eyed furtively, the phosphorescent hands on his wristwatch read 11:04.

The mountain trail rolled bumpily under the wheels; it climbed at first, only to negotiate a zigzag of narrow bends before reaching what had to be the state highway. They were heading north, surely. Bora sat facing forward, although the dark in the car was nearly as solid as in his bedroom. Splintered trees and devastated farms must have been pitching and bobbing up like wrecks in that sea of darkness. Bora imagined them as they kept heading downhill. He was cold, fatigued, yet alert now and totally tense. In and out, he tried to breathe through his diaphragm to relax, but it was no use. Worse. As drowsiness left him, stabbing pangs started in his forearm, a rapid irreversible progression until it became a bloody pain. He folded his left arm against his chest and clutched his elbow, thumb and forefinger pressed hard against the sore flesh-covered bone. Trying to conceal his suffering, he felt the envelope inside his chest pocket – Nora Murphy's note on Red Cross stationery, carried around unopened for a week before he decided to read it. *If I have to die*, he thought, *it might as well be now that she tells me.*

Without turning to the man at his side, he asked, "Where are we going?" And, having received no answer, he sullenly minded the twists and turns of the car. The river valley below, that much he knew, led to a fork in the road, west to Piacenza and east to Parma. The latter route eventually led to Germany. *God always has mercy,* she had written him. *In His wisdom, He has seen to it that my unhoped-for present happiness ...* She did not say so exactly, but he understood she might have fallen pregnant: the side effect of victory toasts on her diplomat husband, in liberated Rome. *I cannot be so bold as to pretend to know what the future holds in store for us, Colonel, but you must promise that you will, between now and then, open your heart to what other love may come your way.* She had underlined *other*, not *promise*. It might mean something. He did not reread Nora's message: only folded it along the crease, replaced it in its envelope and slipped it into the pocket over his heart. In time, everything makes sense. Losing his left hand to a grenade attack, the annulment of his marriage, that brief, impossible passion for a married woman. Even a sort of bittersweet solace for having no impediments, if love ever were an impediment to death.

Half an hour, one hour went by. Through the corner of his eye, Bora perceived the bulk of the man beside him; from the rustle of waterproof cloth, he knew he was reaching inside his trench coat. He held his breath until he perceived the pungent, medicinal aroma of a cough drop.

"May I know why I'm being spirited off?"

Again, no reply. The engine pitch changed as the car reached level ground. Now and then, they went around an obstacle or rode the shoulder. They gained speed, slowed down to a creep. A roadblock came up, and with it a dozen godforsaken right places for firing a bullet through his head. *We shall dissolve into Nothing* – Georg Heym's poem came to his mind. *We shall dissolve into Nothing* – but he could not recall the lines that followed.

A damaged, near-illegible road sign went by – the outskirts of Parma, home to Army HQ 1008. Once again, from here they could go left or right, or ahead to the Po River and its war-ravaged bridges. He settled into his habit of self-control over pain and fear.

By and by, he realized they were indeed coming to the river, where by coincidence or design, docked to a wooden platform on the bank, an unsteady but workable ferry waited to carry them over. Then came a rough regaining of the road, in the eerie distant glimmer of an air raid God knows where on the horizon. Bombed-out villages, bleak detours, shortcuts through the fields and along canals. At every crossing, Bora tried to think of where the next SS or army headquarters might be. As far as he could tell, they kept heading north. He recognized the turn-off towards Brescia, home to three SS commands at least, and to Army HQ 1011. Still they kept going. Every so often, German soldiers or Italian guardsmen stopped them at checkpoints. Bora was thinking of a letter to his parents, whether he should have written one or would be allowed to write one. Whether there'd be time for it after all.

Three wordless hours and more went by, through the damp autumn night, a pitilessly long stretch of time to mull over his life and what lay ahead. At Montichiari Bora identified the last possible turn-off – to an airfield, Ghedi, from where he could be flown off to Germany – but still the car headed north. Sinking into his deepest layer of animal-like forbearance, he found a dull equidistance between resignation and fear.

If not Ghedi, or Brescia, was it the lake they were heading for? Lake Garda, of course. Yes, yes. They would soon seek the steep, narrow Garda shore. Barely visible hills floated on both sides of the car. A downhill stretch, followed by the bristle of shadowy cypresses and a series of curves where palm trees drew the fanciful outlines of exotic belvederes. The lake must be ahead; no, to the right. Below them, to the right. Despite his stoicism, Bora was startled when the car came to a stop by a blind wall, slightly at an angle.

He didn't move until they opened his door to let him out. It seemed forever, with the engine still running. Bora heard the trunk unlock, then the dull sound of his footlocker being dropped on the road. Both car doors slammed shut again.

By and by, he became aware of raindrops tapping the visor of his cap and the shoulder boards of his greatcoat. He smelled the lake, heard the sigh of branches under the rain. It was a swift, dizzy awakening, as from anaesthesia, one sense at a time. The car had gone. The faint sinking of tail-lights far into the night made him suddenly furious. A terrific anger worked its way up inside him at the idea that his anguish had been for nothing; that this was somehow routine army business. The physical urge to pummel somebody kept him there, breathing hard, until he came back to his self-control. Across the road, as far as he could make out in the now pelting rain, several cars sat head-to-tail in front of a garden gate. Barely visible against the glare of a front door ajar, a sentinel at the gate clicked his heels when Bora approached. A scent of wilted flowers and moist leaves came to his nostrils. And the sharp smell of a doused fire.

"What is this building, soldier?"

"Lieutenant General Sohl's residence, sir."

"The town?"

"Salò."

Inside, the bright entryway seemed blinding after the dark. A blue-grey-clad orderly behind a desk sprang to his feet. "Colonel von Bora?" He stared at the papers handed to him. "Lieutenant General Sohl was expecting you tomorrow, sir." Still, he promptly led him into the next room. The confusion of voices that met Bora's entrance alerted him that he was neither the reason, nor the focus of it. Ignoring him, worried-looking air force non-coms left muddy tracks on the carpet as they milled about. A civilian with the frumpy air of a police official, swollen-eyed with sleep, the top button of his coat driven into the wrong hole, strained to hear somebody – an interpreter? – speaking of "thieves" and "Italian responsibilities". Bora overheard an impatient "What?" from the doorway of a third room, a muffled grumble and, "He arrived at this hour?" It *was*, after all, barely three in the morning.

Wearing breeches and boots, but in his shirtsleeves, Lieutenant General Sohl walked over to see him. Tall and rotund, with a shaven head, he resembled the voracious monks you see painted on beer jugs. To Bora's salute he replied, "I appreciate your zeal for the assignment, but we were expecting you tomorrow morning." And because Bora enquired at once about his orders, he let show an edge of anxious spite. "You see, this is not a good time, Colonel. Be so good as to report here in the morning as scheduled. Hager, accompany the colonel to his hotel. Where is your luggage, Colonel?"

Bora resented the tone more than the dismissal. "Out there in the middle of the street, where it was dumped. General Sohl, I wonder if you are aware of the mode of my summons."

"Tomorrow, Colonel: you'll tell me all about it tomorrow." Sohl motioned to the Italian police official to follow him, and turned away.

Just as Bora was leaving the building, a bearded old man in his pyjamas and overcoat was being unceremoniously dragged in from the rain.

Hager, this young but savvy man, was the sort of busybody who thrives in command posts, the sort from whom intelligence officers, as Bora knew well from experience, can learn all sorts of useful details. Driving him down a narrow street, the airman actually relished being prompted. "They threw a hand grenade over the garden's back fence two hours ago. Yes, sir, it does happen occasionally, even here in town. We don't pay much attention as long as it's just noise and a spurt of flames. No damage to speak of, but in the commotion that followed a painting went missing. A large artwork, showing a naked girl in bed. The general is concerned, because the villa and its furnishings belong to Signor Pozzi, and he says there are bound to be complaints. The bearded old man? No, sir. He's just a Jew, an art expert."

They reached a small piazza with a war memorial, by a docking basin. "Albergo Metropoli," Hager announced, coming to open the passenger's door. A dank odour of wet gravel and drenched wood wafted in from the shore. Water made lush, sucking sounds, as if the invisible lake were turning its tongue in its mouth. The road was all a puddle, in which Bora's boots sank to the ankle. His long-repressed anger blew its top a moment later in the hotel lobby, when they assigned him a corner room without a toilet. He had a German colleague thrown out of bed and dislodged at once from his suite, into which he, Bora, moved without even waiting for the other to retrieve his things.

SALÒ, SUNDAY, 15 OCTOBER 1944

Everything was there. Uniforms, handgun, books, letters. Maps, sketches. Snapshots. Condoms, aspirin. His briefcase. Two of the books had broken spines, but his cloth-bound diary was safe. Bora had already gone through his footlocker the night before, still giddy with relief at not having been arrested after all, or shot, but anxious to make sure his belongings were safe. That morning, as he shaved, the face in the mirror had its usual firm coolness; it looked rather dispassionate these days. On the reflecting surface, through a window rimmed with white tiles, the waterline glowed under a sunbeam. Lakes had never been Bora's favourite places. And *this* lake, in particular.

Strewn along its shores, resort towns had become Mussolini's ministry seats, barracks and embassies, as if defeat – inevitable, six months away at most – could be delayed by forcing enemy planes to pick through hotels and luxurious private homes. A last resort, in every sense. The leftovers of Fascism circled slowly like suds in a drain, where everything gathers before being going down the pipe.

Yet Bora had slept soundly a few dreamless hours and awakened perfectly lucid. No more confusion over leaving his temporary command post or his regiment, bled white by the Allies but successful in holding every assigned position in the summer war. They hadn't given up a single stronghold, a single machine-gun nest or inch of territory; Field Marshal Kesselring himself had ordered them to withdraw in the end. As for him, reassignment was a recurrent rude jab in the back, steering him this way and that and expecting him to stay the course. He had learned to accept it, striving grudgingly to do well. Time away from the front line seemed like a waste at the end of 1944, but what nook of northern Italy had not become a front line? You could be killed by a grenade in your back-yard, or while shaving in cold water by the sink. Bora tried to convince himself of all that, quickly passing the razor blade around his mouth; and yet, away from his regiment, he felt like a scab fallen off an open wound.

Mirrors were a luxury up in the mountains, not to mention other items. As with his men, he'd done without. And only after God-awful weeks of fighting, forty-nine hours and twenty-two minutes from the moment he'd read Mrs Murphy's note, he'd taken a sunburned and experienced army nurse to bed. All night they'd had sex with the proficiency of soldiers, without kissing, and in the morning had parted with a handshake. She'd asked for his shaving mirror, "as a souvenir, and because I need a mirror". And that was the sole missing condom from the batch. She, the Nursing Corps officer, whatever her name was, came from Lake Constance. And now here he was on a lake, too. Through the open window, mist blurred the opposite shore, past the waterline glowing like a hot blade tempered in liquid. In the piazza below, the Great War memorial reminded him that in the past generation Italy had bitterly fought against Germany, and won.

Five minutes before eight, Hager led him through the main hallway of Lieutenant General Sohl's residence. On the wall by the staircase, bright oil paintings and tapestries clashed with the French wallpaper, all copses, streamlets and coy shepherdesses.

"That's where the picture was, Colonel." Hager pointed to the top of the stairs, where a massive, empty, gilded frame sat on the floor against the panelling. Bora glanced at it, going past. In retrospect, the anxiety he experienced overnight had been as void and apparently as useless as this frame without a canvas.

Next, he was led into an overly warm studio, heavy with the smell of cigars. An army desk bearing the nameplate "*Generalleutnant der Luftwaffe* Anton v. P. Sohl" took up the middle of the floor. In the couple of minutes he had to wait, Bora took in the details. By now the Flemish tapestries – real? imitation? – were no doubt saturated with cigar smoke. Overhead, the Gothic tracery was beyond elegance, on the carved, artificial edge of bad taste. But it was the fireplace, source of that excessive warmth, that struck him disagreeably: as if there were some danger lurking there after all, when he'd had more than enough of danger and having to face it without flinching. The chimney-piece was a face, vast and angry, snake-haired, moustachioed, its wide mouth gaping red within an arc of stone fangs. A fiery furnace, the jaws of hell, the parched throat of a giant.

Sohl's voice came from behind. "I chose this room because of it." Cheroot in hand, he strode in, impeccably attired this morning. "It has … How to say? An unquenchable, insatiable quality about it. I call it the Moloch fireplace."

Bora greeted him, and then – because the general stared – the mandatory Party greeting.

He'd never met Sohl in the past, and, as far as he knew, there were no air force units on the lake. But they proliferated elsewhere on Italian soil, carrying out their duties in their baggy trousers and rimless helmets. The general could be the highest-ranking German in Salò, or else the representative of Field Marshal Kesselring, himself an old aviator.

Sohl understood that Bora was about to enquire about his summons and raised a hand to keep him from it. When he chewed on his cigar, clearly British war loot from better days, his fleshy upper lip made him look toothless. "You aren't the only one to have had a bad night, Colonel. More about that in a moment. However your summons was effected, we'll both have to make allowances for it. Herr Mengs had been touring the mountains on official business and agreed to give you a lift."

Bora believed none of it. His transfer orders might have been issued orally, but it hardly fell to the Gestapo to carry them, much less carry them out. "Sir, my understanding was that I should lead the regiment to Brescia for rest and refitting. May I view a written copy of my reassignment?"

"Ah! Did you not receive it?" Sohl picked up a sheet from his desk and pushed it towards him with the moist end of the cigar. "As you see, the military governor himself signed your orders."

It did not reassure Bora seeing the signature of Karl Wolff, Himmler's SS envoy and plenipotentiary in German-occupied northern Italy, on the document.

"Why the long face, Colonel? Thank God, good commanders who can fall at the head of their troops are still aplenty. Experienced liaison officers such as yourself are harder to come by, you will agree."

So, that was what it was about. Officially. Despite his own tension, Bora could tell that the general's mind was elsewhere. Smiling covered up some private concern; his prattle acted as padding.

"You young colonels," he was saying, "so mindful of your indispensability." (*The usual stupid comments,* Bora thought. How many times had he heard them?) "You presume to know where you're useful. Well, it's wherever they send you. Riga has fallen; Tito's partisans are pushing on to Belgrade. Would you be capable of stopping all that? Of course you wouldn't."

Bora's sternness prompted Sohl to reach for and hand over to him a slim manilla envelope. "Details of the situation and your duties: read them before you leave. Your previous assignment … Mount Cassio, was it?"

"And the Cisa Pass before that. Although not with the Hermann Göring Division nor the Monterosa, much less the 'mongols'."

"So, no bad conscience regarding civilian casualties. Good for you. You got your five months of hand-to-hand combat, the sort of excitement you army commanders go in for. I hear *Signal* wants to write you up, with photos." Was it the overnight grenade attack that troubled him? Bora watched Sohl mouth the cheroot nervously. He recalled his late brother's contempt for "desk pilots" who crowded offices and high posts while flyers died by the thousand. Despite the warmth in the room, Sohl turned to the fireplace, rubbing his hands. "Anyhow, don't feel guilty about a liaison job. We're not in Rome. No society ladies and no embassy cocktail parties, except maybe Herr Hidaka's in Gardone. Won't you sit down? Cigar? Cigarette?"

"Thank you, sir." Bora stood and declined to smoke.

"Your temporary office is in town, at the Republican National Guard's headquarters. By day's end, a staff car and driver will be assigned to you. I made a nine o'clock appointment for you to pay a courtesy call to Marshal Graziani's aide, Denzo di Galliano, and schedule a meeting with the marshal. Graziani's role is little more than a sinecure, but his exalted rank keeps him happy. On your way out, see my chief of staff, Major Lipsky. He'll show you around as needed and drive you to the Ministry of the Armed Forces." A log in the fireplace hissed and flared up, like a tongue lashing in that burning mouth. "Be back for lunch at twelve sharp, so we can become acquainted. Before then, telephone our deep regrets to Cavalier Pozzi, owner of the stolen painting and textile merchant." No details of the theft followed beyond what Hager had said, but, despite Sohl's superficial calm, a grey pallor came over his face. Bora wondered just how precious the lost painting might be.

Across the hallway from the general's office, from a small room lined in blond wood the chief of staff stepped forward. "Klaus-Etzel Lipsky, Herr Oberst. Welcome to Salò." At once, he came close to undoing Bora's reserve, by adding, "It was my privilege to serve with your late stepbrother in Russia. Commander Sickingen was as fine a flyer as I can envision."

Bora's mourning fortified him against blandishment. "In which capacity did you serve with Peter?"

"I was the squadron's administrative officer. After my flight mishap, that is. A broken back does not interfere with paper pushing. I'm a lawyer by training." Lipsky's deeply set clear eyes discreetly ran over the badges and ribbons on Bora's tunic – a predictable, quick reckoning of his worth. Bora took mental notes of his own. Wide-necked and fair, the major had the tanned looks of a skier or a mountain-climber. From his left ear to the neck, an ugly scar created the strange impression of a welding in the flesh. Campaign ribbons and badges told the rest. "Colonel, my office is at your disposal if you wish to review your orders."

Bora thanked him. Ten minutes later, he rejoined Lipsky and left the building with him. Outside, in the short walk to the gate, the sun eyed open through the clouds, and what had been a single glowing line across the lake spread into a generous sprinkle of brightness.

Lipsky drove a ridiculously small yellow convertible with a civilian licence plate. Only with the top folded back could two tall men hope to fit inside it.

"Is this the sort of car one finds in the German motor pool?"

"No, no. I chose it because I like it." Lipsky reversed the car and headed south. "So, since you come as a liaison to Marshal Graziani, off we go to his Ministry of the Armed Forces in Soiano. You'll see soon enough whether his Republican Army is a true embodiment of what he calls the Italians: *the flower of all races, fragrance of the earth.*"

Bora glanced over. "You cannot be serious."

"He said so in public, less than three months ago." Lipsky smirked, changing gears and flooring the gas pedal with a pilot's gusto. "Doesn't the marshal know *we* are the sweet-smelling bud of the universe?"

Bora did not comment. For a minute or so, he stared at the glossy clearness of the lake. Then: "What about Denzo di Galliano?" he asked.

"You'll see."

"That's not an answer, Major."

"Well, he's an eminent prick."

Such cheek was unheard of. Bora was astonished. How much did Lipsky know about him, that he allowed himself such familiarity? It suddenly came to him that he might be the officer who delivered Peter's belongings to his parents after the crash. Hadn't his stepfather described him as a "former pilot with a Polish-sounding name"? At the time, from his post in Russia, Bora had felt deprived of the right of being there himself, and not a little jealous. He chose not to ask Lipsky about it, and the major did not volunteer the information.

Looking at the map on his knees, Bora noted how virtually every small town on the lake-shore housed one or more ministries. Gargnano, in its scented strip of lemon and lime gardens, was where Mussolini lived. Maderno housed the Secretariat of the Fascist Party and Kappler's Security Service. Foreign officials resided in a hotel at Fasano, not far from the German Embassy. SS General Wolff lived in Gardone, and so on. Southward, where they were going, a number of villas clustered here and there among palm trees and bougainvilleas. Entrepreneurs and militiamen sat side by side with Party devotees and those who only hoped to get out of there alive. Bora wondered how long it'd been since his last visit to La Schiavona, the family place at the northern tip of the lake. Six years at least. A handful of kilometres away from Mussolini's headquarters, his grandparents' summer home now lay beyond the freshly drawn frontier, in newly acquired German territory.

When the car turned right to reach Villa Omodeo, they had to show their papers to the marshal's numerous guards. Waiting for permission to enter, Lipsky pointed to open swatches of land beyond the manicured garden. "Training grounds, and even a landing strip, Colonel. Rather grand. Closely watched day and night, because the marshal fears an attack against his person. I believe those you'll actually deal with are Renato Ricci's Republican National Guard, reined back into the regular army as of last August."

"So I heard."

"But even after Ricci's sacking, the Guard does as it pleases: namely, it takes personal initiatives against the partisans, acts as a police and security force, and keeps the order ... or the disorder. *We* control it, or think we do. Which is probably why you're here."

Once through the gate, Lipsky left Bora at the villa's entrance. No sooner did Bora walk in than an Italian adjutant came to greet him in the foyer. He was natty, polite and smelled of sweet cologne, but the upshot was that Colonel Denzo di Galliano was not in. In fact, he would not return until the following morning. All meetings were postponed. Marshal Graziani, on the other hand, had changed his schedule for the day; presently at his General Staff HQ at Bergamo, he would not be available for an encounter until Wednesday at the earliest.

Bora penned a terse note indicating that he'd called. "Wasn't the colonel aware of my arrival?" he asked.

"Something urgent came up. I'm sure he'll see you around ten-thirty tomorrow." The adjutant had the noncommittal attitude of a bureaucrat, keeping information to a minimum. "It *is* Sunday, you know."

Lipsky didn't bat an eyelid when Bora came out moments later with a frown on his face. Nothing was said while they drove back to Salò. Even while waiting for an ambulance to exit an alley off Garibaldi Street, in a crowd of police uniforms and civilians, they looked on without speaking. Furtively, Bora swallowed two aspirins. Soon after, they came to a glum building with bars on the windows. "Your office is in there," Lipsky informed him. "If you have any further questions …"

Bora was still irritated with the reception at Soiano. Generally, he would not discuss his orders with others; however, Sohl's chief of staff must have been in the know, and his was a second, indirect offer of support. Trust came hard these days, so Bora replied with the first query that came to his mind. "What can you tell me about the overnight theft at the residence, and the painting?"

"The painting?" Lipsky stared at him. "It's not just a *painting*. Why, it's a work by Titian, Herr Oberst. Certified and worth a fortune. A spectacular Venus reclining on a couch, discovered by Conforti, the Jew. Our deep regrets won't be quite enough for the owner. Which is probably why General Sohl is sending you to deal with Signor Pozzi. The general feels your presence here might be useful in that regard."

"Really. How so?"

"He heard of your sleuthing abilities from an air-force acquaintance of yours, Colonel Habermehl."

The talkative sop. God knows what else about me he's let slip. Bora showed no overt annoyance. After all, Sohl never mentioned that he wanted the theft looked into. He decided it was his turn to try Lipsky's reliability. "Who is Mengs? Do you know?"

This time Lipsky reacted with a quick wink. "I have no significant information about him, and I doubt anyone does. His office is at Maderno."

"I see." Bora meant to get his own fact-finding system going soon, since colleagues and trustworthy non-coms he knew were presently assigned to posts in the neighbouring cities. "Major, that cannot be all a general's chief of staff is informed of."

"But it is. I can't imagine why *he* drove you in." Lipsky's arm stretched out in an impeccable Party greeting. "Would it be convenient if I had my things moved to my new quarters later today?" It was the only discreet signal to Bora that he was the very officer rudely dislodged the night before.

The Republican National Guard was aware of Bora's coming. He'd been assigned an office, and he recognized the spur-of-the-moment busyness that often welcomed German officers. Halfway up the stairs, he was surprised, but only so much, to recognize the bantam-sized Captain De Rosa hastening down to meet him. Party salute on one side, army greeting on the other, and soon they were swapping comments about the facilities and the war.

De Rosa acted with a mix of dignity and deference, as if they hadn't quarrelled in Verona a year earlier. The dim state of current affairs and political events had seemingly cut his arrogance down to size. Sombrely pugnacious, his bold moustache grown bushier and shaggier, he spoke vacantly of units and numbers. He lavished on Bora maps, files and typed accounts of military operations, betraying disappointment at being assigned to the RNG from his post in the militia – the notorious Muti Legion. He showed Bora around, bluntly opened doors and slammed them shut; his mouth twisted when mentioning the hated name of this or that politician. It could be an active soldier's intolerance for cramped headquarters, or not. At the end of the tour of the ground floor, De Rosa turned to Bora with a scowl. "My *space*," he said, not "my office", as he unlocked a pantry-like narrow room at the end of which sat an oversized desk. A far cry from his fine digs in Verona. On the wall behind the desk, a gory and tattered shirt stretched spread eagle. "Belonged to a comrade," he explained grimly. "Killed on the eighth of August."

Bora looked from the threshold. "And that thing on your desk?"

"It's a skull."

"I can see *that*."

"Russian front, another comrade." De Rosa half-closed his dark eyes. "We live in the midst of death, Colonel."

"That is a fact. But, I must say, you were less morbid in Verona."

"Morbid? Far from it. I celebrate by collecting photographs of our fallen brothers. Death, blood. Ours, and the traitors'. You must have seen the film of the execution at Verona." (Bora had done, at the German command in Rome.) "Did you notice the coup de grâce fired into Ciano's head?"

"Yes, both of them."

"Three." De Rosa missed the irony. "It took me three. Death is our daily business, and Mussolini's traitorous son-in-law deserved it. Do you by chance recall Marla Bruni, Colonel von Bora?"

"The soprano you were dating in Verona, yes."

"I wish I'd never given her a motor car. She's joined me here."

"Well, bully for you. Does her husband know?"

"Of course not. He's in Switzerland."

Bora followed De Rosa upstairs, thinking of people and circumstances coming together. The circle closed. Being here was like seeking the trap and wilfully stepping into it – something he'd been mindful not to do for the past few years. Pressuring Lipsky before taking leave of him, minutes earlier he'd got out of him a quick piece of advice about Mengs, the Gestapo man. "Ask SS Colonel Dollmann." It meant that Eugen Dollmann was here, too. The perilous intrigues of German-occupied Rome followed that ambiguous officer, who'd once called himself "dissatisfied with keeping his feet in less than three stirrups". Standartenführer Dollmann's acquaintance with Mengs pointed to a connection between the latter and Himmler's office, or worse. Without seeing it, Bora smelled a trap, because the night before he had kept company with the hunters. At any rate, this morning he carried his diary safely in his briefcase. The circle left out its dead and wounded: Bora's old chief, Admiral Canaris, arrested in July after the failed attempt on Hitler's life and the dismantling of the Army Intelligence Service; colleagues and friends tortured and executed. Ranting trials before the People's Court. And now he was being assigned to oversee anti-partisan operations in order to "curb Italian excesses". This made least sense of all.

And what about Mengs? He knew nothing about him, although in June his friend Ralph von Uckermann – himself eventually bound for the gallows – had mentioned a Gestapo man at Salò, a certain Heinrich Müller, who had once been a henchman of the bloodthirsty late Reich Protector, Reinhard Heydrich. Why would SS plenipotentiary Wolff want to "curb excesses" in a fratricidal war?

Suddenly, the words "lovemaking" and "ludicrous" reached his ears from De Rosa's chatter. Bora was startled. He acknowledged them with a "*Sì, sì,*" in Italian, as if he cared.

"I knew you'd understand, being a worldly man. Just think, Colonel von Bora, La Bruni is staying in the same *pensione* where my wife resides. My life has become an inferno."

We all end up in the hell we fashion, there's no doubt about that. "Well, should I feel sorry for you?" Bora showed more amusement than he actually felt. "Some men would kill to have your embarrassment of riches."

"You think it humorous, do you? I'd kill to be free of them both." Grudgingly, De Rosa resumed his role as a guide. Walking to Bora's new office, he quipped, "But naturally you are *faithful to your wife*, as you said in Verona." He looked meaningfully at the German's right hand, from which the wedding band had vanished.

Bora entered the office, strode over to the window and threw it open. "Tell your men that I expect a working telephone by tonight and a set of unmarked, fresh maps of the area and surrounding mountainside. Please have the filing cabinet moved behind the desk, the rug taken out, the windows washed, and do not bother with a motor car. I'll get my own from the German pool."

De Rosa nodded. "I get it," he spelled out in his perceptible southern drawl. "You're here for *him*." Because Bora said nothing, "Cristomorto, right?" he added. "They sent you here to try and catch him: but he's one to steer clear of. He's deranged."

There would be time yet to discover who this "dead Christ" was. Bora answered that he had no details. Yet that name, or nickname, and the way De Rosa, who was no coward, warned him to watch out, struck him unpleasantly, just as the monstrous fireplace in Sohl's room had done. A partisan commander, probably: not the sort of adversary he was interested in facing after real war on the Gothic Line. Leaning out of the window, Bora studied the houses across the street, the clock tower to the left, and the cloudy, moist sky above. "Have a set of office keys made for me. I like to come to work early, and I stay late."

Eleven-thirty, an idea of the organizational mayhem he was to mediate, and a need to breathe the outside air. Bora chose to walk to Sohl's residence. On the way, he noticed that uniformed men and civilians were still milling about in the alley off Garibaldi Street, although the ambulance was gone. The sleepy-eyed police official he'd glimpsed at three in the morning, looking rather awake now, was exiting a doorway, shaking his head. From the open window above him came a sound, singularly high-pitched, like a dog's frantic yelp or a woman's wail.

"What happened?" Bora asked the policeman closest to him.

The man saluted. "A woman killed herself on the upper floor. The one making all this noise is a neighbour: she saw the body and we can't get her to shut up."

"*Ach, so.* And how did she commit suicide?"

"She hanged herself."

The words came from the police official. "Cesare Vismara, Republican Police. May I help you?"

"No, I'm just curious." Bora looked up at the shop sign above the doorway: Antiquities and Photographic Studio, Moses Conforti. "A spectacular Venus reclining on a couch," Lipsky had said, "discovered by Conforti, the Jew." Bora took a mental note and resumed his walk.

Once it became clear that Sohl would not discuss Bora's duties before his conference with Graziani, the conversation at lunch turned to the stolen painting. "Don't you see that's why they placed Lipsky at my side, when I had my own chief of staff until a month ago?" Unexpectedly, over grilled trout, Lieutenant General Sohl took advantage of Lipsky's absence to gossip about him. "Göring himself sent him – this I know for a fact – and had the Venus not disappeared, he'd have made his move to *secure* it next week at the latest. I looked into Lipsky's background, Colonel. Art. *Art.* His father worked for the Keller und Reiner art gallery in Berlin before starting an auction house on the Potsdamer Strasse. Imagine that!"

Disparaging colleagues was not something Bora cared for. He listened because there might have been more to this than chatter. "What then makes you think the Reich Marshal is *not* behind the disappearance?"

"You should have seen Lipsky last night, after the incident. He was beside himself. When you arrived, he'd just finished grubbing through the backyard like a boar, looking for tracks. No. I'm positive he spent the rest of the night on the telephone with Berlin."

"He seemed rather composed this morning."

"Pilots have poker faces. Don't trust him."

Before lunch, Sohl had insisted that Bora examine the frame of the painting. The canvas had been cut from it with a sharp blade, carelessly enough to gash the gold leaf in two places. "Done in a hurry, wouldn't you agree?" The general had spoken the obvious with his lips around an unlit cigar.

Now Bora watched the ever-present cheroot sit like a grub by the general's plate. The heat from the fireplace breathed through the open door of the studio, so much so that he could feel it uncomfortably on his neck. "What happened exactly?" he asked. "And how long was the upstairs left unguarded?"

"Maybe thirty-five, forty minutes. Less than an hour, anyway. There are half a dozen police units in town, ours and Italian, and still someone manages to toss a grenade into my backyard! Nothing but a loud bang, although two rear windows did explode, and a fire started in the trellises. I was asleep – it was past one o'clock – and I must admit the incident did cause a great deal of confusion. When I opened the window, a heap of dry leaves had caught fire and the smoke was suffocating. For a time, my men ran in and out with buckets of water. Then a fire truck came, followed by the police, the RNG and the SS. Thank God it started to rain. We assumed it was a partisan attack, but the thieves must have slipped in somehow, knowing exactly what to go for. Lipsky ran in from his hotel, and it was he who discovered the theft." Sohl stared behind Bora's shoulders, as if someone were watching the conversation. His cordiality sounded insincere. "You must realize this is more than mortifying for me. Signor Pozzi wanted to remove the painting before I moved in, but I told him it'd be perfectly safe with us."

"How did he learn of his loss?"

"He owns another villa up the road, so it wasn't long before he realized where the grenade struck. I had to telephone him about the theft." A white-gloved private removed the empty plates, placed fruit on the table and left. "I told you Pozzi is a textile manufacturer. He owns five of the houses our forces occupy between Salò and Gardone. Little formal education but plenty of good investments. For him, the Venus was a pretty picture that cost him a bundle and was worth even more. Did you speak to him?"

"Briefly, as you ordered. He wants to discuss matters in person, so he's invited me to dinner tomorrow night."

"Capital. You'll see for yourself what sort of fellow he is."

"He could be the sort who takes back what's his," Bora observed coolly. "Herr Generalleutnant, how many people have access to this residence?"

"No civilians. But there's no telling how many art collectors have seen the painting ever since the Jew authenticated the Venus a year ago."

"Conforti?"

"Yes, Conforti. Don't let his Italian-sounding name fool you: he's a Prague Jew. The SS brought him in at my request: I wanted to make sure he'd been sleeping in his bed and meant to see his reactions." Sohl began to peel an apple rather clumsily. "If you're wondering why we let a Jew stay footloose, it's because the German authorities have ordered him to compile an inventory for us."

"Is he married?"

"Not that I should know or care. Why do you ask?"

"A woman killed herself in the building where he works."

Sohl stared at him with his nose in his wine glass. It was possible he was still mulling over reports of Bora's investigative activities in Verona and elsewhere, no doubt exaggerated by Habermehl's bibulous chatter. Unless his days in intelligence drew an all-knowing aura about him, that was far from the truth. Anyhow, the lieutenant general did not openly ask his advice. When Bora asked about the police official, he replied, "Vismara? Keeps to his side of the fence and seems capable."

"How does he intend to investigate?"

Sohl folded his napkin and, holding it with both hands, wiped his mouth from side to side. "I haven't put him in charge of the matter. It's my opinion that Italians are behind the crime, although I don't know whether the grenade attack was part of the scheme or an extraordinary coincidence, clearing the way for someone waiting for an opportunity to enter the premises. Speaking of which, dinner at Pozzi's is a good sign. You'll see what luxury some Italians still live in, Colonel. You are, of course, authorized to hear what he asks in consideration of his loss."

Bora glimpsed a small, second trap in the grass, only inches away from the large one. "So, who is to look into the Venus's disappearance, sir?"

"Why, *you* are. Until Graziani shows up on Wednesday, there'll be time for you to make some sense out of this embarrassing question. Vismara will be at your disposal, and the Jew will tell you all about the painting. My men here were remiss; I'm kicking a couple of them out to the front line, but feel free to question them first if you want to. As for Lipsky, he's off on my orders to Milan. With the roads as they are, and the car he drives, it'll take him hours just to get there. To begin with, I suggest you examine the backyard. Then, after you settle down, go and see the Jew for details of the painting. Tomorrow night, bring our regrets but no contrition. I envy you, Colonel, because you'll eat grandly at the cloth-maker's. He has a handsome daughter, too, which doesn't hurt."

"In my experience, small towns are quick to elect their beauty queens."

"You'll be the judge." Sohl picked up and lit his cheroot. "They say she shaves all over … not just her armpits, you understand."

Bora only half-succeeded in hiding his surprise. "It's unconscionable that such gossip should circulate about a lady."

"Oh, her late husband was a sailor. He once talked in his cups. And in a small town, once is all it takes for such titbits to propagate."

Until five o'clock Bora stayed in his new office, familiarizing himself with the material De Rosa had given him as well as

German intelligence reports on the military situation east and west of the lake. He also read expected but discouraging news about Fascist bickering and infighting, of Denzo's antipathy towards the RNG and vice versa, of Marshal Graziani's outbursts and Mussolini's grumpy silence with most everyone. As soon as the telephone was hooked up, all lines being run and controlled by the Germans, he reserved a call to his old divisional headquarters, to ask about the regiment's advance on Brescia. The operator told him that connecting a long-distance call could take hours. "No less than four, Colonel."

Disappointed, Bora stood up to stretch. His left leg and shoulder ached. The chair was singularly uncomfortable, and the writing implements in the desk drawer sparse and poor. The ugly calendar on the wall, as well as the map hanging askew next to it, suddenly nettled him. He removed the calendar and tossed it into the bin.

It seemed to him that he was preparing for something expected, something for which order and neatness were antidotes. He had to monitor a certain obsessive dislike for shabbiness, for lack of precision and punctuality. Thus, Bora watched himself as if from without at this odd point of his life, neither liking nor rejecting what he saw: a young man determined to keep control even over his tendency to keep control.

Sometime during the summer, he had stopped dreaming about his wife Dikta. Other dreams – often nightmares, or sometimes plain images of riding along Polish or Russian roads – had persisted. Remedios came and went from recollection, along with memories of Spain, where he'd first made love to her. Of Nora Murphy, he had not dreamed in weeks: this, too, might mean something.

It called, for lack of better things, for a cup of coffee. When he left the building, he saw Vismara across the shadowy street apparently waiting for him.

"Colonel, I understand you're to look into the theft, so I've brought you the notes I took on the crime scene." He pulled out of his pocket a folded, typewritten sheet, so awkwardly that it wafted to the ground before reaching Bora's hand. Vismara stooped to retrieve it. "Sorry. Here."

Without glancing at it, Bora placed it inside the cuff of his left sleeve. "I'll let you know."

Had the policeman refrained from entering RNG headquarters because of some power struggle or other? "I typed my phone number on the sheet, Colonel."

"I prefer to communicate in person, if I can. Where is your office?"

"In the *questura* building on the square."

"I'll come tomorrow, as I can."

At eight-thirty in the evening, Bora was finally able to connect with the 362nd ID headquarters. When he left work for good, he found a Luftwaffe private at the door below, with a dated but well-kept Fiat 1100 and a card from Lipsky that read: *I know you said you wanted to pick your own, but this is the best of the lot, and, if you don't take it now, it'll go to Denzo's adjutant.*

By the time he retired, Bora had secured a pack of looted Chesterfields for old times' sake, swearing not to smoke them. Some of his clothes needed ironing after Mengs' minion stuffed them inside the footlocker. He hung the rest neatly. As for his boots, they sat properly shined outside his door.

He lay down dressed as he was, determined not to think or close his eyes. But when the power failed for the nth time that day, he was, whether he liked it or not, consigned to the dark. Flat on his back, he felt blood pounding in his veins, as if the heart muscle were straining, so he sat up in bed. Names and numbers of enemy units and partisan bands flashed before him; his night ride came back to mind in every unnerving detail. In order to fight anxiety, he found himself thinking of the Venus: how to find her, and whether Sohl really expected him to do so. Unknown, unseen, she somehow applied a gentle balm to everything else and provided the safest concern for the night.

A few kilometres to the north, in his deathly quiet Maderno office, Jacob Mengs leafed through pages by candlelight. The files before him were colour-coded, each colour conjuring a response in his mind. Entries dated back seven years, consecrated by bold signatures in black and blue ink; photographs, letters, addresses, names ... Mengs read every page as a piece of the puzzle, to be secured and glued to the rest. *One shouldn't break rules*, he reasoned. *But how I admire those who break them well.* When at last the power flickered back on, he twisted the gooseneck lamp to light up his desk like a beacon and began to write in intricate German script, where C's looked like Z's and H's like F's.

2

SALÒ, MONDAY, 16 OCTOBER 1944

Captain Parisi, Denzo's adjutant, called shortly after eight, to relate that *il signor colonnello* was regrettably detained in his present location and would not be able to meet his German counterpart until the afternoon. Bora, who had been reading reports on the fierce fighting against partisan bands in the Ossola Valley, had just got three guardsmen to haul in a decent desk chair, a radio and a bookshelf. He ordered them to leave so that he could berate the adjutant at his ease but did not succeed in extorting news on Denzo's whereabouts.

Disgruntled, he went back to his papers. The Ossola operation might succeed, yet the existence of an independent "partisan republic" spoke volumes about the situation in the western mountains. By comparison, monthly intelligence from Brescia army headquarters was less sanguine. It signalled activity of the irregulars from mid-August to mid-September along the Oglio River and Lake Iseo, fifteen acts of sabotage against thirty-two recorded in July and August, and twenty-two during the previous period. The air raids, disastrous in the summer, had diminished, too. Intriguing data, difficult to evaluate at this point: of immediate relevance to his charge was the news that seven Germans had fallen prisoner to the bands – three of them officers – vis-à-vis thirty-seven rebels dead and forty-two taken in. If needed, the margin for negotiation, one to six, was reasonable enough.

What surprised him was having received SS field reports as well; it was hardly their style. What was Plenipotentiary Wolff up to? De Rosa added scraps of information by the hour, garnered from a handful of disparate Italian units. Jotted down in the glow of ideological passion, Bora learned more, and less, about Cristomorto than he wanted to know. Reliable data about the size of his unit and area of action were missing. His nom de guerre – Xavier – had emerged in relation to a July shoot-out in Val Sabbia, where two Germans had fallen. He was credited with acts of "beastly violence" against not only the enemy, but civilians as well. To Bora, some of these seemed to be embellished by hearsay and scarcely believable; others – mutilation of the adversaries – he'd last heard of on the Eastern Front, where he'd gathered such gruesome information for the German Army War Crimes Bureau. He scribbled: *Find out if Cristomorto served in Russia*, and, *Unusual that we should know his real name. But is it his real name?*

By nine o'clock, the weather had taken a turn for the better. Bora set up an appointment with Vismara and ordered flowers to be sent to the Pozzis' residence in anticipation of his dinner date. Because the Fiat still had a civilian licence plate, he planned to drive it before lunch to Wehrmacht headquarters, list it as a German army vehicle and carry out a brief reconnaissance of the lakeside to its political northern terminus, Gargnano.

As he left his office, De Rosa approached him. Bora, who was using his teeth to pull up and adjust his right glove, expected to receive one more typewritten sheet, but De Rosa just stood there. "Have you heard the *Radiosender* news? Field Marshal Rommel died of his wounds on Saturday."

"This is called *shivviti*, is it not?"

In flawless Italian, it was the first thing Bora told Conforti, nodding to a small plaque by the door. He added nothing for half a minute or more, looking around discreetly. His nostrils were assailed by the scent of oiled furniture, such as one might smell in old rooms and vestries, and a spicy whiff of dried orange peel and cloves, or perhaps crushed myrtle leaves. In a backroom, he eyed a hazy mirror that played with and distorted reflections, and stacks of nondescript objects on the floor. The spicy whiff flowed from there.

"*Shivviti*, yes," Conforti answered at last, staring at the Hebrew script on the plaque. "*I have set ...*"

Spices and polished wood. Suddenly Bora knew what the scent reminded him of: synagogues in Poland, in the Pale of Russia, where he'd wandered through after the SS Einsatzgruppen had already broken in. He knew the aroma of *besamim* boxes smashed open, with their filigree tower-like tops yanked apart, curtains and Torah cloths torn down and burned to extract silver and gold thread from their fabric. All he perceived in the back room was a heap of intact rods with ornate finials, an indistinct lustre of chalices and plates and the tangy after-scent of silver plate rubbed to a shine.

"... *the Lord always before me*," Bora ended the quote, acknowledging the meaning with the shadow of a nod.

Conforti started to tremble. A small man whose ears seemed flimsy and translucent against the light from the window, he looked at Bora and Bora at him, and the old man's chin and beard trembled.

"You are an antiquarian and a photographer by trade, are you not?" Bora was well aware of the old man's fluster, but German colonels were supposed to act in composed, inquisitive ways.

"Have been for close to forty-six years."

That's something I will never be able to claim. The thought came to Bora with surprising clearness. It was as if the fragility of the old man facing him, so easily shatterable if only Bora were to say the word, had, if nothing else, the solid root of those many decades, while his seven tenacious years of soldiering were no more than shallow foundations under his young life. *We will dissolve into Nothing* ... The rest of Georg Heym's verses, he now recalled, ran:

> *... So that a child can hold*
> *One day all of our greatness*
> *In his delicate fist.*

"My name is Bora. General Sohl sent me to enquire about the Venus."

"The *Venus?*" Uneasily, Conforti groped around in his crowded shop like a blind man, in search of a chair for Bora to sit on. "She is *beautiful* – this you ought to know. I own a copy of the ... of the Venus, I will show it to you. You'll see. Whoever took her knows what beauty is."

"Or value."

"No, no. Beauty. *Beauty*, Colonel." Still staring at Bora, Conforti rummaged through a drawer. "There is so much to say about the *Venus of Salò*. Some must be read and savoured rather than told." He smiled as if apologizing for the suggestion. "Some things can't quite be said. How much do *you* know about the goddess?"

"Her purview is of a sexual nature, I believe, not a sentimental one."

"Exactly. Her nature is darker than the Greek Aphrodite's. She embodies life-giving passion, and its opposite. Which is to say, which is to say ..."

"Stop trembling."

A soldier and an introvert, Bora seldom sought contact beyond a handshake or encouraging pat on the men's back, but now he sternly held Conforti's hand down, against the edge of the drawer. "I cannot begin to understand, as long as you are so frightened. *Calm yourself.*"

MARSHAL GRAZIANI'S REPUBLICAN
MINISTRY OF DEFENCE, SOIANO

Emilio Denzo di Galliano had survived all military and political storms since his first Libyan campaign and was in no mood for a wreck in sight of the shore. Bora's insistence galled him even before they met. Back from a visit to his wife at Sirmione, the German's card, with the hour of his calling punctiliously marked, sounded like a provocation. He turned to his adjutant. "Whether he likes it or not, Parisi, he'll wait until after lunch. What do we know about him?"

"First-rate family and education, *signor colonnello*."

"Military training?"

"As above."

"Age?"

"Thirty-one next month."

Denzo blew his top. "Someone half my age? I fought at Vittorio Veneto, at El-Merg; I was with Mezzetti at Tagrift. The first to enter Kufra, master and commander at Sidi el-Barrani! I have more years of war under my belt than he has been on the Earth. What has *he* accomplished?"

"Spain, Poland, a stint in Crete in '41, three times a volunteer in Russia, Stalingrad included. Active on the Italian front since last September, when he lost his left hand to a partisan grenade," Parisi read. "Two promotions within the same year, the most recent in August, on the battlefield. Kesselring himself recommends him, Colonel."

"Which explains his promotions," Denzo argued sourly with the man's success. "But does he know how to manage politically?" His desk was glass-topped, and he passed his gloved finger across it, as if looking for dust. "When all is said and done, these days that's the soldier's number one skill."

"The *pinkases* community records from Sarajevo and Dubrovnik."
Conforti trailed his fingertips on the engraved silver book
covers. "Hallmarked Pogorzelski, 1867. *Rimmonim* by Stefano
Fedeli, *circa* 1820, with stylized, pomegranate-shaped finials.
This older set is surely the work of Bartolotti, Senior."

To put the old man at ease, Bora had encouraged him to
describe the religious objects; as for himself, he felt angrily
self-conscious for wearing the uniform he did before a Jew. But
was Conforti afraid, really? There was a strange, eerie quality
about him as he moved around, tapping, fingering or stroking
this and that. Imp-like, he captured the glare from the window
and threw a flitting shadow on embroideries and filigrees. He
spoke in a thin voice, dissonant to Bora's sensibility like a tinkle
at the edge of hearing.

"*Ketubah*, a marriage certificate on parchment illuminated
in Ancona, 1651 …"

There are moments when you become aware of having forsaken somehow your surroundings, not physically but mentally,
and though you seek the chink that let you in or might let you
out, you find none. The threshold is not in sight. Unexpectedly,
Bora felt removed from all he'd experienced hours earlier. The
crowded shop – or rather, *what it stood for* – hemmed him in, as
in the Prague tale wherein a mysterious house appears at the
head of an alley once a year, and he who crosses its threshold
becomes a prisoner there forever. Anything but superstitious,
Bora chased the thought away. What was true was that all these
sacred odds and ends bearing exotic names had been thrown
together to be added up and itemized. Their orphaned state,
their coming from countless other places, gave the impression
of a precarious treasure-trove.

"The silversmiths Menazzi and Carlier fashioned these
gilded *atarot*, gifts to the community of Split from the Talmud

Torah Brotherhood in Rome ... You are ... much younger than I expected, Colonel. Much younger, really."

"What does that mean? Does it make a difference?"

"Not to me."

The way Conforti said it was unexpectedly self-assured, so that Bora wondered to whom it should make a difference then. "I'm here to acquire data about the Venus."

"Of course. It is time you saw her."

When the old man stepped aside from the window, a shaft of light reached the mirror in the backroom, so that Bora saw the ghostly reflection of his own uneasy self rise out of the dark.

"Mine is only a copy. But it will give you a sense of what they took from us. Follow me out to the stairwell; we have to climb two floors. You may have heard, perhaps, that Venus's name shares a root not only with 'veneration', but also with 'venom'. Known alternatively as the *Tyrant*, she has a gift for ensnaring men."

Yes, yes. Typical antiquarians' talk. Bora fidgeted as Conforti slowly went up one step at a time. "How much of this would be relevant to a thief?"

"It may mean nothing, or it may be the reason for the theft."

"I have seen the empty frame. The canvas was cut out using something sharp, like a scalpel. Will it not affect the value of the painting?"

"Yes and no. Those of us who handled it know that the original was glued to a second canvas. Cutting it close to the frame would not damage it significantly."

"Those of us ... collectors, auctioneers?"

"And proprietors, Colonel: Pozzi bought it without a frame."

Bora said, "I have seen Titian's works before, nudes that go by the name of Venus. How does this one differ from the rest?"

Conforti glanced back as if he'd heard something extraordinarily naive. "To start with, it is one of three paintings." He wearily caught his breath. "The others are the famous *Venus of Urbino* and the so-called *Santi Venus*, now lost. *Santi* was painted first, the Urbino piece second, and our Venus is to my mind the last and most perfect of the set. It represents a young woman we only know as La Bella, a lover of Francesco della Rovere, or of his son Guidobaldo. Or both, knowing those Renaissance princes. Very young when she first arrived in Urbino, she died in childbirth at the age of twenty-five, one month after Francesco himself expired. The portrait is filled with symbolism."

"Well, the *Venus of Urbino* reclines on a red couch," Bora recollected. "In the back, two handmaidens are either taking out or putting away clothes."

They reached the first landing. A fatigued Conforti halted and caught his breath again. Did he suffer from a bad heart, or some other ailment? He was, after all, a Jew, caught between Fascists and Nazis. Two doors on the landing: the bustle of house chores was audible behind one of them. The other had a handwritten name tag pinned on, which read: *Bianca Spagnoli.*

Conforti saw Bora read it. "A woman died in there yesterday, rest her soul," he whispered and started up the stairs again. "The putting away of clothes has been interpreted as a suggestion of the growing size of La Bella's womb, or else her expectations to pick up fancy dress again after delivery. The myrtle at the windowsill is a symbol of love and fertility. And, of course, the hand gesture at once focuses the viewer's eye on her generative organs."

"But if she died in childbirth, how does the third painting fit in?"

"It was completed after her passing. It was I who authenticated the *Venus of Salò* as a work by Titian, not on a whim but following the judgement of experts like Suida, Venturi, Richter and Berenson. Hourticq was right regarding the meaning of landscape in Titian, and I rather agree with Hadeln, who rightfully claimed the Chesterfield-Gore *Danaë* to be by the Master's hand."

Second landing, at last. "For your commander, Colonel, the theft may be a source of embarrassment." Conforti's face twisted with grief. "For me, it is a crime that goes well beyond monetary value. It is like a death."

Sohl had told Bora that Conforti's family was interned if not already dead. "A removal is not the equivalent of death," he observed unthinkingly, and immediately regretted it.

"I will provide to you a dossier on the history of the painting, including the names of those who have uselessly tried to secure it since the authentication."

The landing led to a single door. There, Conforti stood with a weary shrug. His shoulders were so frail, he seemed easy to crush, and it would be like smashing the antennae and forewings of a delicate insect.

"Please, wait here. I'll turn the light on." The old man entered a hallway even more crowded than the shop below. In the penumbra of shuttered windows, unreadable paintings stood stacked against the walls, while books and boxes formed piles steadied by chairs. The light from the stairwell barely reached the end wall, catching the glint of a gilded frame.

Bora perceived the rich female body languidly recumbing on its side, as if blooming out of the shadows. When Conforti switched on a lamp somewhere, the figure became unashamedly available. Bora was hardly inexperienced, but a flesh-and-blood woman beckoning to him could not have engendered a more immediate, intimate feeling of seduction.

He stepped forward, amid the confusion of books and canvases.

"It is a contemporary copy without provenance or paper-work," Conforti reminded him. "But an excellent work, possibly originating in Tintoretto's studio. I bought it years ago in Florence."

Bora was not listening. He took his eyes away from the painting only so as not to stumble in the clutter. At every step, the female form seemed to shift, unravel, come alive; every curve shimmered like a liquid. He witnessed the lazy flow of those pink and umber surfaces as if in search of a vessel. All too aware of his emotional emptiness, he almost feared the image staring back from the canvas, the crisp halo of her blond-red curls like a filigree glimpsed in the alcove. The Venus looked at him. Her slack gesture, half-caressing, half-sheltering the sweet mound between her thighs, was not unique. Yet this hand, this femininity came somehow before all the rest, primeval and ambiguous, proffering and concealing, saying yes and no at the same time, without contradiction. Bora was rudely reminded of his celibacy by a crawl of nerves down his belly. But no, it was more like a vertigo, a sinking from the cluttered hallway into the Venus's space, in order to become that vessel. The process took only seconds, not enough for Conforti to notice anything but his attention.

"The original is superior to all imitation," he said, handing over a black-and-white photograph. "I took this myself. See the difference? All too often, men fall for the copy ... the likeness of Beauty rather than Beauty herself."

The postcard-sized image was too small to tell. It was true, so far as Bora was concerned. Women, beliefs. He could fairly admit that he'd been passionately fascinated by copies all his life.

Conforti's words placed a seal on his thoughts. "The truth is that Beauty herself cannot be beheld. When you truly find yourself face to face with Beauty, you die. Or become crippled, like Jacob, who wrestled all night with the angelic *shekinah* of God, without knowing."

"Titian was almost a hundred when he died," Bora objected. "And what about scholars and art enthusiasts, or the artists themselves?" Without waiting for an answer, he demanded the dossier. "I will return this after reading it."

He was about to take his leave when there was a rap on the door, and the knocking about of things as someone tripped through the hallway. "*Permesso?*"

Vismara manifestly did not expect to find Bora there. "Good day, Colonel. When you're done, I must ask Signor Conforti a few questions."

"Why? We are looking into the theft ourselves."

"I'm not here for the theft, Conforti. It's about Bianca Spagnoli, since you found her body."

Bora had no interest in a suicide. There was just enough time for him to drive to Gargnano and back, before seeing Vismara at his office. "We meet at eleven forty-five, Inspector," he reminded him on his way out.

At the city limits of Gardone Riviera, cypresses shaded the fancy villa setting of the German *Radiosender*, from which the news of Rommel's death had originated. Across the street from it, Bora stopped by the Japanese representative's residence to leave a note for Ambassador Hidaka, a family friend.

Ahead, past a row of late-blooming gardens, slowing down behind a column of militia trucks gave him time to observe the civilian buildings put to good military use. The trucks must have been coming back from action in the mountains to the west of the lake. Shortly afterwards, two of them veered into one of the driveways leading to a strip of hotels turned into army hospitals: a sad citadel where they had vainly tried to convince Bora to recover after the grenade attack. As God willed, he eventually succeeded in overtaking the trucks, not far from the SS and Gestapo command. He then picked up speed, aware that a string of checkpoints and delays would mark the proximity of Mussolini's residence.

During his return trip, a colleague he encountered while registering the car at the Wehrmacht headquarters told him bluntly, "You say you'll work with Denzo? A fine officer, he is. In Africa, he had rebel leaders thrown alive from aeroplanes. In the Senussi oases, he buried native hostiles up to their necks in sand and blew their heads off with his gun. The German army shouldn't dirty its hands with him."

Bora nodded. "Thank you, but we both know the German army's hands have not been clean in a long time."

Much like Bora's friend Lattmann in Stalingrad, Vismara bit his nails until his fingertips looked raw. He self-consciously kept his hands out of sight as much as possible. He quickly summarized the dynamics of the theft. Rain, the fallen leaves and the footprints of all those who had run about after the fire concealed all traces of the culprits.

"I think there must have been two of them," Vismara reasoned. "There had to be another person on the lookout, in case someone happened to rush up the stairs. By the time we arrived on the scene, muddy tracks were everywhere. Rolling up the canvas, one could easily hide it under a coat or a cape. Do you agree?"

Bora had imagined a similar sequence of events. "The red paint on the metal fragments suggests the grenade was Italian-made. Easy to find these days. Who lives near the residence?" He turned to the inspector, but his peripheral vision captured a light-blue satin belt on the desktop, tagged and slackly coiled.

"There is a maze of shrubbery and passageways all around. Two German officers and three officials live nearby. All of them in Gardone for an all-night party at the old casino there." Vismara wore glasses to scan the ledger in front of him. Bora wondered how well he could see without them.

"I am rather surprised that there are no credible culprits. It cannot be the first instance of theft in this pleasant community. A lack of suspects is like driving in the dark." Bora paused. *Yes,* he thought. *I have done that, too, and without knowing where I was going. I'm still doing it, in fact.*

"Well, Colonel, private cars are scarce, public transportation few and far between. It takes me as much as two days to reach Milan by phone. What is an obstacle for many proves a blessing for criminals. My predecessor was shot dead in the street a month ago: by whom, we haven't a clue. Hordes of bombed-out refugees keep coming. Churches and hospitals offer shelter to anyone who asks. Add to that ten major army hospitals, all under protection by the Geneva Convention and untouchable. Even ministries shelter doubtful guests. Four days ago, a German army truck loaded with ammunition vanished without a trace. Your compatriots are still looking for it in the mountains … if that is where it is." Vismara, who, judging by the nicks on his face, shaved hastily in cold water, shrugged as if to underscore the futility of such endeavours. "*And* two art collectors who recently showed an interest in the Venus, and who are under suspicion of financing the resistance, have gone on the run."

"That's interesting."

"Is it? The theft could have been commissioned in Venice or Milan, or abroad. The painting could already be out of the province or out of the country. Signor Pozzi has been here six times in the past two days, asking for news."

"I'll meet him tonight," Bora interrupted. "Tell me about the man."

In the following minutes, the motion of Bora's fountain pen on a notebook was the sole comment on Vismara's words. However, some details – "He converses with his late wife" – halted the nib in mid-air.

"Thank you, Inspector. How did it go with Conforti, by the way? Any worthwhile details about the woman's suicide?"

"She hanged herself in the bathroom, Colonel." Vismara pointed with his chin to the satin belt on his desk.

"Belongs to a house robe, does it?"

"Yes. But she was naked."

"Completely?"

Vismara tipped his head, a short motion that was less than a nod. The dark hair on his head, carefully styled with brilliantine, was the sole sign of vanity in him. His face was sensitive and patient. A contemptuous Sohl gossiped that he struggled to care for a wife, four children and a mother-in-law. "Don't get too close to him. He stinks of grease and sweat."

Maybe. War told physically on everyone, except perhaps soldiers like Bora, who would rather face inner turmoil than betray discomposure.

Vismara sighed. "I wonder if those who kill themselves ever consider that someone's got to find them."

"They probably don't think beyond the act itself."

"I've seen my share of dead bodies in my career, aside from the war." Hands out of sight even as he sat, the policeman would not look up. "Ugly corpses I can't ever get used to. An ugly corpse is, what can I say, *too much.*"

The admission intrigued Bora. "Are you speaking of this woman, this body in particular?"

"Why, no. On the contrary. She was beautiful." Vismara whipped a photo out of his drawer.

"She *was* beautiful. Is the portrait recent?"

"Yes. And I can tell you she was still good-looking, even hanging there."

Bora noticed the logo, *Fotografie Conforti*, on the picture. "But a suicide is a suicide, after all. Or is it?"

"Oh, the findings are fully consistent. No sign of forced entry, and the house key was in the apartment, on the dresser. But the Republican Guard arrived first on the scene." Bora understood why, given the nearness between the crime scene and the RNG building. "You'd never think the Guard was relieved of police duty, not by the way they rummaged around. When word got out that the body was unclothed, I had to wrest the house key from them."

"I see." The insolent overlapping of ranks and responsibilities seemed to typify life on the lake. It came to Bora that the same building promiscuously housed the Italian Ministry of Interior, the head of the Republican Police and Kappler's SS. Mengs's office, too. He'd recognized the Gestapo car parked there. Eventually, everyone here knew everything about everyone else.

In Maderno, the voice came wavering through Mengs's telephone. He listened with his meaty ear to the receiver, taking notes in pencil. When a typewriter began to clatter furiously in the next room, he went to shut the door, because he needed silence. "It is your duty to tell, Ambassador Coennewitz," he urged when the voice trailed down. "Failing to do so, just because he was married to your daughter, is equivalent to sharing the guilt."

Headed for Denzo's office, Bora had just left behind a pastel-painted cluster of hotels in the ominous hum of American bombers cruising overhead; too high to drop their load anywhere near, they drew countless cottony trails among the sparse clouds. Even with the windows rolled up, the sound echoed back from the hills, a *whoom-whoom-whoom* that must have rattled the dainty sitting rooms overlooking the lake.

The lunch hour had taken more time than he wished. Sohl, whose job seemed easy and undemanding, was anxious to hear news about the Venus. Overly anxious, even. Bora noted it. Sohl's wife, according to the well-informed Hager, came often to visit him from Meran; it was up to the airman to chauffeur her, begging for fuel this way and that. Bora noted this, too. A phone call or a visit to his old friend Colonel Habermehl in Verona might add useful details to his opinion of the general.

Ahead, in a pool of clear sky, the formation's head squadron was slowly veering south; the ribbons of vapour followed, braiding and drifting as the wind took them. Down an empty road, Bora drove at a good clip. At the Manerba crossroads, there was no sign of life but for a truck idling at the stop sign on the left. Bora engaged, never expecting that the heavy vehicle would go through the stop sign and cross right in front of him, giving him no time to brake.

A sign reading Organization Todt flashed by in a blur. Bora heard himself say, "Jesus Christ," and, the next thing he knew, he was ploughing into the back of the truck at an angle, the edge of the massive chassis smashing through his windshield with a fierce thud that jerked his neck. The pain was blinding; he blacked out a moment, enough to know he'd struck his head and could pass out for good, but he was not going to. He distinctly felt the taste of blood in his nose and mouth. The cold outside air came rushing through the shattered glass, and bright red droplets sprayed about when he shook his head to keep awake. Anger at having wrecked the car – hissing and groaning came from the engine – assured him that he was sentient, and shock turned to fury as the door on the driver's side was yanked open by two panicky auxiliaries.

"I'm all right, I'm *all right*, you incompetent idiots!" But because he was uselessly searching his pockets for something to stanch the blood, when one of the girls handed him a neck cloth, Bora grabbed it. "You've bloody ruined this car!" More stunned than he cared to admit, he was not sure whether he was shouting or just saying the words. Beyond the pale young faces around him, he made out the truck, pivoted in the impact; had it been fully loaded, there would have been more injuries, and he would have likely killed himself. He stormed out to view the sorry state of his vehicle and cursed to himself.

"What are you waiting for? Drive me to Soiano, you imbeciles. I'm not going to be late on account of you two!" But he could tell the girls were good for nothing at the moment. He shoved them aside and manoeuvred the truck himself, back and forth until he detached it from the car and could rumble on to the next checkpoint, where he scattered the soldiers before he was able to brake.

As he parked by the ministry, one minute after the appointed time, he was aware of his bloody looks. On the driveway, he answered the greeting of the colonial chauffeur standing by a handsome Alfa Romeo and strode in. None of the cuts were serious, he assured the flabbergasted adjutant, but could he please know where the lavatory was?

"Should we reschedule the meeting, Colonel?"

"On no account. I just need a moment to tidy myself up."

Major Lipsky, back from Milan in his little yellow car, was astonished to recognize Bora's Fiat 1100 in the wreck by the wayside, with two girls in field-grey berets and short socks standing dejectedly by.

Denzo received Bora with his back to the room, facing the window, hands on his hips. "He who leaves notes on punctuality should not present himself in an untimely fashion, Colonel." And, while the German put together a terse apology, he added, "I hear that in the mountains you refused to fight alongside units of the Italia Division."

"It's true."

Since Bora seemed disinclined to say more, Denzo turned on his heel. The sight of a badly scraped face and bloodstained uniform only made him skip an infinitesimal beat. "What is the meaning of this?"

"I would rather not say."

Bora was aware that his own attitude was biased. That same morning De Rosa had handed him an Italian intelligence report claiming that Denzo had accompanied Graziani to the Milan archbishopric one week earlier. "Both in civvies," De Rosa had added spitefully. "They are intriguing to save themselves. Watch out if you find yourself alone with either of them."

Now the fact that Denzo faced him haughtily, elbows squared, provoked him. Yet collaboration was imperative, lest Graziani be further prejudiced in his regard. "I fought very well alongside Italian units in Russia," he mitigated his remark. "Here is a copy of my orders, for Marshal Graziani."

What with bumping his head in the crash, what with the confrontational meeting at Soiano, Bora had a migraine by the time Denzo's colonial chauffeur delivered him to his hotel. Finding an SS car parked by the Metropoli hardly lightened his mood. He forced himself to walk past it without looking inside. When at the front desk he was handed a note from Lipsky enquiring about his health, he felt a queasy sense of exposure. Did everyone already know? Unclasping his collar in anticipation of a shower and a change of clothes, Bora started up the steps to his room.

"Well, if it isn't Colonel von Bora! We said goodbye on a step and meet on a step."

Bora's fingers fastened the clasp again. "Obersturmbannführer Kappler." He turned to the foot of the staircase.

Kappler had been head of the SS in Rome. They had more or less collaborated until the three hundred dead of the March reprisal brewed hostility between them. During the withdrawal from the city, Kappler admitted being disappointed in him, and the last thing he facetiously asked was whether he was afraid of physical pain. Bora said yes.

Kappler joined him on the step, his vulpine face perfectly shaven under the sombre visor. "I thought you were holding the mountains tooth and nail, and, judging by your looks, you must have been. When did you arrive?"

Bora supposed Kappler knew the answer very well, but he told him all the same. He concealed anxiety in a way the SS somehow appreciated or was amused by; his smirk was friendly. "A full colonel, too. I've just come from meeting Dollmann in Milan: had he heard you were here, he'd have gladly motored along."

"Give my best to Standartenführer Dollmann."

Kappler eyed the cuts on Bora's face. "Do it yourself, he'll be here tomorrow." He climbed as if headed for a specific room, but the moment Bora walked into his own, he came down the stairs again.

Half an hour later, Kappler and his car were gone. Bora read the Venus dossier by the open window: comments on its value; letters from other experts; Conforti's doubts that Titian never signed the work, musing that his signature lay hidden by retouching; an account of the 1940 auction, and a list of participants. On that occasion, Giovanni Pozzi had also won the bid on a wall-sized French tapestry of Jacob wrestling with the Angel, the companion piece to a *Tobias and the Angel* that was outbid by a collector from Milan.

Bora recalled Vismara's words about him. "Pozzi's Greek wife, mentally unstable, killed herself in twenty-nine, after an accident permanently injured her daughter Anna Maria. With his brother-in-law, Pozzi went on to prosper despite other personal losses. After he moved back to Italy from Greece, nothing came of an inquiry into the quality of the material he had sold to the Italian forces in Russia. His lawyers got the case dismissed, and he always denied the charges. Now he's busy acquiring bombed-out lots in the northern cities. Officially, the German army pays nothing to billet in his properties on the lake."

"And unofficially?" Bora had asked.

"He enjoys a series of benefits. Your command can better inform you in that regard."

Was there also another daughter, the one Sohl called hand-some? Bora had not enquired, but wrote down key words in his notebook: *son of emigrants to Rhodes – skipped the Great War – Russian Campaign profiteer? – frequents mediums – has a reliable brother-in-law – only son died at three in a boating accident.*

When Bora walked out of the hotel, bound for his office, the cobblestones under the drizzle resembled the scales of a fish, and the lake seemed to bristle. His headache had passed – he credited Kappler's departure for it – and he was ready to send word to Lipsky that he was well. Recognizing his yellow convertible in the car speeding by, in fact, he nodded a greet-ing when the major flashed a pilot's wave from the cockpit.

That evening Bora gave in to De Rosa's offer of a ride to Villa Malona, where Pozzi lived at the southern edge of town. When the captain had heard Radio Roma, now under Allied control, call to "exterminate the Fascists", he foamed at the mouth.

"I'm sure they mean us Germans as well." Bora smirked. "At least, you're lucky enough to have not one, but two ladies vying to console you."

De Rosa sulked. "I'm not going home tonight."

"Why, is there a third love interest?"

"Here you are." The captain braked, and, when Bora alighted, he called back to him. "After a week or two in Salò,

Colonel, you'll appreciate what women you are not married to can do for you."

At the villa, a sandy-haired man in grey flannel came to the door, and to Bora's enquiry, he shook his head. "I'm Pozzi's partner and brother-in-law, Walter Vittori. General Sohl told us about you. Do come in, Colonel."

Behind him, a glorious stairway, all wrought iron tendrils and leaves, had the mark of German art nouveau. With all the lights on, the high-ceilinged entry hall resembled the foyer of an opera theatre. But a gentle, diffuse glare accented the stairs' landing now. There, on a vast tapestry, billows of azure and silvery clouds swept over a sombre wilderness; among gnarled oaks, two small, muscular figures grappled with each other on a riverbank. One of them had wings.

The man standing below the tapestry sported a pan-sized gold watch in his vest pocket and a massive ring on his right hand. By way of a welcome, he said, "Why, 4-A merinos, top quality wool, 180 grams per 10 meters. First rate material and cut."

"I beg your pardon?"

"Your uniform, Colonel. You had it tailored in Italy, eh?"

"… In Rome, as a matter of fact."

"At Caraceni's?"

"Why, yes."

"I knew it wasn't German-made by the crotch. They sew them baggy at the crotch in Germany." Pozzi walked down to shake Bora's hand with the lump of his hefty ring.

"I am here to convey our solicitude concerning the loss of the Venus, and to assure you we are looking into it."

Even in his impeccable attire, Pozzi looked the merchant's part. Smiling was part of the haggling process. "Yes, well, so says the general. But, you understand, I can't put apologies in the bank. I spent one hundred thousand lire on the frameless picture, and now it's worth a hundred times that amount."

"It was insured, was it not?"

"Insured by Lloyd's of London as of 9 June 1940, Colonel, the day before Italy declared war on England! It means I won't see my money before the end of the war, if ever. What do you expect me to do meanwhile?"

"You can't blame the messenger for his message." Vittori stepped in agreeably. "The colonel is a guest, and we have our list."

"What do you mean, *we have our list*? It was *my* painting: I have *my* list."

Bora glanced at the pink-and-grey struggle of Jacob with the Angel – the *shekinah* of God, as Conforti said. There was no telling who would prevail at this point of the wrestling match. "The theft was carefully planned," he said with remarkable composure, "and would have likely happened whether or not you still resided in the villa. So, you have our sympathy."

"Thank you for the sympathy." Pozzi swept a piece of paper out of his pocket. "I'd appreciate if you'd take a look at this, too."

It was a list of German-occupied buildings: from the Grande Albergo Fasano to Villa Zanardelli, plus the ten army hospitals Vismara had spoken of.

"I'm asking to be their exclusive supplier of surgical sheets and bedding, Colonel. I know they go through them quickly." Adjusting his silk tie was for Pozzi a way of showing the ring, or the powerful hand on which it shone. "It doesn't make up for the loss, but it's better than nothing."

Had Bora not been instructed by Sohl to accept Pozzi's request, he'd have bargained to strike out the convalescent homes from the list. As it was, however, he said, "Very well. Now I wish to hear where you were when the painting was stolen."

"What does *that* mean?"

"It means, sir: can anyone vouch for you at the time of the theft?"

"*I* can."

The woman's voice from the stairs caused Bora to half-turn in that direction. The movement reminded him that his neck was beginning to ache from whiplash. He clicked his heels, while Pozzi protested: "You tell him, Anna Maria."

So, this was the daughter whose tragic accident triggered her mother's suicide.

Apparently whole, she was not at first sight the type of woman Bora found attractive. Dark-haired, dark-eyed, she seemed foreign, her features moulded in a flesh so pale as to have blue shadows. On her paleness, the scarlet bow of her lips drew a full and slightly bitter pout. *Turkish or Arabic women must look and move like her,* he thought. *Those blue shadows, round shoulders and remarkably rich breasts.*

"Thank you for the roses." She surprised him, speaking in German as she offered him her hand. "I'm Annie Tedesco ... Never mind Father's bluntness." In Italian, she added, "That night he was here, with dinner guests. We'd gone past curfew, so we decided to sit up with drinks and chat. Isn't it so, Uncle Walter?"

Vittori spoke up. "That's so, Colonel. When we heard the blast, we all rushed to the windows; Giovanni understood where it had come from and rushed over."

"I did *not* rush! I *walked* out."

Hearing Annie speak his language created a small complicity between them. Bora felt that she offered nothing else, but still, it was pleasant. With a gesture of her manicured hand, she invited him into the next room, where a crystal-laden table sparkled like an ice sculpture. "I cannot leave these men alone without having them argue or get in trouble." She smiled. "Any relation to the Boras who used to holiday at Riva, Colonel?"

On her shoulder, where a delicate, narrow strap joined a generously low neckline, was pinned a spike of wheat, perfectly wrought in gold.

"They're my grandparents," Bora said. He knew he ought to be looking up, but his eyes lingered on that single silk strap.

"We haven't seen them in three years or so. How's the old consul?"

In turn, she was curiously watching him, or the scrapes and cuts from the car accident, with a charming upturn of those red lips of hers. It was a mystery to Bora how women could keep their painted lips and nails looking so wet.

"Well for his age, thank you."

"Their house is not for sale, is it?"

Pozzi's question came against Vittori's whispered, "For God's sake, Giovanni …"

Bora turned.

"I doubt it."

"I always liked La Schiavona. If they ever sell, I'd love to have a crack at it." Pozzi spoke with his nose in the glass of an aperitif. "After the war, maybe."

Promptly, Vittori handed a drink to the German. "I think you own quite enough real estate around the lake, Giovanni."

"Says who? You keep buying and planting shrubs and trees: do I say anything to you?"

Bora ignored them, watching Annie supervise the staff around the table. What did Vismara say about her? That she had married against her father's will, and that her husband, a lieutenant with a Jewish surname, had died in the war. That she lived alone, not far. He was still trying to decide whether she was *handsome*, as General Sohl had said. Surely that silk strap, that gold spike of wheat … And he wondered what her illness might be.

"Anna Maria, the colonel will sit here, by Diamantina." Pozzi nodded to the life-size portrait of an attractive woman in Greek costume with a basket of roses in the crook of her arm and the hills of Rhodes in the background. "My late wife." He sighed.

"Half of my life she took when she died. You sit right under her, a place of honour. Just the other day, she was telling me …"

"Father, you *promised.*"

"Giovanni, it's hardly the case."

Pozzi threw up his hands. "Christ, it's never the case, with you two. As if I were dotty or something. *But I know what I know.* Let's eat, then, if you don't want me to make conversation."

Dinner consisted of the best that the black market had to offer. Pozzi behaved, although, when the second course came, he observed aloud, "What are these little pieces of meat, why aren't we having a decent chunk of roast?"

Annie scowled at him across the table. On Sohl's advice, she'd extended a tactful courtesy to Bora, who continued, apparently unoffended, to eat with his one hand.

"Were you ever in Greece, Colonel?" Vittori enquired from his end of the table, where he was picking through his food like a fussy child.

"I was only in Crete, for service-related reasons."

"Really?" Pozzi waved his fork for the maid to refill the German's glass. "Anna Maria's husband died on the island of Kefalonia."

Bora's glance went to Annie, but Annie was staring at her plate.

"War's got nothing to do with it," Pozzi added. "He hit a post while driving drunk."

Coffee was served in a charming oak-panelled parlour, where Bora recognized some genre pieces described in Conforti's list of the 1940 auction.

"If you don't mind," he politely insisted, "I should like to go back to the reason for my presence here."

Pozzi shrugged. "I told the general all I know, just like I'd told him I wanted to take the Venus out of there. Did he listen to me? No. He says nothing leaves Salò unseen, but I know for a fact that there's plenty that comes and goes. The Venus is gone. Gone. All I can hope for is to collect my insurance way down the road."

"And the deal on hospital linen?" Vittori simpered.

"You bet. Why, Walter, do you disagree?"

Vittori had spoken little during dinner. He had complimented Bora's roses (specially ordered in Sirmione) and uselessly attempted to interest the audience in citron cultivation around the lake. He had avoided all alcohol and was now having no coffee. He sat across from his brother-in-law, limiting himself to a sneer. "It is a load of sheets: I suppose I should agree."

Seated on a low sofa at an angle from the corner in which Bora sat, Annie looked at no one in particular. With her thumb and forefinger, lazily, she circled the bangle on her wrist. The shaded lamp behind her cast a glow of amber-coloured light on the slow rising of her breast at every breath. When she moved, the glow ran down her arm.

"Signor Pozzi, did you consider acquiring Conforti's copy?"

"What for, Colonel? The original was an investment, and copies don't cut it. Did people envy me when I bought the Venus, especially after it was authenticated? Did Conforti give you the names of those I outbid? One has moved to Switzerland, but two are still around."

"So I heard. Would they try to secure the Venus by theft?"

"I haven't got a clue, Colonel. They sure wanted it then."

"It could be someone local, too," Vittori suggested.

"The Jew, Walter? Balderdash. He has a bad heart and heaps of trouble trying not to cross the Germans these days. Am I not right, Colonel?"

Bora ignored the question. "I assume no one has contacted you in reference to the Venus."

"Demanding a ransom, you mean? Of course not. All I want at this point is insurance money. And a monopoly on those goddamned sheets."

With her forefinger, Annie kept toying with the bangle. Now and then, she glanced up, never directly at the German's face, but in his direction – an attention that Bora was increasingly aware of. "The colonel was good enough to come, Father. The least we can do is to be helpful."

"Yes, well, it won't give me my picture back, Anna Maria."

There are times … There are times when you suddenly realize what it is that you have been hoping for subconsciously. All evening, it dawned on Bora, he had been quietly wishing for Annie to raise her arm, so that he could spy whether her armpit was shaven or not. But Annie Tedesco was too composed for that, and he still had to wait.

For nearly one hour, they continued to converse, more relaxed as the time to part drew nearer. Vittori spoke of his cotton fields in Egypt before meeting Pozzi, of the Mediterranean Textile Consortium they created together at Malona, and, had Pozzi not interrupted continuously, Bora could have drawn a reliable picture of the two. Pozzi sipped his cognac and kept dropping names of high-ranking Germans and Fascist ministers with whom he affected to be on familiar terms. How true his loyalty might be at this stage of the war, Bora decided he'd ask Vismara later on.

Through it all, Annie sat quietly in her paleness like an odalisque. Her profile gave Bora the lovely, pained impression of a sumptuous woman kept in reserve. He pictured a sensuality made of restraint, reticence: not the prim uprightness of a Mrs Murphy, or the clumsiness of his one-night stand in Berlin. Rather, the unhurried expectation to be chosen, patient or resigned, or dormant. He watched the small motions of her hands, wrists, the slow turn of her neck and torso, and surprised himself, since he was supposedly indifferent to her physical type, conjuring her lazy twisting in bed, all white skin and deep shadows. It grieved him like a fault rather than a sign of virtue that he had not taken advantage of that moment in May when Nora Murphy seemed about to relent, for if she was to fall pregnant anyway, then why not by him rather than her ageing husband? He was ashamed for thinking such thoughts, and even more for not feeling guilty. Only ashamed.

Finally, when Annie stretched her cigarette out for her uncle to light it, Bora caught a glimpse of flesh in the crescent of her sleeveless gown: a preciously smooth curve, like ivory veiled by a tinge on this side of blue. "My late wife, Colonel ..." Pozzi brought him back unpleasantly to the question at hand. "My late wife – and I don't want anyone here to interrupt me – explained to me that the Venus is already out of the country."

Bora stared at him coolly. "Well, your late wife has a privileged observation point. But the nearness of the Italian border is evident even for us who lack that privilege. Any suggestion about the identity of the thief? That, I could use." He spoke as if he'd just heard a credible piece of advice, but Vittori had apparently had enough of his relative's drivel; he waved apologetically and left the room.

Ten minutes later, Bora took his leave as well. To Annie Tedesco, who saw him to the door, he said, "I will share all appropriate or relevant information. My work telephone number is on my card, and you ... and of course your father, Signora ... are welcome to call, should there be news at your end."

Had she caught his hesitation before that precipitous "of course", and how would she interpret it?

All she said was, "It was good of you to come, Colonel. I hope Father's candour will not prejudice you against him. He is what life has made him, but a decent man."

"It was good of you to have me." When Bora bowed to kiss her hand, pain went through his neck like a stab. With it, the discreet hint of her perfume wafted to him, exquisite, as everything was impeccable about her.

Outside, the night was crisp, nearly cold. A slender moon scudded over grey clouds, and only because of it, when the door closed behind him, Bora recognized Vittori smoking in the garden. "Good night, Colonel. Watch your step. The steps are slick with leaves."

"Thank you. Good night."

"Forgive me for leaving the room. There are times when Giovanni's ways become insufferable. Annie is as patient as her mother ... He's a lucky man."

Bora, who had started towards the gate, halted under the trees. "Yes," he said. Then, lest Vittori take it as cheeky compliment to Annie, he added, "It's quite all right."

"Is your car in the street?"

"No. I'll walk." Bora saw Vittori toss away the butt of his cigarette, a fiery glimmer in the air. "The curfew forces me to stay. Giovanni is the only one in the family with a pass to drive around as he pleases."

"One of the privileges he obtained from us?"

"The latest, through General Sohl's chief of staff."

"Good night."

Bora crossed the gate. Lipsky's interactions with Pozzi had not been mentioned even once. Sohl himself had been quiet about them, for whatever reason. The walk in the dark would give him time to think things over, and to take Annie Tedesco's strange beauty out of his head.

At Maderno, mouthing his cough drop, Jacob Mengs placed a long-distance call to Berlin before retiring.

3

The crack of small arms reached Bora's ears as he left the hotel in the haze of a wet day. Front-line practice allowed him, in a handful of tense seconds, to gauge the approximate distance of gunfire: shots from a marksman's rifle, half a kilometre away. He glimpsed a militiaman race towards the noise, musket in hand. A shoot-out ensued, accompanied by the clatter of hobnailed boots on cobblestones.

Bora headed for the RNG building, where the noise seemed to focus, past shuttered house fronts like faces still asleep, or unwilling to look. He unlatched the holster at his left side as a precaution, mindful of peripheral sights and sounds. He walked past Vismara's office on the square; approaching Garibaldi Street, he saw a crowd of armed men in front of the RNG headquarters. By the entrance, the sentinel lay face up in his own blood, among scattered leaflets; a crimson splash marred the wall against which he'd stood watch. A thin curl of steam rose from the hole between his eyes, as if the youngster's soul were leaking out skyward. Blood also flowed from under his black sweater, whose elbows were threadbare. The deadly accuracy of the first shot showed in the way his cap was still on; the other two bullets had been fired into him for macabre good measure, as if to grant De Rosa what he wished for – mayhem at his doorstep. Indeed, the captain was out there, taking snapshots with a pocket-sized Contax camera, barking out orders all the while. Swaggering guardsmen dispersed across the road, kicking doors open or hammering on them with their rifle butts. Bora remained anchored to his self-control. He stooped to pick up one of the leaflets from the bloody ground, and, recognizing the font, pocketed it for later use.

MARSHAL GRAZIANI'S MINISTRY OF
THE ARMED FORCES, SOIANO

"What would you like me to do with this? Data older than twenty-four hours no longer qualifies as intelligence."

Captain Parisi would not argue with Bora. He took back the stack of field reports his superior sent into the room before walking in. Denzo was entering at that moment, fresh from breakfast, and took the German's impatience as mere spite for having had to wait. But Bora was saying, "How familiar are you with passive and active counter-insurgency operations?"

"That is precisely what you were called in for." Denzo chewed on his resentment. "What about them?"

Stormily, Bora stared him down. "Passive measures are to my mind preferable, although they have limited efficaciousness. Active measures accomplish their goals, but lead to heavy casualties, even among civilians. In the East, intelligence favoured sending in well-trained, well-armed reconnaissance and executing random searches and sweeps, but not exasperating the population, in order to point out the difference between our methods and the coercion often used by irregulars to ensure civilian support."

"And your version of *active measures*?"

Marshal Graziani barged into the room with his trademark scowl. Favoured by the Germans although he disliked them, silver-haired and handsome, he combined imposing size with a use of cologne that put Parisi to shame. Without waiting for an answer, he solicited Bora's written orders and let him remain at attention while scanning them.

"Since you speak Italian," he then observed, "everything will be easier. It is your privilege to be assigned to Colonel Count Emilio Denzo di Galliano. You start next Monday."

That "assigned to" galled Bora, but there it was. "*Next Monday*, Marshal? I was hoping …"

Graziani handed the orders to Denzo, who dropped them on the glass-topped desk for his adjutant to pick up. "At ease, Colonel. What about these *active measures* of yours?"

For some minutes, Denzo listened with profound annoyance to Bora's manual-perfect report. "As I see it, active counter-insurgency operations are not more complex: only costlier. They involve moving slowly towards identified areas, by daylight only, covering five or so kilometres a day, so as to spot the enemy camps. Once this is achieved, you can attack the irregulars with air support and corral them down specific escape routes into 'killing areas'. It comes down to containment and liquidation. I needn't stress the necessity of complete radio silence, the use of passwords and badges, and so on. Whenever possible, leaflets must be dropped to warn civilians within the perimeter to surrender the partisans. Any other approach, including the random killing of partisans and their supporters, or blind reprisals against civilians, always has been and always will be counterproductive."

A-ha. Denzo glanced at the Marshal, whose scowl had grown stonier at the implicit critique of Italian operations in the African war. Bora ignored them. "As a soldier, I abhor pointless violence. I served in Russia, and I am convinced it must be avoided at all costs."

"At *all costs?*"

Denzo's question was a leading one. Bora knew this, but arrogance and youth blinded him for a moment. "Gentlemen, you will have to live with these irregulars after the war, unless you plan to kill them all before then." He showed the leaflet found near the sentinel's body an hour earlier. "This morning's *reply* to something we did, and so forth, ad infinitum. What good is it? The handfuls of rebels I faced in the Verona countryside last year were nothing compared to today's bands. Five weeks ago, in the Ossola Valley, moderation allowed us to withdraw in an orderly fashion, regroup and attack successfully."

Denzo exploded. "You, a German, come preaching about moderation! Were you not assigned to the Cisa Pass in July?"

"I was. But I had better things to do than fiddling about with the rebels up there."

"Enough." Graziani raised his right glove (he had not removed it, nor had he shaken hands with Bora). "Colonel von Bora, you cannot serve as liaison with the regular Republican Army so long as you share your office with the Guard."

"I was under the impression that the RNG were now part of the Republican Army. But if the marshal commands that I relocate to this ministry, I will."

Denzo hastened to avoid the likelihood.

"Sir, neither the Military Secretariat nor the headquarters have available offices. May I suggest that the colonel find a completely separate location? Wehrmacht headquarters at Gardone, for example."

"By the marshal's leave, at Gardone I would be far from the Guard but even more so from this ministry."

A shock of white hair danced on Graziani's forehead as he turned vivaciously. "Colonel von Bora, you have a car at your disposal." (Bora actually had borrowed a staff car for the day from the Italian pool.) "If your handicap makes you insecure about driving, Colonel Denzo's adjutant will secure a chauffeur for you."

Bora saw red but watched his tongue. "That will not be necessary. Thank you. May I suggest that I set myself up at General Sohl's command? It would allow me prompt access to Soiano and the RNG as well."

Graziani nodded, and, even though Colonel Denzo seemed dissatisfied, he accepted Bora's proposal.

During his drive back, Bora noticed an American aircraft, seemingly an armed pathfinder, weaving a figure of eight over the lake. Whether the pilot spotted the staff car leaving Graziani's Villa Omodeo or not, it was soon sweeping past, too close for comfort. With no anti-aircraft to be had, it flew brazenly for a time directly over Bora's head at minimum speed, before banking at last towards San Felice and its shoals.

Down the road, driving by the gate of Pozzi's lavish property, Bora was intrigued to see Lipsky's yellow car parked among the palmettos of the driveway. Little surprise, therefore, that he should not sit at his work desk at the residence. Sohl, however, was on the phone, and, seeing Bora in the hallway, slammed down the receiver.

"How did it go?" He solicited a report as Bora stepped in. "Any first impressions?"

"Well, Marshal Graziani …"

"No, not Graziani. We know enough about *him*. I meant dinner at the merchant's."

Again, friendliness concealed an edge of anxiety. Bora only half-relaxed. "Pozzi will keep complaining about the loss of the Venus, while he awaits his insurance money. He insured the painting before its authentication, and, after Italy declared war on England, he had no time to raise the premium. According to both him and Conforti, the value has increased a hundredfold."

"That much?" Sohl toyed with the humidor on his desk. "I had no idea."

"To an interested collector, she may be worth even more." The old intelligence habit of looking beyond appearances, of capturing small changes in behaviour came in useful at times. Bora surmised the general had just received or conveyed by phone a touchy piece of news, which he could not or would not share.

"Anything else?"

"None other than Pozzi went off to Rhodes when he was young and that he made his first money speculating on army blankets in the Great War. In time, he invested in silk production at Como and Lecco. Interestingly enough, only days before Italy invaded mainland Greece, he sold most of his holdings there, making a tidy profit. His brother-in-law brought to the partnership a technical degree, cotton plantations and agave fields along Somalia's Lower Juba; he'd made a fortune in his own right on the markets of Merca and Mogadishu and lived for ten years in Egypt. Together, they had enough funds by 1920 to acquire a number of German- and Austrian-owned villas along the lake; his present home was designed by Schäfer and renamed by him Villa Malona. I believe Pozzi engaged in strike-breaking in the Teens and early Twenties and only joined Fascism when he saw that Mussolini was there to stay. He does business with the regime openly now, but, as with other manufacturers, he may be smelling a change in the wind: millions in funds for the Ossola partisans came from somewhere."

Sohl stared at him. "All of this you learned in one evening?"

"I also learned that Vittori – who is Greek on his mother's side, as is Pozzi's late wife – is now a partner only nominally. His family grew roses in Rhodes, but Walter was soon dispatched to cultivate cotton in Somalia. From the few words he was able to get in last night, I gather he still cares for flowers more than cloth."

The aftereffects of the telephone call were seemingly slow in dissolving. Sohl ponderously picked a cheroot and placed it in his mouth without lighting it.

"What did you think about Signora Tedesco?"

"Nothing."

"Not your type?"

Don't rush to answer, Bora thought, *don't hasten to deny it.* "No, sir."

"Pity."

Sohl glanced at the telephone. Was he awaiting a second call, or still thinking of the one he had received? Bora decided he would provocatively toss a stone in the pond before asking for office space. "General, I heard that Pozzi was granted certain privileges, including permission to drive a private car."

"Yes. That was Lipsky's idea."

"And what does Lipsky have to do with Pozzi?"

Sohl walked over to the fireplace to light his cheroot, trying perhaps to escape Bora's scrutiny. "I see that you, too, Bora, are beginning to doubt the major. Before we had to ... *agree* to his request to supply hospital linen, Pozzi was happy for us to let him keep his textile machines in nearby Roè."

"Quite a privilege. We're shipping everything else to Germany."

"Lipsky was at once taken with the Venus, the tapestries and other pieces of art. In the past weeks, he has been paying social calls to admire the collection, and I daresay the Tedesco girl as well." Bora suspected the general mentioned her again to see how he'd react, and kept silent. "The driving pass is something Lipsky originally offered to her, but she declined in favour of her father."

"If I may say so, sir, you did not have to sign off on it."

"Well, I did. But I also decided to do some more fact-finding on Lipsky." Sohl signalled for Bora to close the door. "I cannot give you details, nor reveal my sources. Suffice it to say, they confirmed to me that he works *directly* for Hermann Göring. And while I have no quarrel with the Reich Marshal's passion for collecting art, I don't care to become involved. So I want Lipsky out. I asked to reassign him as of the first of November. Share nothing about the Venus with him. Stall him until he leaves. God knows there's enough art in this country for Göring to set his sights on. Remember that if he's here when you find the painting, it'll be as good as lost again."

"Finding it may not be easy."

A puff of smoke hovered around the general's stout figure, blurring his features. "Right, and the Venus may be only a piece of the story. A set of paintings went missing from a rural chapel near Nozza. The lord bishop of Brescia tells me the chapel is in the sticks, in an area reportedly plagued by partisan activity."

This *was* news. But not the piece of news that made Sohl nervous. "Take a look at this leaflet, found on the premises." Sohl showed him a sheet. "The printer is a typographer by trade. Cristomorto is his name."

"I've heard of him."

"Commander Xavier, as he's also known. He controls the high ground between Brescia and Lake Idro."

"He *controls* it, sir?"

"I see you're intrigued. See? The assignment will not bore you."

De Rosa's blasphemies filled the stairwell, but out of his cubbyhole, the absurd duet from an Italian operetta streamed from a radio. *Only Fascists could go to their deaths listening to vaudeville tunes,* thought Bora. Compared to the stuffiness at Villa Omodeo, however, even this nonsense was preferable. Fezcapped youngsters loaded with weapons thundered downstairs, stiffening their right arms to greet him.

"Where are you going?"

"To kill us a few, Colonel."

"Where, and how?"

"Captain knows. In a motor bus, Colonel."

Bora addressed De Rosa in German so that the youngsters would not understand. "You're not taking them out in a *motor bus!*"

Avoiding his eyes, De Rosa draped a cartridge belt across his chest and checked the magazine in his pistol. "Well, what else have I to carry them? Let me through, Colonel." When Bora reminded him of the chain of command, headed by Graziani, he burst out, "Fuck him!"

Bora, pale with anger, managed not to raise his voice. "No hare-brained raids while I'm here, De Rosa; they serve no purpose. We already had a casualty this morning. And you're not taking those boys out in a civilian bus."

Aborting the sortie would not do, so Bora, dabbing the cut that had reopened on his lip, ordered the bus to the German vehicle depot; he himself preceded it in the staff car, talking sense into a De Rosa still frantic for revenge. At the depot, he negotiated and obtained an Opel three-tonner, balm on the Guard's poverty of equipment. Chow time at the Wehrmacht mess hall followed, where Bora stayed with the rank and file, then off to the firing range and back to Salò in triumph by three o'clock.

Proud of having also secured for himself a sleek Bianchi S9, Bora knew that three o'clock was the last useful time of day to converse with his hard-drinking Verona friend Habermehl. He hastened to his hotel room to telephone him and found him relatively lucid.

Twenty years older than Bora, the old flyer hadn't risen past the rank of colonel. He addressed Bora by his first name; still, Bora called him Herr Oberst. "Yes, Martin, I know Lipsky. He flew with your brother in Russia, didn't he? You told me to check on him, and I did. Keeps a room here at the Albergo Milano. Alone, to all reports, although he does have female company now and then. Mostly, he stores objects in his room. Art objects, yes. Ships them by courier out of the country."

"To Germany?"

"As far as I know, to the German Reich. The Tyrol, to be precise."

"Meran, by any chance?"

"I'll be damned. How did you know?"

"Bear with me, Herr Oberst. To a private address or an APO?"

"Now, that I don't know. Well, if you insist … Give me a couple of days, Martin … Now, why on earth should I tell Sohl that you called? I haven't told you that he asked me about you, have I."

"The older I become, Colonel," Conforti told him, "the more I realize that landscapes are all that counts. They alone can do justice to the diversity of life. So, although I earn my living taking portraits, landscapes are what matters to me."

Bora found the old man in the kitchen, going through some of his photographs by the open window. In contrast with the twilit ground floor, here the view of a luminous sunset was sweeping. "Isn't a portrait a sort of landscape?" he observed. "Faces are maps after all."

"But a map is not a landscape." Conforti gathered the prints in a folder. He had small, delicate hands, younger than his age. "My desire is to capture a precise moment in a precise place, so representative as to embody it completely. Look outside from where you stand. You can see lines and nuances I could describe to you with my eyes closed. My mind is the photographic plate. The way the sun sinks behind the mountain, a chip in the stone of the windowsill … See? To your left, the eaves of the house next door, its drainpipe loose and removed from the wall just enough to show a belfry on the other shore of the lake, rising like the fin of a fish skimming the water. I have hundreds of such exposed plates in me."

Bora faced the window. With uncanny precision, he recalled one late afternoon near Krasnograd, when he'd sat down to sketch. A farmhouse, lost on a rise, dwarfed by enormous white clouds, had seemed so metaphorical of his plight then. His pencil had followed a crisp mental image of what his eye saw, dividing the texture of rag paper between object and space, assigning solidity to one and emptiness to the other. Where was that sketch now? Curious how he couldn't remember how long he'd been in Krasnograd, how he and his men had left, to what awful next thing. The sound of a distant air-raid siren startled him then, and he was in Russia and here for the fraction of a second, lost and uprooted. Conforti put the photos away in the room filled with the light of sunset. *I will not come out of this alive. How did I ever think I would?* Bora felt neither resigned nor sad. Only weary. Utterly so, but as he stepped back from the window, he forgot both the thought and his weariness.

He asked, for the sake of asking, "How well did you know the woman who killed herself?"

Conforti looked keenly at and then away from the small cuts on the German's face. "Not well, but I knew her." A second folder came to rest on the table. "Would you care to see a portrait photo of her? I took it a few days ago." Nameless black-and-white faces stared back from the prints until Conforti found the one he wanted. "Here." He held it up for Bora to see.

Bora had seen the same print in Vismara's office. A face firm and melancholy, the looks of one who has thought things through and come to a decision. *That is sad resolve, not melancholy.* Bora recognized the feeling, although the time for contemplating suicide was behind him. Destiny needed no encouragement; if Russia had not driven him to carry out the proposition, nothing would. The woman's ears were small, weighed down by antique earrings. She had heard all she was ever going to hear. Nothing would change her mind.

"Was she unhappy? She must have been."

"Or tired of living. She lost her husband in the war, and her house to an air raid. She moved here six months ago, to a room with her mother-in-law. After the old woman died in the summer, she stayed. That's all."

"May I have this print?"

Conforti said yes, and Bora slipped it into his briefcase. Their eyes met across the table. "I suppose, Colonel, that you came to hear what else about the Venus there is to know."

"Yes, that too." Bora did not specify what other question had brought him there. He followed the old man into the hallway, where the painting hung alone on the shadowy wall.

"Observe," said Conforti, pointing to it, "the background resembles that of *Sacred and Profane Love*, or Giorgione's *Sleeping Venus*, which Morassi and Öttinger attribute to Titian himself. A wide-open landscape, not an interior. Cliffs, trees lost in the mist. Clues rather than symbols, Colonel."

Bora faced the canvas with his arms folded. "Clues to what?"

"Riches."

"*Riches?*" Bora turned slowly.

"To wealth nearly beyond reckoning." The sunset glow from the kitchen lit up Conforti's thinning hair like a halo; his bearded face was astute, impish, a breath away from wickedness somehow. Bora had the irrational impression of a conjurer who, by saying the word, could keep him from ever leaving these rooms.

"You see, Colonel, La Bella's child lived to the age of twelve. Who was the father, Francesco or his son Guidobaldo? Francesco called him his own. To avoid a dispute over birthright, he endowed the boy with a remarkable legacy, away from the city of Urbino. The painting is believed to conceal the key to its location."

Treasure, of course. What else? Bora relaxed at once. *He has to come up with something more believable than this.* "The key must be well concealed if no one has managed to find the treasure in the last four hundred years."

"Nobody knew about it. With La Bella and Francesco dead, and the child gone by 1550, only Titian remained. He himself ignored the treasure's precise location, having been ordered to copy the landscape from a nameless sketch. Years later, in the original painting, the master further complicated things by retouching the background, something he frequently did. The copy dates from after the alteration, so it is doubly deceptive. Around 1560, Garcia Hernandez, the Spanish ambassador of Philip II, wrote that, by that time, Titian was so forgetful as to misplace important papers and receipts. I believe instead that even in his old age he knew more than he cared to show."

Bora had with him the postcard-sized photo of the original Venus, where details were unreadable.

"As you may know, Colonel, Titian died in the plague of 1576, at nearly one hundred years of age. His papers, deemed infected, were burned. I did run into a reference, among Vid von Dornberg's diplomatic papers, to a secret agreement between Francesco della Rovere and Titian, but Dornberg failed in learning the details. So, the treasure is still there, and the thief has no inkling that the Venus keeps a secret from him."

"Or maybe he does."

"No, the alterations were too extensive. *I* have my reasons to believe the landscape indicates a place near Naples. The small emblem with the mermaid in the corner, well visible in the original, points to the ancient name of that city. And La Bella hailed from there."

A treasure hunt? These days Naples and southern Italy were solidly in Allied hands. Bora was simply amused by Conforti's tale. "You spoke of *riches*. That is …?"

"Judge for yourself, Colonel. Booty stolen from the monastery of Saint Onofrio's in Rome. When in 1527 forty thousand Imperials sacked the city, the pillaging continued for nine days. The mercenaries ravaged churches and palaces and torched the Vatican tapestries to extract gold thread from them. Francesco della Rovere had orders to contain the sack, but he camped north of Rome instead, waiting to buy the loot from the German mercenaries. Would he return it to Saint Onofrio's for a ransom? Not after he fell in love with La Bella."

"Church vessels, then."

"Ha! Most of the riches at Saint Onofrio's originated in Venice, from where they'd disappeared in the great fire of 1231. I studied the inventories, so I know what survived the flames and found its way to Rome. Byzantine crosses of solid gold, bejewelled reliquaries, an altar of gilded silver weighing three hundred Italian pounds, crystal chalices set in precious metals, and more."

Bora stared at him.

"Does the list surprise you?" The old man chuckled. "I assure you, it is only a partial list. When Titian travelled to Rome in 1545, to visit the pope and Michelangelo, he stopped by Saint Onofrio's. Why? Was he hoping to learn the value of the lost treasure from the good friars?" In the coming dusk, Conforti's gaunt head took on the sinister look of a goat's skull. "Now you see why no copy can ever compare with the original. That's as far as my research took me; I had no means of seeing through the alterations. When Pozzi bought the Venus, I knew I would tell *him* nothing."

The place, the hour, the strange tale. Bora tried to keep to the task at hand. "How did the Venus come to Salò? Who owned it before Pozzi?"

"The painting comes and goes from history, Colonel. When Francesco's son Guidobaldo died in 1574, two of the three in the set were sold: the *Santi Venus* and ours. Aware of the secret value of the latter, Titian tried and finally succeeded in securing and retouching its background. After his death, his heir squandered money and sold off the collection. Our Venus went to the Medicis and remained in Florence for years. She travelled to Rome with one of the family cardinals and was lost for two centuries, only to reappear unexpectedly at the auction in 1940. The seller was anonymous, but we all assumed he was a wealthy Italian Jew from the Brescia area, in need of cash after the Racial Laws."

One flip of the switch, and the light of a shaded lamp awakened the luscious naked figure from the dusk. "Pozzi was looking for 'a big piece', as he said, and I hastened to suggest the Venus. Once I authenticated it, I dreaded a second wave of interest, legitimate and illegitimate."

"So, Pozzi is not aware of the painting's secret. Does anyone else know, beside you?"

"No one."

The question, *Why tell me, then?* became so obvious that Bora did not ask, but everything in him expressed confusion.

Conforti lowered his eyes. "I believe that when we first met yesterday you mistook my emotion for fear, Colonel. In fact, the motive was altogether different. See, I *recognized* you." He clasped his hands until the knuckles went white. "That is, I knew you would come, eventually. I simply did not expect you would be *what* you are." Followed by Bora, he walked back to the kitchen, where evening folded like a wing at the window. "But there's no helping it."

Bora felt exposed, lest Conforti had learned through the Jewish grapevine of his support for the Verona community a year earlier. "Who told you about me?"

"No one told me. You simply don't spend a lifetime studying art and photographing faces without learning to know people. Let's say that when I learned of the theft, I knew the right man would come to look for the Venus."

"Myself, *naturally*." In his anxiety, Bora grew irritable. "Look for her and find her, too?"

"Yes. I admit I expected you would be Italian, and older. Details."

"Details? I hope you realize I have no idea of how to trace the original!"

"That is true. But, Colonel, I trust you will."

Bora swept his cap from the table and left.

The dusky stairwell looked like a cistern. Bora had already gone past the first landing when curiosity got the better of him; the dead woman's door stood slightly ajar. The rustle of objects being displaced came from within. Careless to meet face to face with Vismara or someone from the Republican Guard, he pushed the door open and startled a rumpled little woman from rummaging through a dresser. She reacted in an odd way, too frightened to scream, throwing up her hands with her mouth open. "I wasn't taking anything, honest. I was just looking."

"How did you get in?"

"The door unlocks with the key from the front door below." The woman pulled a key from her apron's pocket.

Bora took the key from her. Fearful of the uniform, she did not resist; she crept sideways to the threshold, past it, and across the landing to her own door.

The sound of boots racing back up the stairs and the loud knocking would alarm anyone.

"What did Bianca Spagnoli live off, do you know?"

Conforti let Bora in, with no other reaction save that quick catching of his breath. Behind him, the Venus was barely visible inside her frame. "She had once been a pianist and music teacher, I believe, but now she eked out a living on a widow's pension."

In the few minutes spent exploring the woman's rooms, Bora had seen the piano, of course, and stacks of scores for an experienced hand. "Why did she stop teaching?"

"I don't know. She saved her piano from the bombs and brought it here. I never heard her play. Colonel ... Colonel, why do you ask? It was a sad enough story."

"It could be even sadder."

Vismara was about to leave his office for the night when Bora called at a quarter past eight. "... The Spagnoli post-mortem?" He replied in haste. "Well, Colonel, a physician verified the cause of death, which was consistent with suicide, and the approximate hour of it, which was seven a.m. Why do you ask?"

"In the woman's apartment, aside from a neighbour snooping around, I noticed that the doorknobs and handles have ribbons tied to them. She owned an excellent piano, which she did not play. I wonder whether she suffered from a disease of the joints."

"What? Such as ...?"

"Arthritis, maybe. My grandfather suffers from it, and, even though his hands appear normal, in the morning he has difficulty even with the simplest of motions." In anticipation of his morning appointment with Eugen Dollmann, Bora was busy pinning badges on his tunic, cradling the receiver between neck and shoulder. "Is there any chance of exhuming the body?"

The extravagant proposal silenced Vismara at first. "Colonel von Bora, the body was shipped off for burial. Surely, you realize ... What's on your mind?"

"That if by some remote chance she could not tie a noose, then someone else did."

Whether it was the last hypothesis he wanted to hear, or he simply wanted to go home for the day, Vismara sighed.

"… And were you aware that she changed the lock, so that she could use the larger key to the front door?"

"I was not aware. But she was locked in, and the key was on the dresser."

"The neighbour got in, didn't she? And did you search for a duplicate key?"

"There's no reason to believe there was a second key. All tenants had the key to the front door."

Bora was dissatisfied but grudgingly let Vismara go.

That night, Jacob Mengs made a new file out of the many.

FASANO, WEDNESDAY, 18 OCTOBER 1944

The morning was warm enough to breakfast at a small table in the garden of Villa Paradiso, where German embassy personnel roomed in style. SS Colonel Dollmann, with whom Bora had had close, politically unorthodox dealings in Rome, pretended not to know who Mengs was, or what he was up to.

"Of course not," he sneered, volubly changing the subject to Rommel's death. "The Field Marshal was *invited* to kill himself, and he obeyed. Never mind, and I quote the Führer's words, that when a government leads a country to ruin, rebellion is not only a right, but a duty, blah, blah, blah. But maybe that doesn't apply to soldiers." He bit into a piece of cake. "Any other version of the story is dung; we both know it, and eat it we must."

The simile was ill timed, but Bora was not thinking of food. Dollmann fussed. "I know you knew and are annoyed to hear *me* confirm it. Well, what other advantages are there to being in the SS if not ready access to the scuttlebutt? Keep it for yourself as you keep much to yourself. I actually liked old Rommel, but he was too ambitious for his own good." He ogled Bora over his coffee. "Have you got yourself a lover?" he asked with a grin. "Cuts and bruises aside – or because of them, they give you a roguish air – you look splendid."

Bora recognized the oblique nature of those compliments. "We are speaking of a dead Field Marshal, Standartenführer!"

"What do you expect me to do, weep? The Gothic Line destroyed your sense of humour, Bora. We need a lot of humour these days." Dollmann paused while the waiter laid a small plate of butter on the table. "I know you're cross at being detached from your regiment, but Brescia is not far, and, as a liaison officer, you have more leeway than most. Besides … Look, I'm not here to discuss field marshals, dead or alive. I'll meet Il Duce in two hours, and the prospect is not so enticing that I'd do so without a pleasant breakfast first. I'm delighted you could join *me*."

Bora watched him butter his toast with dainty dabs of the knife. It was hard to say with Dollmann. In Rome, he'd shown him vapid admiration and daring political support. It could be that today he merely wanted to see him.

"Does Denzo still wear those ridiculous square spectacles to read the small print? For all your insisting that you won't make up your mind about him 'for a week', I can tell you don't like him. Gird your loins, then, because you'll like Graziani even less. *The Butcher of Libya*! If you want to roil him, mention Teutoburg."

"The *battle* of Teutoburg in AD 9?"

"Precisely. Speaking to the Italian troops training in Germany, Graziani deplored Rome's defeat at the hands of Germanic tribes before catching his blunder. We were all laughing in our sleeves. As for your unofficial duty … Sohl couldn't keep the lid on it if he wanted to. News of the theft is out. Il Duce himself showed an interest in the Venus. Whatever else one might say, it's undeniable that he appreciates a good-looking woman."

"How would you know?"

"In February, the Minister of the Interior asked me to convince the owner to offer the painting as a birthday present to Mussolini's lady friend."

Gossip about Mussolini's lover was routine, but already Dollmann was adding, "Il Duce heard of it and grew furious. Had the lady known of the proposal, she might have insisted, being far more spendthrift than His Excellency. Do you have any suspects?"

Bora was wondering whether Dollmann had given him a lead or was simply making conversation. "Yes," he lied.

"I wager that at the top of the list is that spooky little Jew, although I can't think how he'd pull off the heist."

"Or *why*, other than the fact he's Jewish."

Dollmann's amusement fogged over. He fastidiously inspected the rim of his glass and wiped it with his napkin, even though it was perfectly clean. "You still don't watch yourself, do you?" He helped himself to mineral water.

"There's nothing left to watch." At the coming of a second round of coffee, Bora agreeably lifted his cup. "To Rommel, Standartenführer, and to dead men who failed."

"You should not say such things."

"Why not? We're all projections of death."

"But we cast different shadows." When a small yellow leaf floated down from the tree above them and into his glass, Dollmann fretfully discarded the water. "Some are potentially very short."

"Not yours."

Water filled the glass again. "I'm bored with this conversation: let's drop it."

Bora sensed unspoken alarm signals as Dollmann turned to idle chatter, from Sohl's wife – "a pretty young thing in a ratty fur coat" – to the opera season in Milan, all in a frivolous muddle that might have had something to do with the arrival of other officers in the garden. "… If you look at the map, the lake resembles a giant phallus, and we're all playing with it." And again, "Toti Dal Monte is doing *Madama Butterfly* in Milan this month." All he could do was stay serious, hard-lipped.

"And about the Venus, Bora: tell me, who's next on the list of suspects, the partisans? They do need money."

"Yes, and so do my present employers."

This time Dollmann laughed, because Bora meant the Italian government. "Because of Il Duce's interest in the painting?"

"No. Because we present them with a tab of ten billion lire every month." Bora kept mum about suspecting Lipsky and Sohl himself.

"Well! This much I know. You're too testy to have a lover." Holding the glass close to his chest, Dollmann covered it with his hand when a shower of coin-sized yellow leaves rained down. "I thought you'd have straddled our inviolable Mrs Murphy on your last night in Rome. Tell me that you did! She *was* falling for you. I saw her in Switzerland not too long ago: any chance that the upcoming blessed event may be yours?"

Confirmation of Nora's state came so cruelly that, scrambling to maintain his composure, Bora lost it altogether. Dollmann regretted his words. Bora might not have grown haggard with battle fatigue, but tension inside him was parcelled off until it seemed solid instead of shatterable. It had to be a painful process. "That was an unforgivable lack of discretion on my part, Bora. I didn't think it was that serious between you." Whether meant as an apology or to distract him, he added under his breath, "Watch out for Jacob Mengs. He's Kaltenbrunner's man, and a beast."

*

After leaving Dollmann under the mild spring-like sun, Bora had the claustrophobic need to clear his mind. He went for a stroll along the lake, where water plants washed ashore like the tangled hair of drowned women. He listened to the plashing of the waves: a smooth play of advance and retreat under his heels, and now and then the noiseless roll of pebbles below the shifting veil of water.

The sides of the Salò inlet opened a few kilometres away. Hamlets farther off barely rose above the surface of the lake, as if unreachable altogether. Time and space lost meaning in the mundane crowd of villas and guesthouses. Perhaps, what a paradox, it was Russia he longed for – its dwarfing, elating, crushing vastness – or at least the mountains where he'd fought until not long ago. Houses, things, people, were like noise to him, while he needed silence.

Military motorboats ploughed the lake with their foamy furrows towards Gargnano. Passing clouds shadowed the water. A physical need of beauty haunted Bora these days, this morning; he recalled thinking such thoughts when he'd first met Remedios in Spain, when beauty had been the highest expression of order. He was supposed to think of Remedios at the time of his death. It was a fact that seven years, if it was seven years that she foretold, were nearly through. Dying at twenty-three had seemed remote, even while staring death in the face. On the brink of thirty-one, he had devoured the space between himself and death. Yet his stepfather and his maternal grandfather were close to eighty. Perhaps the ladder of his coming close to death was artificial and could be undone.

Clouds cast silky shadows on the lake. Bora tried to think of Dikta, and all he recalled was her profile, the way she turned, the imperious glance of her clear eyes. The rest withdrew as if behind a haze or a thick glass. Little by little, she would be gone altogether. Nora Murphy's charm was unlikely to last, although there were moments when her polite East Coast speech echoed in him. Not enough to indicate love, surely. Today Bianca Spagnoli's face sought his attention more than he cared for, as did the sumptuous Venus from her painted antiquity. Annie Tedesco ... Well, Annie Tedesco he did *not* want to think of, as if he knew that she would bring him unhappiness. Just then, the lake lit up like a fire under a sunbeam, and the things Bora feared were the ones he ran to.

Conforti said nothing when he came to the door and asked to see the Venus. From the kitchen, the old man watched him pull up a chair in front of the painting and sit there in admiration of it, his booted ankles crossed, his arms folded in the wary posture of one who wants to give himself but still holds back.

4

In four days, nothing was heard from Jacob Mengs. Despite Dollmann's words, Bora tried to convince himself that the Gestapo showed its muscle as a mere warning, to keep him under pressure. Yet, ever since the failed attempt on Hitler's life in July, he'd known that it was just a matter of time. This unexpected assignment signed by the head of SS in Italy made him wonder what he was being groomed for. In the summer, his friend Ralph Uckermann had told him, "Pity you're in too much of a predicament already." Nothing else. But Bora had understood that, whatever action was afoot, he could not be a part of it. Even before the days spent in Berlin in advance of the bomb plot, his own stark generosity stood in the way.

After the failure of the conspiracy, he'd followed from the front line the bloody purge of the officers' corps. Friends and acquaintances had been hanged. Mutual trust, the very bond among colleagues, had been torn asunder; it was every man for himself, and there was no relying on accolades or cautions or advice. Bora had all but discontinued corresponding with his parents, lest they be implicated if ever the time came.

He lived day by day, making no long-term plans, anxious for beauty, determined to carry out his duty until they stopped him for good. Only at times, at the edge of sleep, did he have the unpleasant sensation of having lost his balance in a wind that made him heel. Inevitably, despite his self-restraint, mistakes were bound to happen.

*

Gasoline was at a premium, stingily distributed to everyone. Thursday, before dawn, Bora went for a refill at the fuel dump, where he met Lipsky and his little yellow car, which had been washed and waxed to a shine. The twilight was so crisp that it seemed breakable.

"*Very nice,* Colonel. Did she give it to you, or did you take it?"

Bora was instantly annoyed. "I don't know what you mean."

"Why, the car. It's Signora Tedesco's S9. I recognize it even with an army plate."

Did Lipsky seek a confrontation? Bora had simply found the car among the requisitioned vehicles.

"As for me, I'm off to Verona with Turandot."

"*Turandot?*"

"The Tedesco girl, Colonel. I call her so because I think it fits." Lipsky fussily adjusted his cuffs. "Aloof, you know. Refined, alone, just like the princess in the opera. Waiting for the right man to come along."

Bora found the man's self-assurance obnoxious. The thought of the major's hotel pied-à-terre, as described to him by Habermehl, irked him and somehow disappointed him.

"She is due for a medical visit," Lipsky pointed out.

The cold air took on the taste of metal when Bora bit the wound on his lip. "She doesn't seem ill."

"Her illness is of a private nature."

Lipsky was the first to leave, heading south. Bound for his office before going off to the mountains, Bora followed. A private nature? What could it mean? Venereal? Not venereal, not likely. How did Lipsky know? Had the childhood accident permanently injured her? …

He was still mulling over it when he started out for the Tormini crossroads on the way to Lake Idro. De Rosa rode with him, armed to the teeth.

The road climbed among wooded rock walls, past deserted villages and chapels perched on stone spurs, under a sky turning pure blue. De Rosa, map in hand, said, "It's an hour or so to the head of the lake; longer if we want to do some reconnoitring." If he wondered why they were not using a driver, he did not ask; clearly Bora wanted to familiarize himself with the road, as only the man behind the wheel can. Ahead of them, the Opel three-tonner led the way with a Breda machine gun mounted and manned by fez-capped guardsmen.

At the Nozza crossing, Bora asked, "Where does the mountain road lead?"

"To the Trompia Valley, Colonel."

They negotiated curves where the sun never shone in winter, steep pastures, daring little bridges over shingly brooks. *I must memorize this bend*, Bora was thinking, *this jutting rock, this cleft.*

They reached Lavenone, a sprinkle of houses where on a wall one read Mussolini's words: *Discipline, concord and labour for the reconstruction of the Fatherland.* From here on, the valley opened up as they approached Lake Idro. Bora grew interested in the age-old emplacements near Anfo, added on through the centuries until they crowded a perpendicular rock wall. "Splendid hideout. Where do you go from there?"

"Collio, five hours or so on foot, to the Giudicarie and Camonica Valleys."

Thus far, every valley De Rosa mentioned was known for its partisan activity. Bora kept posing questions, but on his own set of maps he'd already marked in red all those narrow and impassable corridors running at a ninety-degree angle from the band-infested territory of Valtellina.

At Ponte Caffaro, by the new border with the Reich, Bora stopped to chat with the German soldiers keeping watch.

By the tapered head of Lake Idro, Storo was a low, nondescript village overlooking a marsh. The mid-morning sun gave the water the glint of tinfoil and made the reeds bristle like a painter's brushes.

It took Bora travelling this far to get De Rosa to admit the truth. When he enquired, already knowing the answer, "Can one get to Riva and back to Lake Garda by the mountain road ahead?" he pretended to have a mind to do so.

"Yes, but it's not advisable." The captain spoke through his teeth. "It's boxed in, very steep in places, dark even at midday. Anyone can open fire from above. During the Great War, they tore each other apart with artillery fire there. Last August, we lost three men near Bezzecca."

During the return trip, De Rosa spoke about the elusive Xavier in hateful terms. "He was in Valtellina with the so-called Fiamme Verdi, but that partisan band kicked him out. The Garibaldi or Matteotti units don't want him either. In spite of our widespread presence ..." – *It's neither a presence, nor widespread*, Bora thought without interrupting – "... he's set himself up in these mountains and has been reported ranging to the west shore of Lake Garda and foraging in herders' huts and hamlets too far to patrol." They had come once more under the Anfo battlements, and, because Bora slowed down, observing them, De Rosa warned: "Xavier may be keeping an eye on us right now. He's daring us. He killed the sentinel on our doorstep; he's the one who scatters leaflets all over to let us know that he's everywhere."

"Or to make us think he is everywhere."

"*Somebody* is scattering the leaflets."

Bora pulled the handbrake. So did the driver in the truck ahead of him, after the fez-bearing toughs hammered on the cabin to alert him. Field glasses in hand, the German stepped over to the edge of the road to scan the mountains. "I doubt he enjoys local support," he said. "If Cristomorto is his real surname, we'll track him down in the records and discover he served in Russia, you see. I heard reports of Russians and Russian front soldiers among the partisans."

"It's hearsay."

A single rifle shot fired from a distance, echoing in all directions, had them both instinctively ducking. The guardsmen wheeled their machine gun this way and that, but no sounds followed, save the papery rustle of dead leaves on the trees.

"Well, it's not hunters," De Rosa grumbled, climbing back in the car.

At the Nozza crossing, Bora told the captain to go ahead with the others. "I have something to do." And because De Rosa warned him against it, he lost patience. "I'll trust your widespread presence on the territory. That is all."

It was hereabouts that, according to the lord bishop, paintings had been stolen from the rural chapel. Bora found and commandeered the local priest to accompany him to the spot, careless that soon the unpaved switchbacks on the mountain trail became too steep and narrow for the car to negotiate. He travelled them now in first gear, now in reverse, trusting his dexterity more than the anxious padre riding with him.

"OhfortheloveofGod, Colonel, we're going to kill ourselves."

"Don't worry, and don't look down!"

But there was no driving the last stretch of the way. The priest leaped out of the car before Bora could park it.

The stale smell of mildew hovered in the chapel. The grill on one of two small windows had been prised loose to allow an intruder to climb inside and unlatch the door from within. "The best painting was the altarpiece," the priest explained. "*The Virgin and St Luke* by Palma, nearly life-size."

Bora studied the floor. "What about the other two pieces?"

"There. You can see where they hung from the traces on the plaster."

Bora stooped to collect and pocket something from the floor. Naturally, no insurance. The chapel remained closed all year, save Christmas, Easter and on the Feast of St Luke, 18 October, which was how the priest discovered the theft. "Why didn't they steal from the church at Mura, if they had to?" he complained. "Their paintings are fancier than ours."

Pointing to an imaginary line at his feet, Bora enquired, "Did you walk as far as this point yesterday, Father?"

The priest looked where Bora was standing, left of the altar. "No, I saw what happened from the door and hastened back to raise the alarm."

"Were you alone, and did you lock the door again?"

"I was alone, and, yes, I did lock the door. You're the first to walk in after the thieves, Colonel."

After they left the chapel, Bora unfolded a map on the bonnet of his car and studied it for a while. Taking his place at the wheel again, he told the priest through the open window, "Sorry I can't give you a lift back to town right now." He backed up to the edge of the cliff, where the down path began, but, instead of taking, it he pressed forward, giving enough gas for the engine to start clambering the sparsely grassed incline behind the chapel.

SALÒ, 12:16 P.M.

Lipsky had already returned from Verona when Bora arrived. Sohl summoned both of them into his office.

"Did you get to the chapel, Colonel?"

Bora said he had done. "Here's dry clay I picked up from the windowsill and the aisle. It came from the threads of mountain boots and originates from a watering trough higher up. I reached it following a goat trail. Pasture mostly, three-quarters of the way. The rest I walked."

Alongside the pinch of dirt, Sohl and Lipsky saw a bit of gilt stucco in the folds of Bora's handkerchief, and a scrap of crumbling red plaster.

Perhaps Sohl said nothing because Lipsky was in the room. Lipsky reached for the bit of stucco with his blond, hairy hand. "So, the thieves came from the mountains; did they leave by the road?"

"Presumably they met by the chapel and carried away the canvases, one of which was large, in a motor vehicle or a mule-drawn cart. There was a certain amount of planning involved, but clumsiness, too. The altarpiece struck against the lintel, nicking the plaster and gilding of its frame." Bora sensed Sohl's annoyance at Lipsky's attendance. Pressure – by whom? – must have been exerted on him to share this meeting with him.

"There are many kinds of clumsy people." Lipsky addressed Bora, who kept his back turned to the roaring fireplace. "You suspect a partisan action? Or am I mistaken?"

"You're not mistaken, but suspicion is all it is."

"That clinches it," Sohl intervened. "We know where the Venus ended up."

"Well, sir, I doubt it. We don't even know where the chapel's artwork went."

"That's for you to discover, Colonel."

Bora ignored Lipsky's dry quip. "At this point, we cannot link the two thefts." Without showing it, he was annoyed because the major had kept company with Annie all morning. He was trying to read on his face what stake in her he might have, if any. How long had he known her? Did he look content, smug, disappointed? ... A chance to find out presented itself when Sohl left the room, as he said, "to dispose of good Italian mineral water, you know ... Stimulates the pipeworks."

"So, colleague, how was the transfer to Verona?"

"Uneventful. I'm having dinner at her house tonight, at Campoverde."

Lipsky took the hint. He was challenging him. Suddenly, Bora was raking his brains to set up an appointment with Annie before him. Campoverde comprised a handful of villas just outside Salò, and he had no idea which one could be hers. Passing by, he had noticed a house on the hillside off the road, with a portico like a Greek temple and medlar trees in the garden. It had made him think of her, but he had no reason to assume she lived there. "Well, good for you," he said coolly. And since the general was still away, he took an opportunity to strike back. "Tell me, Major, what is your real agenda in an assignment so unlike your former duties?"

It was like tossing away a mask and discovering that your counterpart's face came off with it. "It's none of your business," Lipsky snapped back.

"But it is."

"The Venus has nothing to do with it."

"What does, then?"

"It really is none of your business, Colonel."

Bora folded the scraps back inside the handkerchief. "Aside from our military duties, Major, let's make something clear. Beyond the Venus, nothing interests me; I have no time to pursue other objectives. Unless the latest theft relates to the Venus, you and I have no business with it. Do you agree?"

"But you're investigating a possible murder, too, Colonel."

"And how would you know about that?"

"Voices carry in Salò." Lipsky turned to the door as Sohl returned with an unlit cheroot stuck in his mouth.

"*What*'s known in Salò?"

"We were just chatting, sir." Lipsky spoke, glancing at Bora, who kept mum.

"I see. What will we tell the lord bishop, Colonel?"

"All we can suggest is that any worthwhile artwork be removed from remote chapels for safekeeping."

*

When Bora left the building, Lipsky walked him to the gate. The day was pleasant but for a damp sultriness blowing in from the lake. "Sohl is trying to sack me. Did you know? You ought to ask yourself why."

"Perhaps because of your *real* orders."

In the sunlight, Lipsky's fairness had the tinge of dry flax. He squinted in the brightness. "You are completely off course. I have my orders, it's true, but they are not what you think."

"Aren't they?" Bora distrusted him. He knew the aggressive sort, eager to score points whether it was sports, kills or women.

"Forgive me; I am not obliged to tell you." Lipsky opened the gate to let Bora out. The scar on his neck showed in all its crudeness when he grinned. "Your brother did say you could be *difficult.* I imagine you'll have my office after I leave. Just remember not to trust the general, that's all."

A bite at the GNR mess hall and back to the office, where Bora spoke by phone to an SS company commander returning from the Trompia Valley. He knew of Cristomorto, alias Commander Xavier, and agreed on the necessity to learn more through informants. At 3:45, he emerged from the stack of paperwork enough to get the summons to attend the Party Day celebrations on 28 October, his first joint appearance with Colonel Denzo. A jaundiced De Rosa suggested that Denzo would use the opportunity to negotiate permission for top Fascist dependants to reach Switzerland. "Don't let him out of your sight, Colonel von Bora. If my wife stays in Salò, the other wives ought to stay as well."

"What about your lady friends?"

De Rosa's face darkened. "Screw them. They're at each other's throats; they can fend for themselves."

Shortly before four, Bora called Inspector Vismara. Pulling the telephone cord as far as it extended, he spoke by the open window. He promised that he hadn't forgotten the Spagnoli "suicide", but needed different information at the moment. Vismara heard him out and gave him Annie's address without questions. He added that he would be out of town for a couple of days, but they could meet on Monday.

The name of Annie Tedesco's home was Villa Mespilai. Mespilai, Greek for medlar trees. Bora remained by the window, staring at the faded image on the wall across the street, of a Madonna enthroned between two unknown saints. The paint flaked and curled, he could nearly feel its brittleness. These days, he felt everything more keenly. Sounds, odours, light and darkness – everything grew nearly painful to him; he could smell the scent of lemon and medlar trees blooming in distant gardens, the green moss over the pebbles of the shore. He lived so vividly that the thought of lovemaking sounded fresh and novel, like a second loss of virginity. It was a sign, Bora told himself, that he'd guessed right.

He phoned Annie to let her know of his visit. When he reached the gravel path of her gate, the fruity scent of the medlars wafted through the open window of the car. Across the lake, a remote windowpane sparkled with the dipping sun and grew dim, and then another pane brightened and dimmed.

In her clipped Swiss German, the maid at the door informed him that Frau Tedesco could not be disturbed at this time, but already Annie was walking out of a French door to meet him. "It's all right, Liese." She nodded a greeting. "Oberst von Bora."

"*Gnädige Frau.*"

She wore red heels. Shiny high heels and a red rim around her elegant grey shoes. Strange that Bora should notice this detail, when the rest was so heart-stopping. He recognized that she wore *crêpe de chine* because Dikta favoured it; with a scatter of bright flowers on a black background, the silk fit her like a glove. The skirt was loose, however, and he had to imagine her thighs beneath it.

In a luminous living room, there sat a fine Bösendorfer piano. Bora asked who played it, and she said, "Oh, no one, it came with the house. I play the cello, a little." She graciously invited him to sit down. "Father is in the parlour with Signor Bossaglia, his medium. Uncle Walter and I believe none of it, although he's better than I at indulging him. Did you see him in the garden, coming in? No? He must have left. Bossaglia says this place 'inspires' him, so now even my house is open to ghosts." She smiled. The sober elegance of the room reminded him of his grandparents' villa at Riva.

"It is embarrassing, Colonel. At first, Father was only interested in 'communicating' with my late mother; now he's on to other questions, from the workaday ones to the large, unanswerable ones. Imagine, he was just asking how the war ..." Annie caught herself in mid-sentence.

"We are all very interested in knowing how the war will end," Bora completed the phrase. "It would be even more helpful to hear how to win it."

She nodded. "I appreciate your telling me by phone that you now have my car. It's good that it went to someone I know a little. It is an excellent machine, Uncle's wedding gift to me. But you must be here for the Venus, yes? In that case ... Well, I'm glad Father is busy at the moment. It will allow us to speak freely. Coffee, tea?"

"Coffee, please."

Annie instructed the maid and closed the door. "I was with Father when he won the bid, Colonel. I doubt that any of the counter-bidders would plan such an elaborate scheme to steal the Venus. In the last four years, only a collector from Lugano made a serious offer to buy it. And more's the pity:

Father was tempted to sell. The Greek resistance had just destroyed his last storehouse in Rhodes, and he was never one to accept a loss without seeking compensation. Signor Conforti reminded him that, once secured, a masterpiece cannot be parted with."

Bora listened, looking somewhere between her figure and the wide window plastered in paper tape. A reminder of war. Annie, the lake … If he unfocused his vision, she seemed to merge with that world of fading blue and grey. She must be under thirty, just past her mid-twenties, maybe; still, her absorbed composure made her seem ageless. Turandot, Lipsky had called her. Her gown, her neatly upswept and gathered hair – everything conjured the image of that remote princess, cursed, a captive in her own rooms.

When Liese brought in the coffee, Annie served him herself, without raising her eyes, attentive to her task. Her hand was firm and those fingernails bright red, wet-looking. Still without looking at him, she asked, "What happened to your face?"

"Nothing serious. Two RNG auxiliaries and I met on the road: I had a car; they had a truck."

They took coffee in silence, sitting apart from each other. "Feel free to ask any pertinent question," she then invited him. "If I have no answer, I'll say so or give you my thoughts. I'd like the Venus back even more than Father." Her speech was polished, and Bora recognized her Swiss finishing-school deportment, so like Dikta's. Between her cheek and her mouth, delicate as a chiselled mark of bravura, the line of her nostrils drew itself so perfectly that the smallest change would diminish the beauty of it. He studied her because she looked away, although there was no shyness in her.

"I may be out of line, but is your father above absconding the Venus?"

She turned to him. "Why on earth would he do that?"

"To keep it safe from us, or from the war. Or from the aftermath."

"No. He truly is distressed. However ... Uncle always said Father doesn't mind bending the rules."

"They differ, those two men."

Annie smiled. Her upper lip was full and deeply notched, the lower one ridged moist and perfectly red against her skin. "One is my father; the other is my mother's brother. You should have known Mother in order to understand Uncle Walter, who mirrors her virtues, and her weaknesses. I was twelve when she died, and I had to keep them both from going mad with grief, as if I didn't face enough pain of my own. I expected Father would settle for building a rich mausoleum as he did when my brother died. His philosophy is that when something is lost beyond retrieval, some do without; he prefers to get paid for the loss."

"It isn't always easy to find compensation or do without."

The hardness on his face made her uneasy. "I apologize. I didn't mean your hand."

"I didn't mean my hand either."

"Anyway, Father does see other women." She spoke impulsively, out of context, leaving Bora to find the context. "He spends considerably on them, although he often considers them a nuisance. According to him, women painted on canvas are far less troublesome. They cost only once, and grow in value instead of losing it."

Bora was puzzled. Why would she reveal a detail supposedly unrelated to the theft? Because it illustrated her father's way of consoling himself? It sounded like a hint to something he had not yet considered. Women, where? In Salò? What sort of women? He would ask Vismara. This sleepy lakeside, an eye in the storm of war, bred intrigue like a puddle swarming with tadpoles! Bora no longer wondered why Annie had accepted Lipsky's ride to Verona; she had no car, and probably had little choice in the matter. As for Lipsky, of course he courted her, and very possibly had tried to secure information from her. After all, the major might know more than he did about Pozzi, the theft and Annie herself.

"But your uncle …"

"Uncle is like my mother." She gathered the skirt on her crossed legs, swaying a little her red-heeled foot with indolent ease. "Too patient at times. Although he disapproves of some of Father's decisions, he has no real say in the matter. Father lets no one else rule the roost. Uncle Walter prefers living things to art: flowers, trees, exotic shrubs. If you promise not to tell, I'll admit that he and I listen to jazz music on Swiss radio: our private little sin. He's a generous man." Annie passed her forefinger inside the gold bangle at her wrist. "Even in this supposedly privileged community, many have no food, no firewood." She ran her eyes around. "You see how comfortably we live, Colonel."

"Well, you could help those in need."

"Uncle and I do our best, but please do not tell Father. He rose from poverty and has no sympathy for those who do not pull themselves up by their bootstraps."

"Some have no boots left, much less bootstraps." Bora nodded when she motioned with the coffee urn, and watched her refill his demitasse with singular firmness and grace, as though the simple gesture required a ceremony of composure. He asked more questions, and Annie answered without reticence, so easily that he suspected she had rehearsed her story and perhaps told it already. He heard that Pozzi had sold five tapestries and two views of Rome by Corot in order to pay cash for the Venus. When General Sohl arrived, Conforti had just cleaned and reframed the Venus, and, to no avail, Pozzi demanded written assurance of compensation in case any artwork were damaged or removed during billeting.

"We do come across as barbarians," said Bora, glancing away because she was looking straight at him. "As art collectors, my grandparents would shudder at the thought, but there may be troops occupying La Schiavona as well."

Annie nodded, looking away the small bloody cut on Bora's lip. "You could have been killed in that car accident."

Was she thinking of her husband, who'd died in a crash on the island where thousands of his companions, unwilling to serve under German orders, had been mowed down by the Germans?

"Tedesco is a Jewish name in Italy," Lipsky had grinned as he left the fuel dump hours earlier. He'd left Bora wondering whether he meant it in contempt or as an opportunity, a veiled threat, to coax her into a relationship. Annie guarded her emotions well; she could very well be Lipsky's lover and hide it. He admiringly took in the dark sheen of her hair, the blush of coral on her earlobe, the long silk-covered thigh to the tip of that pert red-heeled shoe. He yearned for any claim Lipsky may have on her to fall by the wayside.

"Not likely, Signora, but I appreciate your concern."

For the rest of the conversation, he watched her speak, listen, move, and if a part of him stayed on the lookout for false moves and slip-ups, his soul, or something like it, sought its own truth about her. Her beauty was unlike anything he thought he favoured. Yet in Annie Tedesco he perceived a space, a void, a place to let himself fall into. She was like a brink somehow; possessing her *meant* something. She revealed nothing, and, for that reason, it was as if he'd always known her, perceiving her behind every other; except, maybe, Remedios, who came before all. The process was too quick for review. Bora, who closely controlled his instincts, was inexplicably certain that possessing this woman must signify far beyond the carnal act. It would be entering emptiness in order to claim it, and to discover that emptiness itself *is*.

Outwardly, he was only watching her, aware that she let herself be observed with a kind of mute pain. Crazy, inopportune thoughts rode his blood, and if he could not give in to excitement, he knew full well the risks of involving others at this stage of the war and of his endangered life.

A self-possessed Bora was already standing to leave when Pozzi, whose farewell to the medium had just boomed outside the door, barged into the room. Answering the German's greeting with a wave, he looked around. "Where's your colleague? Signor Bossaglia said there were *two* officers visiting."

"I assure you I came alone." Bora smirked. "And much as I sometimes find myself at odds with myself, I haven't quite split up yet."

"What the devil! He even said that he wore an edelweiss badge. I thought maybe there was someone from the mountain troops calling at my daughter's."

Bora felt himself go white. His brother had flown in Kampfgeschwader 51, the Edelweiss squadron. But so, he reasoned immediately, had Lipsky before his crash, and why couldn't they have gossiped about Lipsky back there, between a phantasmal evocation and another? *Voices carry in Salò.* Still, the coincidence mystified him.

"Well, whatever, not even Bossaglia gets them all right," Pozzi allowed. "The fact remains that lakes, like all bodies of water, attract supernatural events." Seeing there were sweets on the coffee table, he popped one into his mouth. "I wanted to call on the spirit of the woman who killed herself on Sunday, but he said no. Those who die a violent death hang around the spot for days; she would not come. My Diamantina, who drowned herself ..." He glanced from his frowning daughter to the German. "All right, all right, I won't say it. Anna Maria, I thought you invited Major Lipsky for dinner. Is the colonel staying, too?"

The cad. With a courteous nod of the head, Bora took Annie out of the quandary. "No, sir. I will be working until late."

How eventful his return to the office would be, he could hardly imagine.

Two hundred meters up, the pathfinder seemed to be waiting for him. Sweeping down from across the lake, it banked over Bora's car, buzzed it and veered towards the shore and then back. It was unlikely that the pilot recognized the car. But to Bora it was another strange coincidence. He recalled Spain, the fragile aircraft reconnoitring those immense skies, always returning to Riscal Amargo, like God's finger pointing to the stupidity of fighting men. Seven years, Remedios had said: and there were appointments to keep with the living and the dead before the end of December. Near Rome, in the mountains to the east of Rome, enemy aeroplanes had buzzed and harassed him; prudence had called for Bora to pull into the nearest driveway, or seek shelter under the first clump of leafy trees. But Bora was himself playing a game: *If I am supposed to see Annie again, he will not open fire on me.*

The sky beyond the aeroplane had a flat blueness, with remote little stars. It was only three or so kilometres to Salò. There was an anti-aircraft post on the hill behind the RNG building; however, speeding to town might draw fire on civilians, so Bora did not accelerate. When the pathfinder opened fire at last, only by careening into a ditch and the field below did Bora avoid the dense scatter of shells; he distinctly heard them plough and thud into the verge of the road just inches away. Headlights off, windows rolled down, Bora waited for the anti-aircraft to respond or for the plane to leave, whichever came first. The next passage was so low that he could glimpse the open cockpit, the pilot looking down before veering away. A moment later, two booming rounds came from the hill.

Bora regained the road, having already changed the rules of his game: *I am supposed to see Annie again, because he missed me when he opened fire.*

In town, the square at the end of the street was deserted when Bora reached it on foot. Stars had grown bolder over the hills, and a damp breeze blew in from the lake. In front of the *questura* building, Bora recognized Vismara entering a Fiat runabout.

The inspector, already seated behind the wheel, rolled down the window. "Evening, Colonel. I thought we'd meet on Monday."

"I have a couple of questions that can't wait."

"You see, I'm off to Verona."

"It won't take long."

"Is it about the key to the woman's door?"

"No."

Vismara's hand gave up on starting the engine.

Bora walked around the car and sat down beside the inspector. For the next few minutes they spoke, darkness crowding around them in the lonely square. Judging by the spicy aroma rising from the back seat, Vismara's wife had provided loving rations for the trip. The security of affection. Without begrudging it, Bora envied that care. And he understood a family man's desire to travel under the reasonably safe cover of night.

"How much do you know of Signor Pozzi's escapades, and why would his daughter mention them to me?"

"My late colleague could have given you details, Colonel. As far as I know, Pozzi is not a regular of brothels as such." Vismara leaned his elbow on the steering wheel and kept an eye on the phosphorescent dial of his watch. "He might go for this or that wife whose man is at war, or a pleasant widow … You know, the usual."

"Captain De Rosa tells me that his guardsmen rushed to see Bianca Spagnoli's body for the very reason that she was not one of their harlots. But what about the German soldiers? Do you think Germans frequented her?"

"I may have the information by Monday."

Sensing Vismara's haste, Bora was tempted to tell him to go. He chose not to, aware that he could uncharitably impose himself. Nothing actually pointed to a murder or called for asking about Germans and women. He didn't know himself why he was asking, other than Annie's words about her father. For the third time, an impatient Vismara delayed starting the engine. "I will have the information for you next week, I promise."

"Good." Bora alighted, and they shook hands through the open window.

"I'll see you on Monday, Colonel."

"Not Monday morning."

"The afternoon, then."

The wet breeze had grown stiffer. Upturning the collar of his greatcoat, Bora walked away, and soon was rounding the corner of Garibaldi Street. One, two steps down the road. The blast stunned him. A flash, noise, fragments flying, the stench of cordite, shattered windowpanes raining down from the upper floors, ten or fifteen seconds of absolute chaos before voices rose in anguish. Even before turning to look around the corner, Bora knew by the clatter of boots that it was policemen racing out to see what remained of Vismara's burning car. Fuel-drenched fragments – parts of the interior? clothes? charred limbs? – littered the square; the gutted shell bore no resemblance to what it had been only moments earlier. Panic surrounded the unholy bonfire as Bora stared at the whitish thing lying at his feet, whether it was a shard of china or a piece torn off Vismara's skull. *Poor man,* he thought. *Poor wife, poor family.*

He'd seen too much war to share the frenzy of uniforms running to or from the square. Death did this, smelled like this, threw flames around like this. The words just spoken in conversation were sealed as if by centuries of unchangeable fate, committed to eternity by death, despite the fact that one of the interlocutors was still alive. Bora's sense of pity changed into something like concern, for having felt so at ease inside a car about to explode. *How did I not sense danger? Have I lost the sixth sense that kept me alive until now?*

De Rosa met him down Garibaldi Street. He lowered the torch when he realized he was blinding a German colonel with it. "What happened?" he cried out, and without waiting for an answer, he scampered towards the square.

Sohl telephoned within half an hour of Bora's return to his desk. He knew about the explosion, but it was not the immediate reason for his call.

"You should know that Lipsky called at the Jew's this afternoon. Conforti came looking for you here with the news, all bent out of shape ... No, I sent him away." A pause, in case the line was monitored. "His kind makes me uncomfortable, and I'd rather keep my distance. See what you can do about it, Bora."

"About Conforti or about his complaint?"

"Both." Another pause, for the listeners' sake. "So, they killed our poor inspector. A fine state of affairs. Had he stepped on someone's toes, or was it the rebels' doing?"

It was a crude requiem Bora could have done without. He saw no point in mentioning he'd been a breath away from dying in the same blast. God knows why, Lipsky's visit to the antiquarian was what alarmed him most at this time. He tried vainly to reach Conforti by telephone. Leaving the office, he saw agitated guardsmen giving directions to the fire patrol. Smoke rose high, and the last of the flames consuming the wreck gave the night sky a lurid tinge. Although he had the car keys in his hand, Bora chose to walk, and not just because the alley where Conforti lived was nearby.

"You let him *take* her! Why didn't you answer the goddamn phone?"

"My wires were cut months ago, Colonel."

Bora, who'd confronted the old man after throwing him out of an early bed, shoved him aside and strode to the end of the hallway, where an empty wall was all there was. "When did it happen?" He hit his fist on the plaster. "What else has he taken? What was he *doing* here?"

Conforti shuffled behind him in his slippers. "The *atarot* and three of the *rimmonim* sets. The best ones."

"And your Venus?"

Bora was angry for being angry and unwilling to conceal it. He was about to stalk furiously out of there when Conforti added in a small, astute voice, "Try the kitchen, Colonel von Bora."

The kitchen, and the kitchen table. The Venus lay there on sheets of wrapping paper in the half-light, like a secret lover waiting for him; tender and available, yet secure, virginal and unbearably tempting. Anguish met infatuation at some not-so-distant point, past all denials and intentions of denial.

"It's reprehensible, I know," Conforti apologized, looking in. "While the major was downstairs digging through the Sarajevo loot, I sneaked up here to take her off the wall. When he came up, I told him that he was too late, that you'd claimed the Venus already."

"*What?*"

"I'm afraid I said that you needed the painting in order to recognize the original, and ... I was rambling, I realize. As it turns out, the major was looking for religious objects. He unwrapped the Venus and commented that it lacks Titian's flair." In his pyjamas, Conforti seemed even smaller – an elf or a homely ghost. Bora had had enough of darkness and dim interiors, but when he tried the light switch in the kitchen, nothing happened.

"Lipsky may be right, Colonel. Still, I'm not giving her up. Not to him, not to you, not to anyone. I invented the story to keep him from taking it."

"Are you suggesting that Major Lipsky took the original?"

"How should I know? All I know is that he took the *rimmonim* by Fedeli, the beautiful ones not yet catalogued, and the *atarot* from Sarajevo. I am to keep working at my inventory, Colonel. You must intervene!"

"I *must?*"

"I beg you to intervene. The general wouldn't as much as receive me."

Bora was telling himself that it had been a long day. "Calm down, will you? Likely, Major Lipsky was ordered to seize those objects. Your fib about my claiming the copy puts me in an awkward position with him and the general. I will deny it, naturally, which will make things worse." Now that he was composing himself, Bora felt foolish about losing his temper. The difficulties he mentioned seemed petty and idle. He lifted the painting, which proved lighter than he expected but was certainly not easy for an old man to handle, and hung it back in place. "I realize that your well-being depends on the inventory."

"My life, you mean. That is not what I worry about, Colonel. The sacred objects and their destination trouble me. Of my life, I am the sole master: it will end when I decide, not a moment earlier."

"Yes. Suicide is always an option."

"I don't believe in the taking of one's life, Colonel von Bora."

Some days are *too* long. When Bora stepped back from the Venus, he faced an unexpected need to ennoble the lucid and lonesome desire he felt for something to love. Mostly, however, he felt exhausted, irritable; having to walk back weighed on him like a formidable chore. Even leaving this house seemed wearisome. "Well," he said, "did your dead neighbour believe in suicide?"

"I think not."

DIARY ENTRY: 19 OCTOBER 1944, 11:08 P.M.

I may as well use the few pages left in this diary, which I stingily save up, having so much to say. Case of stolen painting more tangled than ever. Tonight I learned that men occasionally visited Bianca Spagnoli. So says Conforti, who is no gossip. Men, at this time of the war, means elders, boys or soldiers. When I pressured him, Conforti added that now and then he heard German spoken in her rooms as he climbed the stairs from the studio. I suggested piano lessons, but he never heard music. Of course, there's no direct relation between having lovers and the suspicion of murder. One doesn't just let oneself be hanged, after all. When I stopped on the way to the hotel by the questura to extend my sympathy for poor Vismara's death, I heard that he had the Spagnoli file with him in the car. So much for that. When I enquired about the physician who executed the Spagnoli post-mortem, worse luck: it turns out he was from out of town, an Italian army surgeon who happened to be in Salò on furlough. It seems I had better forget about Bianca Spagnoli: however she died, she'll have to rest in peace.

At the questura, I unexpectedly ran into Annie Tedesco's uncle, there to denounce the theft of his wallet while he queued in a café. Although he fortunately kept his documents separately, he did lose a fair amount of cash. O felix culpa: a fortunate incident. As curfew time had well passed, and he lives past the Duomo, down from the hotel, I offered him a ride. Was I being courteous or self-serving? Vittori politely said nothing about my driving Annie's car and even invited me to call at his home on Sunday. A pleasant fellow, with some mannerisms I noticed in his niece, mostly a certain choosiness of language, in contrast with Pozzi's balancing act between Italian and his childhood dialect.

I finally heard what the trouble with her health is. While we spoke of the grave loss to Vismara's family, he asked me whether I am married, and when I told him I no longer am, he said he fully understands; his Greek wife chose not to follow him to Italy when the war began. Did my ulterior motive show, or did he simply choose to tell, as family troubles seem easier to reveal to strangers? Anyhow, when Annie was eleven, she was playing with other children, rough Greek boys who dared her to scale the garden gate. Without going into detail, she missed her grasp, and one of the iron spikes caused her serious damage. I understood it to be the reason why she has no children. Perhaps – witness her medical appointments in Verona – she suffers from other after-effects. Is this why Lipsky calls her after the inaccessible, frigid Turandot?

5

The Hotel Regina – Ausserkommando SS Mailand – sat not far from the bombed-out La Scala theatre, awaiting repair under a roof of tubing and tarred cardboard. When Mengs left his car in nearby Cordusio Square, it thundered from a stifling overcast, so low that the spires of the cathedral were lost to view.

Kappler's adjutant, Hauptsturmführer Egon Sutor, awaited him in the foyer. The meeting had been planned without Kappler – unbeknownst to him, Mengs suspected – but the SS commander was there and asked whether the files sent by Sutor had come in handy. Mengs replied they had, very much.

"He was in Berlin just days before the vile attempt on the Führer's life. In the wake of those events, Bora's agenda is all the more interesting." Sutor's hatred for Bora had him tingling with excitement when he passed the additional material to Mengs.

"Did you copy these addresses in Rome, Hauptsturmführer?"

"Yes. Dollmann gave him back the book, but not before we got what we wanted out of it."

Mengs scanned the pages, his eyes racing across them. Kappler watched Sutor address Mengs, still more disappointed than angry at Bora.

"Some acquaintances he cannot help. Take the former lord mayor of Leipzig … Bora *is* from Leipzig after all." (Mengs understood that Sutor meant to draw his attention to Carl Goerdeler, already imprisoned and condemned to death.) "As for Cardinal Hohmann, he'd been his ... What do Catholics call it? 'Spiritual father'? As if a man with a dead father and a living stepfather needed a third." Humour was out of place, and Sutor's attempt fell flat. "The arch-traitors Stauffenberg and Nebe are another kettle of fish. We can't prove that he met them in Berlin, but I'd bet money on it."

"Be sure your sins will find you out," Mengs observed dryly.

An orderly brought coffee. Sutor began to drink avidly and burned his lips, while Kappler blew on his cup without bringing it to his mouth. Mengs continued to read. "May I keep this?" he then asked.

Sutor turned to Kappler, who said yes.

"There's more." Far more deliberate and self-possessed, Kappler reached into his desk and pulled out a loosely bound set of papers. "From my Via Tasso office in Rome. It covers the period from January to early June."

"March through May are particularly interesting," Sutor volunteered.

Mengs slowly turned his head to him, like an ox.

"There's a diary too," Kappler interjected tersely. "You probably know that."

"I do." Mengs sat in his raincoat, neck buried in his shoulders.

After Kappler left the room, Sutor stayed, admiring the Gestapo agent reading and memorizing the data.

A high-pitched sound wailed from outside.

"What's that?" Mengs asked without letting go of his reading.

"Air raid early warning. It means enemy bombers have entered the region. If a second alarm sounds in ten minutes, it means they're in sight. Sometimes that they're already opening the hatches." Sutor was all too aware that Italian air raid warnings were not reliable, but this was not the moment to betray fear. "There is enough in there for half a dozen charges according to headings in the A and B sections of Jurisdiction

IV," he suggested. Mengs paid no attention, so he added, "Well, I mean, A-2 and A-3. B-1 …"

"And E-1." Mengs smiled. "I'll ask for you the next time I am in Milan." Standing from his armchair, he wagged a plump finger at the rattling windowpanes. "I think it's time we went to the shelter."

In the three days before meeting Denzo again, Bora laid down some plans. He instructed the informant enlisted by De Rosa, a curious-looking fellow with an earring in his left earlobe and an umbrella repair kit, to gather details about Xavier. "But," he added, "send word on Sunday morning if you make contact." He spoke in person or by telephone with the commanders active in clearing rebel-infested areas; on Friday, he was in Verona, where he faced those he cared least to meet, Police Lieutenant General Kamptz and SS Brigadenführer Wilhelm Harster. Harster was in, meeting Wolff behind closed doors. As head of all German police in Italy, SS, Gestapo, Sipo, SD, Kripo, he reported to Wolff only nominally. His staff officers were coldly polite to Bora and sent him on his way with some interesting but anecdotal details about Xavier's health.

After spending an uneasy night at Habermehl's apartment in Verona, Bora learned from him on Saturday morning that the pieces of art shipped by Lipsky to Meran went to a given address. "Not a private one, Martin, and not an APO; the Kreditanhalt, the bank on Kornplatz." It was before nine, but, judging from his breath, Habermehl had already downed a few. "Our fly boy beds a maid in the hotel, who will sing for a pack of cigarettes… No, Martin, in Meran there's no 'in care of a given bank employee'; only the number of a safety deposit box, which, if you ask me, has got to be large. In other matters, did you hear from your parents? They have been asking me about you. You've made yourself so scarce, they're worried sick."

Bora expected the question. "Tell them I'm well, Herr Oberst, and that it's best if they do not seek me out for a while."

"Hell, I'm off to Germany! Your stepfather will want to see me and will not let me get away with that. And your mother …"

"Tell Nina to convince the general to stay away from the phone and his outspoken veteran friends, and, if asked, to say they know nothing. Which, incidentally, is the truth."

Habermehl groaned. "'Know nothing'?" Red with drink and high blood pressure, his jowly face seemed ready to burst. "What are you saying? What have you *done*, Martin? I don't understand you."

"Herr Oberst, I know you'll forget our conversation by day's end, so I'll tell you that one can sin by omission as well as by commission. And in every intermediate way."

In Brescia, by mid-morning, he spoke to the Fascist brigade commanders, comparing their data with information extorted from prisoners by the SS. His mauled regiment had meanwhile arrived for refitting, retraining and the mere addition of live bodies. Bora ordered the transfer of the seriously wounded to one of the well-equipped hospitals on Lake Garda and called for a regimental staff meeting in the afternoon. During a sombre farewell lunch at the mess hall, he heard the news that the Allies had taken Aachen, while Belgrade had fallen to the Russians. Closer in, the day before, American bombs had flattened a school in the outskirts of Milan, killing some two hundred children in the stairwell. His colleague Lübbe-Braun, temporarily in command of the regiment, had school-age sons in Aachen and was the picture of dejection.

Bora's final errand in Brescia was at security police headquarters, headed by SS Hauptsturmführer Erich Priebke. Another acquaintance from his Roman days, whom he'd last seen in May when, under a direct order from Field Marshal Kesselring, he'd undergone the humiliation of apologizing to the SS for reporting their intimidation. Priebke was thankfully out for the day, but at his headquarters Bora learned that the British were less than twenty kilometres south of Ravenna. In the wake of all other calamities, the news made him nauseous; he had to sit in the car and calm down, in order not to throw up.

SALÒ, SATURDAY, 21 OCTOBER 1944, 7:37 P.M.

In Sohl's residence, the gold flicker of the empty frame at the top of the stairs was a reminder of unfinished business. The Venus was still gone.

It was not unusual for the door to Lipsky's office to be closed, except for the key in the lock; below, where his yellow convertible usually parked, Bora had caught in his headlights a cat hustling off with a limp field mouse in its mouth.

From his desk, waving with his cheroot for Bora to enter and close the door, Sohl spent two words on the bad military news, and a few more on his good news. "Lipsky will be reassigned as of the first of November ... Where? To Venice."

"That's grand, General. He'll have access to more and better art there."

"At least he's out of our hair."

Our hair? Unless Sohl suspected a personal rivalry between him and Lipsky, he was more than suggesting that Lipsky's presence would hamper the investigation. In light of Habermehl's words, the major's hasty transfer struck a jarring note; Meran, home to Sohl's wife and Lipsky's bank, was on Italian soil but well inside the new borders of the Reich, three hours away. Who was conniving with whom? It was all either very simple or very contorted. If the Venus had one way or another ended up in Meran, sharing ideas with Sohl or Lipsky would help him solve the case or lose the Venus forever. For now, what Bora knew of the general through his old intelligence colleagues was that he had reached the top without taking pointless risks.

It took him seconds to free himself of his greatcoat in the stifling room and figure out a neutral response. "Did the major not come in today?"

Sohl's rubicund face remained serene. The sole source of light was the Moloch fireplace; perspiration beaded his shaven head, yet he didn't so much as unclasp the collar of his tunic. "How did you …? Of course, the key in the lock. How observant. He's using leave time between now and his departure. You can move in whenever you're ready."

"With your permission, I will respect the calendar and transfer here on the thirty-first of October. But won't your new aide require the office?"

The way Sohl eluded the question could mean that, at this stage of the war, he had no need of an aide. Bora did not insist. He reported on his conversation with Conforti, leaving out the lie about his acquisition of the painting; Sohl seemed to know nothing of it, which deposed in favour of Lipsky's discretion. Still, Bora worried about the way in which the major would employ his free time in days to come.

The yellow car was nowhere near the hotel when Bora went to bed past midnight, only to have nightmares of sitting in Vismara's car and being unable to get the door open to escape.

SUNDAY, 22 OCTOBER 1944, 8:23 A.M.

At his NRG office, where he awaited news from the informant, Bora was facing the window with a map in hand and didn't notice Lipsky's presence on the threshold until the major spoke.

"I knew I'd find you here, Colonel. It must be true what they said about you in Russia: that on Sunday mornings, depending, you'd be either at Mass, or at work … or else screwing your wife."

Bora did not look over. "A couple of times I've done all three, not in that order."

"I'm sure you'll have heard that I am leaving Salò."

Bora turned on his heel, folding the map. "Have a safe trip."

Unexpectedly, he resembled his dead brother so closely that Lipsky blinked. Taller than the tall Peter, tough in the same lean, muscular way, his mother's half-Scots ancestry showed less on him. Lipsky was nearly tempted to admit that he'd grieved for Peter as much as a friend can.

"You're giving up already?" Bora's tone was conciliatory, a bit amused.

"I was inexplicably called to serve with Army Coastal Artillery in Venice. Before I go, I want to know whether you really *acquired* Conforti's copy when you could simply have requisitioned it. Jews are not allowed to keep private property, as you know."

"I acquired nothing. He only said so because he did not want to let go of it."

"The sly little Jew. I suspected as much."

"What about the Jewish pieces?"

"The Jewish pieces go to Prague. It's time they took their place in the soon-to-open museum of Jewish Culture there."

Under his breath, Bora's exasperation came across. "That is doubly grotesque. The SS can hardly contrast the insurrection in Slovakia!"

"Well, Colonel, even now the Allies are fifteen kilometres from Bologna. I don't see you packing. As for me, I mean to save face by asking for reassignment to JG1 in Aviano; at least nominally, I'll be among fighter pilots. I'll be waiting to hear if you find out anything about the Venus."

"Oh, I mean to find *her*."

They shook hands. *I hope you do find her*, Lipsky wanted to wish him, but he couldn't resist a last dig. "I invited Signora Tedesco to visit me on the Laguna."

"Did she say yes?"

"She said yes." It was not true, Lipsky hadn't had the nerve to ask her, but he meant to keep a pawn on the chessboard. "We must do what we can, Colonel," he said, placing a spiteful seal on the conversation. "Let's face it: you and I are damaged goods."

"Thanks for the reminder."

Lipsky was driving south on Garibaldi Street when Bora turned away from the window. Clipped inside the map, the black-and-white photograph of the Venus asked that he look at it. He studied it, shamelessly trying to imagine the blond fleece on her belly, the hand cupping between her thighs and forcing the eye to linger on the gentle mound. Languidly folded back, her arm cleared the view of her pert, roused breasts, creating points and counterpoints of light. Bora, who seldom indulged in self-pity, felt miserable in his present loneliness.

The night before, back from work, he'd walked to and entered Bianca Spagnoli's apartment in search of the duplicate key, in whose existence Vismara did not believe. For years, war had given him the right to dispose of things, houses, people; it was hard to envision peace if not as the coming of restrictions. He found nothing of interest but a handful of calling cards, which he deftly pocketed. With the rigid fingers of his artificial left hand, he successfully opened drawers with the help of the ribbons tied to the knobs. In the bedroom, he noted a pair of cufflinks. The bed was unmade as she left it to hang herself, or be hanged.

Afterwards, he'd knocked on Conforti's door. The excuse was to tell him where the *rimmonim* and *atarot* would go; the real reason was to look at *her* again. "I can envision nothing more beautiful than this," he had confessed.

"Colonel, the original surpasses all copies. Your eye tells you. If your eye fails, your heart tells you. Failing that, being a man, the very fact that you're a man tells you."

This morning, being not at Mass, much less in bed with his estranged wife or really thinking of work, Bora was ashamed to acknowledge that the Venus was desirable. He slipped the photograph and the map in his map case and began to straighten his desk.

12:08 P.M.

The informant, due before midday, was late. Bora went down-stairs to see if De Rosa had come in, and he hadn't either. Women trouble, he assumed with a good measure of spite. Two guardsmen were playing cards, muskets resting across their knees, while a comrade kept a vigilant watch outside; in the street, girls in shapeless coats and shawls were making a beeline from the nearest place where they had managed to scrounge coal or bread or whatever was available without notice, even on a Sunday. A lack of hot water and dearth of toiletries lent them the looks of unkempt modesty Bora had seen women wear for years. As for himself, he'd always been drawn to spotless, even fussy women; lately, along with his intolerance for ugliness and disorder, tidiness had become a prerequisite for sexual interest: an uncharitable response, perhaps, but it succeeded in keeping him from temptation.

With the sole perspective of an insipid army lunch, he waited for the informant, stretching his sore left leg under the desk. Idleness forced him to brood, which was in turn fatiguing and inadvisable; so, he turned the radio on, switching stations between syrupy German and Italian love songs and dreary communiques. The thought of starting work with Denzo the following day, the unlikely chance of tracing the Venus through the confusion of police units and archives, the unreliability of witnesses – it all irked him. There was no accounting for all those who had rushed through the residence in the confusion after the grenade attack: Luftwaffe officers celebrating a promotion down the street, guardsmen and policemen, plus those serving on Sohl's staff ... The dynamics of the theft were at the same time evident and obscure. He *was* brooding. *Damn Italians, always late.*

At twelve thirty, Bora decided to step out for a sandwich or send for one. He was putting his greatcoat on when he heard the clatter of boots on the stairs and opened without waiting for the knock. A guardsman handed him a wrap. "A girl delivered your lunch, *signor colonnello.*"

Less than two minutes later, De Rosa rapped on the half open door and stepped in, with ham sandwiches in a paper bag.

His back to the entrance, in front of a similar bag on the desk, Bora was wiping his right hand with the handkerchief folded in the artificial left one.

"Sorry I'm late, Colonel. Damn that Bruni woman and her threats! I brought some victuals, but I see you have anticipated ..."

The words died on the captain's lips when he came close enough to see the bloody human ear in a crumpled square of newsprint, the silver ring on its lobe jellied with gore.

Eating lunch being now out of the question, Vittori's invitation to come and see him "any time on Sunday" offered a possible distraction from Xavier's revenge against the informant. Bora had flushed the severed ear down the drain to keep it from joining De Rosa's macabre collection of relics. No word of a reprisal, as spies ranked low even in the Fascists' book. There was no way of knowing where the man had gone looking for information either. As for the girl who delivered the paper bag, she'd shown up at the door, saying that the colonel had sent for lunch; the guardsmen could describe her only summarily. De Rosa played the harbinger of doom. "Now Xavier knows who you are, Colonel. The message was sent to you personally. You're in for it."

"*Non dica sciocchezze.*" Bora cut him short. "And do not speak of this man as though he were more important or dangerous than he is." But it was possible that news of his assignment to Salò had reached the partisans. Some might know him from the previous year, three months of unyielding warfare with the nascent groups; one or more of them could be those who injured him by tossing a grenade against his car. *The measure of ferocity in our lives*, Bora would note in his diary that evening, *is such that shock and outrage are short-lived. The greatest damage we suffer at war is a wound that becomes its own anaesthetic.*

As he pulled the handkerchief out of his pocket to cleanse his fingers of blood, he had dropped the calling cards found in Bianca Spagnoli's rooms. The night before he'd been too tired to study them, but now one of them drew his attention: to the extent that he hoped to learn details from Vittori, who apparently had nothing to do with them.

In a smock and rubber boots, Annie's uncle stood supervising work in the garden, when Bora drove in through the open gate. Labourers shovelling dirt around a vigorous young fir tree stopped at the sight of the German uniform; Vittori urged them with a wave to keep working and clambered down the grassy incline to meet him.

Soon he was leading the guest to a modern, sparsely furnished room overlooking the lake, a conservatory of sorts. "Glad you could make it," he said. "I hope you do not disapprove of Bauhaus."

Bora replied that he had nothing against Bauhaus style. After the clutter in Conforti's and Pozzi's rooms, the bare walls were welcome. The sole decoration was a tablet representing two monks on horseback, one cowled and the other bare-headed, with halos like straw hats and enormous staring eyes. Vittori pointed at them. "The saints Victor and Macarius, much venerated in Ethiopia. My favourite African souvenir, and the only painting I would not part from, ever. Won't you come to the terrace and enjoy a view of the garden while we talk?"

The terrace had little architecturally to do with the home, but the greenery all around somehow made it blend in. Under a chequered sky scattering random sunbeams, Bora recognized the turreted roof of Pozzi's villa, but not Sohl's residence, lower along the road, nor Annie's house, too distant in its medlar grove.

"Any word about your wallet?" he asked.

Vittori smirked. "You can't be serious, Colonel! I don't expect to hear about it ever again. It's not quite like losing the Venus, don't you agree?"

"As a matter of fact, I was hoping you could advise me in that regard."

The workers' voices issued now and then from below; beyond the rooftops and lush heads of garden trees, the lake had the dull patina of tin. Grey-eyed, grey-haired, Vittori spoke, looking admiringly at the newly planted fir. "If you must know, I found the Venus disturbing, because, aside from the colour of her hair, she resembles my niece." (Bora had abundantly noticed.) "There was something incestuous about having her in the house. Giovanni of course laughed it off."

"Your niece seems to be fond of it."

"She is. And do *you* like her?"

"I only just met Signora Tedesco, I don't think I'm in the position ..."

"I meant the Venus, Colonel."

Bora could have sunk into the ground. He seldom misunderstood Italian, but the blunder was impossible to remedy. Vittori did the only thing a proper host could do: he adjusted accordingly. "Oh, Annie is a dear girl, but a little uneasy around men. Her father and I blame the accident for it, yet the accident can only account for her indecision, not her sentimental despondency."

Indecision in choosing a partner? In keeping him? Determined to avoid other errors, Bora listened in complete silence, leaning against the banister to relieve the ache in his knee.

"One way or another, Colonel, war makes us all despondent. Isn't that *glorious*?" Vittori proudly pointed out a superb araucaria dominating the garden. "You probably think there are plenty of trees here, so why plant more? But mark my words: with the industrial deforestation of the past five thousand years, we're bound to exhaust this precious commodity. It was the subject of my research at the university, although my teachers didn't seem impressed by it. I had it published and translated into French and English anyway. It sold well in London." The notched upper lip, so beautiful on Annie, looked simply odd on Vittori's plain face. He looked around, filling his lungs with the scented air from below. "Trees and plants in general are a blessing. It's no wonder I admire your grandfather's property in Riva."

"The garden at La Schiavona is my Scottish grandmother's doing."

"Well, like her, I'm having sycamores planted next spring. In Africa, they grow to formidable proportions." The soil turned over by the workers' spades glistened in great, rich clumps over the grass. "Are you familiar with *Heart of Darkness?*"

"Conrad's work? Of course."

"It started me on loving Africa, just as Stanley's accounts did with Conrad. If you haven't visited the obscure continent, you don't know what nostalgia is."

"On the contrary, I know very well what nostalgia is. But perhaps I never cared to find Mr Kurtz, dead or alive."

"Or else you knew that homesickness is in everyone, like a measure of lunacy."

"Are you referring to anyone in particular?"

"Why, no. But take Conforti, for instance. A good little fellow, shrewd in his business. But is he as honest as he is shrewd? Take your commander, who saddled you with this investigative predicament; take Major Lipsky: who are they really, and what do they seek? Does Lipsky only want to court Annie? Do you only want to discover who took the Venus?"

Bora felt the comment in the quick. "But you spoke of lunacy."

"Yes, however you define it. I do not eat green vegetables; only roots or tubers, freely given by the living plant at the end of its season. I am fond of, and despite all prohibitions listen to, Cole Porter's music. My brother-in-law calls it crazy. Yet he claims to 'commune with the departed'."

"We all have our druthers. As a cavalry officer, I could never, not even in Russia, bring myself to eat horsemeat. For me, it's somehow cannibalistic."

Vittori called out to a thickset, red-headed workman below and dismissed the crew for the day. "Take Annie, who married a Jew shortly before the Racial Laws of '38. She could not know, you will say. They let him keep his citizenship because he was an army officer, but his drinking habits were no mystery to her. *His* mother fiercely opposed the marriage, as did my brother-in-law. But our proud and self-destructive Annie took him in spite of it all."

"Marrying the wrong person is no sign of insanity."

"No, but I can never forget what her mother's self-destructiveness led to."

Turning away from the garden and the lake, Bora looked at the heights behind Salò, leading to a perilous no man's land. "May I ask whether your brother-in-law gave his wife a reason to self-destruct?"

Vittori rolled up the sleeves of his smock, because the sun glowed warm between the clouds. "Colonel, I fail to see the connection between the stolen painting and Giovanni's private life."

"There isn't any." From the shiny rim of a cloud, a wandering sunbeam swept across the roofs and up the green hillside. Bora smiled to downplay his observation. "Mine is mere curiosity; sometimes we build something for the sake of taking it down."

Still, the level of Vittori's ease had lessened. Bora asked to see the garden and showed such interest in it that his host was soon appeased. "Ah, birch ... Russian birch, is it? Its branches are as pliant as a willow's, and it withstands the heaviest snowfall."

"And it is a fast grower, Colonel. Let me show you the Norfolk Island pine, a relative of the araucaria. You see the araucarias by the gate ..."

After the visit, Vittori led the way back to the conservatory. He called Bora's attention to a massive radio cabinet with the turntable door open.

"Take a look at my *forbidden* records," he said. "Acquired in London before the war, when I studied botany and attended Cole Porter's revues."

"Your sin is forgiven. I don't usually admit it, but in Stalingrad I was saved by Cole Porter." He removed his army cap, to signal the unofficial nature of his statement, or else that he was in no haste to leave. "Imagine, I found the record collection of a Soviet officer, which included American music. There was a gramophone, too, and one particular night I just listened to that dear music, those dear, sane words, and thought of all that anchored me – and my men, wholly dependent on me – to life." He placed "Night and Day" on the turntable and lifted the tone arm to check whether there was a needle under it. "Only days earlier our army surgeon told me that it was all over. He added, 'It's your worry now,' put a gun in his mouth and pulled the trigger. Of course. The Russians were at our doorstep: they were already in the building where we were holed up. We heard them pound and threaten. Chances were a thousand to one against us. Had the song's words not reminded me, 'Night and day, *you are the one*,' I'd have probably raised the gun to my head a third time – and fired. But there was that *one*: that *one* hope, belief, woman … I wasn't sure, except that there was *one thing left*, and I could not and should not let go of it. I gathered my men, who must have thought me drunk or demented, listening to music with a loaded gun behind closed doors, and told them, a thousand to one or not, to hang on to the one thing they held dearest and get ready to break out."

"Which you did."

Bora placed the needle on the record but did not turn it on. "We did, all of us – and Cole Porter, too. We escaped when our 71st Division and the entire Sixth Army had already surrendered, and made it to the German lines in the Russian winter. Mine was a form of benign lunacy, compared to what else went on in that campaign."

Vittori seemed troubled, or perhaps moved, by the account. "The times make us fragile. You did put a gun to your head twice."

"I did, yes." When Bora took out a calling card from his breast pocket, Vittori stepped closer to read the name on it.

"My brother-in-law's card, I see. What about it?"

"A widow named Bianca Spagnoli was found hanged last week."

"Yes, we heard it was a suicide."

"Well, this card comes from her rooms."

"I don't understand. How would you know, and what does it mean? Did you ask Giovanni? I'm sure he has an explanation for it."

"I will surely ask him."

"But ... Why? Don't you believe the woman killed herself?"

"No." Bora wondered whether he was lying or had built something for the sake of tearing it down.

DIARY ENTRY: SUNDAY, 22 OCTOBER 1944, 7:08 P.M.

Useful stopover at Vittori's. It took me a good hour and several records to make him admit that Pozzi had a lover among his factory workers in Rhodes when his wife drowned herself in a well; but, according to him, she knew of his affairs and took them in her stride. Vittori believes Bianca Spagnoli got Pozzi's calling card from someone, hoping for employment at the Roè textile works. But if my own theory about Spagnoli's arthritis is correct, she would never have secured a position. However, Vittori added an interesting titbit. Despite the pervasive presence of army units on the lake, there is much to and fro in Salò. Annie came up in conversation, but only because she is unwell these days. At least she's not in Venice with Lipsky.

After Vittori, I stopped by Conforti's. According to him, local gossip has it that Vismara was killed because he was investigating the Spagnoli case. Has word of a possible homicide leaked out, and how? What nonsense goes around in small towns!

Tonight, I am supposed to attend a reception at the Gardone Spielcasino. I expect I'll hear more nonsense. I hope to meet Prince Borghese, of the submarine branch, whom I was introduced to in Rome years ago, when he was a young navy officer. While I fought on the Belchite front in Spain, he was successfully attacking HMS Havock, *and went on to sink the* Valiant *and more. Although I lost a British second cousin in the wreck of his submarine, I maintain that Borghese's feats remain formidable ones.*

SOIANO, MONDAY, 23 OCTOBER 1944

Denzo's purview before his arrival on the scene, as far as Bora could ascertain, was a desk job. Italian soldiers might have to be coerced to carry out searches and violent reprisals alongside German SS and police units, while Denzo's feelings about that possibility remained unclear. From German hearsay, Bora knew that after the collapse of the Italian front in Africa, the colonel had spent months at his country home in the hills above Chivasso, officially to cure a tropical fever; in September 1943, only because of Graziani's insistence had he joined Mussolini's Republican Army. At the Gardone reception, a Wehrmacht aide from Gardone tattled that Graziani had discovered Denzo locked up with provisions in the outbuilding of his country home. "I was there," the aide said, "and you should have heard the colonel claim, fresh as a rosebud, that he'd never even heard of the king's surrender. I thought Graziani would burst a vein in his neck!"

The first workday began uneventfully. Aside from his strong aftershave, Parisi was palatable – both punctual and efficient. By midday, having examined a prodigious amount of paperwork, Bora concluded that it would be wise to sound out moderate guerrilla leaders in an attempt to isolate the more extreme partisan groups.

"That's brilliant," Denzo sneered. "Giving yourself up to men indoctrinated to shoot you."

"Me? I was thinking of both of us."

Denzo appeared suddenly less amused. "The marshal will never agree to it."

"Plenipotentiary Wolff will."

"I am not under his command."

"We all are. Including the marshal." Through the corner of his eye, Bora detected how Parisi, head low on his papers, was listening intently. He said, more agreeably, "We have the Church on our side: that is, local churchmen favour negotiations. That is a considerable advantage. The Church is tied to class interests; it abhors the Left and all that smacks of lay culture. We ought to keep it on our good side. As for the factories, the workers, socialist or no, communist or no, prefer the general strike to sabotage. I don't think we'll have to battle them on the assembly-line floor as we did in Stalingrad."

Denzo sat on the corner of his desk, dangling his elegant boot. "Listening to you, we face nothing but a stroll in the woods."

"Not at all. Still, Italy is not Russia; we can choose our enemies. Armed partisan bands count a few hundred at most; they're politically divided, and I say we capitalize on the division. It's true that they control some mountain passes and valleys, but, if we avoid unnecessary harshness, we can manage nicely until next month, when I wager the Allies will halt under adverse weather conditions."

Parisi's expression must have shown some form of unspoken agreement with Bora's words, because Denzo dismissed him. "Parisi, get the marshal on the phone." He tossed onto his desk the memorandum Bora had just summarized, and, as he was not wearing his spectacles, he probably hadn't noticed it was written in German. "I don't care about your judgement of the Church."

"It's how I see it. I dealt well with the Church in Russia. After all, less than two weeks ago, His Eminence Cardinal Schuster supported the creation of the Rebirth and Reconstruction Battalion, which, unless I am mistaken, is comprised of former shirkers *and* partisans."

"I demand deference towards religion."

"And I demand common sense."

Denzo squared his shoulders; tall, narrow-shouldered but straight-backed, he cut a fine soldier's figure. "Let us be clear with each other, Colonel von Bora. When I joined the Republic following the marshal's example, it was not my intention to fight against other Italians."

The statement, Bora could tell, was meant to impress. He thought, without saying it, *It isn't our fault if your countrymen switched sides.*

"However, Bora, if I have to fight other Italians, I will not want for severity. I know how to deal victoriously with rebel forces. I don't need a German to tell me how to lead a campaign in my own country."

There it was. Graziani's dissatisfaction with the prospect of a civil war resulted in leaving the dirty work to his protégé, or rather, his protégé's men. Bora suspected it from the start and, having seen it in Spain, recognized the combination of religiosity and aggressiveness.

"Well," he objected, "where is your memorandum? I saw nothing that comes close to a plan of action. I spent three days with German *and* Italian commanders, from the cadres of SS Leibstandarte Adolf Hitler to the units employed at Lovere, Bagolino and Mount Baldo. By midweek I will send my recommendations to Marshal Graziani, with a copy to Plenipotentiary Wolff, and you are free to sign off on them or not."

Lunchtime, spent separately, kept the situation from degenerating. Bora had been running a slight fever ever since the reception, and, having hurt his knee in Berlin back in July, he could not rule out a reinfection. Since no office space had been set aside for him at Soiano – although he had not insisted on having one – Parisi shared with him a two-desk room. It was he who in the afternoon informed him that an Italian officer was asking by telephone for Colonel von Bora. "I'll take it here," Bora said. Parisi left the room.

The caller identified himself as the army surgeon sought by Vismara in relation to the Spagnoli death certificate. "Given the inspector's unfortunate demise, I was told to call you. I can't add much to what I told the police, except that the bruise on the woman's neck was technically a 'soft furrow', and her facial cyanosis was marked. The findings are consistent with criminal strangulation, but also with self-hanging. Regarding her hands and fingers, an early stage of arthritis is possible. What? Sorry, the line is disturbed. No, not impossible: I said *possible*. When I was called in, there was considerable confusion, as the body had been taken down by the RNG. The Guard wanted me to write down 'accidental death', but it'd have been preposterous. So, since there was no sign of forced entry or struggle, I put down 'suicide'."

"Yet you do not rule out foul play?"

"No. The knot was not a noose per se: more likely to have been tied by a housewife than by a sailor or a Boy Scout. Given the crowded conditions and the curiosity around, I refrained from an intimate examination and cannot tell if she had sexual intercourse before her death."

"I was about to ask."

At four Denzo left for Desenzano, where Graziani had summoned him. Bora worked one more hour, sketching the week's schedule: the two colonels would join a German–Italian operation already underway in the mountains, while Bora would test the waters with a view to a meeting with moderate partisans through the mediation of Cardinal Schuster in Milan.

At five, Bora left Soiano under the Allied bomber formations flying high in a patchy sky. Annie's car felt familiar and safe, as if she'd let him in, taken him in metaphorically. Driving by her place, Bora could not tell whether she was at home. Somehow, he thought she was not. The thought of her chafed him slightly, as all things that attracted him; the response of a busy man who against his better judgement finds distraction hard to resist. Chasing the idea that she could have followed Lipsky to Venice after all, he went out of his way not to imagine intimacy between the two. If Lipsky nicknamed her Turandot, things had not got that far; the prospect paradoxically made him edgier, and more pressed for time.

Back in Salò, Bora worked on a message for Wolff, and phoned the cardinal's secretary in Milan. When he came downstairs with the intention of seeking a cup of coffee somewhere, he glimpsed a handful of militiamen leaving De Rosa's office. De Rosa himself tensely joined him at the foot of the stairs.

"Two German Security Service men were gunned down in Breno."

Breno, nestled in the tortuous Camonica valley, was one of the places Bora had marked in red pencil as unsafe. "And what the hell were two men doing alone in *Bandengebiet* territory?"

"According to the militia, they had been detailed to keep watch over a couple of hanged partisans. The worst of it is, they were strung up from the same tree after being shot."

Breno is not in Xavier's area, Bora was thinking. "It was an accident waiting to happen! Has anyone claimed it? Were the executed taken away by the attackers?"

The partisans' bodies had been removed, and there was no claim so far. De Rosa's moustache trembled with excitement.

"There's activity reported at the Tormini crossroads. I think there's something afoot by way of a reprisal."

Bora returned upstairs to place a call – "Holy Christ," De Rosa heard him mutter on the way – but all phone lines to the Brescia SD command were busy, and no one answered at Maderno. He tried uselessly until eight, when he stopped by his hotel before driving to Gardone to check on his wounded men at the old Rosenhof inn, now a German surgical ward.

The telephone was ringing when he entered the room.

"Bora? Dollmann here. I have no time for details: Field Marshal Kesselring was seriously injured near Ferrara. A car accident. He's alive but unconscious at the local hospital. There's nothing you can do, but *I know how he cares for you*, and thought you'd want to hear this."

Bora sat down on the bed. He had served under Kesselring even as the field marshal had done under his stepfather decades earlier; he couldn't bring himself to accept that the old man could die now. Dollmann, who often wasted words, but never concepts, was implicitly warning him to watch out. How? From the Russian days, a measure of political safeguard had depended on Kesselring, and now matters could come to a head, whether or not the field marshal were to die. Only two weeks earlier, a car accident had been used as an excuse to eliminate Rommel – a chilling thought. He wondered how one prays for wounded field marshals.

Only after leaving for Gardone did Dollmann's words come back to him. "No time for details." Why? Did "there's nothing you can do" mean the impossibility of being of assistance to Kesselring or the futility of trying to protect himself? The last thing he wanted was to be halted by tight-lipped SS men at the fork in the road; they asked for papers, waved a dance of torches around him and let him go. Militiamen stopped him half a kilometre ahead on the outskirts of Barbarano. "What happened?" "*Ordini, colonnello.*" It was past nine-thirty when Bora reached the surgical ward. It was beginning to rain; fir and palm trees rustled like gigantic tails overhead. He parked, found his way in through the darkened entrance, and spent the next hour at his men's bedsides.

6

"Your face is bleeding."

Jacob Mengs spoke when Bora walked by his office, bound for the end of the hallway reserved for the Gestapo and SS.

A merchant on the threshold of his shop, a well-fed butcher whose stock is abundant: it was unusual for Bora to judge others purely on physical grounds, yet the association between Mengs and slaughtered meat was as odd as it was overpowering. He felt repugnance at being addressed.

"On your cheekbone," Mengs pointed out. He watched Bora dab the cut reopened by shaving and walk off with a barely spoken acknowledgement, a reaction that made him smile, because the aversion was mutual.

Kappler, on the other hand, listened for two minutes before interrupting Bora. "You ought to thank us, Colonel. Wasn't one of your informants killed, too? We saved you and the Guard the effort of a reprisal."

"Obersturmbannführer, if you explain to me how shooting three farming families will solve our problem in Breno, I *will* thank you for it."

"We also plan to torch their houses and declare Breno *Bandengebiet.* Of course, you yourself were gallivanting through an area under rebel control a few days ago. Had a German colonel been killed, there would have been a heftier reprisal on our part. You of all people, who worked *so closely* with Field Marshal Kesselring, ought to admit that we scrupulously applied each of the five points he set for us on the twelfth of August. Reprisals are being contemplated. And since we're on the subject, how much do you know about Xavier?"

Kappler's mention of the field marshal was not wasted on Bora, who showed no emotional response. "Mostly anecdotes," he said. "Reports that the structure of his command is anomalous. His less-than-company-size group is spread out, yet we have no word of a second-in-command: only hand-picked liege lieutenants. Until last night, I'd have ventured to say that his foraging area extends from Lonato in the south to north of Riva, and from this lake-shore nearly to Lake Iseo, but not as far as Breno. He likely controls a fraction of that, mainly trails and observation points. Anfo comes to mind. If Breno is part of his territory, we have to rethink his mobility, or his collaboration with other groups. I heard from Italian intelligence that the road from Brescia to Tione is at risk."

"It is."

"For the rest, he has access to a rudimentary press and advertises his actions in flimsy pamphlets, using such military euphemisms as 'striking down' and 'execution' for brutal killings." Under Kappler's stare, Bora struggled to control his tension. It was like slogging through mud, knowing that the trap yawned nearby. The sense of listing under a great load became unmanageable for a moment. *Am I about to commit an error? And if I am, when?*

"Xavier," he went on, "sounds politically and psychologically extreme, an ideologue rather than a patriot, closer to Russian models in that sense. In fact, he served in Russia." Out of his briefcase, Bora pulled an Italian army record book. "If he is this man, we know everything about him, from his parents' names to his qualifications."

There. Kappler was quick, but the way he eyed the other contents of the briefcase did not escape Bora, who snapped it closed.

He was looking for the diary. Carrying the diary in his briefcase was a habit; only during the summer, in the mountains with his men, did Bora trust Fate enough to part from it occasionally. Now Kappler had seen it, and finding another repository became a pressing need.

"Ingenious," Kappler was saying, apparently immersed in the army book. "Congratulations. Clearly, this fellow does not care if his real name is known. No women are allowed to follow his group, did you know? Another peculiarity. Has a younger brother with him, but it is unclear in which capacity he serves."

Well before stepping into the building, Bora had considered how much information about him the Gestapo and SS could be sharing. Save his last month in Russia, he'd had less to do with Gestapo officials than with SS and Security Service forces, but now men and things met perilously as they circled the drain in Salò. "I wonder about the girl who delivered the informant's mutilated ear." He continued to speak calmly, hoping to convince. "A girlfriend, maybe, or an innocent bystander told to carry the wrap, no information given. His illnesses during the service are telling: fevers, bouts of vomiting – it could be related to his work as a typographer."

"Lead poisoning? Ah, of course. Your family owns a publishing firm."

"There are rumours of his erratic behaviour, another possible symptom. He has his men shot for minor infractions. A peasant in the Sabbia Valley claims his eardrums were pierced when Xavier fired a gun close to his head, mock execution-style. There's no question in my mind that he killed my informant *and* your two men."

Kappler reached across his desk for a typewritten sheet. "Well, I have here Plenipotentiary Wolff's signature indicating that you are our liaison with the Italians, so what is your plan for Xavier?"

"Capturing him. He's probably already overextended. Last month, the militia fell upon one of his abandoned camps. Going after Xavier would effectively truncate the band." Through the open door, Bora recognized Mengs's heavy tread and forced himself not to look over.

"Secure clearance from Marshal Graziani. Then we can discuss a combined action." Mengs must have been standing just outside the door (Bora thought he heard him breathing laboriously); still, Kappler kept a friendly demeanour. He extended his right hand to shake Bora's, who saw through the ruse and made the Party salute instead. "As for us, Colonel, we follow our own directives. With all respect for your band-fighting experience, we still plan to torch those farms. I'd invite you to come and watch, but I know you're busy. Oh, and whatever business you have with the Jew in Salò, make haste. We no longer need him."

It had begun to rain. In Soiano, Bora found a message from Schuster's secretary, setting up an appointment with the arch-bishop at his Milan residence for the afternoon. Parisi reported that Marshal Graziani had authorized a three-day joint search in the Trompia Valley, beginning 29 October. A German company from Brescia was to rendezvous with RNG units at the Tormini crossroads and head north by way of Sarezzo, where it would link up with Security Service forces. Denzo came in, peeling off his gloves and cursing the rain; he did not share with Bora the reason for his summons to the marshal's the day before but brought maps of the search area. He premised that his duties would detain him in Milan until the 28th, at which time they would meet there to celebrate Party Day.

At the Curia, Cardinal Schuster, sad-faced, looking taller because of his slim figure, listened to Bora's proposal and promised to have an answer by the end of the month. "Anything can be arranged, Colonel, if there's goodwill on both sides." As he spoke, he handed Bora a copy of his *Catechism on Marxism*, which the German received, bowing his head. "Anything, even a meeting between fire and holy water. Which does not mean that I see you as the latter. But there are worse devils about."

That this antique room saw all kinds of postulants come and go was a known fact. Bora found himself having to trust the German–Italian Schuster, a philosophy graduate like him. They discussed the necessity of parleying with non-Marxist partisans before touching on private matters. As soon as Bora entrusted him with a handful of private letters, Schuster smiled. "They will be safe. The Bishop of Verona told me of your tête-à-tête with him a year ago."

It was bad enough that churchmen gossiped about his initiatives in favour of Italian Jews. Bora said boldly that he recalled no such encounter and left the palace in a troubled state of mind. It would be past eight before he reached Salò, and somehow or other Conforti had to be *told* of Kappler's plans.

SALÒ, 8:17 P.M.

Conforti was in the back room of his shop. Bora found the door open and walked directly in. The orderliness of the interior surprised him; the sacred vessels were neatly boxed or in the process of being so. He assumed the bad news preceded him, and when he learned that it hadn't, he did not know what to think.

Conforti showed him the "completed hand-written inventory", as he said, placed it on a capricious Victorian side-table and sat down, his hands on his knees.

"Why should I hide? There is no point, irrespective whether the Church would kindly take me in; I am not interested. Thank you for offering."

"What will you do?"

"What I have started doing: putting things in order. I still have to organize the photographic equipment, the collected prints and the artwork upstairs." Conforti politely bridged an imaginary gap between wisdom and resignation. "You do not have four thousand wings, as the esoteric tradition says, but you make a credible Azrael."

"If I were the angel of death, I would not come to warn you."

"Yet there are similarities between you; he, too, wears boots, and medals. You may be one of the *malachim ha-Maveth*, and not know. Weren't you just now at the fateful western window?"

Bora was startled. The old man could not possibly have noticed him stopping outside by the screened little window and wondering if he was inside.

"Can't you see, Colonel? It is time for us to part. In three days' time, I will stop my heart."

"Would that dying were as easy as that."

"It is in my case."

As if to underscore the strange words, the power failed and darkness became total. Bora had no electric torch with him, and neither man made an effort to strike a match against the box or flick a lighter. "And the Venus?"

In the heady scent rising to his nostrils from the spice boxes, Bora took a single step forward, towards the corner where Conforti sat. Instead, he crossed a phantom threshold, beyond which a chasm seemed to open and claim him; he remembered this was what he had dreamed of in Russia. Over and over, even in the good days, when victory seemed possible. He'd stir from sleep with his heart in his mouth, wondering why he had no fear of sinking down to an unreachable bottom. But it'd never happened to him in a waking state. The old man's words reached him but were incomprehensible. Bora wanted to leave, his useless errand here being done, but the effort was superior to his strength.

Finally, Conforti's speech curdled into an intelligible sentence. "If you do not find *her*, it will be your fault."

WEDNESDAY, 25 OCTOBER 1944

By Wednesday morning, Denzo had got a Defense Information Service interpreter to translate Bora's memo and, having deleted references to the Church and added a few considerations of his own, hand-delivered it in his name to the marshal's residence at Desenzano. Bora went from astonishment to rage when, during an icy telephone conversation at noon that same day, he heard from Graziani that his recommendations, just received by courier, did not differ appreciably from the brilliant analysis already presented by Denzo di Galliano.

Bora's first reaction was to get in the car and barrel towards Sirmione, where Denzo lived, to defy his colleague, but a look at the fuel gauge warned him that he did not have enough for a round trip. Soiano was closer, though, and, within the half hour, Captain Parisi received the brunt of the German's anger. All he could do was stand by while Bora telephoned the interpreters' office in Salò and then the SID external office in Milan, to learn the names of all accredited translators there. As for Denzo's private number in Sirmione, it was out of bounds.

Bora paid no attention to De Rosa's absence from work when he returned to the RNG building. He spent the rest of the day, swallowing aspirins for the severe pain in his arm and leg, preparing for the three-day search operation. Only when he came downstairs to confer with the captain did he hear that no one had seen De Rosa for hours.

Bora returned upstairs and locked himself in his office. On a blank sheet of typing paper, he made a "to do" list of all that demanded his attention. In Russia, drafting lists of duties and responsibilities had allowed him to check them off punctiliously one by one as he carried them out. Today he jotted down: *Venus, diary, Cristomorto, Denzo, Sohl, Meran, Lipsky, Nozza, Conforti, Spagnoli. Missing key, calling cards, red marks (on Verona hotel maid's neck: kisses, or?), girlfriends (Pozzi's and ...?), stolen church paintings, diary, bank deposit box.* When he had finished, he saw that he had written "diary" twice, and not once Annie Tedesco's name. Or Mengs's.

It felt like a sea of unstrung details, dangerously floating after a wreck.

Late into the night, Bora studied the maps of the mountain region. Sipping lukewarm coffee from a thermos cup, he waited for the intricate charts to speak to him under the glare of his table lamp. He sought a detached, quiet state of mind, close to animal instinct. It had worked in Rome, in Russia and in the bloody mess of the emergency room: if only he could reach it; it never failed.

On one side of the desk, underlined in red, sat German and Italian intelligence reports; on the other, his list of duties and concerns. When at last he reached a state of deep inner quiet, beyond all logic, the jumble of symbols and pencilled remarks began to unravel before him. Disparate places, trails and mountainsides coalesced into a pattern until Bora confronted an exhilarated sense of what to avoid and what to look for, as if there were drops of blood on the maps, some of which were friendly and some inimical. Scraps of paper and disconnected pieces of information fitted together, not in the way of a puzzle that needs to be arranged, but as a foreign tongue that suddenly becomes intelligible. He came so close to understanding Xavier's thoughts that he chose not to go the frightful last step.

The office was icy cold. Numb from having sat so still, Bora pushed back his chair. The watch read one o'clock on Thursday, 26 October. No more coffee, and the maps no longer spoke. The steel trap of logic was on.

When he opened the window, a brutally cold wind rode the street like a wave. Slender, colourless clouds were all that was left of the overcast. Weariness made him ache, and he needed a shave. He reached into his breast pocket, where he kept a fresh razor blade ready for these overnight stays. The razor waited in the top drawer of his desk. Standing in front of a small mirror, he freshened up, in order to look impeccable as he walked past the sentinel by the door.

He'd just fallen asleep, still in his clothes, when the phone rang. De Rosa was at the other end, his voice choked and unrecognizable. "Colonel," he whispered, "I must see you at once. May I join you?"

Bora's watch said that he'd slept a matter of minutes. He'd been dreaming. What had he been dreaming? Weariness fell off him like a wet rag, leaving him perfectly lucid. "Where are you? Is it about work? We can meet at the RNG."

"No. Personal, a personal matter. Very urgent."

"… Come, then."

In Verona, a year earlier, De Rosa had once shown up after hours as he did now, without his uniform; and in that case, too, the issue at hand had been women. Staring at Bora, he said breathlessly, "Do you recall what I told you about my troubles, and Marla Bruni's threats?"

"No."

"I told you when you were looking at the severed ear."

"Well, I was probably thinking of the severed ear, then."

"I never told you that the third woman was Marla Bruni's maid …"

"Christ, De Rosa, I'm tired. Get to the point, will you?"

"Well, I'd given her a gun to protect herself, because of La Bruni's temper. Even after sacking her, La Bruni slapped and abused her in public, and lashed at me, too, for 'bedding a servant'. Now she – her name was Fiorina, Fiorina Gariboldi – she's shot herself with my gun."

Bora scowled at De Rosa, who looked considerably less martial in civvies. "You definitely have no luck with domestics," he observed.

"That's below the belt, Colonel! I'm a desperate man, I don't deserve it."

From the jumbled narrative that followed, Bora understood that Fiorina Gariboldi, a professional lady's maid, had become pregnant by a former employer. She had raised her young son alone until the winter of '43, when she answered an advertisement for "a profitable situation" with La Bruni in Salò, courtesy of Captain De Rosa. She'd left the boy with her parents near Milan, and the unconscionable air raid of 20 October claimed him as one of the young victims.

"I'd given her a PP 7.65-calibre civilian model because La Bruni made her distraught: only as a precaution, you understand. I gave her no ammo. A few days ago, when news came of the boy's death, I demanded the gun back, lest she do something crazy. I was to get it from her at six-thirty tonight. Good God, Colonel, I found her in her room, with her son's photograph on the bed, as if she'd been kneeling before it when she put a bullet through her head."

Bora simply had no desire to get involved, although he

came across as insensitive. "Well, what do you want from me? She clearly found ammunition somewhere."

"But if it should be known that it was my gun …"

"The Police Pistol is German. People will think it was one of us who gave her the weapon and ammunition. As it is, they blame us Germans for all that is unpleasant."

Still in his overcoat, as most of the rooms in Salò were frigid, De Rosa was the picture of bundled exasperation. "Colonel, please! They saw me with Fiorina at Gargnano, at Gardone … I used to bring her to the Spielcasino. Some colleagues weren't even aware that I was having an affair with La Bruni."

"Why keep the prima donna here, then?"

De Rosa let out something like a horse's snort. "In Brescia and Desenzano, it'd be La Bruni."

"And the wife in Salò."

"Precisely. That's the way it was. Colonel von Bora, for the sake of your past investigations, come along and tell me if in your judgement it is *undoubtedly* a suicide."

Bora said neither yes nor no; unhurriedly, he took his greatcoat from the wardrobe. "Has anybody seen her, other than yourself?"

"No. She lived alone, and much as I was tempted to conceal the body, I was afraid I'd be found out. You're the only one I could call on."

Thanks for nothing, Bora thought. "Do you have an alibi?" he asked.

"I was at work until six. At six-thirty, I found her dead. After seven-thirty, I was with La Bruni. You can imagine my state of mind. I couldn't even get an erection."

"Spare me the details. And between six and six-thirty?"

"I stopped briefly to see how the wife was. But I hope to God she won't be involved."

*

Fiorina's home was in the outskirts, towards Barbarano; an old, isolated farmhouse at the end of a lane screened by tall canes, here and there withered by autumn. In the glare of Bora's torch, the upper windows looked broken down and forlorn. De Rosa used his key to open and let the German in first.

"Holy Christ, you didn't tell me she was naked!"

"I shouldn't have thought it would shock you."

"It doesn't. But do you really think a woman would remove her clothes before killing herself, in front of her son's picture?"

The cold in the room condensed the men's breath into small clouds. Bora placed his electric torch, a flat, square Daimon issue, on the bed, at an angle that allowed him to view the body. Next to him, De Rosa fretted.

"You must help me, Colonel. My honour as an officer and a Republican Fascist …"

"Screw your honour. You should have thought of it earlier." Crouching by the body, Bora placed two fingers across her neck. "Did you touch anything?"

"No, but my fingerprints must be everywhere in the room."

"Was the door closed when you came for the gun?"

"It was open. She was waiting for me, so I paid no attention."

The stubby pistol nestled in the woman's fist, slackened as if she were reaching out for something. Bora held his breath, so that the vapour would not dim his view. With the gloved right hand, he lifted the hair from her face; she was fair, remarkably attractive; the intact left temple and cheekbone, lips and chin had the glossiness of alabaster under the crude light. The small freckles on her shoulder pointed faintly to the half-hidden swell of her breast. Bora pulled back when De Rosa's own jumpy torch lit up from above the handful of blondness between her thighs.

"She's way cold, isn't she, Colonel? She …"

Bora interrupted. "Is there a physician you can trust?"

De Rosa's torch searched the corners of the room, perhaps to make sure he'd left no personal items around. "I know a surgeon at the civilian hospital: I could fetch him."

"If he's not on call."

Twenty minutes later, escorted by a gloomy De Rosa carrying a kerosene lamp, the physician walked in. He was an old man, a retiree forced back into active service. The captain must have explained things to him on the way, because he greeted Bora without additional comments. He took his hat off in the presence of the dead woman and crouched to examine her in absolute silence.

Bora looked on, feeling numb. He had neither eaten nor really slept in twenty-four hours; even his anger at Denzo seemed foreign and remote. While waiting for the physician, he'd compassionately draped a sheet over Fiorina's body. His second care had been to inspect her clothes, neatly stacked on the chest of drawers: shoes at the bottom, woollen stockings and garters, underpants, bra, skirt and blouse. He found nothing worthy of notice in the drawers or inside the iron stove, where wood shavings and old newspapers waited to be lit.

At the foot of the bed, De Rosa looked shrunken, the dark moustache a scrawl on his pallor.

"She's been dead eight or nine hours." The physician spoke in curt sentences, with a southern accent Bora could not identify. "The hypostatic stains are evident. When did either one of you gentlemen last see her alive?"

"Wednesday afternoon," De Rosa said hastily.

"I've never seen her before," Bora spoke up, but somehow that was not true, either. At the Spielcasino he'd seen several women, and, for all he knew, Fiorina could have been one of them. It was as if someone else were standing in his place; he experienced only an impersonal sadness that linked him to the misfortune of others. *Why did I not tell Conforti that by asking, "And the Venus?" I meant his copy, not the stolen painting? Whether or not he can die at will, his collection faces an uncertain fate.*

"That's all I can say for now. I will need the body for a full report." Ignoring De Rosa, the physician turned to Bora. He stared at his mutilation as if he'd just noticed it was there, and it called for a professional, assessing look. "I will phone at mid-morning, Colonel."

At daybreak, Bora was already at his desk when De Rosa came in, looking the worse for wear but ready to discuss the joint operation in the Trompia Valley. A steaming thermos cup in the German's hand was the sole indicator of his need to keep awake; his countenance and uniform, down to the sheen of his spur-bearing boots, were spotless.

"If Denzo comes along, Colonel, I will not take responsibility for my men's reaction."

"A commander should *always* take responsibility for his men's behaviour."

"Well, we don't trust him."

Bora's face did not change expression. All he showed was stern forbearance. "I will not have a brother officer disparaged in his absence." He would have said so regardless of what he thought, which was a little consolation to De Rosa. What De Rosa noticed, enviously, were the good looks of the man before him; what seductive use one could make of such looks, such uniform, such rank. He was no longer wearing a wedding ring, so for all his primness he, too, might be taking liberties.

Bora's question startled him. "Did you really *not* give her the ammunition?"

"I swear it, Colonel. She didn't know the first thing about guns."

"That would not mean much. At five I loaded my stepfather's Parabellum and shot the prisms off the chandelier with it."

"Ammunition can be purchased anywhere in Salò."

Bora had to agree. He'd found one cartridge in the pistol and recovered a shell from the floor. On it, the lower-case "wa" code indicated wartime manufacture (Leipzig, incidentally), while the single P on the cartridge dated a few years back. This late in the conflict, he carried rounds by different makers in his own P38, so the detail meant little per se. "Whom else did she frequent? Did she have friends?"

De Rosa's grumpiness promised a response of the I-was-more-than-enough-for-her type, so Bora added, "It's German ammo. Could one of the officers at the Spielcasino have given it to her? She was attractive, she can't have gone unnoticed."

"Your colleagues *flocked* to her. Although she spoke no German, she was their type, blondness and all. What can I say? Given the right circumstances, a man could end up giving a woman a souvenir he ought not to."

Bora could not disagree. In Prague, during a furlough, an acquaintance of his had given his sidearm *and* holster to a buxom girlfriend, racing to take it back once his intoxication abated.

"It wasn't my fault if she shot herself, Colonel."

Vittori is right. Bora looked away from De Rosa's self-absolving figure. *We're all made fragile by the times. I think myself steel, but I may be glass for all that.*

Once De Rosa left, nearly one hour went by before the telephone rang. General Sohl was on the line, speaking with a cheroot in his mouth, judging by the distorted sibilants. "Bora, what's going on with the Jew? I hear he's being deported in two days. Did you get out of him all you were supposed to?"

"I did, and shall report to you in due course, Herr Generalleutnant."

"Good, good." Sohl's attention faded, as if he only pretended to care. "What I really wanted to tell you is that my wife will be here early next month, and I would appreciate your showing her around. Compatibly with your duties, it goes without saying, as a personal favour."

Often, when superiors spoke of "personal favour", some public or private catastrophe was at hand; Bora's commanders had resorted to the expression in Stalingrad whenever they had mistakes or bad decisions to cover. He was instantly wary. Still, the woman was from Meran, where Lipsky's bank and security box were located ... Trap or opportunity, why not take it as it came? He'd ask Hager about her, under the pretext of finding out what sights the lady had already seen.

"Major Lipsky has returned, Colonel, but I'd rather not ask *him*."

All Bora heard of the sentence was that Lipsky was back in Salò.

THURSDAY, 26 OCTOBER 1944, 10:48 A.M.

"Death came between five and six p.m.," the surgeon reported. "The entry hole shows no significant bruising, nor a ragged appearance. Sometimes, smaller calibres exploded point-blank resemble stabbing wounds, although automatic weapons do more damage generally. I submit that the pistol was not fired directly in contact with the skull. Even though people can hold a gun away from their head, we are here speaking of an arm's length. No, the fact that the bullet entered behind the ear does not exclude a suicide. I have seen more bizarre self-shootings. It's the distance that gives me pause."

The call from the hospital had come precisely at 10:45, and for the last three minutes Bora had been listening carefully.

Then he observed: "The clothes on the dresser make *me* wonder. Shoes, stockings and underpants were stacked in good order; but the bra should have been on top of skirt and blouse, don't you agree?"

"Only if she laid down her clothes as she took them off. She could have stacked them as you saw them on second thought."

Bora pulled the telephone cord to its maximum length, to look out of the window as he spoke. "But why undress in a room cold enough to make one shiver and risk missing the shot? Why undress at all?"

"She might have imitated the woman who hanged herself two weeks ago. There's no accounting for troubled minds, Colonel."

Out in the street, identified by the twin runes on its licence plate as an SS vehicle, a truck came slowly down Garibaldi Street. Tensely Bora expected it to pull up by Conforti's doorway, but it kept going and went out of sight.

Through the receiver, the surgeon's voice came with the hum and whirring of static. "To be honest, I am slightly unsure about the hypostatic stains on her right wrist. The position of the stains is consistent with her lying on her right side. Yet, on her wrist the blood clotting under the skin forms a tight reticle; it could point to a bruise caused before death."

"Really? Could she have been *forced* to fire?"

"The reasons for a bruise can be many, Colonel. I'll do my duty and draft a death certificate with my post-mortem. I expect the matter to end here."

In the afternoon Bora was informed by Denzo's aide that all the commanders heading units involved in the joint operation would meet within the hour.

Anxious to precede Denzo and confront him before Graziani's arrival, Bora lost no time. While he sped down the last stretch before the Soiano turn-off, he was confident he would be the first to arrive. The hairpin road leading to Villa Omodeo called for a reduction in speed, especially as it had begun to drizzle, but Bora pressed on. Out of nowhere, Denzo's car, which judging by the blue guidon on the hood carried Marshal Graziani as well, overtook him on a blind curve; Bora made out the profile of the Askari soldier at the wheel and little else, before being left behind in a whirl of rainwater. Moments later, seeing the two Italian officers cosily chatting as they walked into the building nearly had him veering off the slippery driveway. At the risk of being soaked, he parked at some distance, to keep them from seeing him struggle to compose himself.

Still, resentment made him see red. Hearing his memorandum freely quoted and elaborated by Graziani enraged him. He was unusually quiet during the first part of the meeting, so that the marshal eventually turned to him in a huff. "Are you not interested, Colonel?"

Bora swallowed his pride to say that he was.

As soon as Graziani was called out of the room, with an excuse Denzo tailed him to avoid facing Bora alone. But the German was ready for the contingency, and followed him to the gleaming hallway, where he sidestepped him to look him in the face as he held up to him a typewritten sheet. At the top of the sheet, in capital letters so that anyone could read it without glasses, was the name of the interpreter who translated the memo.

"Well, colleague?"

More than Denzo's words, it was the way he flicked the sheet that brought Bora within an inch of physical reaction. "See that you do not cross me more than you have done, Colonel Denzo. I am in a foul mood after a year in Italy."

"You are? Gentlemen do not make threats in Italy."

"Gentlemen do not appropriate the work of others in any country."

"Well, it is your word against mine, isn't it?"

Captain Parisi realized what he'd stepped into the instant he saw them facing off. He froze, as if trying to remember to which room he ought to be taking the folder he had in hand. How much he'd heard mattered nothing to the indignant Bora, who made a smart about-face and stepped back into the marshal's office.

The rest of the afternoon dragged on. Graziani sensed that something was seriously amiss, but he made no effort to enquire. At six o'clock, other officers joined in; Priebke for the SS, two representatives of the Resega brigade headquartered in Milan, and De Rosa for the RNG. On the long table, ashtrays and bottled water marked the men's spaces, as did fountain pens, pencils, cigarette packs and notebooks.

"Shortly after you left the office," De Rosa whispered to Bora, "a lady who wouldn't leave her name phoned, asking for you. Said you'd know, and would you call her back." A cold stare quashed any familiarity on his part, but during the first break Bora asked for a private telephone from which to place first a call to Brescia army headquarters and then one to Annie Tedesco.

He re-entered the smoke-filled room in time to find some of the spaces rearranged, and, worse luck, the only empty chair left was beside Colonel Denzo's.

"We were about to continue without you," Graziani quipped from the head of the table. Bora hastened to take his seat. He swallowed a sip of water from the glass in front of him to chase down the first retort that came to mind.

"My apologies."

Until nine in the evening, in various positions of controlled slump, the officers suffered at the hands of the number-crunching Parisi. Blue-grey layers of cigarette smoke formed a fictitious ceiling above their heads; only Graziani, on his feet, towered head and shoulders above it.

Bora, who had quit five months earlier, drifted from desire to open his virgin pack in irritation. He envied the others' relative alertness. As for himself, he simply ached to curl up somewhere and close his eyes. Words droned in his mind, and he had open-eyed flitting dreams of things seen and heard during the day and the endless night before: Fiorina Gariboldi's dead body and blond hair, Sohl's inane demands that he entertain his wife, Lipsky's yellow runabout sitting in Annie's driveway like the token of a parlour game. The Venus ... Well, *the* Venus was God knows where.

At long last, with a synchronous squeal of chairs pulled back, the meeting was over. On his feet as everyone else while Graziani retired, Bora was tempted to sit down again and go to sleep right where he was. Denzo saw through his weariness. "We'll be due here again early in the morning, Bora. Make sure you're not late."

A moment later, the marshal walked back in with a whiff of cologne and a leather portfolio. "At seven hundred hours tomorrow, the two of you will report here. The subject of the meeting is restricted, and I forbid all speculation about it on your part."

Only by running cold water over his head in the bathroom sink did Bora clear his mind enough to drive to Campoverde. He travelled with windows open to stay vigilant and disperse the cigarette smell that no doubt impregnated his uniform. Above the lake, a black well of clear sky yawned among the clouds; brilliant stars studded it like gold nails. From the street, no lights showed in Annie's house; the garden gate, however, gaped open, and beyond the blooming medlar trees, dogs barked in gardens far and near.

"Please come in." She dismissed his apologies for the late hour. "You said you'd come whenever you could, so I assume this is the earliest you could be here. I took the liberty of phoning you because there really is something I wish we could discuss."

Bora clicked his heels, took off his cap. The lights were low, and, in his weariness, she appeared as images do in dreams; when she stepped back to let him in, her paleness and dark hair were to him like ivory and night itself. He'd heard Italian soldiers speak of the starlit African skies as "the coming of the Ethiopian bride", and the expression came back to him; he unexpectedly felt longing and solace in her presence, and something like anticipatory lovelorn chagrin at having to part from her after this.

The unwelcome sight of a suitcase by the door caught his attention, like a pinch on the heart.

"Are you leaving?" His concern that she would answer "Venice" was so keen; he feared she would know why he had asked.

"Why, no. My maid Liese will spend the nights in town from now on. I gave her a suitcase of mine to pack her things; she'll be back for it in the morning. I knew it might happen: Father's seances unnerve her, and, if that weren't enough, yesterday a friend of hers unfortunately did away with herself."

Annie must mean Fiorina. Bora's relief at hearing that she would stay was tarnished by the mention of a violent death, as if something impure were coming between them.

She led the way through a French door to what must have been the room for the seances; details escaped his dulled attention, but the surroundings bespoke discreet luxury. Nothing was excessive, or wanting. He found himself admiring her hips; when she turned on her red heels to invite him to take a seat, he looked elsewhere, perhaps not quickly enough.

"May I get you something to drink, a cigarette?"

"Thank you, no."

"Coffee, then?"

"Please."

While she was gone, Bora tried to see through her reasons for inviting him, and his own for accepting. But his lucidity stumbled, and wherever he looked in the room, he was met with tempting low armchairs and furry Greek rugs. He sat down after all, finding instant comfort across his shoulders and back. Sconces diffused an even, unobtrusive light, and everything was as he expected it to be around her: furniture, books, hues and textures. He felt at peace, resting his head at the centre of that orderly collection of things. Light, shadow, wood, glass, leather and heavy cloth, dull, rounded shapes. The silence was welcome, and deep enough for him to slip into.

He awoke with a start. Annie sat on the sofa, watching him. Pouring coffee, she smiled. Bora felt blood rising to his face. He straightened himself. "I apologize. This has never happened to me ... I'm terribly embarrassed."

"Why? You must have been exhausted. There's nothing wrong in letting go. You only closed your eyes a moment."

Bora, fully alert, could not imagine having been drowsy, although this, too, was a reaction to fatigue. Her coffee was too strong, but he praised it, upright and square-shouldered as he drank. The silk she wore, the hair slackly knotted on her neck were new to him and, at the same time, familiar; it nearly pained him to behold them. *A maiden from always,* he thought, *a silhouette on an ancient relief, she is luxuriant and safe from me.*

"Uncle Walter told me that last Sunday you showed him a calling card. He did not go into detail, but he seems concerned that you are somehow linking Father to the woman who hanged herself."

Bora did not raise his eyes from the white flokati covering the floor between them. Had he counted on the fact that Vittori would tell her, or his brother-in-law? He took time, not answering.

"Perhaps I do not understand your role among us, Colonel … A hanging death has nothing to do with the Venus."

Not looking at her, perceiving her only through the corner of his eye, Bora unhappily tried to protect himself from attraction.

"Why does it trouble you, Colonel von Bora?"

Coolness ran under her words like water: not callousness nor contempt (Bora sought those responses); rather, a serenity that made him look up. He all but saw the small stream of her coolness surge back, grow muddled. His heartbeat quickened in his throat. It throbbed in his retina, as if he'd been running hard to reach her.

"Why does it trouble you? Taking one's life is not the worst choice one can make."

Bora opened his mouth without thinking. "I have been here a few days. I have no friends. Two women have died during this time, and it worries me."

"But why?"

Reaching for the briefcase at his feet, Bora took out the Venus folder. *I have no friends.* What a stupid, unrequested admission. A motion of Annie's hands on the sofa flushed him under his uniform like fire.

"Liese told me her friend was desperate; the first woman had her troubles as well. What can possibly disturb you or make you wonder, when you must have seen so much death?"

"I'm convinced they were murders and intend to have them prosecuted as such."

They were both lies, or close to it. He heard the clear tinkling sound of the bangle on her wrist as she reached for Bianca Spagnoli's photograph, which he'd laid on the sofa near her. "I don't know who she is," she said, but she must have understood very well why she was being shown it. "You cannot mean it. Uncle thought you'd come to check on some details ... You can't have called at his house with the intention of discovering *things* about Father!"

"I call where I please, Signora Tedesco. Where I must, and where I am summoned. You did summon me here."

"Because ..."

"Perhaps because you, too, feel that things are not as simple as that."

Annie bit her full lower lip. "I was hoping you would confirm they were suicides." Her lip-biting revealed more concentration than fear. She had over him the advantage of having been awake while he slept, a psychological edge they were both aware of. When she crossed her legs, the movement drew her thigh under the silk – a long, shapely thigh, but already her hand smoothed the fabric over it. "I'm not familiar with Father's girlfriends." Annie reached for an amber cigarette box and moved forward when Bora held a lighter to the cigarette she had placed in her mouth. Unexpectedly, she changed her mind about smoking, and he hesitated for an awkward moment before pulling back. "Would *you* ever kill a woman?"

Bora thought of the spring, of Rome. "I did."

In silence, Annie stared at him with an inscrutable lack of expression on her beautiful face. "What can you do for me, Colonel von Bora? I need to know what happens next. I'm not fond of my father, which I'm sure you'll find inexcusable." The cigarette she had been fingering broke in her lap. She dropped its blond shreds it into the ashtray and chose another. "The schooling he secured for me makes me contemptuous of him. But it doesn't follow that I would stand by and watch him fall."

"If he has a credible alibi, why should he fall? I have just begun to look into the deaths."

Now that he was awake nearly to an excess, he captured how she was the focus of this room. He recalled Vittori's words about Annie, Conforti's words about the Venus. The similarities were not in features but demeanour. Annie, too, was available by sensuality alone. She could, there was no question about it, make men come unstrung.

"You can't believe my father would kill." She spoke from within the frame of her fine things, precious and fine as they were.

"I don't know."

"That's rather noncommittal of you."

"I am committed to other things."

She glanced away from him the time needed to light her cigarette. "What has Uncle Walter told you about me?"

7

De Rosa, at work uncharacteristically early even for a Republican Fascist, stepped over to the threshold of his cubbyhole when he heard the front door opening. "*Martha?*" he called.

Already midway up the stairs, Bora halted with a questioning look.

"The classical opera, Colonel. You were whistling the aria 'She appeared to me' just now, were you not?"

"I didn't realize I was whistling."

Judging by his spit-and-polish appearance, De Rosa was practising his role in the parade of the following day. "This morning the men will try out their routine," he confirmed. "It's grand that I have enough fuel for the staff car *and* the three-tonner!"

How pathetic to hear him rejoice for so little. Today it was a full tank, when victories should be what warms the heart. Bora nodded and continued to his office, where he reserved a long-distance telephone call to Meran for later in the day. To be sure, De Rosa had recovered quickly from Fiorina's death. There he was downstairs, trying out, with the door open, a pep talk for his troops, taken with the enthusiasm of celebrating Mussolini's takeover in Rome, as if Rome had not fallen to the Americans in June.

Denzo had slept at Villa Omodeo, but the advantage did not avail him; Bora showed up at the gate at 5:58, forcing the sentinel to let him in, and was waiting with briefcase in hand when Graziani came down for breakfast thirty minutes later. Denzo, with a somnolent Parisi in tow, was taken aback when he joined in shortly thereafter. As for Bora, a few hours of sleep had returned him to an enviable clear-mindedness. Waiting for the marshal, he'd already perused the medical report on Fiorina's death, collected at the hospital on his way there, and jotted down an entry in his diary.

The conference lasted an hour, during which, aside from Graziani's words, you could have heard a pin dropping on the floor. A pale October sun was beginning to draw wraiths of light on the wall when Bora, notebook in hand, posed two brief questions.

After remaining alone with Graziani – Bora having returned to Salò to start his day there – Denzo gave vent to his disappointment in a not so roundabout way. "*Signor maresciallo*, the irregular format of a conference with partisan leaders … two high-ranking officers going out unarmed, without an escort … When all is taken into account, how advisable is such a conference?"

Graziani smelled Denzo's fear, and his sympathy for him was veined with contempt. He stood with his head low, like a bullock about to charge. "The conference does not contemplate communist partisans, Emilio. They're former officers of the Italian royal army. One of them is Garolfi. Do you remember him? He was my chief of staff in Addis Ababa. The group is led by Lorenzo Carlevaris, a former mountain troops officer who goes by 'Vittorio'; he is a thick-headed, uncompromising combatant, but half of his men answer to Garolfi. You are to strike a separate agreement with him *personally*." His frown met with a tight-lipped, unconvinced Denzo. "If Garolfi agrees, we'll have an edge over the Germans, whatever Carlevaris decides. If he refuses, we won't lack German help to wipe them all out."

"And how am I to reach a separate agreement with Bora on my back? The man speaks perfect Italian."

"Garolfi has already been unofficially contacted by me through the Curia of Milan. You'll travel to the appointed meeting place in separate vehicles. Garolfi, who goes by 'Italo', will not be identifiable as a commander. He will sit next to you in the back seat, and you will parley on your way to the mountains without Carlevaris's overhearing. Officially, you and Bora will then present a joint proposal more than likely to be rejected by Carlevaris's men. With any luck, you'll already have negotiated a separate truce by then."

Denzo's concern about the dangerous operation was becoming a spited need to whine; he suspected that Graziani was using him for his own intrigue. He clumsily tried to suggest alternatives. "*Signor maresciallo*, wouldn't Colonel Lanzetta be a more appropriate emissary? I am more than ready to go, but he *does* command army headquarters."

"No."

"What about Lieutenant Colonel Zingoni, or Colonel Di Leo … Zingoni could use a promotion."

"No, Emilio. I want *you* to go."

As for Bora, he placed relative trust in the operation; he knew it had to be attempted, in any case, and was indifferent to the risk involved. Once he left Soiano, he went directly to the NRG headquarters and asked for the latest intelligence on non-communist partisan units. Then, his reserved call to Meran being still an hour away, he put the interval to good use.

He ascertained that De Rosa had an alibi between 6:00 and 6:30 on Wednesday evening; the concierge of his hotel confirmed his presence during that time. Marla Bruni, the soprano, had had her neck massaged by a hotel maid until 5:45 (no gratuity), and then at 6:20 or so she'd asked for assistance with her corset. It was unlikely that in the interval she could reach the outskirts of town, wrest the gun from her rival, load it, fire it, wipe it clean and return after staging a suicide scene in time for her date with De Rosa.

Annie's maid, like most women in Salò, was queuing for food items that morning. By having her name called aloud by the salesman, Bora was able to trace her, take her aside and confront her. Asked specifically, Liese insisted that she knew nothing of Fiorina's love life; they had become acquainted standing in a queue for soap some weeks earlier, but all Fiorina spoke of was her young son and how she planned to have him come to the lake for Christmas. Since leaving her employment on the 17th, she had moved to the end of town, too far to keep in touch regularly. They'd only met briefly on Sunday, the 22nd, when Fiorina had appeared demented with grief at the news of her son's death, and – oh, yes – the previous Thursday as well, when she'd mysteriously hinted at "a woman who hated her".

Bora was less successful in his enquiry with the Kreditanhalt director in Meran; although tamed by the intervention of the local Platzkommandant, he was willing to state only that his bank provided the clientele with safe-deposit boxes of various sizes.

DIARY ENTRY: 8:12 P.M.

All day spent preparing for the operation at the end of the month. A company from my regiment (under Captain Johannesquade) is coming from Brescia, as it is my wish to have the German army flank the Security

Service and Republican Guard. A handful of mountain troops (Alpini) from the Intra battalion are participating, under Denzo's command.

I met Commander Borghese at his X Mas HQ. Our cordial conversation, in English, confirmed my impression of this heterodox soldier. Unfortunately, because of an ongoing conflict between him and the Security Service, I was unable to secure the participation of some of his men.

Too tired to write an entry last night, I add a few considerations below. Namely:

I don't know what to make of Annie's sudden recollection, while we were already saying goodnight (having spoken of many unrelated things during one of the best hours of my life), that her father was "away on business over the weekend of 14 October". By coincidence, it was when Bianca Spagnoli died. Then she added: "You haven't asked and Uncle does not know, but Father was out all last night as well." Why did she tell me, and is it another coincidence? She explained that the previous afternoon her uncle dropped her at her father's, and, it having grown late, she decided to spend the night there. At eight in the morning, Pozzi was still away. His car was gone, his bed still made. "Did you see him come in?" I asked, to which she said no. She had heard the door opening and met him for breakfast thirty minutes later. "How did he look?" My question must have sounded as invasive as it was. Still, with her curious way of not quite looking at me, she answered: "Like someone who spent the night out." Five minutes later, owing to something unexpected that occurred between us, I had forgotten all about our conversation and the doubts it caused me.

As for Hager, whom I saw tonight with the excuse of enquiring about Frau Sohl's upcoming visit, I must say he's a wily young fellow; in a Latin play, he'd have the role of "servus callidus", the clever man-servant. He seems in two minds about escorting the lady to Milan, as he gets that time off other duties but must wait in the car. He tells me that, of course, Frau Sohl has already seen the Duomo in Milan, so – given the wreckage caused by bombs elsewhere – my challenge will be

devising an itinerary. There isn't much shopping to be done anywhere,
so I hope she doesn't expect to find glittering display windows.

What Bora did not write was Hager's titbit about having
taken Frau Sohl twice to Cordusio Square, "at the corner of
Brolettostrasse", and having waited there upwards of an hour.
According to the map, three banks – Credito Italiano, Banca
d'Italia and Cassa di Risparmio – stood no more than two
streets away from the square.

After the ink dried on the page, he closed his diary and left
the hotel. Ever since his reassignment, Lipsky and his telltale
yellow car had made themselves scarce; Bora didn't know what
to make of the man who had been his brother's friend: parts
of him remained enigmatic, and, despite his northern fairness,
a shadow seemed to follow him.

Tonight, as he filled his lungs with the wet breeze, Bora
had the distinct impression that multiple traps had been set
around him in the dark, as if space were a field of steel jaws
ready to snap. Two weeks after riding with Mengs, the perception of danger had intruded into his waking life, making him
spasmodically intuitive.

He began walking along the shore until by counting steps
he knew where to turn off towards Conforti's home. Ever since
Tuesday, he'd worried about the old man; on Wednesday and
Thursday, stealing moments from his daily errands, Bora had
stopped by and knocked on his door. To his frustration, Conforti
had neither opened nor replied. He stood for all those who
would find no mercy, no help, and his keeping stubbornly
out of touch thwarted Bora's sense of justice. Tonight was no
different: no response at home or at his shop. The silence was
absolute. Fearing the worst, Bora stepped outside on the alley;
there, the western window of Conforti's shop had a dark drape
pulled across it, but a gap in the folds allowed a tall man to

peer inside. He made out Conforti sitting by candlelight, and the pendulum-like motion of his head davening in prayer. *It's not so easy to die at will, is it?* Bora grimly understood how being who he was had sentenced him to stand outside, shut off and powerless.

MILAN, SATURDAY, 28 OCTOBER 1944.
TWENTY-SECOND ANNIVERSARY OF
THE FASCIST "MARCH ON ROME"

The trip with Denzo to Milan was an awkward experience, made worse by detours and roadblocks. The nearly 150 kilometres between the lake and the city crossed three regional partisan commands and three unwritten but agreed-upon areas of influence, in a foggy farmland threaded by irrigation canals as veins crisscross the back of the hand. Air raids had hardly missed a train depot or a bridge; indiscriminate attacks had scarred insignificant villages as well, isolated farms, single buildings lost in the yellows of autumn. A taciturn Bora looked out of the window, while Denzo napped part of the way or bade his colonial chauffeur "step on it" or read a Great War classic, General Maravigna's *The Art of War*, volume four.

They were close to their destination when Denzo put away the book and asked briskly, "Is it true that you disregard your family title, Bora?"

Bora turned from the window. "Well, the Reich is not a monarchy."

"And German barons are a dime a dozen, aren't they? As our surname suggests, we Denzos descend from Frederick II through his beloved son Enzo: *imperial* blood, *imperial* land."

A bombed-out factory went by, and a wooden sign listing civilian targets destroyed by enemy planes. Men and women in the distance seemed to be picking roots or stumps from the earth, alongside channels steaming like sewers in the cold air. The mauled but functioning railway junction at Lambrate appeared in the haze. Everywhere the eye turned, land was being churned up, chewed up and vomited out by war, overrun and split and heaved up and taken away. Land might well be what wars are all about, but it was no commodity to trust in wartime. For months, Bora had tried to keep himself from thinking what Germany must look like after five years of war. *It's all coming back to us, as if through an evil mirror.* The odour of dismantled walls and crushed bricks could not possibly enter the closed car, but he recognized it still, as if the ruins lay in his lap. Wandering sunbeams, hemmed in by clouds, seemed capable of incinerating the fields. He observed, as a delayed comment on Denzo's words, "It must rankle you to serve in a republic then."

Bora had not seen Milan since childhood and remembered it as a severe city of rails and marshalling yards within a glum industrial belt. In his diary, he would later call the Fascist parade by the Duomo "a bivouac of the Dead". A palsied reactivation of defunct nervous terminations – nothing else. It overwhelmed him, when he had believed himself hardened to bad news. Volunteer corps and Republican Guardsmen, marines, auxiliaries, police units and youth associations paraded under a grey sky hung low like a circus tent. Old slogans, old songs, the useless old stomping of feet, yet everything had something senselessly brave, even heroic about it. Black cheviot, black silk. Black wool. Young women in black tops and sandals.

De Rosa and his fez-capped toughs filed by the podium, singing loudly. At their passage, girls waved kerchiefs. Bora stood sternly, as a German officer was expected to stand, nursing his dejection. Spruce in his grey silk twill uniform, Denzo was thick in conversation with a bespectacled colleague. To Bora's left, a boyish lieutenant beamed at the sight of muskets and machine guns. "Have you ever seen anything like it?" he cried out in the fullness of his pride.

Bora curtly said no. Most weapons were German surplus, and the equipment mixed and matched at best; and the faces, the faces ... He thought he'd seen grim faces in Salò, but these were unspeakably resolute and wroth. Only the lieutenant beamed. "You just wait until the Americans dare show up in the Po Valley, Colonel!"

This time Bora turned at the lunacy of the words, doubting that he'd heard right. *He* had fought against Clark's Fifth Army and could laugh at the pitiful boast.

Whatever other ceremonies the Milan Fascists had planned, Bora was anxious to leave. At the end of the parade, when Denzo joined some friends from the 205th Regional Military Command, he asked De Rosa, about to depart with the Guard, to give him a ride back.

Past Treviglio, having thus far proceeded in tandem with the Opel truck, the captain signalled to its driver to go ahead. Bora cringed at the thought of hearing more nonsense about sentimental troubles, but De Rosa kept at the wheel, driving tight-lipped and with a hard frown. When he applied the brakes, pulled over at the edge of the road and turned the engine off, mumbling about an urgent need, he had looked so out of sorts for a while that Bora thought nothing of it.

He waited in the car five minutes and more. Ten minutes having passed, he began to worry. Men had been surprised and killed in similar circumstances before. Bora alighted and, looking towards the shrubbery where the captain had gone, walked in that direction, pistol holder unlatched.

The cawing calls of distant crows gave the countryside a semblance of life. Haze rising from the ditches created a false ceiling, and a white heron took flight from it with a glorious and silent unfolding of wings. Closer in, a suffocated human noise put him on the alert. Bora reached the shrubs and parted the branches with the P38 in his fist.

De Rosa sat at the edge of a ditch with his feet in the mud and his face buried in his hands, bitterly weeping. Bora holstered his gun, more ashamed than he would be had he surprised him squatting with his trousers down.

"De Rosa, *was ist los?*"

Addressing him in German was meant to create a buffer to emotions, but even so, De Rosa kept crying, sobbing and making the "uuh uuh uuh" sounds of a disconsolate infant. From the broken words Bora was only able to make out that he grieved for Il Duce.

Yes. It was over; they all had known for a while. Bora remained by the ditch with his arms folded, gazing into the haze. Trained to swallow his grief, he did not know what to do. Out of decency, he walked back to the roadside; there, leaning against the side of the car, he gave up on abstinence and lit himself a cigarette.

SALÒ, 6:00 P.M.

Bora returned to Salò after dark, in time for one last surprise on a difficult day. Finding Dollmann's car in front of the RNG building was the preface; while De Rosa went directly inside, Bora walked over to the car to see what it was about. "Standartenführer," he greeted the SS man through the lowered window.

"Colonel. Back from the celebrations?" Dollmann opened his door and rested his booted foot out of it. "As it happens, I was driving through Salò at around five o'clock. I was in no hurry, and you know I am by nature a patient man; however, as we drove down this street, the sight of an ambulance piqued my curiosity. I ordered my chauffeur to stop, because a small crowd had gathered by the very alley where the Jew Conforti used to live."

Bora had never given Dollmann Conforti's address. He had found out somehow and decided to call at his place before his SS counterparts did.

"Naturally, I enquired, Bora. Someone says, 'Heart attack, nothing we can do.' Uninterested in the shuffle of those hauling a stretcher, up the stairs I go, and find myself in a shabby parlour, where a frump stands with a handkerchief to her face. I see from the nameplate on the door that it isn't Conforti's place. But there's a little fellow slumped dead on the sofa, over whom a medical man is leaning. The frump blubbers about a phone call come for the Jew. You *are* listening to me, aren't you, Bora?"

"I'm listening."

"To cut a long story short, she tells me that a call came for the Jew, that messages reached him at her flat, because his line had been cut, and so on. 'I was standing right here,' she informs me. 'One moment he was talking on the phone and the next he was grabbing his chest and gasping for air.'" Changing his tone to different pitches, Dollmann illustrated the conversation in Italian, vis-à-vis Bora's sombreness. "Then the frump seems to remember something and asks me whether I am Colonel von Bora. Imagine that. No, I reply, but I will see him later in the day. Why, is there a message for him?' Just then, the physician declares, 'Massive coronary. Struck him dead in five minutes flat. Someone should inform his relatives, if he has any.' The frump whispers something about there not being any relatives, and, in fact, that was what killed him: news about his family. I impose myself, and learn: one, that Conforti's daughters were interned in a Bolzano camp; two, that they have recently died there. 'A funereal piece of news,' quotes the physician. He must have stayed awake at night to think up such wisdom."

The lake breeze cut like a knife; it felt as if it could sever house corners and overhangs. Bora raised the collar of his greatcoat. "Who was the caller?"

Dollmann sneered. "Good question. Why is it that after a moment even compassion becomes self-preservation? The frump vows that she has no idea, she didn't know Conforti that well, and so on. All she knows is that it was a woman's voice that said to 'fetch him quick'. Then I want to hear when Conforti gave her a message for Colonel von Bora ..." Dollmann was visibly enjoying his Italian role-playing. "Won't you come and sit inside, Bora, instead of standing on the pavement?"

"No, thank you."

"As you please. Well, the frump swears she understood what was happening the moment Conforti staggered away from the phone, because her husband, too, died of a heart attack. She helped the old man over to the sofa. All he told her was to 'give the copy to Colonel von Bora and tell him to keep looking'. Which is why I waited for you on your doorstep, postponing my dinner. Will you join me?"

"I thank you, no."

Fastidiously, Dollmann adjusted his left glove. "I advise you against going there now. The Security Service are clearing up the Jew's rooms."

Bora stayed on the pavement in the bitter wind until the SS car was out of sight. He then went in to call General Sohl.

"Well, Colonel von Bora, what can we do; the Jew was sickly, or so he said. I wonder if your inquiry didn't have a role in it. If he was in any way involved in the theft, now we'll have a devilish time getting the Venus back ... Hager, more wood in the fireplace! By the way, this morning, when he came to take leave, Lipsky told me that he'll be in touch with you next week. He said he has a surprise for you, which will give you a wholly different perspective on Conforti. I was right after all: the little Jew did keep secrets from us."

I must not think of what the SS are doing in Conforti's rooms, or what they're piling up in their trucks. Bora sat down behind his desk. "Any anticipation or details, Herr Generalleutnant?"

"Only that the Venus conceals something."

In a state of anxiety, Bora paced the floor as he waited to enter Conforti's house. When he arrived, there was no sign of life in the alley; the door to Conforti's shop stood wide open. The two rooms had been emptied. The *shivviti,* yanked from the wall, had been crushed underfoot. Bora raced up the dark stairs, past the first landing and to the next flight of stairs. Here he knocked over someone coming down the opposite way. A shriek followed when his torchlight floodlit the nosy neighbour, Dollmann's "frump", trudging with a chair aloft, which she now dropped and let tumble down ruinously. She scrambled for her door and, once inside, she tried to push it closed, but Bora was quicker and placed his foot in the crack. "*Aiuto, aiuto!*" Hysterical and with a bad conscience, she shouted, as though anyone would come to help her.

"Stop carrying on, I'm Colonel von Bora."

The door gave way. Bora halted just inside, as he recognized other chairs from Conforti's flat. Whether he looked threatening or else, the woman hastened to say, in the high pitch Dollmann had imitated so well, "Take it, take it, it's in there!" She pointed to a musty backroom where, wrapped in newspapers and tied up with string, something large and flat stood against the wall. "He brought it down all by himself two days ago," the woman added while Bora peeled back a corner of the parcel to expose the frame. "Asked me to keep it until Saturday. I saw no harm in it, but mind you, I've got nothing to do with Jews, never did. 'It's a copy' is all he said. 'A copy of what?' I asked. He said it didn't matter. And now ... please, take it away, for the love of God, and let me be." She started to sob angrily. "The chairs won't do him any good now. I figure he owes me for dying in my house. First the Spagnoli woman hangs herself, then the Jew dies in my parlour. If Jesus doesn't put an end to it, I don't know what I'll do."

"Where did they take his body?"

"To the civilian hospital."

Upstairs in Conforti's flat very little remained; his photographic equipment was gone altogether. Bora saw a few empty frames and worthless knick-knacks. All the drawers had been ravaged. In the kitchen lay a scatter of negatives, envelopes and paper scraps, which, one by one, Bora picked up and set aside. Strange how, after Conforti's death, these rooms had taken on the impersonality of an empty shell. Gone was the magical threshold of an alchemist's lair, and little did it matter whether illness had killed the old man or he really did stop his heart at will. Bora returned below and, from the frump's telephone, asked De Rosa to drive over, on the double.

While Bora waited for the captain to help him salvage Conforti's papers, Jacob Mengs resumed work in a good mood. A Hauptsturmführer named Lasser had just wired in a report about an escape of Jewish prisoners the previous autumn, and, although it related to Bora only in part, it matched the rest of the puzzle with aesthetic finesse. He was still missing data for November and December 1943, but the pattern was nearly complete.

DIARY ENTRY: SUNDAY, 29 OCTOBER
1944, 11:59 P.M.

*Just notes. West of Lake Idro, above the valley. First night of round-up
with my men and the Italians.*

    *As always when I am out in the field, life feels real again. Yet we
came to it through a God-awful summer when we hemmed back like a
wave, leaving our dead behind us like debris. And the dead – my men,
the enemy's, the civilians – matter more to me now than they ever did.*

Bora took a drag from his second cigarette in two days. For a
moment, the taste of American tobacco brought back an image
which he desperately tried to keep from intruding – Dikta's
eyes after they'd last made love, in Rome. She'd already told
him she had asked for an annulment, so lovemaking had been
generous on her part, obstinate on his. He had been confident,
good lover that he was, despite the gravity of his wounds. How
do you hide the loss of a hand? "It has nothing to do with it,"
she'd said, cigarette smoke trailing blue across the shaft of
morning light. "I'm just tired of our marriage, Martin." Naked,
as Manet's Olympia, as Goya's Maja. But not like the Venus.
He'd never made love so well, and still she'd left him.

*Night after night, I wonder if I loved her, when I so seldom grew angry
with her. I can see now that all was fragile between us, that my stoicism
concerning her was only stolid lack of care. It was always the object,
the idea that bound me fast: all else, everyone else, even Dikta, were
substitutes for that abstract passion that alone will never disappoint
me or betray me or leave me behind. Thinking that I was in love, that
she loved me, freed me to pursue that other love.*

In the morning, near Lovere, the SS pulled away for their own
operation to the north. Shortly afterwards, Bora's and De Rosa's

men did run into a well-armed partisan force, which engaged them in fierce small-arms and hand-to-hand combat. By late afternoon, they succeeded in reducing them, not without losses. A cache of weapons, several of them German-made, was recovered. By Monday evening, a joint German–Italian communiqué announced the capture of thirty-four "bandits", nine of whom Bora felt he could tentatively ascribe to Xavier: a first blow that promised to yield information.

Denzo agreed that they would attempt no prisoner transfer until appropriate security was arranged, and, while De Rosa stayed behind to mop up, Bora moved quickly ahead to set up an interrogation centre in Storo. Denzo, who'd been given by Graziani exclusive charge of the prisoners, resented the interference. Despite the foul weather, anxious to beat the Germans to the Storo crossroads, he chose a mountain shortcut in the *Bandengebiet* area west of Collio.

At daybreak on Tuesday morning, Bora did not expect to meet the Italian convoy trundling down the mud from the heights. He stepped out of the truck with a mind to forbid hasty initiatives and squelched his way to the convoy's head car. Denzo flung the door open. It was pouring, icy raindrops running down from their visors as the officers faced each other.

Denzo's concise news was that the convoy had been treacherously ambushed and, during the shoot-out, the prisoners had lost their lives.

"*What did you say?*"

"You heard me. No point making that face, Bora, as if it were my fault."

Bora went from consternation to rage more precipitously than he'd had hearing of the plagiarized memorandum. "But *how?*"

Denzo faced him with immense coolness, his narrow face set hard in the lashing rain. "We were under attack. Naturally we had to machine-gun them."

From the truck, Captain Johannesquade saw how close Bora was to a physical reaction. Dropping his gloves in the mire, he ran over, shouting, "*Herr Oberst, bedenken Sie es,*" to call him back to his senses.

"*Machen Sie mich nicht wütend, Johannesquade!*"

Bora, however, restrained himself. Once out of the mountains, he reached Soiano at breakneck speed and, after hearing that Graziani was in his fortified home, Villa Tassinara, carried on to Desenzano.

In the face of Bora's intransigence, the marshal was unsympathetic. His long, square-jawed countenance betrayed his vexation at a German's formal complaint. "You'll have to get along with your senior colleague better than you're doing, Colonel. Squabbling never helped an army."

Bora found the comment outrageous in view of the rag-tag quality of the Republican army, and Graziani's own contention with his counterpart and adversary Badoglio. "I wouldn't refer to my reaction as 'squabbling', Marshal Graziani. Colonel Denzo could have at least refrained from leaving the executed behind for the partisans to exploit."

"Why, would you have behaved differently? You sound sour because Denzo suffered no losses during the ambush."

"The magazines of the escort were nearly full. I personally checked them and believe there never was an ambush. They merely machine-gunned prisoners who were a bargaining tool and a source of invaluable intelligence. As a result, we've wasted two days. I insist that Colonel Denzo be sanctioned for such lack of competence and military ethics."

The imposing Graziani rose from his desk. "Colonel, may I remind you that you are in my house? I do not know much about you other than what your record and your mutilation suggest. I have known Count Denzo di Galliano full forty-five years, so I intend to carry out my own inquiry before I take any action. I understand your frustration but not your arrogance. Hold on to your incident report: I will ask for it when the time comes."

Bora swallowed the bitter pill. "And how does the marshal expect me to relate to Colonel Denzo in the meantime?"

"I hope as a high-ranking Italian officer is used to being treated: with respect and collegial politeness."

TUESDAY, 31 OCTOBER 1944, 11:00 A.M.

At the Tormini crossroads, where Johannesquade and De Rosa waited for him, Bora said only that Graziani would not take any immediate action.

"*That asshole!*" De Rosa burst out. After the German trucks started south towards Brescia, he poured out his venom against Denzo, and this time Bora let him rage at will.

"In Africa he and Graziani lied to Il Duce after the attempt on the marshal's life. They killed nearly four times as many natives as they wrote in their report ... I heard it from a Bersaglieri lieutenant who was in Addis Ababa that February. Denzo steals from the Military Secretariat, we have it for certain, and his chauffeur has orders to thieve fuel from the Desenzano German depot."

"Christ almighty, Captain. What do you say of me behind my back?"

"Nothing I wouldn't tell you to your face, Colonel. You're a little too educated for a soldier, and by my standards probably don't fuck enough."

Bora entered his car with a half-smile. "By your standards, I ought to risk what you just went through with your three-way game? I'd rather have one woman, De Rosa."

"As long as you've got one in mind."

DIARY ENTRY, 31 OCTOBER 1944, 9:06 P.M.

There is always a precise time when we lose our heart to another. On Thursday, after leaving Annie's house I stopped in the garden for no particular reason; other than, presumably, regret for parting from her after the way we said goodbye. Quietly, I sat down on her doorstep. No light showed from her shuttered windows, but she was still up – I could tell, by I don't know what disquiet of mine. And when she began to play (she practises very late, she did tell me that), I recognized Mozart's variations on a French song: "Hélas, j'ai perdu mon amant." A cello score I know well, having played it often on the piano, the last time in Russia, at old Larissa Malinovskaya's, because she asked me, because she excelled at the violin, and because she had been my dead father's lover and loved him still. So, on Thursday night I let go of my heart as one drops a sheet of paper into the river. Letting it float until it becomes sodden and sinks just below the surface, continuing to drift.

The SS were not due back from the mountains until the following midweek. Bora was to join them on 2 November without Denzo and continue the round-up. Having met their commander, a middle-aged, soft-spoken Swabian, he was favourably impressed. It counted as something, after Denzo's behaviour made a meeting with royalist partisans so doubtful that he suspected an intentional strategy.

He was typing a detailed report on the combined operation when the telephone rang in his office. Lipsky's voice, from Venice, came wavering as if from a distant planet. The first words out of his mouth were, "So, the Jew beat us to Valhalla, Colonel. If Jews go to Valhalla. You've probably laid your hands on the schmaltzy copy, no?"

Bora gave himself the privilege of not answering, although the Venus sat wrapped in his hotel room at the foot of the bed. "How's *your* collection?"

"Touché." Lipsky said that he had heard from a Munich art historian, who had corresponded with Conforti through the years. An "additional value" had been mentioned in regard to the Venus, but no more than that. "I believe there might be a different portrait under the Venus," Lipsky speculated, "perhaps by someone even greater than Titian. Reich Marshal Göring is fascinated and wants me back in Salò in two weeks' time. The Jew would keep things from us only if he was involved in the heist, don't you think?"

"He told me that the loss of the Venus was like a death to him. An art lover would not remove a Titian with a knife."

"It would be exactly what he would do to shift suspicion away from himself and his *in-house accomplices*."

"In-house? Consider what you are implying, Major."

"I no longer work for General Sohl." A surge of static drowned out whatever Lipsky said next. "… And how is our cagey Signora Tedesco?"

"I'd prefer it if you didn't speak of her in such terms."

"Why not? I rather like her."

Bora set his face hard, as if Lipsky could see him. "An inquiry and personal concerns don't go hand in hand."

"Speak for yourself, Colonel. You're in charge of the case."

After the conversation, Bora was in a black mood. He busied himself, preparing for the transfer to Sohl's residence, and, in the pelting rain, did not notice that something similar was taking place downstairs.

That same night, dining with Graziani, Denzo had a bilious need to vent his resentment for being brought to task by Bora, who insisted on confronting invisible and merciless rebels in a war without rules. Surviving through these last months of war mattered more to him than playing improvident and risky games.

"I put you in charge of the prisoners precisely to avoid useless bloodshed." That was the extent of Graziani's reproach to him. Still, Denzo took it personally. "I did," he protested. "We suffered no losses."

However, if he hoped that the death of the prisoners would prevent the meeting with Carlevaris and Garolfi, it was not to be. Graziani insisted on it. Denzo left the table with a profusion of complaints against German interference, just on this side of whimpering. It was Bora's fault that prisoners were taken, Bora's responsibility that the operation had been planned to begin with. You could not deal with the Germans, nor share ideals with them; too long and too rooted was the historical antagonism between the two countries, and so on. Graziani heard him out in a silence tinted with leniency.

After leaving for Salò, Denzo ordered the chauffeur to drive to General Sohl's residence. There, with unrehearsed arguments in mind, he barged in to match Bora's strike against him.

In his hotel room, Bora freed the Venus from her wrappings. Crouching before the painting, he undid the string with great care. As the opalescent figure began to emerge, he knelt, because kneeling was more comfortable or somehow required. Her seductiveness warned him that he was at risk of falling in some kind of impractical love, because he needed to be in love mostly, in safer ways than he had been in his life. As if requiting him, against all hope she came to stay with him. Without grazing the canvas, Bora ran his fingers down the pale curves of her body with a great need to let go and be safe.

8

On his last day at the GNR building, Bora wondered at the sound of hammering from below. It came from De Rosa's cubbyhole, and when he walked there, he was surprised to see that flags, guidons, bloody memorabilia and all evidence of the captain's presence were gone. A guardsman was driving nails into the wall to hang a framed photograph of Mussolini on horseback. Seeing Bora, he turned on his heel and made a Fascist salute, which with hammer in hand rather made him into the icon of a socialist worker.

The short of it was that De Rosa had physically and administratively transferred back to the Muti Legion. He left a note for Bora in which he explained how the "unacceptable drafting of the Republican National Guard into the regular army" made it imperative for a Fascist to join those whose loyalty to Mussolini was "unquestioned". Denzo's behaviour during the joint operation had broken the camel's back. He meant to fight alongside proven militiamen, trusting that he would share with them "victory or death".

It was a sudden and curious getaway in the wake of Fiorina's death, but true to the man's character; the comings and goings with the militia behind closed doors now made sense. Within the hour, Bora himself was ready to leave the RNG.

When he stopped by Sohl's gate, a narrow sunbeam sliced across the lake; the land beyond it, veiled by haze, resembled a mythical, serene harbour, a sight capable of ennobling the litigious paltriness of their lives in the Republic.

Just then, the general was taking advantage of the break in the weather to leave for a stroll and invited Bora to join him.

They reached town, following the shore, while above the lake the single-engine plane buzzed like a meat fly. With round sunglasses on, Sohl resembled a bald owl. He chattered about this and that, pointing out this or that house, where Germans or Italian politicians resided. His wife would arrive on Friday. Would the colonel have an itinerary for her by then? Bora said yes.

Where the promenade curved inward between the Casa del Fascio and the Metropoli, Sohl stopped to sit on a bench. Like so many buildings in town, the Casa del Fascio had once been a guesthouse. Now loudspeakers on its façade broadcast gushy war bulletins every evening, which people had to hear, standing to attention.

"Colonel Denzo came to see me last night."

Bora had expected a statement of sorts. After all, German generals don't stroll along without an additional reason. Sohl spoke with his eyes gazing at the lake. "He was rather rancorous towards you. Promised to go as high as it takes unless I *talk* to you. No, not his words exactly." (Denzo had demanded that Bora be put in his place.) "He plans to take his grievance to Ambassador Rahn, and even to Il Duce himself."

"Did he explain the reason for our conflict, Herr Generalleutnant?"

"I was hoping you would enlighten me. This morning Rahn's office called, and I do not appreciate it when people go over my head." Sohl measured his words with such relaxed care that Bora suspected it was a technique and remained watchful. "I wouldn't worry about Mussolini: he's all bark and no bite for us. But Ambassador Rahn is like saying Himmler, Colonel."

"Well, Wolff brought me here, and *he* is like saying Himmler."
Bora was annoyed but kept his temper in check. He related the
events of the previous three days as sparely as possible. "What
I don't understand is why Marshal Graziani, who supposedly
dislikes a civil war, chose Denzo to show the iron fist to the
irregulars. The man is merciless and a coward, and he might
get us both killed."

Sohl listened, stretching his trousered legs and toying with the
gold-and-red paper band of a cigar wrap. *Why is it that I have the
impression Sohl knows more than he's letting on? He's ill at ease, or else
talking in bad faith. Was he asked about me? And if so, what did he say?*

"Denzo blames you for embarrassing him before Graziani."

"A potential loss of intelligence from prisoners is well worth
a colonel's deserved embarrassment."

Sohl played with the bright cigar band, covering and uncov-
ering his wedding ring. "Perhaps it would be best if you stopped
investigating the theft, Colonel."

Bora's reaction did not go beyond a deep intake of air.

"You see, I have come to the conclusion that it's unfair
to saddle you with an investigation while your duties are so
time-consuming. It is not your responsibility, after all. The
Jew is dead, and he took with him whatever he knew about
the Venus. The SS have taken the rest. Frankly, the theft of a
valuable painting, distressing as it is to me personally, is nothing to the plight of Army Group North in Courland. Yesterday
the Yugoslavs entered Zara."

Reacting was useless. Bora felt a stabbing pain at the pit
of his stomach. *The hell I am abandoning the task, whatever you
say.* He perceived the moment as a turning point. Everything
around him became starkly clear: the shadows in the water,
as if the lake were breathing; the distant aeroplane. When a
motorboat sped by in the distance, small waves wrinkled the
shore. Sohl stared at him through his smoky lenses.

"Thankfully, Colonel, the call from Rahn's office merely authorized Giovanni Pozzi to be the sole purveyor of bedding for our infirmaries. Inform him before you head back to the field. It will sugar the pill of his having to write off the Venus."

Bora would say neither yes nor no. Disappointment made him tight-lipped and aware that he was giving off the impression of obstinacy.

"I overheard," Sohl continued, cigar band firmly on his ring finger, "that you are also 'looking into' the suicide of an Italian woman."

"If the source is Major Lipsky, General, he is short of one 'suicide'."

"Whatever. I am not telling you what to do with the little spare time you have, but is it wise?"

And this from the man who told him to give up on the Venus but to escort his touring wife. Bora's irritation came close to brimming over. "I thank the Generalleutnant for his concern."

Given his return to the field in less than twenty-four hours, Bora used part of the morning settling down in his new office. Through the window, left open to dissipate the heat from Sohl's fireplace, he could make out Pozzi's villa past the lemon groves and espaliers in neighbouring gardens. Who knows, from the second floor, Annie's tall-standing Mespilai might be visible as well. "There's a plant in Rhodes that children call 'forgetful-ness'," she'd told him on Thursday night. "Nobody knows what it looks like, because, as soon as you step on it, you begin to wander. You ramble aimlessly without a care, and sometimes forget the way home. Once they found me so far, they didn't understand how I could have walked all that distance. Has it ever happened to you?" Then, without waiting for his answer, "Sometimes it happens where there's no sprig, no field, but you get lost all the same."

Before lunch, Bora made an appointment to see Pozzi, enquired about Field Marshal Kesselring's transfer to a hospital in nearby Riva and wrote a few lines in his diary.

I'm reporting these facts in scattered order. Not without difficulty, before leaving the RNG office this morning, I called the Bolzano transition camp to enquire about the fate of the Conforti girls. They transferred them there in July. It is true that they are no longer detained in the Resia Street Durchgangslager; in August, they shipped them from Bolzano to an undisclosed camp in the Reich, but there is no indication of their death. Certainly, they did not die in Bolzano. So, either the woman who called Conforti had incorrect information (possible), or she purposely gave an ailing elder news that might literally break his heart. Who would possibly benefit from his death? Did someone fear Conforti had more to say about the Venus? Most of all, who is this woman, and how would she have access to the news?

Bora found himself suspecting Lipsky or even Sohl for the call to Conforti, for reasons of their own. It was like an itch he could not scratch or disregard. He thought of one of the major's girlfriends, or even Sohl's wife, who reportedly spoke Italian well. Why had Sohl exonerated him two weeks after charging him with the task of finding the Venus? Or it could be another woman altogether. And did she call from Bolzano in the first place?

Last night, wrought up as I was after meeting Graziani, I decided to go through Conforti's papers. Aside from the clippings in Czech, which I cannot read, I collected the Italian and German notes, placed landscapes and art reproductions on one side and studio portraits in a single folder. Curiously, among these, one greatly resembles Fiorina Gariboldi; a graceful, sombre face scrubbed clean. Why, when someone dies, do we seek in his portrait the signs of impending destiny? And why do I want to see a murder in the end of two beautiful women?

Spent a grotesque quarter of an hour with Pozzi, who behaved as if the monopoly on linen were due to him. His brother-in-law tried to talk some civility into him and thanked me. I gave no update about the Venus. What could I say? I am just fishing around for ideas.

Before leaving, however, I whipped out of my briefcase Bianca Spagnoli's photograph, and showed it to the men as I did to Annie. "Who is she?" they both asked, and Pozzi tried to snatch it from my hand. Why? Did his brother-in-law (or daughter) tell him of the calling card, or is the sight of a suicide distressing to his widowed state? He does not seem so sensitive. I enquired whether Spagnoli had recently sought a position at the Roè textile works. Pozzi told me to go to Roè and ask, if I want to. As for Vittori, he assured me he has not told him of our conversation but admitted sharing it with Annie. This, I knew already.

At the local restaurant, where the militia gathered to dine, Bora met De Rosa's latest incarnation as a Blackshirt. With a glance at the portrait the German showed him, he confirmed it was Fiorina. "Nice photo. I wonder when she had it taken. She's wearing the blouse I gave her last month."

"I hope I didn't make you lose your appetite, De Rosa."

Soup was on the table, and De Rosa dug his spoon into it. "It takes more than that. Imagine, La Bruni moved out of her hotel room while you and I were chasing partisans. In a note she wrote me that, given her public rows with Fiorina, she 'wants to stay away and be above suspicion'. No, I don't know where she went. She has her passport and may try Switzerland."

"You do not seem crushed."

"On the contrary, I stay awake at night, thinking that I gave that girl the gun that killed her."

Fiorina had already been downgraded to "that girl".

"And your wife?" asked Bora.

"She keeps out of my affairs, as she ought to."

2:14 P.M.

Annie Tedesco came now and then to have tea at the Metropoli, sometimes with friends, sometimes with her uncle. Today she sat alone.

Bora's entrance startled her, because he was clearly looking for her. Having made eye contact, he strode over to her table and saluted. "I can only stay a minute, Signora Tedesco: may I sit down?"

She nodded her assent. Bora seemed troubled or in haste – probably both. She judged him rather pale in his field grey; the rim of his shirt that was visible over the clasped collar had a dazzling whiteness. There was a scar at the side of his neck, which she had not noticed before. His cropped hair lent him a foreign, archaic look of soldiering, with shaven temples and a swatch of bare skin above the ears.

The waiter, about to take the order, thought better of it and remained at the other end of the room. The other tables were empty.

"Did you discover something about Father?" she began.

"No. I had to see you."

"Why?" Annie swallowed visibly. On her throat, round and white, a dark blue vein pulsated slowly. They addressed each other formally, playing a tense game as insecure adversaries.

"You kissed me." Bora placed the small claim like a pawn between them. "I would not be here had you not kissed me on Thursday night."

Relief, self-consciousness, a searching of the eyes not quite downcast, to conceal embarrassment or a need to smile. "Thursday night you needed comfort. I saw it. It was a trifle on your way out, you reacted as though it were a trifle."

Bora maintained absolute control over his expression. Paleness could not be helped, but that, too, conjured an image of calm. He stood, saluted again with a courteous lowering of his head. "It was not, Signora Tedesco."

From the *Soldatensender*, the radio in Bora's office was broadcasting *Drei hundert Rosen* when Habermehl telephoned at three. He was back from Germany, which meant he had met his parents. "Come and visit before the end of the month."

Bora promised, aware that the Luftwaffe was withdrawing from Verona and Vicenza. Then a call came from the Cremona Italian SS command – Bora turned down the radio as he spoke to the commander in charge – and, as soon as he put down the receiver, it rang from the German Security Police headquarters in Brescia, by which time, stretching across his desk, he turned off the radio altogether.

DIARY ENTRY: 3:39 P.M.

Why did I tell her I could not stay? It was not true, at least not for the reason I gave. Had she invited me not to leave, I'd have stayed, although it meant she'd be seen with a German soldier. The other night I had to react as though it were a trifle because things would have got out of hand otherwise. I think she knows. The attraction between us is overpowering. There was a moment, while we conversed, when we began to tremble because of our nearness to each other. I told myself: This is like the first time with Dikta, when we lost our heads (that is, we lost control over our senses). No, I see it now. It was more like meeting Remedios and discovering that loving her in the flesh was only a way to love what's beyond it. Annie's words the other night, spoken out of the prison of our mutual loneliness, created a glorious intimacy I have never experienced before, although we did not touch until she kissed me on the doorstep.

She is going away to Como for several days, she told me, which somehow lightens the burden of not being able to see her, as I myself shall be gone.

At four, determined to observe at least part of his day off, Bora left the residence for Gardone. There, he was soon parking by the ornate gate of the Japanese embassy.

The following week made him feel better. The pettiness of office politics melted in the reality of long drives, hikes, interrogations, the setting up of advantageous "staging points" for the combined operation. Two of his company officers had served in the Balkans and had experience of mountain guerrillas; once he had laid out for them the acceptable moral limits of a raking search, he was satisfied that discipline still held. In the past months, he'd too often heard of "matters getting out of control" as an excuse for massacres and unmilitary behaviour. That sort of lie concealing what his general-rank stepfather termed a soldier's "pig-headed lack of invention". As always, the left-wing formations resisted being brought to reason. And Xavier's shadow dimmed all good intentions. Bora's men were attacked and fired back, broke into farms and rounded up peasants; they terrified villages they were just passing through, armed to the teeth. Xavier was spoken of everywhere, although he could not be everywhere; civilians feared him more than they feared the Germans and dared not give information.

NOTES FOR A DIARY ENTRY: TUESDAY, 7 NOVEMBER 1944, IN THE FIELD

It is patience, the meekest and most animal-like of virtues, that most moves me about men. A ruminant quality of taking upon oneself the weight of life, which my soldiers and the poor folks of these valleys share fully. Even physical pain does not score or nick it. Xavier follows us and flies ahead of us, figuratively speaking, a Nosferatu who kills ten and, by the way he does it, makes it appear as one hundred. We finally secured an informant, an elder whose son died at war, and, thanks to him, we discovered two of Xavier's ammunition caches. I know there's a larger one somewhere. Returning, we discovered that pieces of him were scattered near the farms across the valley, as a warning. In an hour's time, we caught up with those who were carrying out the macabre distribution and hanged them on the spot. What about the ruminant quality, patience? Justice flies in the face of patience, I say. Yet the farmers, in their fear of Xavier and of us, totter under patience until they crawl.

This morning I found myself – not by accident, as the charts told me – scouting a trench of the Great War. Rusty gun carriages from thirty years ago lay side by side with shells recently fired. Patience endured and was blown to bits here. But I think that I chose soldiering because I am capable of great patience. Rams and bulls are ruminants, too.

The combined German–Italian units returned on Thursday from Costa to Gargnano. From there, Bora continued north, to visit Kesselring in Riva.

RIVA, THURSDAY, 9 NOVEMBER 1944, 6:29 P.M.

The field marshal waved him closer to the bed. "Don't say my face doesn't look like chopped meat. I know it does. Who won the election in the United States?"

"An unprecedented fourth term for Roosevelt, Herr Generalfeldmarschall."

"Just our luck."

"He may not last the course. Will the field marshal stay in Riva?"

"No. It's off to Meran after this, and then to Germany. I'm out of commission for the next two months, Martin." He familiarly sought Bora's hand and shook it. "Behave yourself between now and then, for your family's sake, if not your own."

It was too late for advice. "If the field marshal would consider my request for reassignment ..."

"You are not here at my bidding, and my successor, General Vietinghoff, is not inclined to reassign you. *Na*, Martin, what is going on? Come and see me in Meran as you can."

FRIDAY, 10 NOVEMBER 1944

Bora's day began early at General Sohl's, then at Soiano, where he left a sealed mission report for Graziani and enquired about Colonel Denzo. He was not expected until later, Parisi informed him, as the marshal had dispatched him to Gargnano with orders to persuade the "head of government" (the captain did not refer to Mussolini as Il Duce) to call back the Italia Division from Germany.

"The decision to send back Italian trainees rests with *our* government," Bora quipped. But he did not venture beyond the comment. He knew from Sohl that Mussolini's ambassador, Anfuso, had complained bitterly to the German foreign office about recent atrocities against Italians. "*Anfuso anfacht.*" The general had smiled, playing with words. "As with my fireplace, the ambassador *fans the flames.*"

By eight, Bora was ready to escort Frau Sohl. It was an imposition in more than one way: in the wake of a demanding seventy-two-hour military operation, touring Milan in the rain was scarcely at the top of his list.

Dollmann's description of her as a "pretty young thing in a ratty fur coat" was not true as far as the fur coat went. For the rest, she had the racially prescribed looks of a pencil sketch by Willrich; her blond hair, braided under a Tyrolean hat, accentuated the impression of peasant wholesomeness. A gap between her front teeth made her self-conscious, so that she covered her mouth when she smiled. Bora found her pleasant and uncomplicated, the typical second wife of an older widower, or impenitent bachelor. She carried a small wicker suitcase, which she insisted on keeping in her lap. Dikta had been similarly punctilious about hatboxes and necessaire bags; war made even affluent women defensive about goods so hard to replace.

The day's itinerary, approved by Sohl, included the Sforza Castle, Saint Satiro's, the palaces Clerici and Belgioioso, the arches of Porta Nuova. After visiting the arches and the castle, however, Frau Sohl asked to see Cordusio Square. Confident that an army colonel would not be left waiting like a chauffeur, Bora obliged her and had his first surprise of the day.

"You won't mind if I do a little shopping, will you?" she said, her foot already out of the car. Bora understood that his presence was not required. She added something about being back in an hour, opened her lilac umbrella, and vivaciously stepped off towards Broletto Street, Hager's "*Brolettostrasse*".

Bora had been on the point of suggesting a restaurant, as it was midday and any shops and offices still open would close soon, but, having visited the city before, she probably knew that black-market goods were available at any time in unsuspected places. Fresh touts were transacted in the interpreters' office, and American films could be bought at the top floor of Villa Elvira, the residence of the German propaganda official.

Choosing understanding over impatience, Bora reached for his briefcase and pulled out a selection of the correspondence found in Conforti's house. Arranging the German language letters by date, he'd already noted that between 1940 and 1941, only a single writer appeared regularly throughout: a no-better-identified Dr A.L. Broeck from Lugano. Art lover, antiquarian ... who could say? He replied to Conforti's enquiries relating to specific artworks. One letter, mentioning the 1940 auction, somehow connected Broeck to the Venus. The text mentioned the legend that La Bella was buried in a monastery overlooking her hometown, Naples, but questioned its source. "*I* have my reasons to believe it is a place in or near Naples ..." Bora recalled Conforti's words about the della Roveres' hidden treasure. Judging by the last three letters Broeck had written, the question between them had remained unresolved.

The car windows had meanwhile fogged due to the dampness of his greatcoat. When Bora opened on the driver's side, cold air floated in with the raindrops, carrying the sharp odour of damp bricks and plaster, the stench of bombed cities.

For security reasons, and because Bora carried a modified Gewehr 98, Frau Sohl rode in the back seat. It was now, as he wiped the rear windows, that Bora's eye fell on her small suitcase. During the trip, he'd heard her open it by snapping the locks, so it must be unlocked. Out of he knew not what spirit of impertinent curiosity or professional inquisitiveness, he followed the inexcusable impulse to check its contents. Outside, the end of Broletto Street was deserted, and so were the other two streets, Dante and Tommaseo, from which Frau Sohl might return from her errand. In ten seconds' time, Bora had opened and inspected the suitcase, in which lay a Lenci doll in Lombard costume and a grinning mechanical monkey with cymbals.

*

Two streets away, at the Hotel Regina, Jacob Mengs spread his paperwork on Kappler's desk. "Under Blaskowitz's command in Poland, he was one of the hard-nosed army brats who fed him material for his charges. Early in October 1939, it was he who came up with the smug definition of bestializing to describe police operations in the East. We nearly lost sight of him while he went gallivanting through Russia, until he surfaced again near Kursk by publicly splitting hairs about the necessity of preventive measures. Nearly came to blows with an SD commander then. He led a charmed life until today, and the charms were variously called Blaskowitz, Reinhardt, Senger und Etterlin, and Kesselring. He's got none of them on him now."

A few minutes after the appointed hour, Frau Sohl returned in the drizzling rain. Slightly flustered, a couple of hairpins out of place in her braid, she had just sprayed more cologne on. She explained nothing; Bora asked nothing. A lunch of empty chatter followed, and a quick visit to the Church of Saint Satiro, before heading back.

By four-thirty, after spending a few minutes with her husband, she was en route with Hager to the train station.

Sohl straddled the floor by the fireplace, hands clasped behind his back. "So, Colonel, what did you and my wife discuss during the trip?"

"Other than the sights on our list, sir, the usual things: Frau Sohl asked me whether I am married or have children, if my parents are still living … the usual."

Exponential acceleration in men's fluster was something Bora had become used to in the army; its warning signs were as predictable as its reasons. When the general further asked him where else in Milan he'd taken his wife, Bora saw no warning signs. He answered truthfully.

Showing the tour guide he'd been clasping, Sohl demanded to be shown the specific places. "Did she go anywhere on her own? Shopping? Where, for how long? Didn't I tell you not to let her out of your sight?"

"I assumed the advice was not literal."

"Have you seen her walk into the store? If not, how do you know she went shopping?"

"She told me so, Herr Generalleutnant."

Sohl's temper frothed like wine under a cork. "Well, a colonel's silence cannot be bought off or imposed as it can be on a private. I am asking you to tell me, *if you please,* where you dropped Frau Sohl in Milan, and where you waited for her."

"I waited for Frau Sohl at Cordusio Square, near the Clerici palace."

"How long was she gone?"

Bora lied outright. "I couldn't say, Herr Generalleutnant; I had taken some paperwork along and busied myself with it."

"Did she bring anything back with her?"

"Sir, I would prefer if any additional questions relating to Frau Sohl's visit were posed directly to her."

"By God, I am asking you if she brought anything back from the store!"

"Only her handbag."

"Then where did she get the toys, will you tell me that?" From Sohl's hand, the tour guide made a flip in the air and fell.

Bora did not even blink. Frau Sohl's chattiness and voluble smile had reminded him of Dikta before their marriage, when they emerged from hurried intimacies of which his family would hardly approve. Whatever he thought of Frau Sohl's fluster upon returning to the car, he kept under seal of impassiveness.

Pacing with his fists tight, Sohl stumbled over the tour guide and kicked it. "By God, Bora, my wife deceives me with Lipsky.

Twice she went to Milan, and twice Lipsky was out of the office for the day; today, I had a call placed to Venice, and they told me that the major was away from his desk." His booted feet drew a fretful zigzag. "The slut, with two small children at home! She knows I can't do anything about it, unless I'm ready for a scandal and to have the children suffer." He spoke with his head cocked towards Bora, still pacing. "You're not covering for your colleague, are you?"

"Herr Generalleutnant, this conversation is making me uncomfortable. I have no knowledge of what the general implies and beg to be excused."

"No, of course you're not covering for Lipsky. Forgive me, Colonel. It's just that I consider myself a good husband and a good father, and these things are hard to take."

"I beg to be excused."

Once in his office, Bora closed the door, locked it and went to breathe the lake air in front of the open window. The buzz of the reconnoitring plane, which he could hear without seeing it, irked him as a hidden threat can vex a fearless man.

Before long, a call from the GNR informed him that the new head of police had been trying to get in touch with him all day. Immediately, Bora phoned the *questura* and promised to go in person. It was less than a kilometre away, yet the obnoxious aeroplane, having banked widely over the water, was making again for the Garda road. Bora saw it flicker from afar in the sinking sun, nearly vanish as it turned sharply, and then head arrow-straight for the road.

How many times had he driven under strafing aircraft? It was not the best afternoon to remind him of the relative impotence of ground troops before air power. Steadily he reduced speed, braked to a halt, set the car at a right angle across the road. The plane had grown to the size of a blowfly and closed unwaveringly. Far from leaping out to safety, Bora reached for the Gewehr 98 and adjusted the graduated sight to two hundred meters.

Policemen were looking out of the windows when Bora arrived in Salò. Across the square, people hastened towards the lake, and there was excitement even inside the *questura*. The new head of police, Inspector Passaggeri, a burly man with an obstinate forehead and a warm, dry handshake, came to greet him in the hallway.

"What a sight. You must have seen it as you drove in, Colonel. They say it was a grenade launcher that brought it down."

Bora kept mum. After the first moment of exhilaration, he'd watched in a sweat until the stricken aircraft, madly careening landward over the town, veered off and sounded the open water like a vertiginous dying fish.

The office had changed in no appreciable way since Vismara's tenure. The desk was more orderly, perhaps, a circumstance that disposed Bora favourably. Passaggeri said, with the indefinable accent of one who has travelled and lived in many places, "I served in Verona before this; we never met last year, but I heard of you from Inspector Sandro Guidi, whom I know well. Lord knows what happened to him; I haven't heard from him since."

"He was in Rome when I left the city," was the sum total of Bora's response. In his judgement, Passaggeri stood to Vismara as a bulldog to a setter, an impression confirmed by the words that followed.

"I try to do my job, Colonel, whatever the circumstances. I was informed that you and my predecessor discussed the death of one Bianca Spagnoli. Since his notes on the incident were destroyed with him, I wonder whether you'd be willing to help me fill in the blanks." Bora's nod encouraged him to go on. "Shortly before my arrival to Salò, there was another suicide ...

A sensitive matter, owing to the deceased's relation to an NRG officer. It is no longer the Guard's job to investigate crime, but it took me some doing to get the evidence I needed. The physician who penned the Gariboldi death report mentioned your name, hence my phone call to your old office. I thank you for coming."

"You're welcome."

"About myself, Colonel, this is what I have to say: I'm a bachelor, without attachments. I soldiered in Russia, where I did not expect to survive, so I don't fear death. I have no taste for politics: never had, doubt I ever shall." He squared a significant look at the medals on Bora's tunic. "I believe the war is lost. If I could prosecute anyone who claims the contrary, I would."

"Understood." Bora snapped his briefcase open. He took out some typewritten sheets, which he lay on Passaggeri's desk. On them, as a paperweight, he placed a metallic cylinder about thirteen centimetres in length, marked in bright yellow on the propelling cartridge. "Gewehr-Sprenggranate". "There are many ways of losing a war."

BARBARANO, SATURDAY, 11 NOVEMBER 1944

Bora's diary entry for Saint Martin's Day was concise: *Vienna heavily bombed by the Allies. Today I am thirty-one years old.*

The morning air was clear above the surface of the lake, motionless like the shard of a giant mirror. At every shot he fired, the muzzle of the P38 barely nosed up before returning dead in line with the target. With his gloved artificial hand, Bora placed the gun against his side to slide back the grooved magazine guard, release the empty clip and drive a full one in its place. He resumed shooting, and the SS orderly waited until the second clip was empty before giving him the message from Dollmann, who was waiting at the edge of the road and waved when Bora looked over in that direction.

"It is always pleasant to watch a man demolish a target without anger. Or shoot down a plane. Too early or too late for breakfast, Colonel?"

Over a precious soft-boiled egg at nearby Albergo Galeazzi, Dollmann said, "I could not let your birthday and name day go past without a little celebration. Too bad you missed Ambassador Rahn's party on Thursday, when there was a to-do between Anfuso, that dear Pavolini and Buffarini-Guidi, whom you know and love from your Roman days. Ministers! Oh, the usual lamentations about the engagement of Italian soldiers. Twenty-four thousand of them will remain in Germany, thank you, to man the anti-aircraft. How can we trust them? There was mass desertion from the Monterosa Division. Well, what can we do? At the party, I had the pleasure of meeting your General Sohl. His real name is Antonius von Padua. Did you know that?" He spoke as usual with disparaging humour. "A fine Catholic specimen with a half-Italian wifie his daughter's age. And you took her to Milan, you rogue. She'd be your type, too, except for the vacancy on the top floor. I couldn't help teasing Sohl about having a purported Titian stolen from under his nose. Are you making headway in your inquiry?"

"There's no inquiry any more."

"No!"

Bora dipped his spoon in the delicate yolk. "If you have privileged information about the general's role in this matter, Standartenführer, I wish you would share it."

"I have none. Well. A teensy fourth-hand titbit, after Rahn's reception. I overheard it from a friend who got it from Kappler, who learned it from someone else. It concerns a painted canvas deposited in a Milan vault on the eighteenth of October and a curious bank director. No name of the bank, nor of the man, who was arrested for political reasons and tried to buy his life with the information. You know how exuberant special police units can be." With the right hand, simpering, Dollmann made a slicing motion across his neck. "Don't look at me that way. That was your birthday gift. I'm not getting involved. It could have been anyone who deposited a painting for safekeeping in one of Milan's many banks." His back to the window, the SS man carefully studied Bora's face. "So, you're off in two days for your parley in the mountains. Don't look surprised. It isn't a legerdemain. I was the interpreter between Wolff and Graziani when they discussed it. I hope you tried an olive branch for size before you put it in your beak. Is your blue-blood counterpart up to the task?"

"We'll spend tomorrow making ready for it. I'll have troops stationed just outside the perimeter, with orders to intervene fifteen minutes after the appointed return time from the conference, or in case of a shoot-out. Cardinal Schuster swears by his contacts, but one never knows."

After scooping the fluid yolk from his egg, Dollmann neatly emptied the shell of its white. "Tomorrow I am at Il Duce's. Vietinghoff is meeting him. Oh, the agony of having to hear them squabble over thousands of Italian soldiers – as if it mattered!"

NOTE FOR A DIARY ENTRY:
12 NOVEMBER 1944, 10:42 P.M.

Annie Tedesco returned from Como, where the family's town home is occupied by refugees. She told me so when I went to see her at eight. Our good breeding stood in the way, as did the embarrassment of having kissed once. Officially, I was there to ask about this A.L. Broeck, whose name she had heard from Conforti, who corresponded with many art experts during his process of authentication. Poor signor Conforti, as she calls him, told her once that many sensitive people cannot behold the splendour of the real thing and seek a reflection of it. He told me much the same. She then quoted her mother's belief that only at the bottom of a well does the sky show its true colour, unfaded by the sun. Informed by Vittori that she drowned herself in a cistern "near the church of the much-venerated Madonna of Kaminula", I made no comment. But Annie light-heartedly showed me her Greek earrings in the shape of small enamelled boats – the same her mother wore when she committed suicide.

She spoke of her childhood next, weaving recollections with tales she had heard in Rhodes, as if she needed to keep in a fabled, safe container the years before her accident, of which she said not a word. I responded in kind, from the same physical unease – much stronger in me, I wager – and ended up telling her my own silly episodes, only so that she would keep me there. In our reciprocal unwillingness to give in, nothing else happened, more's the pity.

On the threshold, she asked me if I ever heard of the "shepherd's hour". Thinking about what awaits me tomorrow, I said no. "It is a sudden clearing that opens at sunset in a rainy sky, so that sheep can be safely brought into the fold." And then night comes, I thought.

ABOVE VAL DI DAONE, MONDAY, 13 NOVEMBER 1944, 11:50 A.M.

When the army driver disappeared down the serpentine mountain track, Denzo trailed the personnel carrier with a glance.

All around, a hovering moisture bridged the states between fog and rain. The agreed-upon landmark was a dismantled blockhouse from the Great War, on a ridge from which it must have pitilessly swept with its machine guns thirty years earlier.

Blasted windows and scarred cement were all that remained. "Could they be hiding in there, Bora?"

"No."

The ground lay pocked by puddles rimmed with crusty ice, where every single raindrop from the overcast created multiple concentric circles. Uneasily, Denzo stood in a greatcoat and Graziani-style bulky scarf. Bora wore none of those, preferring to retain his freedom of movement. For ten minutes, they waited silently, watching the two ends of the solitary track.

Under the cliff, a miniature geometry of farmhouses dotted the valley towards Pracul; the distant Chiese River ran grey in its gravel bed, here and there splicing into branches. Dosso dei Morti, "dead man's rise", showed its pastures, still green, against a background of racing clouds and wind-torn fog. Northward, the barren crags rose, capped with snow and shrouded in a blizzard.

Denzo stole a glance at Bora, who paced over the dead grass along the track. The calm of his gait and the daring vulnerability of his shaven nape irked him. Graziani had made them shake hands and demanded that they forget their differences, but Denzo had vowed to himself: *This is the last joint venture I let the marshal volunteer me for.* When he turned to the blockhouse beyond the track, the chilly wind crowded his eyes with tears.

Three minutes past the appointed time, the drizzle left off just as two shabby vehicles emerged from the same curve travelled by the personnel carrier. A crumpled Italian flag bearing the royal crest hung from the front window of the first car. Bora squared his shoulders, and Denzo stared, visibly relieved.

His reaction seemed curious to Bora, who was on guard. *Who knows*, he thought, *his gumption may be of the second-wind type, surprisingly available under stress.*

Unless others were keeping cover nearby, there were eight men in all. A youthful, bearded man with the insignia of a lieutenant colonel and a Royal Alpines feather-bearing cap, fair, light-eyed, came forward to meet them. Army greetings followed on both parts.

Carlevaris, Denzo thought, meanwhile recognizing his acquaintance Garolfi in the second group, a few feet away. Italo wore a sweater and jodhpurs and was careful not to cross glances with him. "I am Commander Vittorio," the lieutenant colonel said. "You will ride separately to the appointed place, for your protection as well as ours."

Bora felt the familiar thrill that predicted trouble. He tried to discount it as mere dislike for having to parley with irregulars. Still, there was something about the blockhouse, the mountains and the valley wind that warned him. Even Denzo's change of mood was ominous.

"If you don't mind?" After searching him, Vittorio blindfolded him. Bora overheard Denzo spunkily make little of having his sidearm removed. His own holster was unlatched, and out came the P38. "It will be returned to you after the meeting, Colonel."

It was unpleasant to be shoved into a vehicle for the second time in a month. Bora sat wedged between two men whose muskets crowded his lap. Given his mutilation, no attempt was made to secure his wrists, but surely the guards would restrain him in case he tried to remove his blindfold.

The doors slammed shut. Bora heard the car behind, where Denzo must have been sitting just as uncomfortably, start its engine. They moved off, tyres crunching the gravelly edge of the track, and up they went. Within minutes, they made a sharp turn and changed direction, and so three or four times more, until Bora lost his bearings.

The first thing they saw once their blindfolds were removed was a curve overlooking a conch-like valley. Fog half-filled it with fleeting wavy peaks. Out of place in the wild setting, a table and four chairs awaited them. Vittorio and Italo sat on one side, Bora and his colleague on the other. Men with automatic weapons stood watch from a stony spur, while beyond them turbulent clouds drifted by.

To Denzo's surprise, Carlevaris, after some haggling, did agree to an immediate truce, negotiated over single positions across meadows, crests and Great War trenches. Xavier's name never came up, although Bora imagined him threateningly standing there. Garolfi, annoyed perhaps at being upstaged by his companion, asked at one point whether the Germans were parleying with other groups. Bora said no.

"That means that elsewhere you will apply your usual methods."

"That means we will respond to provocation as needed."

Nevertheless, they shook hands and agreed to a second meeting when springtime would once more fan the fires of war. "If your army is still in Italy by then," Vittorio added, still grasping Bora's hand.

"Springtime comes early in Italy."

It had gone easily enough, and when they piled into the cars to return, they were just under one hour ahead of schedule. Bora, whose pistol had been returned, was beginning to think that his sixth sense had grown unreliable. In the general relaxation after the parley, cigarettes were passed around repeatedly, until smoke made necessary the lowering of all windows.

They had driven downhill for twenty or so minutes, as the blindfolded Bora calculated, when the brakes slammed hard. The men in the car exchanged whispers in dialect. "*Ostia, ostia, mira!*"

Bora understood there was an obstacle ahead, nothing else. The car stalled, ground its gears, started in reverse, stopped dead. There was the lifting and metallic readying of weapons on both sides of him, and a sudden sense of alarm. Doors opened.

All Bora could hear was the clack-clack of pebbles dislodged under many boots, a sign that a number of people were assembling around the car. When he lifted his right hand to remove the blindfold, no one stopped him.

A dozen men stood on the track. Vittorio alighted, banging the car door. Whatever he was saying to them was inaudible from the car. The men wore mix-and-match equipment, the expected patchwork of Allied and German uniforms, sandals on their feet, or boots, or even city shoes. Some wore shoulder-length hair; others, wild beards. The only thing they had in common were red kerchiefs about their necks and automatic weapons. Bora guessed that some were Slavs.

There. Xavier's men, the thrill had been telling him from the start.

Through the car's back windows, rifles poked against the partisans crowding Bora. A mistake, being so close as not to handle weapons well. His right arm was wedged so that he could not reach for his holster. Doors were jerked open from the outside, and Bora's guards ordered to get out. It was then that a wild-haired, moon-faced young man peered in. "Hey, look what we got us here!" he cried out.

Bora made no effort to move, angry as he was for having fallen into a trap. "*Was suchen Sie?*" he snapped back, as if the youngster and the crowd behind him were not armed with Sten guns and grenades at their belts. Through the corner of his eye, he saw Vittorio, who, inaudible above the wind, appeared to be angrily protesting and trying to negotiate his way through. Confronting him squarely stood a tall and meagre man. Cristomorto himself, the name raced to Bora's mind, with a rise of anxiety but interest too, in meeting him. Pale and long, unshaven, the Italian word *spiritato* – "possessed" – came to Bora's mind by way of a description. The red cloth at his neck resembled the bloody cut around John the Baptist's severed head.

As for Colonel Denzo, he shakily stood disarmed, hands raised. Bora's temper rose at the sight. "Out of the car, out of the car!" The youngster prodded him with his rifle. "Get out of the car!"

What with Denzo's loss of heart, what with the shouted command, Bora angrily forgot the risks. He perceived trepidation beneath the youngster's bluster, but his rifle poked hard, ready to fire.

"Fuck you! Get out of the car and put your hands up!"

Bora exited the car and stood next to it. An attempt to unlatch his holster was promptly forestalled. "*I'll* take this. Hands up, or I'll blow your head off!"

Xavier looked this way. Without intervening, he chewed on a stalk of grass, careless of Vittorio's protests. The one with the moon face stole a tense look at him but received no encouragement or advice. Grimly, he returned the rifle to Bora's chest. "Hands up, or I'll shoot."

"Just tie him up," Xavier ordered.

Outnumbered four to one, the blue-scarfed men still clung to their weapons. A suicidal shoot-out could ensue at any moment. Bora glimpsed a grim-faced Denzo being unceremoniously bound by the wrists and jerked forward. The youngster tried to do the same with him. "Hey," he called out. "This one's got a dead hand," he spoke up. "How do I do it?"

Xavier suddenly paid attention. He approached, staring. "Ah, but this is Bora, *il comandante* Bora. Aren't you *il comandante* Bora?" He took the P38 from the youngster's hand and gave it to a stocky giant. "Off to the Russians for execution."

Being dismissed as a mere accessory was for a moment more insulting than hearing he'd be shot. The banality of it all surprised and galled Bora. This was it? How different from the Spanish days, when he'd met his first Marxist face to face, and an American at that. *Seven years*, Remedios had predicted.

I will think of Remedios when I die. I am thinking of her now. Passing the rifle strap over his shoulder, Xavier turned Bora around and tied his arms above the elbows, sending a sharp pang up his spine. Soon he and Denzo were standing at the centre of the motley group, where Xavier and Vittorio faced each other.

"We agreed that you'd let us through." Carlevaris stood his ground.

"I did, on your way up."

"These officers are envoys. I gave my word they'd be returned safely." Vittorio's hand hooked the belt, where his pistol still lodged. "We have an agreement. My men are up the road, ready to intervene."

"Mine are here."

Noticing how Denzo's face had gone white, Bora said to him under his breath, "Remember who you are."

A step away, the confrontation between commanders grew into a more and more agitated exchange of nervous shoves and recriminations, until Xavier unslung his rifle and discharged it directly under Vittorio's chin. Bora was closest and was showered by a scatter of blood and brain fragments. He thought Denzo had been struck, too, by the way he went down, eyes closed, crashing onto his knees.

Shots erupted everywhere next, a burst of deadly, disproportionate crossfire that felled Vittorio's royalists, a chaos in the middle of which Xavier coolly pushed Bora towards the Slavs. Bora stumbled over Denzo, huddled at his feet, into the spot where Vittorio's exploded skull fed the dirt with fresh, steaming gore. Out of the din, the thrill inside him toned down, as if he hadn't been turned over to those who would shoot him. "Get up," he told Denzo through his teeth. "For the sake of our rank, get up."

Denzo muttered something, and, when the moon-faced youngster leaned over to jerk him onto his feet, he clasped the German's booted leg with his bound hands.

Bora kicked him off. Just then, Xavier's rifle dangerously scraped Bora's temple as he wheeled around to gather his men. "*Via, via, via!*" Soon he was scrambling across the track and downward, into the conniving safety of the fog.

GARDONE RIVIERA, 4:20 P.M.

Jacob Mengs had never visited Villa Besana. In the presence of its resident, Plenipotentiary Wolff, the affability of those who wielded real power made him envious. Wolff, pleasant and dismissive at the same time, observed, picking his words, "I regret to hear this. I spoke to Colonel von Bora occasionally and judged him to be a fine officer."

"The truth is often unpleasant, Obergruppenführer. I would not trouble you for your signature unless I needed it."

"Well, get Ambassador Rahn's signature. He is Reich plenipotentiary."

Mengs had no choice but to assent. How many plenipotentiaries did a puppet government require? Bureaucratic trammels embittered him; he saw through them and still had to swim through them. Once out of the ivy-lined seat, he wondered what women found in Wolff, who only looked like a dapper bureaucrat, despite the tales of his bedroom talents.

Captain Sutor was waiting in the car. "So, did you get it?"

"No. We're off to Fasano."

"To Rahn? Why to Rahn?"

"Because he's our plenipotentiary for the day."

9

The Slavs, only one of them Russian as far as Bora could tell, did not shoot them on the spot, which was not necessarily good news. They made them hike blindfolded to the higher ground – a strain for the aged Denzo – and lie face down precariously, rifles pointed to the napes of their necks, while they discussed their next move. Bora's knowledge of Russian let him capture enough words to start hoping. There was talk of ransom and exchange. He thanked his stars for not having worn ribbons indicating service on the eastern front. Denzo, on the other hand, seemed at the end of his tether; Bora felt nearly sorry for him. "*Animo,*" he encouraged him, and got a nasty prod of metal at the base of his neck for it.

It began to snow as they resumed climbing, and before long sleet lashed against them. The last stretch, on a difficult, steep incline, was made slippery by surfacing rocks. By mid-afternoon, the prisoners found themselves facing a crudely built wooden hut in a squally clearing among ragged firs. The firs quivered and roared in the gale.

The exhausted Denzo wheezed in his bulky greatcoat, blindfold still hanging from his neck. "This disaster falls on you, Bora."

"If they meant to shoot us, they would have done so."

"Shut up, both." In bad Italian, the Russian drove the Sten between the prisoners to separate them. Seeing his sidearm in the man's belt vexed Bora, and being searched in quick frisking motions even more so. Off came their wristwatches, and likewise Denzo's signet ring, scarf and greatcoat. Next, unbound for the time needed to relieve themselves, they were escorted to the fir grove by the Russian with a machine gun. Denzo groaned. "See? They'll kill us like dogs."

Instead, they made it safely to the line of trees and past a watering trough amid frozen mud and chipped stones. With the help of his teeth, Bora removed the right glove. His back turned to the Russian, he tried to eye something he could use to free himself later, anything. Ash-like, icy snow spiralled around him. He looked over his shoulder and asked with a gesture if he could wash the drying blood from his face.

"Quick about it."

Next, Bora was dropping his glove; as he clumsily bent over to retrieve it, he grabbed a piece of flint from the ground and pocketed it.

"Get up, get up!"

On the side of the hut was a lean-to, little more than the size of a chicken coop. Once inside, Denzo was secured in a half-prone position, his back to the wall. Bora fared no better. Not only his right wrist was secured, but his left ankle as well, so that it was impossible for him to do more than sit cross-legged with his face to the wall. Once they locked them in, they could barely see past their noses.

Graziani waited for a call from Denzo until evening, although by six-thirty the entire German–Italian command structure was already on alert. It was difficult to remain optimistic, and when Captain Johannesquade, who was to intervene in case of a delay, reported in, the bad news was confirmed.

At eight-thirty, Mengs reached Gardone with Rahn's signature in his folder. On his way back, he drove to Salò and the Hotel Metropoli, where he climbed to Bora's first-floor room.

It was no use trying to reach his pocket and the flint inside it. Denzo was tied down, unable to be of any help to Bora, even if he had wanted to. In his exasperation, before cold and inertia set in, he'd vomited his venom against the German for "bringing him here". Now he wheezed and shuddered in clothing unsuited for the mountain chill. As for Bora, increasing frustration at being unable to free himself was getting in the way of clear-headedness; still, he kept trying. "Quit squirming," Denzo rebuked him in the semi-darkness. "God damn you. You haven't a chance to get loose."

"What's that to you?"

Bora rested his head against the wall, to calm down and think of something else. Outside, the wind gave a voice to every chink and fissure. He smelled mustiness, the wet, roughly hewn timbers and Vittorio's blood on his shoulder. His muscles ached in the unnatural position, after Xavier's first binding. A fierce urge to escape made him curse the useless piece of flint chafing his leg through the pocket's lining. An inventory of his uniform seemed equally pointless, until it came to his left breast pocket. There, tucked away in case of a hasty shave, was a fresh razor blade. The notion went through him like an electric shock. How could he forget? It was so small and flat that frisking had not revealed it.

Reaching it was another matter, let alone making use of it. "Colonel Denzo, did you notice if the door was bolted from the outside?"

"I want nothing to do with you, Bora. When I get back to Soiano I will have you relieved. I will have you sacked. I will ruin you."

"... I don't think it was bolted."

Time wore on. Denzo's reproaches became a troubled murmur and then the heavy breathing of fatigued sleep. Outside, a few wind-borne words signalled a changing of the guard. The coming to life of chinks and fissures meant a torch was being waved about in the dark. The door, so low that you had to crawl through it, cracked open just enough to let the beam search inside. Denzo did not awaken. Bora could not pretend to sleep because his position was too constrictive, but he was careful not to react when he jerked the cord to check on its hold. "Damn you," Denzo grumbled in a twilight of consciousness. "There are guards outside, don't you know?"

For all Bora knew, there were several more inside the hut. He let minutes go by before renewing his efforts. Back and forth, twisting at the risk of dislocating his collarbone, hindered by the stiff cavalry boots, he was at last able to use his bound right hand and unbutton the flap of his left breast pocket. But he could not stretch his fingers enough to reach in and grasp the razor blade. Stretch and turn as he might, Bora came short of success, and the cord bruised the skin of his wrist. Muscles trembling, he leaned over until his torso was parallel to the ground, the sore left knee sending sparks of pain up the thigh to his groin, all the while fumbling with his artificial hand to keep the flap of his breast pocket lifted. It took more stretching and grinding of teeth before the tip of his forefinger met the blade's wrapper, only to lose contact with it. Bora swallowed tears of physical pain and disappointment. A spasm of the left knee caused him to jab Denzo's side. "Stop it," Denzo mouthed loudly in his sleep. Bora held his breath, lest the guard outside take another look through the door. Nothing having happened, he set about his work once more.

His pianist's hands had always been sensitive. Ever since his mutilation, the touch of his right hand had acquired an even keener tactile intelligence: controlled, accurate, strong and subdued, as it needed to be. At long last, he succeeded in reaching the blade and pulling it out. Careful not to drop it, he held it upright between middle and ring finger while he peeled off the wrapper with his forefinger and thumb. It took time, as his hand was stiff with cold and constriction; he risked cutting himself – and did so. But when he had the thin wafer of naked metal firmly in his grasp, he felt the unadorned, heady sense of power that comes from holding the proper tool.

His bleeding fingers worked at severing the cord that fastened wrist and ankle to the wall, but it was a struggle to maintain the angle needed for the blade to bite into the fibres. Halfway through the desperate effort, he noticed that Denzo had awakened.

"Bora, what do you think you're doing? You must be *mad*. They surely hold us for ransom … Don't even think I'll come along."

Blood raced to Bora's face with strain and anger. "Another word and I'll cut your throat."

The cord frayed one fibre at a time and finally snapped. Bora breathed out, slowly changed position, and slipped the blade back into his pocket.

"You're mad," Denzo protested. "Don't you dare touch me, or I call out. I'm not coming."

"And I don't give a damn." On his knees, Bora crawled to the door. Through the chinks, he smelled the icy night air with animal eagerness, trying to capture the sound of steps outside. No crunch of snow underfoot, but the stomping of one who tries to warm up as he keeps watch.

Denzo cringed at the idea that gunfire could erupt against them at any moment. Until the cold flowed in, Bora's silence kept him from knowing that he'd pushed the door open to leave.

A deep roar came from the fir trees. The time it took the guard to realize that someone was standing by him, and to reach for the rifle at his shoulder, was two seconds in all. Too slow. Bora hadn't broken a human neck since Russia, but the jerk-and-twist motion came easily enough.

For a demented moment, Denzo was tempted to shout the alarm, but his voice refused to come. He gasped for air like a fish on the hook at the thought that Bora had slipped away. In Africa … Well, in Africa he'd hanged natives for less than letting a companion escape.

The books in Bora's room were useless to Mengs. Commentaries on ethics, a collection of poems called *Tristia* and a selection from Hölderlin – staid stuff he leafed through in search of notes before returning them to their shelf. There was nothing in the uniforms, nothing under the mattress. The footlocker was empty except for two snapshots of Rome and a watercolour sketch of Russia signed "MHB, 1942". In the drawer of the side table lay pistol clips, a sealed packet of prophylactics and a wedding ring. It was a great disappointment. Before leaving, Mengs drove his hand inside the pillowcase and behind the cushion of the armchair.

DESENZANO DEL GARDA, 9:00 P.M.

Annie, who did not expect to find her uncle waiting on the railway platform, was frightened when he told her he had just picked up her father at the police station.

Vittori was smiling, however. "Nothing serious, darling. He was brought in by a zealous policeman for driving without his papers and resisting arrest. The new *commissario* is a martinet, so there we have it." He kissed her hand.

Annie found the story disagreeable. "With all his privileges, Uncle, he ought at least to be observant of the law." She spoke without looking at him, her red lips bitter or impatient. "Is he at home now?"

"Yes. Furious, but safe. I came to tell you in advance. How was Verona?"

"Rainy." In a high-collared, ample red overcoat, she made the few men around stop and stare. There was no travelling after curfew, so they would have to spend the night in town. Tired after one more doctor's appointment, Annie unprotestingly followed her uncle to the restaurant of the closest hotel.

Vittori handed her the wartime menu. "He is unhappy that you went to Como without telling him."

"Oh, please!"

"He worries, Annie."

German officers entered and sat down at a nearby table in a sparkle of shoulder boards and medals. Vittori saw his niece glance over. "Anyone we know?"

"No, Uncle, no one we know." But she was simpering. "I was thinking of Father, red-handed at the police station, and you bailing him out."

"I know he doesn't deserve it," Vittori admitted. When laughter came from the Germans, he seemed ruffled. "It's you I was thinking of."

Under her pert little hat, drawn tightly around her temples, Annie's hair had the sheen of finely wrought metal. Everything about her was composed, secure, as if behind a resilient partition. "Thank you. I don't need protection."

"Well, I'm glad to hear it. Not even from the German major, or the German colonel?"

Annie did not reply or change expression. She amusedly studied his face and saw it was friendly, even engaging.

"Of the two, the colonel is the better-looking one. He has *grace,* if men can have grace. Are you a little taken with him?"

"Should I be?" Having said so, Annie was cross at herself, since she did not mean it and had decided not to think of Bora in those terms. She did not blush – she never did – but heard her own voice grow resentful. "You ought not to ask such questions, Uncle."

"Heavens, Annie. Why not?"

TUESDAY, 14 NOVEMBER 1944

At midday on Tuesday, Bora stopped an RNG patrol just below Ponte Caffaro, looking no worse for the experience but for his need to shave and change uniform. "They must be looking in all the wrong places," he said dryly, when he heard that a search for him and Denzo had been ongoing. "I haven't run into anybody until now."

From the radio shack at Storo, he hastened to alert Graziani's office. Parisi told him that Johannesquade, alerted by gunfire, had rushed to the place of the ambush moments after the main body of the royalists discovered what had befallen their commander. Germans and Italians nearly came to blows before reality set in: Vittorio, Italo and the others dead, cars abandoned, no trace of the two colonels.

In an army truck bound for the commissary in Gardone, Bora started back. His leg hurt. In fact, as the excitement wore off, he could hardly walk on it.

He was waiting uncomfortably for a ride outside the commissary, when a leathery medical officer drew near with a cup of coffee in hand.

"I'm Zachariae, Il Duce's physician," he informally introduced himself. "I heard from a colleague that you're the young man who got away from the rebels. Drink this, and let's have a look at your fingers and knee before you go."

*

Graziani would not hear of postponing a debriefing. Zachariae had taken Bora in for X-rays, but, no broken or fractured bones having been discovered, he bandaged the cuts on his fingers and discharged him. By telephone Bora asked General Sohl to lend him Hager as a driver and, without even changing, rode to Soiano.

Marshal Graziani had blotches of red on his cheeks, a sign of repressed anger. Bora's answers were judicious and unassailable, and he knew his friend Denzo well enough to believe he had chosen not to escape. He was nonetheless piqued at the German for telling him, and for the way he had stared straight at him, his eyes sourly green and clear in his hastily shaven face.

"You say that, despite all, the parley was successful ..."

"His Eminence Cardinal Schuster confirms it," Bora interjected.

"... And yet here you are safe and sound, while your colleague's fate is unknown. You claim to know the mountains well enough to climb down to safety. Did you not consider that your escape, despite the likelihood of a prisoner exchange, might cause a reprisal against your colleague?"

Bora did worry about Denzo, for reasons different from Graziani's. "It was my duty as an officer to escape imprisonment, especially as I placed little trust in an exchange."

"You speak Russian, yet you did not try to communicate with your captors!"

"Had they known of my Eastern Front service, Marshal, they would have certainly shot us both. It goes without saying that I am willing to lead the search for Colonel Denzo." *Had he not lost his nerve, he'd be here, too,* he was thinking. *Now he's either dead, or ready to talk.*

Waiting just outside the door, Parisi feared that Graziani might repeat what he'd told him: that he suspected the German had negotiated his way out, if not traded Denzo's life for his own. He held his breath, but the accusation did not come. Shortly thereafter, in the rain, he was escorting Bora to the car, in the parking area where Denzo's colonial chauffeur waited impassively by the Alfa Romeo. "He's been there since we heard, Colonel. Won't eat, won't sleep."

Bora sighed. "Let me go and talk to him before he gets soaked." Handing him his briefcase, he added, "Will you place this in the safe for me? ... I *am* sorry about your superior, Captain Parisi."

"You are? I'm not." Denzo's aide placed Bora's briefcase under his arm so that he could unlatch his wristwatch. "If the colonel comes back, I'm asking for reassignment. Take this until you replace yours. I noticed you're without."

Before evening, Bora stopped at the embassy of Japan to retrieve the diary he had prudently left there for safekeeping. He copied down the notes taken during the combined operation and wrote a brief entry.

14 November 1944. Two years and two days after the Red Army's counteroffensive on the Don, I have escaped imprisonment for the third time.

By six-thirty, thoroughly exhausted, he fell asleep on the bed in his hotel room.

WEDNESDAY, 15 NOVEMBER 1944

What a difference twelve hours of sleep make. Upon awakening, for the better part of five minutes, Bora did not remember that he'd escaped with his life, that Denzo was lost and, until pain shot through his leg, that he'd promised to search for him.

If he lay still, the pain lessened considerably. At the foot of the bed, out of place in the Spartan room, the Venus was a fleshy knot coming undone smoothly before his eyes. *If you do not find her, it will be your fault.* Had he not promised Conforti to seek the original and failed thus far? He derived seductive blandishment from the painted image; he wished he could step into it, removed from anxiety and the passing of time. Why should he feel safe looking at the Venus? He did not investigate, lest he discover one more trap set for him.

When he sat up in bed, fully awake, he noticed two things that had escaped him the night before. The Venus's frame had been slightly moved (the maid had instructions not to touch it), and a piece of paper had been slipped under his door. In a familiar, minute handwriting, it read, quoting the old German hymn, "*Als aus Ägypten Israel.*" Followed by: "*Welcome back – E.D.*"

No doubt Dollmann had heard of his adventure and, perhaps driving back from the Mussolini–Vietinghoff conference, decided to leave a message. A risky Biblical quotation these days, comparing him to the Jews fleeing Egypt, but that was like Dollmann.

It was seven o'clock on Parisi's watch when Passaggeri phoned him, apologizing for the early hour and asking for a meeting "regarding the women's deaths", to which Bora agreed.

"Eight o'clock in my office, Inspector. By the way, do you happen to have acquaintances at the San Vittore prison in Milan?"

Punctually, at eight o'clock, Passaggeri arrived at Sohl's residence. He wore no hat – Bora wasn't sure whether this was a habit of his or so that he wouldn't have to doff it before a German. Invited to sit, he stood, and Bora did the same.

"Colonel," he began, "these aren't suicides. In both cases, the circumstances can make one suspect a voluntary act, but the details don't add up. I have failed to have the Spagnoli woman exhumed, but I did trace her family doctor in Verona. He confirmed that nearly a year and a half ago she was diagnosed with rheumatoid arthritis, and her finger motility was impaired. In Gariboldi's case, there is evidence of threats against her by the soprano, who has opportunely sought refuge in Switzerland. And there she can stay. I don't believe she went beyond the public scenes she made. In my mind, it's immaterial whether the weapon provided by her lover was with or without ammunition; even loaded guns do not fire by themselves. The *teatrino*, the mise-en-scène of the son's picture and her nakedness don't convince me as evidence of a suicide, although it seems contorted for a murderer to take such pains just to do someone in. I'm not ready to say the two incidents are related; however, the first death bears the hallmark of cleverness, no more than that. The second seems to want to impress with its ingeniousness. *If* we are facing one murderer, we can expect other deaths. The third will be cleverer yet, or else ..."

"Or else?"

"Or else it will be a mess. Do you mind if I smoke, Colonel?"

"Be my guest." But Bora made no effort to point out there were no ashtrays in the room.

Passaggeri took a cigarette from his breast pocket and lit it with an aluminium army lighter. "Now it is a question of seeing whether the victims had anything in common. They were women, alone, and in difficult circumstances. Thus far, a typical profile of female victims, but also, generally, of many women these days. They were beautiful, but beauty is in the eye of the beholder, et cetera. The fact remains: their one common detail is that the murder was made to look like a suicide."

After three drags, the cigarette formed a frail cylinder of ash at the tip, which Bora observed, standing with arms folded behind his desk. "It has been done, in political settings."

"Lacking in Spagnoli's case, as far as I can tell. In Gariboldi's case, none of the three people who might want to eliminate her – lover, rival, lover's wife – lacks an alibi. The 'political' lover could have sent someone to do his work for him, but the method would have been far less complicated. Why, it was even in Matteotti's case." Having mentioned a socialist leader murdered by Fascists years before, Passaggeri looked directly at Bora as he spoke. The latter said neither yes nor no. The cylinder of ash had grown longer and unstable, but the policeman took another long puff. "One second characteristic the victims share is that they both frequented Germans, at least occasionally."

"So I heard."

"Well, an occasional killer gives in to an impulse and cares little about creating puzzles for the investigators, who stand a slim chance of catching him anyway. A close relation, or else a killer with a good gaming mind, may well indulge in complicating matters."

"Yes." Nearly half of the cigarette had been smoked. The firmness of Passaggeri's hand, held in front of his face with a delicate pinching grasp, kept it together despite its advanced consumption. Bora felt a smile coming to his lips. "However, when complication aims to conceal the crime, rather than merely mislead, the game is entirely self-serving."

"Unless the killer considers society at large – the world, destiny, what have you, as the ideal counterparts of his game. Not the police. And he naturally wishes to continue his crimes undisturbed." In the twinkle of an eye, Passaggeri's left hand cupped below the falling ashes. "Not even what the victims share may be determinant, but we have to begin there. Fiorina Gariboldi had a lover in the Republican Guard and two acquaintances among the German officers frequenting the rest and recreation centre ... the 'Spielcasino', as you call it."

"Do we know their identity?"

"One is a Lieutenant Wilfried Mack of the *Radiosender*. The other, a junior physician named Reiner, from the military hospital Villa delle Rose, the old Rosenhof."

"Do you know either of them?"

"I am slightly acquainted with the surgeon."

"Were you aware that he rooms in Barbarano, within walking distance of the old place where Gariboldi was killed?"

"I was not. And the lieutenant?"

"He billets in Salò."

Bora jotted down the names in a notebook.

"Both of them have odd work shifts as far as I could ascertain." Passaggeri spoke with the cigarette stub in his mouth, as steady as a mason piling bricks.

"Any word about who Bianca Spagnoli's German acquaintances might be?"

"The neighbour across the landing seems to think it was you."

"Me?" Bora knew better than to laugh openly in the presence of a police official. But he must have looked amused enough, because the inspector stayed straight-faced while asking:

"When did you arrive in Salò, Colonel?"

"You cannot be serious!" Nevertheless, Bora added, "On the night between the fourteenth and the fifteenth of October."

"At what time?"

"I don't recall exactly: two-thirty, three o'clock? I was driven by an army driver to my quarters at the Metropoli, where I stayed until the morning."

"And on the evening of the twenty-fifth?" Seeing the German's irritation, Passaggeri placed his heavy, square-fingered hand on the desk. "Forgive me, Colonel. The evening of the twenty-fifth?"

Bora had to think it over. "I stayed in my Garibaldi Street

office until a few minutes past one o'clock in the morning. The sentinel saw me exit at that time."

"No breaks, no dinner?"

"No."

"Why not, if I may ask?" Careless of burning himself, Passaggeri extinguished the depleted butt between his fingers, and put it in his pocket.

"I never take breaks when I study charts and maps. If the neighbour took me for someone who had been there earlier, at least one other German must have visited Bianca Spagnoli."

"Well, whoever it was, he tried a few notes on the piano as she heard you do."

Ever since coming to the lake, Bora had never enjoyed a confrontation so much. "Inspector, there are a few other details I have not yet shared with you …" He was thinking of Pozzi's calling card and his various absences. "But before I do, we have to agree on a price."

Passaggeri wagged his head. "It depends on whether I can pay, Colonel. Namely, if it has to do with San Vittore. What do you wish to know?"

VILLA MALONA, 1:08 P.M.

While Bora readied to lead the search for Denzo with a Republican Guard unit, Pozzi said he could not understand why Annie was not home for lunch. "You phoned her, and she's not coming?"

Already seated at the table, Vittori shook his head.

"Well, isn't that grand. I get kicked out of my house by Germans, stolen from, detained by that prick of a policeman, and my daughter doesn't even talk to me. What's on her mind? What the hell is going on?"

"Ask her."

Pozzi snatched a bun from the bread tray and bit into it, swallowing the crumb in ill-mannered haste. "I'm not going to." He rinsed his mouth with wine and stood there stormily.

"She likes Bora," Vittori threw in casually.

"She *what?*"

"Just what I said. I can tell."

"Well, I won't stand for that!"

"It's for her to decide, don't you think?"

"She sure has got the sense of a cow." Pozzi spoke in dialect. "First the Jew, then the scarface pilot, now this. No, sir! With all I spent educating her, I won't have her opening her legs to a German like the rest of 'em. You've got to talk to her, Walter."

Vittori, who had taken a sip of water, slowly dabbed his lips with the napkin. "What really surprises me," he said in a deliberate voice, "is that my sister lived as long as she did as your wife."

The mountains between lakes Idro and Iseo crawled with SS men and Fascists. Past the place where the bodies of the royalist partisans had fallen, all Bora could remember clearly was the first tract leading to the higher ground. It wasn't until the second day out that they reached the wind-beaten clearing bordered by the grove of towering firs. The hut had been abandoned – nothing but empty food cans inside. The lean-to was deserted as well. In a shallow grave at the edge of the grove lay the Russian whose neck Bora had snapped in order to escape. No trace of Denzo anywhere. In the bitter cold, the guardsmen poked around and, having turned up nothing, sat around to rest and wait for further orders.

Their commanding officer took Bora aside. "This is how I see it, Colonel. Had they wanted to kill him, they'd have done so right here. So, either they decided to take him elsewhere for an exchange, maybe even from a distance, or else they returned him to Xavier. In which case, he's as good as gone."

Bora agreed. He musingly watched the guardsmen come and go from the hut, piling up pieces of old wood to make a fire. He was anxious to return to Salò. With the imminent danger of Denzo's spilling out strategy and numbers, going after Xavier before the winter became a priority: two weeks' worth of guerrilla warfare, taking advantage of the truce with the royalists. When a guardsman called out from the hut and everyone reacted by grabbing their weapons, he envisioned between regret and hope that Denzo's body had turned up after all.

Seeing a brightly dressed woman appear on the threshold with a child in her arms mystified him for the moment it took him to realize that it was a tall altarpiece, held aloft.

DIARY ENTRY: THURSDAY,
16 NOVEMBER 1944, 9:31 P.M.

What a surprise, stumbling into the canvases stolen from the chapel. The frames were battered, and the figure of Saint Luke, with brush in hand at the foot of the Virgin, damaged by a nasty rip. I had the hut all but taken apart in the dim hope of finding the Venus, but to no avail. Ransom was never asked for those pieces. Was it then one of Xavier's dares, or the Slavs' bright idea? Speaking of them, a more sobering discovery awaited us down a piece from the fir grove. The disarmed bodies of my captors lay side by side, shot through the napes of their necks. Executed by the royalists – so thinks the RNG commander. I rather think it was Xavier. Our watches were still on the wrists of the Slavs. Denzo's signet ring, however, was missing. Before dark, we regained the valley road. The SS and some Fascists are still up. The smiling Swabian leads them.

Tomorrow the altarpieces travel to the Brescia archbishopric for safekeeping. At least someone will be celebrating!

VILLA TASSINARA, FRIDAY,
17 NOVEMBER 1944, 9:19 A.M.

Bringing up the issue of Denzo's possible collaboration with his captors was a task Bora could gladly do without.

"We have to consider what a man can be made to say under duress or torture," he reasoned. "I have no intention of charging Colonel Denzo with treachery, but we must be realistic."

"Coming from a German, I find it an interesting concern."

"Sir, the situation forces us to contemplate the worst-case scenario. Whether or not we hear of a possible exchange or ransom, I suggest we move at once against Xavier, even at the risk of endangering the prisoner's life. No, sir. I have no clearance from Plenipotentiary Wolff to start operations until I receive yours, but the Security Service has already started its own round-up. Unless I am empowered to move out with the Guard, the Security Service will follow its own directives."

All Bora walked out with was a twenty-four-hour moratorium to allow Cardinal Schuster to become involved. It was clear that the Blackshirts and Republican Guard had taken the likelihood of Denzo's unreliability much more to heart: De Rosa headed the discontent and threatened to take matters into Fascist hands. "*Wir müssen realistisch denken*" was what Bora, unwilling to berate this colleague, allowed himself to say.

Like a dog that won't let go of a bone, De Rosa insisted. "Thirty-five men, Colonel von Bora. The Guard has lost thirty-five men in the last forty-eight hours! Look at the map! Xavier is getting his information from somewhere."

"Maybe."

"Maybe? I tell you, it's Denzo! Why didn't you drag him out with you or put a bullet between his eyes?"

Angry as he was, Bora found himself snickering. "Don't raise your voice, and don't speak nonsense."

"The bastard is spilling out our deployment and will spill out our strategy, too!"

"Winter is upon us. And he may be dead already."

"Don't count on it. Judas's kiss, I'm telling you." In a passion, De Rosa surged from his chair while Bora sat behind his desk, massaging his sore knee.

"*Wohl.* I'm moving out in twenty-four hours. Are you coming along?"

"The militia leaves now, Colonel. And all the volunteers I can scrounge up."

12:40 P.M.

Bora had lunch at the Metropoli and then, while a perfect ray of sunshine parted the clouds over the lake, went for a walk. On the way, he recognized Vittori in an English-style trench coat admiring the same view. They greeted each other, although Bora made no effort to further a dialogue, tending his own thoughts. Vittori had been talking to him for a time before he even became aware of it.

"... Were you chosen because of it?"

"Because of what?" Bora realized he was glancing over with an uninvolved half-smile.

"To seek the Venus, because of your grandparents' passion for art. They favour Flemish painters, if I'm not mistaken."

"Also a few of our Saxon Romantics, like Friedrich and Carus. The answer is no. I happened to be on hand, that's all."

Vittori nodded. Ribbons of sunlight ran across the surface of the lake, and both men stared at the reflections. "Yes. You strike me as a concrete man."

"Only because I have a concrete profession. I like art very much."

"Surely more than I do." Sun and shadows fired up, darkening the water. "Forgive me for saying this, but do you think you ought to visit Annie at her house?"

"Yes, if Signora Tedesco invites me there."

"I'm speaking for her sake: these are difficult times."

Bora wondered if she had told him, or if Vittori had seen them together in the restaurant two weeks earlier. "All my calls are justified by the investigation."

"I hope you will not take my words as an inference that there may be more between you."

Bora did not. "I'm a responsible man, Signor Vittori. I realize how precarious these times are. Any concern about your niece is understandable but unnecessary."

"Her father and I don't want Annie to be hurt, Colonel."

"*I* don't want her to be hurt either."

"Except that she is attracted to you."

Now that Vittori had said it – *because* he had said it – Bora did not believe it. He faced the water, apparently in control, but shaken and self-conscious inside. "My apologies," he said brusquely. "I am due back to work."

HOTEL REGINA, AUSSERKOMMANDO
MAILAND, 1:30 P.M.

In Milan, clouds brought rain, and rain brought about cottony fog that padded the streets and made the skinny lampposts resemble hanging trees. Kappler, Sutor and Mengs had to turn on the lights while they discussed the general strike.

"We pre-empted trouble by closing the Marelli, Caproni and Falk works on Monday, but, judging by what happened two days later, such measures may no longer suffice."

"No, and a shut-down factory doesn't produce more than a struck one."

Hauptsturmführer Sutor grew bored with the talk. He found an excuse to leave the room and go and yawn somewhere else in the hotel. When he returned, the topic of conversation had changed.

"He's entitled to a warning of some kind," Kappler was saying in his monotone, and at once Sutor knew what this was all about.

"The hell he is." The words escaped him.

Kappler looked surprised. "I beg your pardon?"

"The hell he is. He's had five years, plenty to know what's coming."

"Well!" Kappler's surprise gave way to a virtuous sneer. "You may foster a grudge against him since your days in Rome. But this is not Stalinist Russia. We have rules."

"Yes," Mengs intervened. "They're gangster methods you're suggesting, Hauptsturmführer; we do not bump people off in the back seats of cars."

Sutor swallowed his frustration. "What do you suggest, then?"

"Well." Mengs's blank eyes turned to him. "I suggest you listen to Obersturmbannführer Kappler."

10

In their last conversation, Lipsky had mentioned a visit to Salò by mid-month, possibly the coming weekend. Bora brooded over the reason for it: overseeing things for Field Marshal Göring, or making good on his suspicions about Sohl's role in the theft. In light of Sohl's distrust and jealousy of the flyer, the likelihood made Bora edgy. He was still edgy when Commander Borghese rang him, to express his contrariety at having the militia take over the search for Denzo. "It would be far better if my men or yours went, Colonel."

"I agree, but I can't move until Marshal Graziani authorizes me."

Borghese complained about the stranglehold of bureaucracy and vowed to send some of his commandos after De Rosa. Shortly thereafter, General Sohl summoned him to let him know he'd be in Meran until Monday. Patching things up with his wife, or spying on her, or because he wanted to avoid meeting Lipsky, Bora could not say. All he knew was what his calendar said: that on 18 October, when, according to Dollmann, someone had deposited a canvas in a Milan bank vault, he'd had breakfast at Fasano with Dollmann himself, and the general was not in Salò.

"You ought to take the weekend off, too," Sohl told Bora engagingly, as if desirous to be forgiven for his jealous scene days earlier. "Your Italian colleague is either alive or dead. If he's dead, then *sine ut mortui sepeliant mortuos suos*, as we read in

Luke. Let the dead bury the dead. If he's alive, there isn't much you can do about it. Look at yourself. I don't see how you can even manage to dial a number with your fingers bandaged."

"I use a pencil, Herr Generalleutnant."

"But you can't use a pencil to shoot, can you."

The odour of Sohl's cheroots and the warmth of the fireplace followed Bora out into the hallway. There, the unexpected dazzle of something bright red at the head of the stairs, like a tongue of flame, made him so sure he'd glimpsed Annie that he jostled an orderly as he hastened after her.

She was still inside the gate when he reached her, and she looked up ever so briefly from under the small shade of her hat. The scarlet coat around her blazed against her pallor; Bora nearly expected her to burn with it. Instead, it shielded her flowingly: Medea standing in a merciful bonfire. The greyness of day turned irrelevant around her even as the landscape behind the Venus receded. She answered his greeting, but she had in her something of a young prisoner pretending self-composure so that she can find a way out.

"I thought you were still out of town." Bora could have slapped himself for the banality of his words.

"No. I simply did not answer the phone."

After the meeting with Vittori, this had the makings of a godsend – or a disaster. Bora began feverishly to think of a good reason for her not to leave at once. "May we have lunch?"

"No, thank you."

"Dinner, then?"

"No."

Bora blushed in embarrassment and disappointed hope. It had happened in Berlin back in July with a girl called Emmy. Girls were starting to say no to him … But then Emmy had come to his room. "Please."

"Another time, Colonel. I left something for you."

He should have asked what that "something" was but did not. Suddenly her haste, her reticence were readable even from his disappointment. Bora was granted the grace of reading her truly, how everything in her betrayed desire in response to his own, which was so shamefully strong. A slight push and they would be over the fence keeping them apart. "Tonight, please." He had not been *wanted* in so long that he couldn't believe his good fortune, never mind that she was saying no to him and might continue to do so for a while.

As for her, she looked at a place between his shoulder and the gate, a hazy point separating what was not Martin Bora from what *was*. Her longing was well guarded, yet in his presence a weakness, a languor overtook her that made her want to lean against the pillar and give in to him. She felt awash. Past the bloody surge of cloth around her, the medals and badges on Bora's tunic reminded her of who he was, what he was. And yet she had to keep herself from a sinking vertigo. Now that they faced each other, she felt powerless before the way things would turn out. Seemingly, she did no more than give him her gloveless hand. "My home, at eight."

2:18 P.M.

What Annie Tedesco had left for him was a packet of letters and a handful of photographs of the Venus taken by Conforti for the 1940 auction. The letters, sent to Pozzi by antiquarians and collectors between 1940 and 1942, concerned other purported Titian works, pandered for exorbitant prices. Bora noted down the names and placed the envelopes into the Venus folder. If he flipped quickly through the photographs, held together by an elastic band, the small figure seemed to flicker and move before his eyes.

When the operator rang back from Wolff's office, Bora was able to speak to the plenipotentiary himself. Wolff sounded annoyed at Graziani's postponement and inclined not to release troops on demand. "If the marshal wants twenty-four hours to haggle through the Church, he'll have to do without us afterwards. Yes, *natürlich*: go up if you wish, Bora, but out of your own goodwill."

Only because he'd returned in a slight euphoria after speaking to Annie, Bora had left his office door open. Now, as he put down the receiver, Mengs's voice came from the threshold with a rap of knuckles on the jamb.

"Have you got a moment, Colonel?"

Bora looked up. "Yes, of course," he said, feigning indifference. "Come in."

Without stepping in, Mengs leaned his shoulder against the door-frame. "No need to take much of your time. We would like to set up an appointment with you. Just routine questions to those who served at headquarters in Rome, nothing personal. We understand you're a busy man, so will you look up your schedule now?"

We. The use of the plural, along with civilian clothing, had an ill-omened quality of diluted responsibility. Bora, who was looking at the Gestapo agent, saw him blurred, like a target in the fog. Having entrusted his briefcase to Parisi was the only thing that kept him from slipping into a parallel dimension, where another Martin Bora, having led a different life, came to the fatal conclusion of a series of choices and events. This Martin Bora reached for his calendar. "Next Wednesday, at four o'clock?"

"Perfect." Leaving the jamb, Mengs approached the desk, ostensibly to take a pencil and mark the date on his pad. When he was in front of him, he stretched out his hand. "Oh, we'll need your sidearm as well: I'd like to have it now."

Bora made an extraordinary effort to stay calm. "My sidearm?"

"Just a routine check."

Ribbed handle first, the P38 was handed over. Mengs took it, checked the clip and pushed down the safety catch. "Do you always carry it ready to fire?"

"No."

The gun sank into Mengs's pocket. "It will be returned to you Wednesday evening in my Maderno office. Of course, you are welcome to secure another weapon for temporary use."

On certain days, bad news accumulates like tangles of hair and dirt blending to clog the drain. Sohl knew that Bora had left in haste. "Where is the colonel?" asked Hager, busy carrying his luggage down the stairs.

"He did not say, sir. Said he'll be back in forty-five minutes."

At Soiano, where an agitated Parisi had asked for his presence urgently, Bora kept telling himself that it had to do with Denzo's fate, or Graziani's bad temper. Oddly, he found the aide waiting for him at Villa Omodeo's entrance.

"I preferred not to tell you by telephone, Colonel, and did not want to leave the premises. I found it strange, but they showed a signed slip from Plenipotentiary Wolff, and I *had* to give them the combination to the safe." He preceded Bora to the room where sensitive documents were kept. "Would you verify if anything is missing from your briefcase?"

Bora would rather not speculate on the implications. He first scrutinized the files on counter-insurgency measures and the sheets of intelligence messages. "It all seems to be here," he said. His briefcase was in order, still locked. Ordinarily, he wouldn't act in the presence of others, but time was short: Parisi watched him unlock the briefcase, look inside and remove it from the safe with a look of relief. "Everything seems fine."

"I still can't understand what they were looking for."

Out of the thoughts racing through his mind, Bora reached for Mengs's words – "Just a routine check" – as to an absurd life preserver. Checks and controls were run constantly, on everyone; had Dollmann known of anything directly related to him, he'd have given him a hint ... Bora walked away from the safe in a state of self-possession, anticipating his date with Annie and asking himself whether the cologne Parisi wore was vetiver.

"Colonel," he was saying, "the marshal will not like it. This is most irregular."

Bora changed subject. "If there's no word from the Curia by morning, I'm going up with a platoon of my men. Here's your watch back. Thank you. I recovered mine. Could I impose on you for a P38 from the lot we captured last month?"

Sohl had left for Meran when Bora returned to the residence. He went through his briefcase once again to ensure it had not been searched and decided to walk to the *questura* down the street.

Passaggeri was haranguing someone behind closed doors. With a sedate gesture, Bora kept the police orderly from knocking and announcing him, and waited outside while the bawling went on, the usual reprimand all of them had given or received as soldiers. Later, not even the sight of a German colonel succeeded in composing the inspector's stormy look, although he mumbled a greeting and lost no time before informing him of Pozzi's brief detention.

"What can I say? I wanted to see him eye to eye. Please take a seat, Colonel. I noticed you don't smoke. Mind if I do? I have to smoke when I talk. What can I do? It's a vice." Shaking hands with him, Passaggeri had of course felt Bora's bandaged fingers. Bora obliged his curiosity by resting his forearm on the desk.

"The news isn't much, Colonel. It's a fact that Bianca Spagnoli sought a position at the textile works in Roè, where Pozzi produces parachute cloth for you Germans. No, Fiorina Gariboldi did not apply. In any case, the superintendent denies giving her a calling card. It is not policy. After all, calling cards are made to change hands and can be found anywhere."

"True."

"On the other hand, Pozzi denies having been away on the days of the murders. All he worries about is being prosecuted for some of his money operations." Spikes of precociously greying hair around Passaggeri's face enhanced his watchdog looks. His age was impossible to estimate even by approximation: well above thirty but below fifty, somewhere in between. "Pozzi doesn't strike me as a homicidal maniac, but the folks he surrounds himself with, fortune-tellers and so-called mediums, don't depose in favour of his sanity."

A needling rain had begun to fall, ticking against the windowpanes. Roofs across the square bristled and turned shiny. Out of his briefcase, Bora took the folder of women's photographs from Conforti's studio. "It's best if you keep this, Inspector."

Bianca Spagnoli's portrait was the first of the batch. "This one," Passaggeri said, "for all of her neighbour's gossip, was as close to a recluse as it gets. No friends, no acquaintances. The portrait seems to be the only luxury she allowed herself, unless that Conforti fellow did it for free, which apparently he now and then did. The Germans – boots on the stairs, recognizable voices – visited her three times in all, after curfew. But she died at seven in the morning." Carelessly, Passaggeri let ash float down from the cigarette, because he no longer needed to impress Bora with his self-control. "You've seen the alley. Narrow, dark even at midday. Anybody can slip by, German or Italian. And she *was* good-looking."

In less than four hours, I will meet Annie. In less than twenty-four, I might be killed in the mountains, looking for Denzo. Wolff's men could have been spying on Graziani. Why not? In any case, Mengs will learn nothing from my sidearm.

Bora looked away from the window. He promised he would try to test the waters with Lieutenant Mack of the *Radiosender* and the young army surgeon regarding Fiorina Gariboldi. "I will let you know. What else have you learned about her?"

"For one, that she was not exactly the pathetic single mother who raises her son alone. The boy's father, a furniture wholesaler from Lissone, paid good money to keep things quiet, until he decided to risk telling his wife and save the expense. That is why the girl had to go back to work, in due course becoming Marla Bruni's maid. The rest of the story is as you know it. Few female acquaintances. The Swiss chambermaid Liese Cassli …" – he mispronounced Klaeusli – "… knows remarkably little for a 'close friend'. Seems that Gariboldi picked up clothes at charity sales and fixed them up nicely. But if a girl wants to look good at the Spielcasino … eh?" Someone knocked on the door. Passaggeri roared, "*I'm not here!*" Then he continued, "She, too, had her picture taken by Conforti. Who knows whether the coincidence is meaningful? Besides, the old man's studio was ransacked – but you know this already."

Bora nodded. "Gariboldi's portrait was paid for two days before her death: here's the receipt. Is there any chance you might identify the other sitters, Inspector? In the folder, there are eighteen portraits in all."

Passaggeri pinched his moribund cigarette off and set it aside. "Colonel von Bora, even in the fantastic hypothesis that this folder were somehow a tool for the prevention of other murders, we can't follow up on women whose names we don't know. Keeping tabs on people only seems easier these days; the net has a tight mesh, but the clever fish always finds the rips."

I hope so, Bora told himself.

"One piece of information I must ask you to keep for yourself is that in Gardone we have a former inmate, a felon who during his draft period, more than twenty years ago, was investigated after six women died in the space of six months. He spent a couple of years in and out of courtrooms and did some time, which was all they could saddle him with. Lives by doing odd jobs, including dish-washing at the soup kitchen where Spagnoli got her meals twice a week – and keeping the flowerbeds at the Spielcasino."

"I see." Bora sat up, suddenly intrigued. "How does he get around?"

"Like everyone else. Takes the tramway or walks." Passaggeri was careful to douse the excitement he'd started. "Unless I can place him at either of the crime scenes, I don't expect much from this coincidence either."

"How do I recognize him?"

"With all due respect, Colonel, it's best if you let me do my job, and I will keep you informed as I go along."

"I will let you do your job, but how do I recognize him?"

Passaggeri blew air through his hairy nostrils. "Small, bow-legged, rock-solid, red hair." He wrote two lines on a slip of paper, which he pushed across his desk to the German's side. "My part of the San Vittore bargain. The names of the banks, and of the banker executed in Milan."

MESPILAI

When the bell rang, Annie Tedesco doubted it would be Bora, since she had not heard a car drive up the hill. But it was eight o'clock, and Bora stood on her doorstep. "You did not walk, Colonel!"

"No. I left the car at a colleague's billet, down the road."

She was flattered by the courtesy, which, however, denoted the private nature of this call. "I hope you will forgive my fickleness for deciding not to dine out."

"I'm grateful to be here." Bora followed her to the room where corners were rounded and lights discreetly low. The flowers arranged in vases were those he'd sent. On the low table lay two books, one of them in Greek, whose title at first he could not make out while he stood there, waiting for her to sit down. He'd insisted on meeting her but had no preconceived plans; on the contrary, he saw the awkwardness of the situation now. When she offered him cognac, he said yes.

"Major Lipsky phoned me," she informed him, handing him the drink. "He is flying in on Tuesday. Did you know?"

"I did not. Does he call often?"

Annie sat at one end of the sofa, visibly pondering the motive behind Bora's question. "Not often. Is he your friend? He speaks of you as though he knows you well."

The Greek books were Bacchelli's *Mal d'Africa* and Kazantzakis's *Odyssey*. Bora, who had uncharacteristically taken a couple of drinks before coming, downed the cognac in the hope of relaxing. "He does not, Signora."

"Of course. I'm sorry. You told me you have no friends in Salò." She sat with legs crossed, toying with the gold bangle around her wrist. They looked at one another, regretting that they had chosen to meet, because now they had to conceal what was on their minds.

I feel what I feel, he thought, *there's no point in hiding it. What about her?*

When a timely short double ring of the doorbell, followed by a long one, brought Annie to her feet, Bora imagined at once who it was.

"Excuse me. It sounds like my father."

Pozzi's booming voice came next from the entrance. "How was I supposed to know? That uncle of yours is buying himself another tree, so I had to drive him to Limone and back. Thought I'd stop by." In a moment, he was in the room. "Oh, but it's the colonel! How's life, Colonel?" Did he expect Lipsky to be here? When Pozzi plunked himself down in an armchair, as the lapels of his coat drew apart, Bora glimpsed a leather strap across the front of his shirt, and a bulge on the left side of his chest. "What news of the Venus?"

"None."

Whether she was relieved or annoyed by the inconvenience, Annie was walking back and forth in the vestibule. Under Pozzi's scrutiny, Bora felt lonely overhearing the sound of her gentle steps. It was the sound of home, of family life ... Perhaps his existence had been strange, and wasteful.

From across the room, Pozzi kept an evaluating stare on Bora, who tried to appear unconcerned. As many hefty men do, Annie's father sat with his knees far apart, and the lump of his genitals was evident against the left thigh. There may be some challenge in that too. Bora quickly looked away. Alcohol was beginning to have its effect, and he too sat at ease, legs extended, his boots crossed at the ankles. "What size is your calibre?"

Pozzi placed both fists on his knees, elbows squared. A salesman's smile rose to his lips, the same he must display with a competitor. "7.65," he said, without asking why Bora wanted to know. "You must be closer to a solution than you were, Colonel."

"Not really."

"So, you have nothing to tell us?" Which meant, *What are you doing here, then?*

"No." Bora got to his feet when Annie re-entered the room.

Eyeing the flowers, Pozzi, having come from the greenhouse, must have been calculating how costly they were. "Is he telling you any more than he's telling the rest of us, Anna Maria?"

"I haven't had time to ask the colonel any questions." There was wholly feminine annoyance in her tone and in the sweep of skirt past her father. She returned to the sofa, letting him pour himself a drink. Bora felt her sinking back into the inertia of his first visit, when in the presence of her relatives she'd seemed indolent or weary. He thought of the Venus in his hotel room, which he now and then covered to avoid distractions. Annie, too, was veiled somehow, opaque. Whether he or her father left first, the evening was lost, and he might as well accept it.

"Well, I know when I'm not welcome." Pozzi swallowed the last of his liquor. "Don't bother seeing me to the door, Anna Maria." He stood with a knowing look, which Bora took in good part, but Annie resented.

"I *will* see you to the door."

When she returned from the vestibule, Bora was already wearing his greatcoat. "Why is your father carrying a pistol?"

"Is he?" Annie said she had not noticed. "There have been small thefts at the factory. He may feel more secure with a pistol." She watched him retrieve his cap and place it under his arm. "You could have asked him. Why didn't you?"

"Because it is not my job."

Annie took the comment in her stride. "I'm sorry about the way the evening turned out." In the subdued lighting, the high, opulent curve of her breast filled the silk of her dress. But she did not encourage him, and he did not encourage himself. "I'll walk you to the gate."

She threw a fur over her shoulders and preceded him out. Above her, the Ethiopian bride sparkled in the bitter dark. No longer in bloom, the medlar trees crowded the garden path with their jagged heads of leaves.

"Uncle Walter says you are divorced."

Was she seeking the complicity of the night to speak and, at the same time, the safety of an open space? Had Bora thought she was really interested in knowing, he'd have grown self-conscious with pleasure. But it was only a polite enquiry.

"It is not true."

"Are you married, then?"

"My wife secured an annulment."

At the bottom of the hill, lights off, Pozzi's car was still parked on the road. Annie stopped with a small swallowing sound, somewhere between spite and a sigh. "Sometimes it's safer not to love people."

"Or countries, or ideals. Or other things." Bora placed a quick brushing of lips on her hand. "I understand what you say. But it's not safer, only easier."

"What are you committed to, really?"

"Other things, Signora Tedesco."

Now, because *he* wanted to go, she kept his hand in hers, testily. "What are they?"

"Not people."

"Ever since you spoke to us of the Venus, *our* Venus … I think you're in love with her."

"I think I am."

Vittori, who had been left behind in the back seat of Pozzi's car, flew at him after Bora went by with an ironic salute. "Have you no sense? What a faux pas! How embarrassing. Didn't you at least consider that the colonel could be useful to you?"

"I don't want him to lay my daughter, that's all."

SATURDAY, 18 NOVEMBER 1944

Bora's decision to join the search did not have to wait for the end of Graziani's moratorium. At dawn on Saturday, five days from his capture, De Rosa radioed in the discovery of Denzo's body by the militia. With a few men Bora took the mountain road, and in three hours' time, part of which was travelled on foot, he stood with De Rosa on a ridge, not far from an isolated farmhouse.

"Shot dead like a pig, Colonel."

Bora looked at the body, heaped on a half-dug hole as if a grave had been started but impatience or haste had felled him at the edge of it. "Is that how they kill pigs in Italy?" Denzo had been kneeling, hands bound behind his back, and, judging by the raking of dirt around him, he'd thrashed about not to die. "He must have four or five bullets in his head."

"Has a whole clip," De Rosa specified, showing a handful of casings.

Bora avoided looking over. A scent of snow blowing from the heights erased all other smells. He, who did not suffer the cold, felt the mountain wind like a thief searching him; if he closed his eyes, a mortified sense of being exposed took hold of him. There had been colder days in his life, but he was chilled now.

Fierce in his cheviot and black wool, De Rosa seemed compelled to give details. "Looks like he was locked up in there the past days." He pointed to a stone barn behind them. "They must have shot him when they heard us coming."

Bora observed nothing in return. Denzo's body had drained itself in the hole, like an animal sacrifice. The back of his head had turned to mush. Only by turning him around could Bora identify him by what remained of his face. His ambivalence must have shown enough for De Rosa to speak up. "Why, you could have ended up the same way. It's not like we should care about him either. He got what he deserved."

"He was certainly punished." Bora stepped away from the hole and went past the hatchet-faced group of militiamen to the barn. He walked with full appreciation of the place's solitude, reprehending himself for "not caring", as De Rosa put it. It was like Xavier to execute Denzo as the enemy drew near and clamber to safety in time. Of course it was. Bora wondered whether arriving here a few hours earlier, in defiance of Graziani's orders ... Looking back, he saw De Rosa turn the body over with his foot.

Bora radioed the news to Graziani before the remains were composed and hauled down. From Soiano, the news spread quickly across the command posts. In Milan for the swearing-in of auxiliaries at the castle, Dollmann knew it already when Mengs contrived to run into him at the Caffè Centrale, where he had sat down to a late breakfast. It was not hearing him repeat the news that set him on edge. In the pale morning light, other small words spoken by Mengs caused Dollmann to face him squarely. A mask of detachment came over him from the astuteness of his soul, moulding like glass on his face. In comparison, Mengs looked limp, but it was Dollmann who was afraid.

"Why ask me?" He shelled words out like marbles for Mengs to count. "Since when am I Bora's keeper?"

Mengs accepted the impossibility of shattering the mask. Tapping on it was enough to send vibrations to the man beneath it, over the empty coffee cups.

SOIANO, 4:06 P.M.

Despite the presence of the lower-ranking Parisi, Graziani called it a "failure of comradery" and "tantamount to desertion of a fellow officer", so that at his return Bora found himself defending De Rosa's conduct. "All that could be done was done, Marshal Graziani: three different attempts to locate him in five days. We have unfortunate precedents for the spur-of-the-moment execution of prisoners."

"You are a living exception to that!"

"Only because I did not give them the opportunity."

"You should have forced your colleague to come along, then, or the militia should have been careful not to alarm the enemy! It should personally shame you – *shame you* – that it took a hero's death to belie your obscene hints of betrayal. *Si vergogni, colonnello!*"

For the first time since his wounding, Bora had had to stop by an army hospital and ask for an injection of painkiller. Standing cost him an effort of the will. He had thus far let the marshal berate him, telling himself he'd only react to Graziani's use of one word: hero. When he heard it, his cup overran. "Allow me to observe that it all depends on how a man dies. Per se, there is nothing heroic in getting a head full of lead, especially when one can't help it."

For a dreadful moment, Parisi envisioned the marshal striking Bora. He froze on the spot, jaw locked in expectation, but the twitching right arm never left the marshal's side. His voice was, all the same, like a knife lifting a layer of live flesh. "I entrusted a friend and colleague to your *experience*, and you left him behind to be murdered. I hold you responsible, as if you had pulled the trigger yourself, and regret only that your appointment protects you from sanction. I have to stomach you on my staff, Colonel, but do so with all the loathing of my blood for your uncivilized breed!"

Bora stood still until Graziani stormed out of Denzo's office. A moment later, with a blow to the dead man's desk he smashed the gleaming glass top and, under Parisi's gaze, sent sheets of it flying across the floor.

SUNDAY, 19 NOVEMBER 1944

Denzo's funeral took place in Milan on Sunday, in the presence of bigwigs, units from the 205th Italian military command and a truckload of Marelli workers who'd been "volunteered" to attend. For the Germans, Wolff and Dollmann were there, and Kappler and Bora as well. Buffarini-Guidi, Pavolini, Graziani and Zingoni represented the Italian government and armed forces. Mass was sung in St Marco's church, wedged as it was with its false antique façade between two streets. Commander Borghese, in fatigues, sat on Bora's left and now and then whispered to him during the homily. It rained hard as the funeral procession formed outside, reinforced by the influx of Catholic Action affiliates, among them Countess Denzo di Galliano herself.

Civilian umbrellas jammed the space at the sides of the hearse, while the military men had the privilege of getting soaked. Although Kappler, Dollmann and Bora did not exchange more than a greeting, afterwards Wolff addressed Bora as they waited for their cars. "Well, Colonel, there must be better places to meet than at a comrade's burial."

"Indeed, Oberstgruppenführer."

"Last summer, Field Marshal Kesselring told me of your request for reassignment from Italy. Whatever became of it?"

Tucking away his unease at facing the man who'd ordered the safe opened and searched, Bora answered truthfully that he had heard no more about it and did not feel the field marshal was inclined to grant it. Wolff laughed. Despite his name, he had little narrow teeth – the teeth of a sheep. "With your expertise of the East, you'd probably end up there. Perhaps the field marshal wants to keep you alive."

*

Denzo's sombre-faced colonial chauffeur drove Bora and Parisi back to Villa Omodeo. There, Parisi explained that *he* had got his reassignment, which Graziani had taken as a sign "of loyal mourning". "It's just down the road in Padenghe, at headquarters with Colonel Lanzetta."

Bora congratulated him.

"Thank you, Colonel." Parisi breathed in the rainy noon hour. "Now I can tell you that I cannot abide aftershave. Now that Count Denzo can no longer force me to wear it in order to ingratiate myself with the marshal, I'll be able to smell like a man."

Bora had a little smile. "May I ask that you take care of the colonel's chauffeur? He is a good and faithful man."

TUESDAY, 21 NOVEMBER 1944, 11:07 A.M.

On Tuesday, when Lipsky flew into Ghedi airport, he was not a little surprised to find Bora waiting for him on the runway. Rain turning to sleet accompanied them as they drove away together.

"May I ask why not?" Lipsky asked before long in his vibrant tenor voice, struggling to hide his irritation.

"Because I forbid it."

"I fail to see how my meeting Signora Tedesco might intrude on your investigation."

"Your personal preference can create prejudice. As a lawyer, you don't need me to explain it."

Look who's talking. Lipsky's gloves slid off his hands and impatiently sought his pocket.

Past Brescia, the road skirted the hills; wind and sleet blew across the fields and the road. The presence of roadblocks at regular intervals, slowing their advance, allowed the officers to discuss business at length. Lipsky said he'd learned surprising new details about the Venus's "secret"; he speculated, much as a hopeful prospector does. "You've gone through the Jew's correspondence, I expect?"

"After you cleared his paintings out? Exhaustively. It all amounts to letters from other scholars. He kept no copies of what he sent out, or, if he did, I did not find them."

"And he never mentioned to you that the painting is a map of sorts?"

Until this point, Bora had been minding the drifting sleet outside. Now he looked over. "Is that why the Reich Marshal is interested?"

"Colonel, *please.* Let's not pretend with each other. I heard that Sohl asked you to abandon the inquiry, and I am offering my collaboration."

"How magnanimous."

"What I mean is: I do not *necessarily* have the appropriation of the Venus foremost in mind. Should we succeed in finding her, I would even go so far as delaying her transfer to Germany. Keeping details from each other will not expedite things." Lipsky had noticed Bora's way of withdrawing from conversation by using short sentences, flatly spoken. "Please talk to me, Colonel."

"I haven't sought your help to get to the bottom of this, Major. I have no more interest in collaborating with you than I have in abetting the thief, and largely for the same reasons."

Lipsky blushed until his scar shone white. "I am under orders, as you are, but I am not dishonourable."

Bora felt sudden disgust at the hackneyed excuse of superior orders, a repulsion that turned his stomach. At the following checkpoint, while the car queued with other vehicles awaiting inspection, he flung the door open and stepped out into the storm. The SS men ahead looked his way inquisitively, saluted and walked up to him. "*Herr Oberst, Ihre Papiere, bitte.*"

Bora handed them his papers. Flakes of ice sprinkled his greatcoat when he re-entered the car. "The SS say there's trouble ahead. Are you armed?"

"Yes."

Less than ten minutes later, they slowed down by a burning Italian truck, beyond all help. Lipsky insisted on hearing more about the Venus, and at last Bora silenced him by saying, "If you must know, I am closer to knowing who took the Venus." Which was less than half-true.

The weather started clearing as they drew alongside the lake. It was barely raining in Salò when Bora dropped Lipsky at the Metropoli.

In his office, a message from Borghese awaited. A badly wounded partisan had been taken prisoner during a furious gunfight in the Val Camonica, and, to Borghese's disappointment, transported to the military hospital in Riva – Reich territory, off-limits to Italian units. There, he lay unconscious and about to have surgery. He carried a handful of leaflets on him, some of which he'd been desperately trying to swallow when they had overtaken him.

Bora called in at once, asked Borghese for a description of the man and the leaflets and assured him that he would start out for Riva immediately. "There's no point going there now, Colonel," Borghese objected. "He's about to have surgery. If he makes it, it may be days before he's able to speak again. We offered to keep watch at the hospital tonight, but yours wouldn't hear of it. Above all, do not inform the Republican Guard or the militia of the capture."

Lipsky was sitting at the bar of the Metropoli when Bora joined him after dinner. "Major, I hope you made a detailed inventory of Conforti's paintings before shipping them out."

"Not *before*." Lipsky lifted his glass in a greeting. "After. There were nearly one hundred."

"Ninety-eight, without counting the prints."

"You could have spared me a good amount of work."

"You did not ask. I could have also given you the key to his door."

"Well, screw it." Slightly altered by drink, the major was in a conciliatory mood. "Won't you toast the Venus's health?"

"With pleasure."

They poured themselves brandy, and, because both held liquor well, they did a generous amount of drinking. Whether one was trying to make the other talk, they drank to soldiers' honour and Bora's dead brother, to winning and losing the East and trying not to lose the West. Before bringing up Sohl's wife, Bora had to graze the edge of intoxication, watching Lipsky fall over his.

"The sop thinks I'm doing his wife? So that's why he wanted me out of here so desperately! It's amazing, the reputation we pilots have. I'm not screwing her, but I know who is."

"Keep it to yourself, Major."

"It's Wolff. I saw them walk out of a doorway on Rovello Street."

"I'm not listening."

"They then strolled to the Credito Italiano, she in her furs and he in civilian clothes. Entering the bank from Porrone Street, lest they be seen by Hager, who was waiting in Cordusio Square."

"I don't know that any of that is true."

"Tsk, tsk. You're not as virtuous as that, Colonel; I've heard spiteful remarks coming from you before. You'll agree that not even a general's wife would be so brazen unless her lover were above prosecution." Merrily, Lipsky lowered his voice. "You see why neither you nor I, to say nothing of poor Hager, will inform Sohl on his marital difficulties. I'd much rather he thinks I'm screwing his wife, even though on principle I never bed the woman of a superior officer."

Out of Lipsky's gossip, the detail of the *Credito Italiano* bank captured Bora's attention. But Lipsky was telling him, with a pout, "You just don't want me to see her, that's what it is."

"If you're talking about *Signora* Tedesco, you're right."

Lipsky laughed a mean laugh. "I can't believe you're trying to keep me from her! If she were in any way a suspect you'd have never allowed yourself to grow fond of her."

"Now I know you're drunk."

"Well, you're a little over the top yourself. And aren't you *fond* of Annie Tedesco?"

With a controlled reach of the hand, Bora moved the empty bottle away from himself. "I'll break your neck if you don't stay away from her."

"Well! I broke it already. And besides, the regulations won't allow it." But Lipsky was not so intoxicated that he missed the genuine hostility in Bora's words. He straightened on his stool with exaggerated gravity. "As we're civilized men …"

"This late in the war, neither of us is particularly civilized."

"Damn it all," Lipsky mumbled in sodden agreement. The scar on his face, now that drinking had relaxed his muscle control, caused his left cheek to droop a little. He buried his head in a shrug. "Very well, then: Signora Tedesco does not care for me." He grinned, glancing at Bora's hard-set face. "I suppose that's what you wanted to hear. I flew all the way from Munich to find out this afternoon. And what would it be to you if she did? As Peter said, you want it your own way, when, after all, neither of us is looking for more than a …"

"Don't you dare say the word, you self-important paper-monger." Bora took a deep breath, lest he shout at his colleague in front of the Italian bartender. "You haven't the faintest idea of what I'm looking for."

11

No power, no hot water. From the open window a grey, chalky line drew the boundary between Monte Baldo and the sky, and you couldn't tell at this hour that a lake lay in between. But Bora felt as if he could smell water, stubble fires in the fields and the earthy odour of leaves rotting in the drainpipes. Braces dangling from his waist, he put down the razor and went to answer the phone, blotting his half-shaven face. Passaggeri's rough voice left him no time to wonder what the matter was.

"... If there weren't something I want you to see, Colonel, I wouldn't be calling so early. It's on the left-hand side of the street, coming from the Metropoli. And be quick about it."

Through the receiver, the policeman's voice was a hook pulling him into everyday reality. The Venus, at the foot of his bed, looked his way and coyly rested her hand between her sweet thighs. *The hotel maid swore she never touched the frame in my absence. Who did, then, the other day?* Bora felt his chin with his bandaged fingers. *My days are hard enough,* he wanted to say, *they are counted. I must try to avoid my own death, not solve those of others.*

"The time to finish shaving," he told Passaggeri. But then he sat on the bed. Another killing, another woman killed. What the devil ... He'd finish shaving later. With his eyes closed, he fastened the buttons of his tunic and clasped his collar. Getting ready was automatic and quick, regardless whether he felt energetic or was carried by sheer momentum; soon he was out of his room, and, before leaving the hotel, two steps at a time, he stole upstairs to see whether Lipsky's boots were outside his door, waiting for a shine.

When he parked by the kerb at the place indicated, there was no sign of Passaggeri, no police car. Bora knocked on the door in vain. Only then did Passaggeri emerge from the twilight in a crumpled trench coat, hatless and with his hair up like a wolfhound. "You told me it was on the left side coming from the hotel," said Bora irritably. "Did you want to check whether I *accidentally* went to the house where she was killed, despite your instructions?"

"Sorry, Colonel. I have to be impartial in these things."

"As if I couldn't think of better things to do with a woman," Bora grumbled to himself in German.

The house across the street sat on a diminutive fenced garden. There wasn't enough light to see out of doors, much less past the entrance. Passaggeri said, "It's in the corridor back there. Watch your step: here's an electric torch."

Bora stumbled on a footstool as he went. No other noises followed, and the only sign of his having found the body was, "Oh, Christ."

Passaggeri found him holding the torch close to his chest, so that the glare reached the ceiling. He had stepped into a puddle of clotted blood, but it was a low ceiling, and blood spattered it, too.

"See, Colonel, if her wrists weren't slit, I'd have said it was the same hand that killed the six girls back in twenty-three." The inspector stayed a few steps away, smoking. "It's the smell that still gets me about these things. It helps if I smoke."

Bora returned the beam to the body crumpled at his feet: hair–skin–wounds–eyes–blood–hair. Teeth showing white. He followed the trail of blood in the narrow corridor up the walls where it drew blotches and long chains of drops. "Who is she?"

"Judging by the stuff around, a higher-grade seamstress. The name is Miriam Romanò; we're looking into her background."

"Is she rigid?"

"Totally. The body is at room temperature. She'd have screamed to the high heavens, had the first blow not cut her throat … Well, maybe after the cutting of her wrists. Not that screaming would have done her much good. You saw the house stands alone."

Bending over, Bora took a closer look at the dead woman's face.

"Pretty, wasn't she?" Passaggeri forestalled his comment. "I noticed it too. I brought along the Conforti dossier, but her portrait is not there. Looks as if she tried to get away and was done in halfway to the front door. Nothing under the night robe. Note that she's wearing only one slipper. The other is in the bedroom, where she was attacked. Has been dead between ten and twelve hours."

By the way he kept him busy listening, the policeman might have thought him unnerved and in need of distraction. The truth was that Bora had long ago humbly confronted his horror before death. Now only grief remained, or rather a sad sense of outrage. "What was the detail you wanted me to see?"

"It's in the bedroom."

Seeping under the doors from the corridor, blood had run into the bathroom and the parlour, leaving black spiders on the tiles. Bora's light swept steadily around as he sought the bedroom.

"Well, this *is* a German shirt," he admitted, once there. "Not my size, if that's what you're thinking. And it's air force, not army." He brought the cloth to his face. "But it's been laundered," he said, adding, "so a German officer could simply have brought his shirt here to have another one made." *The fact that Lipsky didn't leave his boots outside the hotel room doesn't mean he could not have gone out.*

"She was a ladies' seamstress."

Last night Lipsky was too drunk to take them off, thought Bora. "The weapon?"

Passaggeri shook his head. "Razor-sharp, double cutting edge, wielded with enough strength to cut through bone. Her arm all but came off. The killer waded in blood and wiped his feet on the parlour rug before going out. No fingerprints so far."

Electric power returned. Suddenly the scene seemed acceptable, nearly banal in its dreadfulness. The men breathed more easily in the plain sight of it. Squashing his cigarette butt on the bloodstained wall, Passaggeri took in Bora's weariness without comment.

"We were alerted by a customer who came for a fitting yesterday afternoon. She knocked, received no answer, but, listening through the door, she heard the radio on. You know how it is: at first, she thought she'd come on the wrong day. She returned home, checked her calendar and phoned Romanò. No use. Since it was the second-last fitting for her wedding dress, the customer wouldn't give up. To cut a long story short, she compared notes with friends who'd also mysteriously missed their Tuesday appointments, went from snit to worry and called us last night. After discovering the crime, we spent the night working on it, but you saw the body pretty much as we found it."

"What did the physician say?"

"That judging from the scar tissue she'd tried to cut her wrists in the past. This wrist-slitting, however, is a ruse, or at any rate somebody *helped* her to commit suicide – in excess of what she wanted." A notebook emerged from Passaggeri's pocket. "Thus far we know that she was married. Her husband became a prisoner of war in Germany after the Armistice. According to the customer we spoke to, there had been no news from him for a long time, although Romanò seemed frightened of him. A jealous bastard, it seems. She didn't speak of him fondly."

"Could he have re-entered Italy with one of the units we remustered?"

"We'll see. Trouble is, the evidence links this to the other two murders. Only, here there was no time to go through the routine of taking all the clothes off, as she apparently resisted." Flipping a page of his notebook, Passaggeri stifled a yawn, a flaring of nostrils on his shaggy face. "Guess what radio station she had on, when we broke in?"

"The *Radiosender*?"

"Precisely. Besides, there's a diploma on the parlour wall from what seems to be a professional school in Germany: you'll be able to confirm it. Romanò possibly spoke or understood German. Did she know Lieutenant Mack, or the army surgeon? We'll find out. The physician, who is the same that was called in for the second post-mortem, doubts a surgeon would be so sloppy. Our signor Pozzi was not at home when I sent a man to check at ten o'clock last night; his car was gone as well. His relative Vittori knows nothing of a scheduled overnight business trip. No trace of Pozzi yet." The pencilled notebook waved from side to side like a fan. "Colonel, it's no mystery that you're overseeing the inquiry into the stolen painting. Am I to assume, as Vismara suspected, that you see a connection between the theft and the murders? If so, tell me."

Bora saw no point in lying. "I don't even know who stole the painting. I thought of a connection, but why should there be one, and *how*?" He had suddenly had enough of the scene. "Do you mind if I open a window?"

"We can do better. Let's go to my car. I have a flask of hot coffee in the front seat. What time must you be at work?"

This being the morning Bora would travel to Riva to confront the wounded partisan, he said he had some leeway. He'd need the rest of the day to prepare emotionally for the four o'clock meeting with Mengs. Anyhow, no one would miss his presence: Graziani was incommunicado since Denzo's funeral, and, as for Sohl, he'd telephoned from Meran to say he'd stay there until the 22nd. De Rosa seemed to have fallen off the face of the earth.

Outside, the clean chill of the rainy dawn was welcome. Coffee had seldom felt as comforting as did the bitter, mediocre brew in Passaggeri's thermos. Bora drank quickly and was grateful for another serving.

The policeman was flattered. "No sugar, half coffee and half whatever else, but strong enough to do its job. Well, Colonel, that's the way I see it. As with the others, the victim knew and let the killer in. But you don't open the door while you cut your wrists, do you? Romanò lived alone and had some troubles. Unlike the other two, however, she was reasonably well off; her customer brags that she sewed gowns for several wives and girlfriends of the regime. Even for Emmy Göring. As in the other cases, there was no rape, and no intercourse before the attack."

"Are you sure the killer is a man?"

"No." Passaggeri savoured his coffee. "Nothing in these three deaths necessarily excludes a female culprit. The blade used here was so sharp, it'd cut through steel. But I do think it was a man, all the same."

"His cuffs, his trousers … they must have been drenched in blood."

"We know he washed his hands in the kitchen sink. Although he wiped his shoes, he tracked some blood to the front door, and rain washed out the rest."

Bora finished the second capful of coffee. He felt an unwarranted sense of security, sitting there. Caffeine was beginning to enter his bloodstream, and energy came with it. "I want you to know that I do not discount the possibility that the culprit may be German."

"Whoever he is, in a town this size, it's a matter of time before we find him. Keeping him from killing again is the challenge." Passaggeri had been drinking from an old teacup, which he now put away. "See what you can do about Lieutenant Mack's and the army surgeon's alibis last night, Colonel. My red-haired felon in Gardone told a credible story, but I've kept him on the hook. One thing is certain: there will be no squashing the news with propaganda. Women will be double-latching their doors at night."

At the first light of day, on the dashboard of the car, a magnetic medal showed Saint Christopher wading the river with the Christ Child on his shoulder. Bora stared at it. *If we could only be borne so safely across life.*

Back at the hotel, Bora used toilet paper to wipe blood from thet soles of his boots, filled the sink with soapy water and finished shaving. An army truck would soon stop by and take him to Riva, so he simply waited, updating his diary.

Ten minutes later, the phone rang. "Any relevant news?" Bora asked, surprised to hear Passaggeri's voice.

"You be the judge. Miriam Romanò was Anna Maria Tedesco's personal seamstress. Colonel? I thought the line had fallen. Yes, Romanò has been sewing gowns for Pozzi's daughter since returning from Germany seven years ago. Pozzi often gave her rides to and from Signora Tedesco's. He's still gone, but I have men waiting for him at his home."

The knock on the door, and an orderly's voice informing him that the army truck was idling below, forced Bora to terminate the call. He left Salò in a tense mood after Passaggeri's words, unwilling to elaborate on them for now.

*

Borghese's men, armed with pistols, Beretta machine guns and fixed bayonets, stood at the border with the Reich, north of Gargnano, inches away from scuffling with the German guards. When Bora left the truck to enquire, their lieutenant came up to him in a passion, asking him to intervene and let his men through.

"It's policy," Bora said. "No Republican troops are allowed beyond the border. There's nothing I can do."

"But you must let us through, Colonel! Xavier led a commando raid against the hospital and freed our prisoner!"

There were moments when, to Bora, it seemed he was chasing objects wildly rolling away and, no matter how he kept at it, he would fail to grasp any of them. He radioed from the border for details.

"The volume of fire was absolutely disproportionate to the goal of the rescue," the post commander explained. "It was so sudden. Why, it was genial, in its own way! They brought in a fainted girl in a civilian car, and in the confusion they muscled their way in."

Bora heard the story with a growing sense of defeat, because if – as Borghese described to him – the wounded partisan was none other than the moon-faced youngster he'd seen in the mountains, he must be Xavier's brother. And he'd risked everything, coming into the wolf's den – not to save him, as a violent removal after surgery could finish him off, but to make damn sure he would not talk.

There was a smell of explosive in front of the hospital. The door to the emergency room had been blasted open. Everything seemed deadly still until Bora entered. Inside, medics hastened with stretchers, a babel of voices flew from the wards as the nurses' anxious small faces looked out or held back patients who crowded to see what had happened. A path of blood led Bora upstairs, where the shooting had been vicious and the walls were marred by the zigzags of machine-gun fire. A glass door gaped, shattered. White-clad orderlies went to and fro, and there was crying in a back room. No one stopped him or asked questions. Bora straddled an overturned metal cart to enter the prisoner's room, the odd eye of the storm. There, nothing seemed to have been touched. The empty bed was relatively undisturbed, medicines stood in a row on a side table. Voices from the corridor came to the room like pieces of overheard arguments, none of them relevant.

A physician addressed him from the door, saying something apologetic. Bora did not turn to reply. Only when familiar, coarse voices alerted him that German soldiers were climbing the stairs did he return to reality. An army sergeant snapped to attention on the threshold.

"It's the damnedest thing, Herr Oberst. I don't know how it happened."

SALÒ

By ten o'clock, Bora allowed into his office a rabid De Rosa, who'd come with a couple of toughs in tow to vomit injuries against Borghese in reference to Denzo's death. "You have to intervene, Colonel von Bora, for your good name as well as mine. After you and I risked life and limb for that traitorous asshole!" Livid with rancour, he hammered his fist on Bora's desk. "He has the gall to accuse me in front of Graziani, actually accusing *me*. But I have Il Duce on my side, he'll see!"

Bora had reached his own conclusions well before Borghese whispered his suspicions into his ear at Denzo's funeral. Bitterly, he watched De Rosa's performance. "As if I could ..." the captain spluttered in a strangled voice. "As if could ..."

"I think you *did*." Bora echoed him in German, so that the lumbering toughs would not understand.

De Rosa swelled up and shrank in a matter of seconds, the strangest mutation in a man's countenance. That he believed himself to be in the right, there could be no doubt; Bora's reply must have struck him as incomprehensible. "But then ..." he protested flatly, almost without interest.

"Do not worry. I won't take this any further, with Graziani or anyone else. But from now on, I do not want you at my side for any official or private business ever again."

The unpleasantness of the meeting affected him afterwards. In his inconsiderate fanaticism, De Rosa had been more loyal than Denzo. Having to uphold the primary rule that a soldier will not murder another, Bora tasted the sorrow of disintegrating rules, a chaos in which all of them walked among ruins, and De Rosa was not the guiltiest.

Passaggeri's gruff voice, when he telephoned after lunch, took him back to the sight of the small heap of broken flesh lying in her blood. It seemed like centuries, a remote past.

"Pozzi showed up as fresh as a rose at eleven. Was in Milan, he said, on urgent business. What business it was, he's not telling. Resisted having his automobile searched, called two lawyers and the minister of justice, made a general fuss, and we had to let him go. No blood on him or his clothes, but, as he owns a pied-à-terre in the city, he could have changed there. We're following through in that direction as well ..." – Passaggeri yelled away from the phone, "*I'm not here!*" – "We'll question Signora Tedesco next. After seven years of fittings, she must have got to know her seamstress better than most. As for Vittori, the brother-in-law, he called at the *questura* of his own accord to say that he met the deceased at his niece's home. Not only that: Romanò was trying to talk him into helping her get papers for her husband to escape to Switzerland."

"From *Germany?*"

"No, Colonel. From the great void where shirkers and deserters fell after the Armistice. He made it to the lake and is hiding somewhere around here."

MADERNO, 4:58 P.M.

Hearing someone entering the building, Mengs peered out of his office. At once, he sat down at his desk, and, after Bora entered, he invited him to sit.

"I'm glad you could make it," he said, as if Bora had a choice.

"Duty bound," Bora replied in the same tone. But he kept himself from looking directly at the paperwork on Mengs's desk.

"Please," said Mengs, motioning lazily with his right hand to the drawer, before extracting and ceremoniously handing back Bora's P38 across the desk.

"Thank you." Without checking the clip, Bora held it on his knee. Mengs suspected that he was carrying another pistol and had no room in the holster.

"The reason for our unorthodox request is the assassination of a Gestapo informant in Rome back at the end of May. Like other German personnel, you were on the scene. You may recall that we requested to inspect the weapons of all those who were present; somehow we didn't get to yours." Bora only nodded his head. "It turned out that the informant in question was a double agent. You mentioned this fact at the time. May I ask how you knew?"

"I found out later, from a leaflet. As the Gestapo did, I believe."

Mengs smiled. He shifted a cough drop from one side of his tongue to the other. "True. She was killed by a 9-mm bullet from a Walther P38, 1943 Model."

"Not this one, I presume." Bora replaced his gun in the holster.

"No, Colonel von Bora: not that one. Have you ever seen a picture of the informant?" Without waiting for Bora's reply, Mengs set a photograph before him. "A vital list of Jewish undesirables was taken from this person at the time of the killing."

"I saw one of your men searching the body. Are you sure there was a list?"

"Yes. It's puzzling, too, since you were the first to reach the body." Mengs swallowed his cough drop, visibly relaxing when Bora latched the holster. In a muted, artificial tone, as if speaking through a cardboard tube, he continued, "You're a cultivated man, Colonel. Your options in life were hundredfold. Why did you choose the professional army?"

"It is a strange question to ask in the sixth year of war. The army is a family tradition."

"Your father was what they call a 'great musician', was he not?"

"My grandfather, as you know, was a field marshal. We have many soldiers in the Bora family."

"And your mother's?"

Bora took what he deemed a little too deep a breath and exhaled it slowly. "And my mother's."

"The British Army, that is."

"Some British, some German. I have plenty of cousins."

Mengs looked up with a forced smile. "It must be nice, being born to the international set. You've travelled widely. Even to America in '38, on a visit to West Point. Salò must be confining."

"Not really." It was a plain answer, but the question deserved nothing better.

"What a healthy attitude." Mengs stood, and Bora stood with him. "Well, that is all, Colonel. As you see, it was quick and easy." Coming around the desk, Mengs escorted him to the door. "And you're Catholic," he added indulgently on the threshold. "You often acted as liaison with the Vatican in

Rome. Were you aware that one of your acquaintances, a former teacher of yours, in fact, had close ties with Stauffenberg's band of traitors?"

Bora's hesitation was short-lived. "You must refer to Cardinal Hohmann."

"The one who was killed in bed by a whore. Precisely." Mengs gave his hand for Bora to shake. "So, you practise your religion? You believe all that Rome teaches?"

"I ought to, if I don't."

"A philosophy major? Come, you don't mean that. What about the commandment 'thou shalt not kill'?"

"There are exceptions to that commandment. The principle of double effect, indirect voluntary ill effect, not to mention other issues."

Mengs rested his back on the jamb of the door. "In simple words, sometimes it's all right to commit murder."

"It depends on the motive."

"The motive must be more relevant than the person you kill, that is."

"I could suggest excellent theological writings on the subject, beginning with Aquinas."

"Oh, no. I'll stay ignorant as I am. Philosophy is not my game." Mengs backed into his office, smacking his lips. "Have a good evening, Colonel von Bora."

5:25 P.M.

Skilfully, Bora drove off the country lane and parked in the high yellow grass. There was a breeze, but rain had fallen sparsely here, and it was not cold. He left the car, and it was a minute or two before he began to *feel* himself walking. He emerged from the numbness of the blow, after expecting it long enough to forget it had come. Waiting made things worse. Razor-like, it breached the flesh but did not go in.

It was to tie up again what inner strings had come undone that Bora needed to walk off and make sense of where he was, how he was, what came next. He recalled other walks, years and years earlier, a green solitude, a naive sense that the world was tameable and that it only took courage to face it. All had changed since then, but he hadn't. Out of numbness came a lucid, unresigned sobriety. This might be the last time he would feel Death so kindly near.

Behind Bora, the trees were squat and naked like chicken claws. He walked along a ditch that meandered in a slack curve, before turning back in the rain that began to fall.

SALÒ, ALBERGO METROPOLI, THURSDAY, 23 NOVEMBER 1944, 0:59 A.M.

Bora was still up. He'd been reading Hölderlin, reviewing Conforti's letters, his notes about the Venus and the murders; he had called Annie three times before she answered at half-past nine. She was unwell, she said, did not wish to converse, and, please, would he not call again. Lipsky on the other hand had sought him "everywhere". A note of his left with the concierge read: *We have to talk. I had to leave urgently. What about meeting in Verona tomorrow, at 3:00 p.m.? Habermehl wants to see you too. Leave me a message at his number if you can't come. Otherwise, I'll wait for you at his flat.*

Darker than ever, the wooded landscape behind the Venus exalted her at the foot of his bed. Bora refused to look at it, because tonight the Venus would make him restless, just as Annie had taken away his peace of mind. There were other things, besides. Immense *other things*. He blamed himself for letting Mengs's eyes – the eyes of a dead animal – keep him from closing his eyes to rest.

SALÒ, 12:03 P.M.

It was lukewarm and sunny at noon. Usually, Bora would lunch at the mess hall closest to wherever he worked, but today he wore his greatcoat and went for a walk along the lake. He had last met his wife at the railway station in Rome on such a day, the very same day she told him she no longer wanted him. It was strange how he had felt no mortification at first, no offence, but astonishing pain, as when in the autumn of 1943 he'd looked at his bloody arm and the hand was gone, and gore poured black from it instead.

Those were the times of his fragility, when he had felt paper-thin and vulnerable, even beyond breakability: something that could be shredded and thrown away. In both cases, he had held onto that resilient sliver of determination and come through. But there was always something new, filing away at the laborious rebuilding of strength. Bora kicked pebbles as he went. He reached the edge of the water, where pines stood and there were shrubs and dainty bushes and gravelled paths.

On an impulse, he looked over the raised collar of his coat, seeing no one. The wind brought the scent of citrus fruit and evergreens. The street and the pavement were empty. Yet he felt life energy quickening his veins and muscles from a state of alertness to elation, a life upon life of his flesh. He could tell she was nearby before he saw her, before he recognized the blaze of her red coat.

Annie strolled in the park, unaware or ignoring him, except that Bora would not be overlooked or ignored today. He crossed the paved grounds towards her and Annie was alarmed. Surprise made her less unattainable, slow to react.

"If you don't let me, I'll die," he heard himself say when she pulled back, arching her neck without stepping away, caught in the embrace and too weak to free herself.

And of all the women he had kissed, including his wife, Annie was the hungriest and the most reluctant; Bora felt he was breaking through her defences and urging her through the sweet red slit of her mouth, unsealing it with his tongue until she let him in. A great wave of blood hurt him more than it gave pleasure; it was like a roar coursing through him. And while by this time Benedikta would have offered him a little well of moisture with tongue retracted, waiting to bite back, Annie's tongue came to meet his and for a moment they vied between them, running against each other's clean edge for supremacy.

Bora was not accustomed to giving way. He forgot where he was and whether people were watching. He savoured her mouth, holding with his right hand the fleecy nape of her neck until it yielded to him.

Vittori and his brother-in-law were driving from Pozzi's lawyer in Desenzano, bound for the Metropoli for lunch. Compelled to supervise the installation of a jersey machine at Roè, Vittori had recompensed himself buying a twenty-foot spruce. At a snail's pace, they emerged from behind a column of German trucks, and Vittori broke the silence he had kept so far. "Isn't that Annie?" He nodded towards the lakefront.

Pozzi did not look away from the wheel. "So what?"

"Bora is with her."

"Well, didn't you say he could be useful? Let them talk."

"That's not what they're doing, but so be it."

Finally, Pozzi glanced over. He braked hard, stalling the car. "What the ... By God, can't he wait to do it indoors?"

"Women like aggressive men," Vittori sneered back. "You ought to know that."

VERONA, 3:04 P.M.

Habermehl was as sober as Bora had ever seen him. His packed bags were one more sign of the German withdrawal from Italy. The drinks cabinet, once the family altar, stood open and empty. Lipsky rose from the chair the moment Bora entered the room, and, because their handshake was cordial, he did not expect to hear, "Were you in your hotel room last night, Major?"

"It is really no business of yours. I wasn't with anyone you know."

Habermehl made an appeasing gesture of the open hands. "Boys," he addressed them with the old army endearment, "no arguing over ladies."

"There was another woman killed in Salò last night," Bora said.

"And you're looking at *me*?" said Lipsky. "Colonel, you're off your head. Maybe you're killing them yourself in your sleep."

"Honestly, Martin!" Habermehl intervened. "Sit down and listen to what Klaus-Etzel has to say."

Bora sat across from Lipsky. Three hours after Annie Tedesco walked off from their kiss, he was still muddled. Leaning back, ostensibly resisting him, her hips had met his, and the step where she stood – compensating for the difference in height between them – made that closeness simply perfect. He'd grown too aroused to follow her as she hurried off on her red heels. He wondered now if Lipsky could read it in his face.

For once, the flyer was not thinking of women. "Our common friend, here, tells me you've been making enquiries about me." (Bora looked stormily at Habermehl, who renewed his peace-making gesture.) "Let's be clear: I did acquire several artworks for the family firm while in Italy. This not being a good time to ship fragile items to the Fatherland, I deposited them in Meran, care of the Kreditanhalt. The Venus is not one of those fragile items. The Jew's collection, I relieved on the Reich Marshal's behalf, and, whether you like it or not, it was perfectly legal. I like bedding women, but I already told you that Frau Sohl is not one of them. If you are thinking, as I believe you are, that she is somehow involved, it isn't with me that she's operating. I suspected General Sohl's connivance from the start, and I'm convinced she's letting Wolff under her skirts to protect her husband's dealings. In fact, the Sohls, who should be squabbling over me, are spending time together in Meran even as we speak."

"You haven't made me come to hear you rehash your story."

Sitting straight-backed, Lipsky reclined his head against the back of the armchair. "No. I'm offering to trace the Venus in Meran, if that's where it is."

"And why would you do that?"

"For your brother's sake, you arrogant son of a bitch. And because if you do not watch yourself, Wolff will crush you. Or do you really think your disagreements with the SS in Russia went unnoticed? What's picturesque on the front line is plain dumb elsewhere."

For half a minute Bora sat brooding. Under no circumstance would he acquaint his colleagues with his summons by Mengs. Habermehl could not be trusted with confidentiality, and Lipsky didn't need to hear that he was right. "The lieutenant general and Frau Sohl are staying at her parents' house, on Pfarr Platz," he said. "How do you propose to trace the Venus?"

"Through an antique dealer in the Meran borough of Obermais, and my bank there, the Kreditanhalt. I am *friends* with the director's wife." With a wink, Lipsky rose again from the armchair. "Well, gentlemen, my Junkers takes off for Venice soon. I know you two have family matters to discuss." When Bora walked him to the door to thank him, the flyer smirked. "You're welcome," he whispered. "Just let me know how much fun it is fucking Turandot."

SALÒ, 5:27 P.M.

The mark of Passaggeri's coming was a notebook page, folded neatly and stuck between the jamb and the door of Bora's office. In cramped characters, with tall capital letters, the message informed him that *il nostro tenente* – clearly Lieutenant Mack – had on 12 October answered an advertisement concerning a "privately owned, concert quality upright piano" and, for that reason, had gone with a colleague from the *Radiosender* to view the instrument at Bianca Spagnoli's place. He had paid a deposit on it, agreeing to complete payment within a month, at which time the owner had two weeks' time to relinquish the piano. As the instrument had never been delivered, he had shown up at the *questura*, asking that Italian authorities force the seller to return his money. *When I told him that Bianca Spagnoli died suddenly more than a month ago*, Passaggeri continued, *he demanded that the piano be turned over to him. Either he's devilishly clever, Colonel, or he has nothing to do with this – and probably the other murders, too.*

Bora pocketed the note. "Hager," he told the orderly as he came down the stairs, "I'm off to Gardone for a medical check-up. Should the general call, take a message and reach me at this number."

"*Jawohl, Herr Oberst.*" Hager opened the door for him. "But I doubt the general will be calling. He is travelling to Venice with Frau Sohl."

Reiner, the young surgeon, inspected Bora's fingers. "Zachariae himself sewed them up? You must have friends in high places to get Il Duce's physician to look after you."

"It was just an accident."

"Where have you been lately? We had some film showings at the Spielcasino, including a couple of juicy American pictures." Despite his bloody smock, Reiner sounded like any empty-headed German officer, waiting for the end of the war. "Tuesday night we had a live show, and, as master of ceremonies, I bathed in beauty from six in the evening to three in the morning. You should have been there!"

Bora was not ready to see another possible suspect about to disappear. "You don't mean that you were at the Spielcasino for nine hours?" he observed with a grin.

"Just ask anyone in the ward. Tonight we have something classy planned, and if I find someone to take my place in surgery ... Do come."

"Thank you. Speaking of women, have you heard ..."

"... of the women killed? Who hasn't? I knew one of them, the pretty blonde who came with the pint-sized Fascist. Not in the biblical sense, you understand, but I did know her, and if she hadn't died, I'd have had time to inspect every inch of her, the poor thing. You must have met her too?"

Bora said he didn't remember. "I can't make it tonight. Another time, maybe. Where do I go for X-rays?"

He stopped by the *questura* on his return from Gardone. Having seen from the window Bora carefully locking his car, Passaggeri quipped that one exploded automobile was all the Salò police would countenance on its doorstep.

"I appreciate it," Bora smiled back. His pleasantness did not fool Passaggeri, who read enormous tension behind it. But as it was neither his affair nor his inclination to gauge the emotional health of German officers, he merely took note of it.

Within minutes, they exchanged updates on Mack, the surgeon, and what else the *commissario* had learned. "I move fast when I move," he said, "when they let me move. Signora Tedesco was shocked to hear of Romanò's death. She added that she is not surprised that Vittori was asked to help the seamstress with paperwork for her husband, who, although in hiding, is still imposing on her. The problem is: *where* is he? Does he come to town? Is he here already?" Passaggeri lifted his thick forefinger to stress the importance of his next words. "There is also the story of Pozzi's pied-à-terre. We found blood in the toilet bowl. No results from the analysis yet, and we have kept mum with all involved. We also discovered that he illegally carries a pistol, which we have confiscated. He exploded and claimed you 'snitched' – his words – on him. Did you know he carried a pistol, Colonel?"

"I did."

MESPILAI, 7:31 P.M.

Annie stayed at her father's house until late. At the foot of the hill, where Pozzi braked to let her out, she glimpsed in the dusk the tail-lights of a car parked in front of her gate. Alone as she was, she started homeward without hesitation, and, even before recognizing the vehicle, she read the letters "WH" on the plate. Bora was standing next to it.

"I leave in the morning and don't feel like entertaining tonight, Colonel."

"I'm not here to be entertained, Signora. I have something to deliver and have no intention of staying after I do so."

It was an odd reversal of roles since the morning she'd come to his office. But their feelings had altered, grown strained. Beyond his polite explanation, Bora did not seem disposed to apologize for the kiss any more than Annie was to recriminate. "All right. Can you give it to me here?"

"No."

In the glimmer of headlights, she handed him the keys to the gate, which Bora opened. "I have two domestics staying overnight. Uncle imposed them on me. They will take whatever it is from your car."

Bora shook his head. "It is the Venus that hung in Conforti's flat. I will bring her in myself."

"The copy? Why? I thought that, for lack of the original, you were in love with her."

"It would surprise you how I can do without."

Soon, the wrapped painting stood against the wall of the room where wood, glass, leather and heavy cloth, corners rounded and smooth accepted the gift in their orderly midst.

"Why did you bring her here?"

Bora did not answer. How could he say that he'd begun to rid himself of things and that, if it was true that most men could not contemplate the original, the Venus transcended all imitations? He wished Annie good night and started to leave. Her voice followed him into the vestibule. "You did not call."

"I did call. You did not answer."

"You should have insisted. I don't always answer the phone."

"I don't always call someone three times." Cut out of the dark, his figure stood square-shouldered, tense, feigning assurance but not so much that he'd look at her. He was shamelessly hoping she would ask him to stay. Annie hugged her elbows, looking at the night behind him rather than at him. "You should ask," she said.

Bora left.

12

Like a noose at the end of the year, December slipped around them all. Bora spent the last week of November in the mountains, with a mixed force of German and Italian troops. Before going into the field, he spent a day contacting former intelligence colleagues wherever he knew them to be in the area, a pilgrimage meant to avoid the use of telephone lines. He had a physical need to get out and be bruised again, grow tired, stop thinking about complications. He'd rather be shot at by Xavier's men, while De Rosa and the militia scouted the mountains on their own, looking for their hideouts.

Shooting echoed in Salò and Gargnano, from Riva and even Torri across the lake. At night, flares and reflectors yellowed the western sky, where the heights rose from the dark and faded again. In the valleys, mortar fire hammered with a dull staccato. Bora followed reports of a desperately wounded man, hauled on improvised stretchers from one hideout to another. Surely, Xavier's brother was slowing down the group and sooner or later they would abandon him somewhere. Bora expected it, and so it was, hours before the end of the operation. By the time they caught up with him, in a hovel reeking of death, gangrene had devoured the moon-faced youth. German medics came out, shaking their heads.

And if the fishnet technique of containment and liquidation won out, Xavier himself and a couple of companions had slipped through the fingers of their pursuers. Bora took it badly, given the success achieved otherwise. He supervised the transport of the dying partisan along goat trails made impassable by squalls of icy snow. In sight of the valley, he was so close to the end that they stopped in a clearing to let him die. Not one to gloat over death, Bora surprised Johannesquade by saying, "Take care that this man's photograph be printed and widely circulated."

Upon his return on 1 December, in a sickening cold, Bora discovered that the Liguria Army Group command had moved to Vidigulfo near Pavia and that Graziani now commuted there. So, he went directly to the residence. Although it was only ten o'clock in the evening, Sohl had retired, and the heat from the fireplace had abated. On his desk, telephone messages piled up; from one of those that Passaggeri had left, he evinced that Annie was back from her trip. As for Lipsky, he had called the previous day, from a private number; this was the sole call he returned.

Once in the hotel, troubled by his desire to see Annie, and the imprudence of doing it, he told himself that he could not stand the idea of lying alone with his thoughts. Much as he cherished solitude, he feared the lowering of tension. His mother's and stepfather's letters, entrusted to Habermehl, written separately, read over and again in the past days, sickened him with worry. "Against all hope, your mother Nina expects you home soon," Habermehl told him. "Your grandfather is under surveillance. I tried to hearten her. But, Martin …"

Seated on the bed, Bora unbuckled his holster, laid the P38 on his bed table. For years, he had kept loaded guns at his bedside. For years, every rudimentary thought had implied a moral choice. Now there was nothing but waiting, sifting through the guilt of things not said, not done, as if the sum total of his sins were a great number of omissions.

When the telephone rang two hours later, still awake, he reached for it without haste. It would be bad news, one way or another.

But of all people, it was Annie Tedesco. Her voice was urgent, low. The first words she whispered made no sense. Bora listened to her voice coming through like a warm liquid pouring in, melting whatever was rigid and breakable inside.

"Thank God you're back. I'm frightened. There was noise at my window, and someone is tampering with the lock. The neighbours' dogs are going mad ..." Bora overheard furious howling in the background. "I'm afraid someone is trying to get in."

Bora kept calm, to keep her calm. Weariness had completely left him. "Are all the windows locked? Good. Have you called the police?"

"Yes, but no one has come yet. Father isn't home, and Uncle isn't answering. I don't know who else to ask."

"Try your uncle again. I'll be there in a few minutes and ring four times."

There was still much barking in the yards nearby when Bora arrived. Only after hearing details from her, and wondering why she sounded less afraid, did he realize that Vittori was in the house.

"I came running as soon as she reached me at Giovanni's home, Colonel, but I'm glad she called you first. There's no one out there now that I can tell."

"How did you get here?"

"As I said, I'm staying nearby at Villa Malona; my heating system gave up. I was asleep and didn't reach the phone in time when she first called. Then, given what we're hearing in the news, I grew worried and called her to ask if she was all right. From Villa Malona, I cut across gardens and low retaining walls. It's much quicker that way." In an undertone, so that Annie would not hear, he added, "I picked up the sound of branches being disturbed when I entered the garden."

"Could it be an animal, a large dog?"

"I doubt it."

Bora looked Annie's way. "There was someone in the garden," he told her, careless of Vittori's unspoken disapproval. "It is best if you know and spend the rest of the night at your father's. I'll take a look at the windows and the lock before I go. Signor Vittori, will you join me?"

The garden wall was low, overgrown by vines. In the back, Vittori showed him that only a hedge separated the property from the others. Invisible in the dark, villas dotted the hillside, each at the centre of its own green belt. Together, the men inspected the medlar grove, the flowerbeds. The only visibly broken branches were at the north end of the garden, by the hedge. "But in my haste, I could have snapped some of these myself," Vittori admitted. Scratches on the shield of the lock were the sole evidence of tampering at the door, although the bedroom shutters had been badly scraped in an attempt to force the latch open.

"What do you make of it?" Vittori asked.

"It was a clumsy or brazen approach, nothing like the others."

"Are you *sure*? I am very worried."

"They would have cut the phone wires had they wanted to succeed."

Annie was pacing the vestibule when they entered. "Signora Tedesco," Bora said, "would you show me the window that was being forced when you phoned me?"

She led the way through the house and down a hallway to her bedroom.

"Yes, this corresponds to the one tampered with. Of course, he'd have had to break the glass had he made it through the shutter. Did you call from here?" Bora glanced at the bedside telephone.

"Yes."

The bed was wide – her wedding bed, he thought – and not slept in for the night. A heap of silky underwear lay on the rug, which he could not help noticing. Annie saw him stare at the floor. "There was warm water tonight," she explained. "I practised the cello and then took a bath." Bora looked away from the silk.

From the threshold Vittori said, "If you no longer need me, Annie, I'll be walking back. You're in good hands. Should you decide to come, I'm sure the colonel will be so good as to drive you over."

While Annie saw her uncle to the door, Bora stayed behind. The moist imprints of her feet on the floor and the carelessly thrown handful of silk, her bed: seeing them intoxicated him. Things around him were a haze of shapes. *I kissed her*, he thought, *and, by God, she kissed me back.* He thought he could recognize the taste of her kiss under the thin scent of bath oil, intimate and irresistible, the sweet fresh odour of married life he knew so well and felt he could not do without. The sight of the translucent handful spoke of her power to make him lovesick at the foot of her bed. The closing of the front door came to his ears as if from a distance, bringing him to, so that he walked out of the bedroom and went to retrieve his cap from a sideboard in the vestibule.

Annie's voice reached him from the room where she sat among her slick surfaces, hands in her lap. "I hope you will honour my wish not to inform the police."

"So, you did not call them."

"No. I was afraid, but after Father's experience, I didn't want them here." She lit a cigarette, which she abandoned after a first drag. "I followed your advice and called my uncle again, even though the poor man came over armed with a ridiculous walking stick. Fortunately, you came as well."

"I am better armed," Bora agreed tersely.

For the first time, he saw Annie without make-up. The whiteness of her face was like a frame to her dark, frowning eyes, and her mouth pouted nearly as red as when rouge layered it. Bound in her robe, she showed nothing but the shimmer of cloth, little shimmers as of water running down to her feet. Around her, the room sank into an undifferentiated haze, where shapes failed as when one leaves dangerous shores at night. The watery shimmers washed over her until she was shell-smooth, shiny, hard and safe. Bora trembled with an immense need to let himself go into her safety. He stepped forward. Annie's head twitched, like one who is jerked awake and frightened by the touch.

"Please take me to Father's."

She was not safe, even to herself. Her fear was obvious to him, like something excreted by a shell in self-defence, a thin ooze that would not protect her from men's hands. Like metal in his mouth, he tasted things not done out of pride, virtue or propriety, which he should glory in but instead regretted. He stepped back – a military step that brought him back into line. "Dress warmly. I'll take you to your father's and notify the police."

Later, his insights were scattered and awry. And because tonight Annie had seemed so cold, he was no closer to her for all his longing. He replayed in his mind what he could have done instead, and there was nothing. He could not – *could not* – take advantage of a frightened woman. The question was: *who* had frightened her? Why was her uncle so worried, as if he knew something more? In the morning, before work, he would inspect the lanes and passageways behind Annie's house, looking for clues. As was his habit, Bora, preparing for the night, reached for his briefcase, swung it on the bed, unlocked it and snapped it open.

All within him became still. Breathlessly, he stared at folders, letters and papers. *His diary.* It was impossible for his diary not to be there. Since returning from the mountains, the briefcase had been with him. He'd walked out of the office with it, and in the car the briefcase had lain in his lap. Overturned on the bed, the leather case spilled out his calendar, notebook, documents and papers. He should have felt the difference in weight but had not done. Like a blinding headache, anger was trying to rise and unsteady him at the worst possible time. Bora struggled to keep it down, to stuff his anger beneath his fear, which was the much more appropriate reaction. Every mistake he had committed had been born of overwrought distraction, especially in Rome. Tonight he had committed the worst. The most dangerous, and the worst, leaving his briefcase in the car while he was inside Annie's house.

SUNDAY, 3 DECEMBER 1944, 7:15 A.M.

Bora was on the telephone with Dollmann when Passaggeri arrived at the residence. This was the earliest the inspector, who had a cold and kept a handkerchief bunched against his nose, had been able to meet him. It did not surprise him that Bora looked weary, given the operation west of the lake; what puzzled him was his distracted welcome. Noticing a map of Leipzig on the desk, he inferred that Bora hailed from there; as fifty and more Allied bombers had been shot down during a raid over that city, he assumed the German was thinking of home.

"Should I close the door, Colonel?"

"Never mind."

Because Bora invited him to sit but asked no questions, Passaggeri blew his nose and began to speak. "I don't know if you heard the blast yesterday morning at around eleven. No? Well, someone had the bright idea of tossing a grenade through the window of Pozzi's brother-in-law while he listened to music in his conservatory. He's lucky he escaped with his life. A Brixia grenade, a *red devil*, a dime a dozen these days. The front part of the house is badly damaged. We're looking for tracks in the garden, but rain and all the gravel and dirt from planting make things difficult. Vittori spent the night at the hospital, and it'll be a miracle if he doesn't lose his hearing. Had he been by the gramophone at the time, we'd be picking up shreds of him. He repeats that he's 'very worried' about someone trying to harm his niece. Did you know that someone cut his phone lines on the night of the attempted break-in at Signora Tedesco's? She could reach him only because she called him at her father's."

The mention of Annie, the policeman noticed, seemed to shake Bora out of indifference, but he remained unresponsive.

"About the blood in Pozzi's pied-à-terre, it's another false lead. Female blood, all right, but the analyses say it's menstrual. And although Romanò looked younger than her years, she was past menopause." Judging by the thuds in a nearby room, someone was tossing wood into a fireplace. "When Vittori recuperates, I will grill him for details, as Romanò's husband-in-hiding could have a hand in the attack. Her customers reported how the seamstress feared he might discover some indiscretions on her part. And if she approached Vittori in the hope of securing papers, a jealous husband might have mistaken their involvement for a love affair. On the other hand, do you know where Pozzi claims to have been on the night of the break-in? At dinner with an untouchable and uncheckable politician."

Bora listened with arms folded, head low. When Passaggeri placed the photos of Vittori's blasted house on the desk, he stared at them in silence.

Maybe it's because they lost Belgium and the Saar, the policeman thought. "Minutes before the blast, Colonel, I called Vittori to inform him that we'd found his wallet. His main worry is that his niece has returned home and wants nobody to stay with her."

Reaching for one of the photos, Bora studied it close up, then tossed it back. "Very interesting."

Yet Pozzi and Vittori had made a point during their statements of telling the inspector that Bora showed a keen interest in Annie Tedesco. "I'm afraid he'll make her unhappy," Vittori had told him, to which Pozzi asked outright if there was a way to keep them apart.

PORTESE, 8 A.M.

The modest *pensione* on the promontory facing Salò looked grey in the misty morning, and an unlikely place for the finicky SS officer. Dollmann, however, sat drinking coffee by a cheerful little stove. He did not acknowledge Bora's presence until he came to sit before him. "Care for some black coffee?"

"No, thank you."

Dollmann acted as if this rendezvous had not been his idea. "What I have to say is soon disposed of." Fastidiously he folded his napkin first into a square and then a triangle. "Barring a miracle, we won't be seeing each other again. As of today, I re-enter the anonymity of my career and leave the burden of heroism to those who can bear it. It's for the best. I take my little hollow gourd of shame and begin my own pilgrimage."

Bora had expected similar words. He'd come to the meeting with little hope that Dollmann might have his diary, or at least let him know what had happened to it. It surprised him only that Dollmann had taken the risk of speaking. He said he understood. He did, in fact. After a sleepless night, he felt an irresponsible tipsiness, like a thinning of the blood after surfacing too quickly from deep water.

"Your request for reassignment has been a dead letter since last spring," Dollmann continued, "but at least they haven't thrown it away. Kesselring no longer opposes it, and it may yet go through."

Bora disbelieved this and said so. He watched Dollmann pensively stir the sugar in his coffee. "Will you support Major Lipsky in the last part of the investigation if I am prevented from it?"

"I couldn't if I wanted to, Bora. Find someone else. You knew that if it came to this I'd let you down completely: the shadow detaches itself from him who casts it." He smoothed his napkin. "I only have a small viaticum to give you: you should have left your diary in the safe at Soiano."

"Ah." Regardless of what insane irony Bora felt, his hope had taken a headlong plunge. "The safe that Plenipotentiary Wolff authorized his men to get open?"

"Don't be sarcastic." Dollmann resented the guilty need to get away from him. If Bora was afraid – and he had to be, unless he had deadened himself to his emotions – he let no sign of it transpire; he still clung to the habit of fastening civility and soft-spoken control over whatever went on inside. One of these days, Bora might lose control, but not now. "You have options, you know."

Bora looked at him calmly. "Except that I don't see them as such."

"Even though they're quick and honourable?"

"They're quick, not honourable."

"Pity." Dollmann wanted to end the conversation, because he understood Bora's motives and shared them, but not enough to stand up for them. "No one will help you," he blandly confessed. Bora's nearness troubled him. He looked away from those stern eyes; the smooth razor-scraped skin of Bora's handsome face unnerved him into wanting to confess something, something ... the unspeakable something else, as if Bora didn't know. "No one will help you," he repeated instead. Desire scooped him empty, and he was unable to admit even his emptiness to Bora.

"Well, Standartenführer, God will have to."

In his forced composure, Bora seemed still capable of pondering other things, unrelated to his own safety. He held before the SS man a card with a name written on it. "As things stand, then, you owe me at least some answers on this person." And while Dollmann, having read it, visibly considered whether he'd tell or not, Bora opened the stove door and threw the card inside.

The acceleration of events was a phenomenon Bora had witnessed on every collapsing front. Time contracted, then flew across the arc of a week; stimuli and information overlapped and came from all sides until one lost count. The lakeside had turned inwards, becoming a gigantic interior like Conforti's dark house; days resembled rooms, his duties were steps leading up or down, around blind corners. Occasionally he caught himself as if standing somewhere else, so that Russia and Spain, Rome and Cracow, his wife's bed and the emergency room had the power to claim him for a few disconnected seconds, taking him away from the present.

Attentive as he'd always been to light, weather, the minutiae of his surroundings, Bora found himself walking in a fog after meeting Dollmann. It dulled even the ever-present pain in his arm and leg. Only the Venus reached mercifully out to him from the dusk. *I need to understand; she will make me understand somehow.* The hints of a solution, hidden by a shroud dense enough to conceal the brink, had the Venus as its sole ghostly guide. She drifted in and out of sight to remind him he must not give up, because there was much more at play than art and wealth. Death and more death, she seemed to say. The duty of preventing more death.

At his return to the residence, he smelled cigar smoke and saw through the door that, having somehow replenished his stock of cheroots, Sohl was irritably puffing away while a workman crouched by the Moloch fireplace, examining it closely. "Ah, Colonel," the general called over. "See? So apparently solid, you'd never think it would crack."

"*Troppo fuoco*," the worker observed, gesturing to indicate an excessive blaze.

"Must get it fixed before the owners find out," Sohl muttered to Bora. "Well, Colonel, you've done us proud by cleaning up the irreducibles. Seems we haven't talked in weeks, eh?"

ABOVE SAN MARTINO, 3 DECEMBER 1944, 2:59 P.M.

In the afternoon (Bora had uselessly tried to reach Annie by phone), a radio message from Johannesquade, patrolling on Mount Spino, caused him to speed out of Salò. At the Fobbiola Pass, a young woman who made disconnected statements about Xavier had approached the Italian SS, asking to see a German officer. The captain sensed who she might be and detained her until Bora had decided what to do.

Bora drove to San Martino, where Johannesquade waited with the girl in a weather clear and frigid, limning every peak and tree branch. *The end of things and people,* he was thinking. *How familiar.* The spook that Xavier had been – bloodthirsty, mad, one of the many whom the Russian front had chewed and spewed out – had fissured like Sohl's fireplace and might have fallen into pieces into his hands. Having planned and anticipated this possibility, Bora was still nearly disappointed that broadcasting the death of the young partisan had succeeded. Not that he'd hoped for a final battle and blaze of glory between them … But yes, he *had*, after all, as if Xavier, who'd disdainfully given him away to be shot, deserved more than betrayal.

The girl had been crying. Restive, bony like a plucked bird, she had the face of misery and passion. *How could I forget that women can hate so much and act upon it?* Bora did not have the heart to ask her if she was the same who had pretended to faint during the raid at the Riva hospital and who had carried in her hands, as a warning, a severed human ear.

Johannesquade, who spoke no Italian, could tell by the earnestness of the exchange that Bora paid an intrigued attention to her. The girl made agitated, wide gestures towards the heights. Bora let her speak and then questioned her watchfully, leaning towards her. He nodded twice to what she answered. Next, he was spreading a map across the hood of the car.

When he learned of the conversation, the captain stood, staring. "Herr Oberst, were you serious when you gave her your word?"

"Of course."

"Even though you know who she is?"

"Oh, yes." Bora always carried cigarettes for his men; they were the last of his plundered Chesterfields. He proffered the pack to Johannesquade, who eagerly accepted a smoke. "I can be generous, if she leads me to Xavier. He is the one I want."

"You seem convinced she's not a decoy."

"I stake my experience on it. She lost her man because Xavier dragged him out of the hospital. She says Xavier himself is ill, as I suspected, and now I know how to get him. She goes free, and, when I capture him, I will not hang him."

Johannesquade took a long, ruminative drag. The small area Bora marked in red pencil pointed to a farmhouse halfway up

Mount Pracalvis. The mountain loomed before them, its foot already in shade, solemn and not appreciably different from other peaks at the close of day.

"I want all the men in place by sundown," Bora ordered. "We close in on him tonight."

Lipsky, who'd sneaked away from his Venice post at noon on Saturday, reached Bardolino after dark to meet Bora, as they had agreed by telephone. All he found was a private with a note from the colonel asking him to wait until morning. He assumed there was a military operation in course, although he had no way of knowing that Bora was at that time leading a patrol towards Xavier's isolated hideout.

Resolved to avoid familiar places and faces along the lake, Lipsky went inland to Affi, where he secured a room for the night.

BARDOLINO, MONDAY, 4 DECEMBER 1944, 7:39 A.M.

Bora struggled to keep his eyes open, but that was not why he had no desire to speak of the night raid on Mount Pracalvis. "Nothing to brag about," he told Lipsky, who seemed alert and pugnacious, in case the colonel wanted to quarrel. "When we barged in, he lay sick on a pallet, but was quicker than any of us. He pulled a sub-machine gun from under the blanket and shot himself with it. He waited until the beams of our torches were on him. It was ghastly. As the burst took his head off, one of my men passed out. First the tension, then *that*. We had to revive him, and he's at Gardone under medical care now. And Xavier must have known he was betrayed, because he'd already killed his two companions. My boys felt robbed of their victory."

"God almighty. And you?"

"Banality will have us all, sooner or later." Bora shrugged. "What do you have for me, Major?"

Aware that he'd been staring, Lipsky looked away. In Russia, towards the end, Bora's brother too had seemed under untenable pressure; but Bora had a harder shell and hid it better. "Confirmation that my would-be sweetheart, Frau Sohl, deposited a large suitcase, presumably of valuables, at the Meran Kreditanhalt, on the sixteenth of November."

"Really? Under her husband's or her maiden name?"

"Her maiden name, Grössner. But she withdrew the suitcase a week later, on the twenty-second."

"Hmm." Bora drained his coffee and rolled his aching neck. He kept from Lipsky that his old intelligence colleagues reported how the call to Conforti on 28 October had come from Meran. "Any chance you might check the Meran train depots, both at the central station and at Untermais?"

"Yes. But it will require a few days: I can't exactly be seen doing it myself."

"How many days?"

"I should be at work as it is … I don't know."

"*How many days*, Major?"

Lipsky heard the earnestness, without understanding it. He would not commit himself. But he did say, "I'll see what I can do."

"Thank you. Any idea of where I could find a room around here?"

"The Moscal at Affi, if you don't mind the thin covers."

Through Monday, and a good part of the night, Bora slept in the small *albergo* with a pillow on his head and his greatcoat over the bed. At dawn on Tuesday, after a change of clothes and a shave, he was at the Ministry of the Armed Forces in less than an hour. There, Graziani had called a staff meeting; on the agenda, among other items, were Bora's report and the deployment of the newly repatriated Monte Rosa division. In the interval between the morning meeting and the marshal's arrival, Bora made a couple of telephone calls. Annie was not in – or did not answer. Passaggeri said he had news that he wanted to discuss in person.

"I will be in Soiano all day, Inspector." The many hours of rest had done him good, but although he was perfectly awake, Bora felt off guard somehow. He wanted no additional duties today.

"Well, I have an errand to run in Soiano at three o'clock, Colonel. Will you be able to see me after that?"

Bora scribbled on his calendar. "I have a conference at three-thirty: you'll have to be very much on time."

The morning went tediously well. After lunch, Bora sipped lukewarm coffee over the report he'd compiled for Graziani, when Parisi, there with Colonel Lanzetta and the headquarters staff, asked him if he wanted a fresh cup. "No, thanks. Please show me to a typewriter; I wish to add a few things."

At two fifty, Graziani walked in, looking glum and keeping to himself the news of mass desertions in the Monte Rosa division. Three minutes later, Parisi hauled in an armful of maps. An orderly brought a tray with mineral water and goblets, followed by a stack of heavy glass ashtrays.

A 2:58 p.m., two Gestapo plainclothesmen came to the building and asked for Colonel Martin von Bora.

Bora looked away from the door where the men stood. With a calm gesture, he took the sheet out of the typewriter and laid it on the desk, smoothing it with his hand. "I suppose it cannot wait until four o'clock?"

"No."

"May I then leave a message for Marshal Graziani?"

One of the men waved for him to get up. "Let's go, Colonel." The other reached for the paper Bora had just typed and crumpled it in his pocket. As they walked back the length of the corridor, they stopped by the open door of the staff room and, heedless of the officers' surprise, they swept Bora's briefcase from the chair and took it along.

Summoned by Parisi, Graziani stepped out of his office in a high dander. "What the devil is going on?" he shouted in the agents' wake. All he faced was Passaggeri's unfamiliar countenance at the top of the stairs.

Mengs had coffee made. Bora's address book and diary were in front of him, studded with markers. There were also, to Bora's surprise, photographs and packets of letters. "Ah, Colonel," he cordially said. "Have a seat."

Like a postmaster accepting one more piece of mail, he stretched his arm out to collect Bora's briefcase from one of the agents. Without opening it, he placed it beside his chair. Two plain white cups sat without saucers on the corner of the desk and he filled them. "I know what you're about to ask and hope you'll refrain from it." Eyeing through the markers he'd placed in the diary, Mengs chose one, opening at the corresponding page. He did not read from it. Instead, he said, "We have a series of problems, Colonel."

"I should say. You pulled me out of a staff meeting with the minister of the Italian armed forces to come here. Is this going to take long?"

Mengs did not detect enough irony to make an issue of it. "It'll take as long as it takes."

His sinister affability disconcerted Bora. It was nearly cold in the office, but perspiration started to bead under his clothes. Looking at Mengs cost him a visible effort.

Mengs puckered his lips. "Nobody likes giving bad news,

Colonel." He lifted a sheet from the desk and wrote something on it in pen: date and time, Bora judged. "The first problem is with your maternal grandfather. *Der Junge* ... Isn't it what you call him in the family?"

"Yes. Why, what's happened to him?"

"He needs a talking-to. Urgently."

Bora guarded an unwise surge of temper. "About what? He's an old man of eighty."

"You must surmise what it is, being his favourite grandson. And the only one, after your brother's death."

"On the contrary, I can't imagine the problem to which you refer."

"Non-observance of publishing directives. Guidelines clearly spelled out in Adolf Spemann's *Solitude and Community*."

This was not the reason for his summons. It annoyed Bora that Mengs tested him this way. "I am not familiar with the book," he objected.

"It defines the responsibilities of publishers in today's world, as do the articles by Kummer and Taupitz in the *Journal of Library Science* and *Library*. For nearly ten years, the Bora Verlag has carried far too much sail under your grandfather; even the most tolerant of governments runs out of patience with relapsing intellectuals."

"If you refer to the translations of foreign authors, you are aware how difficult it has been for readers to obtain foreign currency and acquire books abroad. Superb translations are what the Bora Verlag has always done, as a service to the German public."

"As a service to the coffers of the Bora Verlag, for over two hundred years. We expect you to make the old man see reason and shut up shop while he's ahead."

"I have no such authority."

Mengs actually laughed. "Why, Colonel, that's a silly thing to say. Authority is what you *are*. The Bora Verlag must go. And shall go, one way or another. That your grandfather is in error, you will hear from a trustworthy witness. We've arranged for a long-distance call from Germany: you will learn how things are from your mother. Be so good as to tell her to hand over the keys of the firm to my colleagues. Have your coffee."

When Bora did not move, Mengs started sipping from his cup. Casually he pushed back his chair, exposing the ill-fitting cut of his suit. When his eyes slowly wandered to the window, the drab afternoon light seemed to die in them. They reminded Bora of the dull eyes of the cow he'd shot in Poland. "As for you, on the other hand, ever since Spain your good, long record of involvement with counter-intelligence has rewarded you well." He pointed to Bora's medals. His fatty hand fished out of a stack of photographs a snapshot, which he showed. "Do you remember this?"

"Yes. It was taken in the summer of thirty-nine, near Brest-Litovsk."

Mengs looked at the back of the photo. "Indeed. And the people in the picture?"

"Myself and First Lieutenant Valery Gerasimov."

"Of the Red Army."

"We were attachés to our respective commands during the talks that summer."

"You must have spoken Russian well."

"Serviceably. I spoke it *well* six months later."

Mengs put the snapshot away and began viewing others. "It's one of the things that gave you an edge in the East. Polish, you did not speak; still, you managed to get into our business even in Poland, under Blaskowitz."

Mengs continued to smile, with unnerving monotony. Bora was in a cold sweat. Photographs and letters came from his trunk and elsewhere; some he had sent to relatives, others he thought he had disposed of or lost. It was uncanny to see them piled on the desk like flotsam from the past.

"Here's an interesting shot, Colonel. Your former wife, eh? Who's the man with her?"

"Her father."

"Yes." Mengs seemed to have suddenly remembered the real reason for summoning Bora. "We received a concerned phone call from Ambassador Coennewitz last month."

Bora frowned and hardened considerably across his shoulders. "Why should my ex-father-in-law express his concern to the Gestapo?"

"Well, it has nothing to do with marital issues. He called regarding – how shall I put it? – your political reliability." Gauging a measure of powerless anger in him, Mengs pushed Bora's cup towards him. "He told us how, during your first furlough, you confided to your wife that you felt 'anguished' – your words – for the way racial policies were applied in the East. Your father-in-law asked you on that occasion if you liked Jews." Mengs flipped through a notebook of his. "Your answer was: 'I don't think it's relevant.' Since he insisted, you replied that, and I quote, 'Human life has an inherent dignity over which we cannot arrogate irresponsible power.'"

Bora said coldly, "I did not know my father-in-law was a Gestapo informant."

"The fact is, Colonel, we found the report strange in view of your record. After all, you were a featured speaker on Eastern campaign issues before the Army School cadets in Berlin. The cadets thought you were stirring. So, you diverged from the truth either while lecturing to them, or when you spoke in private to your father-in-law."

"I was speaking strictly of military operations in Berlin."

"Yet, asked point-blank if you liked Jews, you refrained from answering. That's an odd thing for a German officer to do."

Bora lowered his eyes without knowing why. He felt no shame whatsoever, although Mengs might have read it as a sign of his relenting.

"Now you're talking neither to the cadets nor to family. Suppose we get the matter squared away. Do you like Jews, Colonel von Bora?"

"No."

"I fear you may be telling an untruth." Mengs paused to drink.

"I'm not often told I lie. And I don't have to like someone not to want to butcher them."

Mengs contracted and then relaxed his jaw in a surge of pink flesh. "Have your coffee, Colonel. It's going to be a long afternoon."

Passaggeri had been bodily ousted from Cremona for ideological reasons and believed he knew a thing or two about hauling people off besides. Since Parisi seemed the only approachable officer in the bustle that followed Bora's removal, he enquired of him, because – one never knows – the colonel could have even been detained for the three murders.

"I think he has *political* troubles," Parisi said. On his face, the policeman read fear, distress, the usual reactions of the times. He added something about a safe opened by the SS and returned to the meeting room.

Mengs's voice had a way of trailing off that forced Bora to pay a nearly painful attention to his words. "You are a puzzle to me, Colonel. Why do you write diary entries in English, when your native tongue is German and we are at war with English-speaking nations?"

What light remained of the day had curdled and waned. An orderly came to shutter the window and turn on the electric light. The office looked bleaker under the artificial glare. Bora's papers lay on the desk like dead leaves. Mengs had not abandoned his condescending sociability, and the call from Germany was late in coming.

Bora was guiltily thinking of his mother. "I grew up speaking it," he said. "You have seen it is nothing but a conventional diary."

"Conventional? I wouldn't go as far as that. Well written. The pages devoted to your wife's desertion are *poignant*." Mengs stared at Bora in long spells, up from the densely written pages before him. Without looking away, he took from his pocket a scrap of paper, which he presented on an open palm. Bora recognized it. Under the tunic, his shirt no longer absorbed sweat and stuck to his torso like an icy second skin. "This, we found on one Aldo Sciaba in the German wing of the Rome prison. You were the only one who visited him there. Come, come. Being quiet won't do, Colonel."

"What is the question?"

"Do you admit giving this note to the Jew Sciaba from his wife?"

"Since I don't believe in materializations, it stands to reason that I gave it to him."

"And why?"

"Because it cost me nothing."

"Some prices are exacted after months, or years. But let's go back to Russia. You and Gerasimov spent a week together in Brest-Litovsk. What did you discuss?"

"Neither politics nor military matters."

"Would you have me believe that for seven days you discussed the weather?"

"We talked about music."

Mengs held his coffee cup under his chin. "You *talked about music.*"

"Gerasimov was a graduate of the Leningrad Conservatory. We discussed piano techniques, blind octaves and rounded binary form."

Mengs sighed. Bora's performance reports were accurate, he took stress head-on. He stood under pressure like an animal, with stolid resolve.

"You took Gerasimov prisoner two years later and interrogated him. Did you learn anything worthwhile?"

Where is this going? Bora couldn't tell. "All that could be expected of a prisoner. He was not a political commissar."

"But you shot him."

"My men fired on him as he attempted to escape. It was his right to attempt it; it was our duty to prevent it."

"Why did you keep a photo of him?"

"I did *not* keep it. I don't know where you found it."

Mengs seemed suddenly to regain his good humour. "You know, Colonel von Bora, you might just as well start telling the truth. You have been under surveillance since your arrival in Italy. We know everything. Whom you've seen, what you've said. Even the kind of sex you like to engage in. This neat trick you have of having an orgasm without necessarily ejaculating, which makes you *resilient* ... A trick your wife told her friends that she would miss. How do you exactly do it? I'm curious."

Bora lost control of his breathing. "How would you know?"

"Be assured, we know. You bedded an Austrian whore at the Hotel d'Italia eight weeks after your wife left you. You laid her from eight in the evening till three in the morning, confessing that you didn't think you could live without your wife, et cetera. After becoming worried about risking a venereal disease, you submitted to tests at the military hospital on Vescovio Square. The results were negative, but you refrained from sexual activity in Rome from then on." Out of an envelope, Mengs dropped a piece of lead and a brass shell, which he rested on the open diary. "As you see, we're well informed." He no longer pretended friendliness. "These belong to the Walther P38 that killed our informant in Rome last May."

"You inspected my sidearm."

"We inspected the sidearm you carried when I asked you for it, yes."

In Soiano, Parisi waited for everyone to leave before calling Bora's office. As he expected, he was told that the colonel was not in. It was now nine o'clock and very cold. An hour earlier, Graziani had left, still incensed. "I will let them have it tomorrow!" he had growled. "Kicks in the arse, that's what these Germans need! Disrupting a meeting I attended in person … Kicks in the arse, I say!"

"Another question concerns your agenda. Names, surnames, addresses, all black on white."

Bora's mouth went dry. Uselessly he tried to swallow. "I haven't seen most of the people listed in years."

"I believe it. But some of them are people arrested or executed in the past months for the criminal plot of the twentieth of July. And, while we're on the subject, aside from the fact that you were friends with Uckermann, one of the traitors, what did you do out in the field to stress the importance of the Führer's survival?"

"On the Apennines we were under heavy enemy fire from the seventeenth of July to the twenty-third. I had more immediate concerns."

"Not more important, I hope."

"More immediate. On the twenty-fourth, I instructed the men as by orders. We adopted the Party salute, and the rest."

"Hmm. You spent some days in Berlin before the crime. How did you personally react to it?"

Bora wetted his lips. His left arm had been aching for the past two hours. The elbow felt numb with pain. "I am a creed-bound officer."

"It depends on the creed, Colonel. At any rate, while we're waiting for your mother the baroness to call from Germany, you may help me clear up a few more questions. We have time, so I wish to show you an educational film the cadets in Berlin have already had a chance to watch. Have you ever visited the Plötzensee detention camp?"

Bora said that he hadn't. But Plötzensee was where the conspirators had been executed, and he knew at once what the film was.

WEDNESDAY, 6 DECEMBER 1944, 5:00 A.M.

A single, exceedingly bright star shone in the hazy eastern sky when Bora walked out of Mengs's office. He did not see the star, only its brightness, as if the two things were separate. He smelled and sensed things around – he could smell the lake in the dark – without appropriating them to his mind, like an animal. The darkness was still perfect; the wind cut like glass. He found he was shivering in it.

"*Ihre Papiere, bitte.*"

The soldier had come out of nowhere. Bora turned with automatic heed towards him. The torch in the soldier's hand danced like a will-o'-the-wisp. In order to take the papers out of his inner pocket, he put down the briefcase and was startled when it fell on its side with a thud.

(Half an hour earlier, Mengs had still been rummaging through it. Without a word, he had flipped through pages, unfolded letters, shifted files. Then he had rested the briefcase on the desk with its handle turned to Bora. Allowing him to rise for the first time in nearly fifteen hours, he said, "You may go for now.")

The soldier shone the light in his face to match it against the photograph in the pass. "*Was tun Sie hinaus, Herr Oberst?*"

(Bora remembered the strain of rising steadily from his seat. "I would like to have some coffee now." Mengs's eyes showed some slow, admiring amusement at the words. He'd ordered coffee to be made and a car to be brought for Bora. They sipped it on their feet at the opposite sides of the desk, concealing their different weariness.)

Bora said now, "*Ich gehe arbeiten.*"

"*Um fünf Uhr morgens, Herr Oberst?*"

("We'll let you know when we need you again, Colonel. By the way, did anyone ever tell you that you remarkably resemble Stauffenberg? You could be his younger brother. You didn't meet him in Berlin, last July?")

Presently Bora said, "*Ich gehe arbeiten, Gemeiner.*"

The soldier returned the pass. "*Vielen dank, Herr Oberst.*" And he let him go.

The star dilated into a flickering stain. Bora's eyes ached when he looked at it. Tension left his muscles with a shiver, of which he was ashamed. His mother had wept over the telephone, because she *knew*. His stepfather would stay in Leipzig under the bombs, come what may. The keys to the publishing house had been surrendered. The sole reason for Mengs to involve his mother was to remind her that her son was in a Gestapo office at three o'clock in the morning.

Nina had said, "I beg you, Martin. You are all that's left." She *begged* him. Who was standing with her? Who had been threatening her? "I beg you, Martin." But he could do nothing for her, or himself.

He closed his eyes not to look at the star. He needed to lie down. Neck, arm, leg, his whole body crept with sharp pain. Rape could not hurt more.

("Let's go through nineteen thirty-nine again, Colonel von Bora.")

Even now, saliva rose to his mouth with the need to vomit the humiliation of being pried open and scraped inside, reamed into remembering.

("And then you did what?"

"I don't recall."

"And then you did what?"

"I do not recall. It's been five years."

"*And then you did what?*")

Words had come out of him painfully measured, until he knew what he hadn't said but not what he had said. How many times had he slipped up? Now everything ached, and Bora felt sick. When he reached his hotel room, he had just enough time to reach the sink and vomit Mengs's coffee into it.

At seven-thirty, Sohl was surprised to find him at work.

"Good morning." He stopped by his door.

"Good morning, Herr Generalleutnant," said Bora, standing. He was clear-eyed and neatly shaven. The general noticed that he was wearing all his medals, including the Knight's Cross.

"You may want to phone Marshal Graziani."

"I've tried already. He is in Vidigulfo. I will apologize for my absence, rest assured."

"I know I shouldn't ask, Colonel, but …"

Bora's lips set firmly. The jawbone became visible under the lean sheath of skin. Sohl had seen wounded men similarly hold back agony. Bora stared at the map squared on his desk, and, whatever internal process was going on, it was private and silent, not to involve others. "Sir, I will call Marshal Graziani again on the hour."

13

On the telephone, Graziani swallowed Wolff's nasty retort like a bitter pill. He'd never been spoken to so haughtily by a German.

"I don't believe you heard correctly who I am, *Generale* Wolff: I am *Maresciallo* Graziani."

"I know who you are, Marshal. I'm still telling you not to interfere with German internal matters. You call enough damn conferences and meetings to make up for a disrupted one."

"This is unacceptable!"

Wolff clicked his receiver down. Before he could call back to continue the argument, Graziani was informed that Colonel von Bora was on the other line and had tried to reach him all day Wednesday. "Tell him to get his righteous arse here before noon, with all the paperwork he had in his briefcase when he left on Tuesday!"

Bora was in Soiano for nearly two hours, during which he heard in all possible variations that his absence had disrupted the staff meeting. The accusation ranked poorly compared to his other troubles, so he took the outburst with a straight face. Under Graziani's anger, the mindless euphoria of the past days gradually returned to him, until he had to keep himself from smiling at each new recrimination. *I'm as good as dead,* he thought, *and here's this hysterical old man spraying saliva on a corpse. What damn difference does it make to either of us?*

How little his hilarity had to do with amusement he found out after leaving Graziani, when his nervous release became impossible to control. He had to stop in a fit of laughter at the entrance of the ministry, where a staid staff officer waited until he was done to give him the schedule for the following day. Bora glimpsed the sheet and tossed it over his shoulder. "Good. I'm taking tomorrow off."

FRIDAY, 8 DECEMBER 1944, 10:07 A.M.

The rest of Thursday, and all day Friday, Martin von Bora was not to be found anywhere. When enquiries about him reached the *questura* from Sohl's and Graziani's offices, Passaggeri himself was away, supervising the blasted music room in Vittori's house.

After five days in the hospital, Vittori, unhurt but for some minor burns and scrapes, and wearing cotton wads to protect his aching eardrums, stumbled around the devastation. "My records," he bemoaned the loss of his collection. "My African violets, my Albers armchairs."

What with the acrid dust, what with his cold, Passaggeri sneezed. "The least you can do, sir, is tell us where Romanò's husband is hiding."

"How would I know where he hides?" Vittori's voice sounded like a deaf man's. "I told you all I know. I didn't even say a definite yes or no to his wife when she begged me for help. She moved me, but securing paperwork is not my forte. I saw him only once at the end of November, when he sneaked into the queue at the soup kitchen I patronize; or, I should say, he saw *me* with his wife, who wanted me to take a look at him before saying no. He's a brute of about forty. Keep him away from my niece, that's all I want."

"Well, that's not going to be easy, if she insists on living alone. What about convincing her to stay here?"

Vittori covered his right ear, because the inspector's voice rang out in the hollowed room. "She won't. By tonight, I'll have this room sealed and the radiators functioning again. The phone is still out of order, but I can live with that. Should Annie change her mind, she's always welcome."

After the visit, which added nothing to his first impressions of the incident, Passaggeri was annoyed to find Pozzi's solicitor in his *questura* office. He heard that he could choose between relinquishing all unreasonable harassment of his client and being sure to face his second sacking in a month. "I have it from His Excellency the minister of justice, Commissario. In this envelope you will find the names of reputable citizens who will vouch for Cavalier Pozzi's alibi during his absences from Salò."

The minister was a shoal too big even for the headstrong policeman to knock against. He was still in a foul mood when Annie Tedesco telephoned later in the day.

"*Ma no, Signora!* I haven't seen Colonel von Bora since Saturday." He did not tell her he'd seen him in the hands of plainclothesmen in Soiano, or that he'd heard the worrisome formula: political troubles. "May I ask why you wish to know?"

Annie hung up. Sitting with his head tilted back, in hopes to clear his plugged nose, Passaggeri mulled over Bora's disappearance. In Russia, he'd heard of a Grenadiers commander who strangled two women in a drunken rage and actively sought the culprit among his officers before realizing he was on his own tracks. Now, why in blazes should the idea come to his mind? The commander, the legend went, had walked unarmed into Russian fire, dying a hero to boot.

It took him until evening to trace Bora in a room at the Tre Corone in Bussolengo, where he'd reportedly spent the day alone. "Did the colonel ask for anything or anybody?"

"A sheet of paper, Commissario, and needle and thread."

"It's Martin," he said. Every other time he had announced himself as Colonel von Bora, or Bora, but tonight was sacred and demanded the shedding of earthly titles. That her door was ajar would to him have been cause for alarm, had the sound of her cello not flowed so steadily from within.

Oh, the sweet G minor of the music. From the vestibule, he saw Annie look up from the instrument, with a slow turn of the head over her lovely shoulders. *Is she unhappy? Does she not care that someone could come in from the night to harm her?* On the threshold of the room, Bora listened, greatcoat on his shoulders, watching the small resolute motions of her chin while she played. '*Au bord d'une fontaine,*' went the words of the French song. He said, without entering, "I have come to ask."

He hoped, speaking the words, that she'd sense the acuteness of his desire across the narrow space between them. And, because the front door was still open behind him, that the cold of night would rouse the delicate tips of her breasts under her clothes, if desire did not. "May I enter?"

"Yes."

Bora closed and locked the front door. He removed his cap and came forward until no distance was left between them. Details, neat angles of him flowed to her: his paleness, small glints of metal. The cool of night stood with him. Annie let him undo the clasp of her fingers on the bow, lean the cello aside, make her stand. Instead of kissing it, he brought her hand to his chest, where even under the heavy cloth, the pounding of his heart could meet her touch.

"Please allow me to spend the night here, Signora Tedesco. Grant me the honour of making love to you; I've been wanting to ask for so long. Don't say no. Please."

Annie could have cried and laughed at the same time, because Bora spoke to her in his perfect Italian, yet was so formal in asking her to make love. On an impulse, she kissed him or let herself be kissed, caught in the push of his hips, and though she said, "Not with the light on, not here," and he, "Yes, yes, here," she let him dip his fresh, impatient tongue into her mouth to tempt her.

"Even if you don't love me." They felt each other awkwardly, she much bolder in touching him than in letting him touch her, Bora ashiver with longing under the uniform, determined not to let himself go too soon. "Even if you don't love me, tell me yes."

Her shoulders and torso were still rigid, thrown back, but, from her belly down, her flesh turned as soft as water, yielding, easy. Annie felt herself grow deep and formless. Not telling him yes, she let him seat her back and turn the light off, kneel against her knees. *Bless the grace of a woman who does not take her clothes off, but lets you undress her* ... Piece by piece, Bora freed her of her things, down to the underclothes; imagining the scar on her belly, he hungered to feel it and find comfort in it to his own fears. Holding her firmly, he was able to lay his mouth on her and seek the wound with his lips, following its cruel scar down from her navel, to the place where she must be all sweetness and tender folds. But when, as in the Venus, he met the modesty of her hand, there was no kissing or wooing her fingers apart.

In his Barbarano residence, Obersturmbannführer Kappler had a headache, and the last thing he wanted to do at this hour was talk on the phone to Mengs. He said, "Sure, Bora would quote Military Law, especially Article 47, Clause 3. Refusal to obey 'criminal orders' is what the army marches on when it suits them. As early as June I told *others*," he avoided using Dollmann's name over the telephone, "that I doubted he could be intimidated. It was my professional evaluation then, and it remains so now. It has nothing to do with being afraid. He'll make mistakes but won't give in until different methods are employed with him."

"*On* him, Obersturmbannführer."

"Semantics. When you're drilling through hard timber, you get yourself a tougher bit." Kappler swallowed a yawn. "Talk to Wolff, if it is clout that you want. I'm not about to meddle with army administration."

"Wolff won't talk to me. Should his reassignment go through, Bora stands to get away with it."

"He stands to get away from you personally. I don't believe he'll get away from us, here or elsewhere." Kappler adjusted the pillow behind his neck and yawned again. "You had fifteen hours to put the fear of God in him. You have the man's diary and agenda, plus whatever guts he spilled in those hours. What more evidence do you need? I could have had him shot half a dozen times in Rome. Each time something intervened."

"That's why we mustn't give him time to do anything else."

"Well, *you* let him go. Now it's between you and luck, if you get to nail him before his reassignment."

MESPILAI

"You don't love me?" In her bed, Bora heard himself moan at every deep push, even though it cost him no effort, for the pleasure of forcing each time a tight, exhilarating seal within her.

"No."

"You like me, then."

"I like you, then."

He enjoyed lying on the dark buds of her nipples – cool, sensitive to the touch like violets, with the scent and taste of flowers – besieging the little knot inside. "You are still closed, deep inside. Tell me why you're afraid of it, Annie."

Her answer made him humble. It sobered him into kissing her more tenderly than he'd done with his wife. "But why? Why do you think that way?" Sounding and measuring himself inside her, he spoke small words on her arched throat, her chin. Life was here, spending the night with Annie Tedesco. Life within life. Death crouched around him all day, but could not draw near the bed where life was.

"Because they taught me so."

With eyes closed, Bora kissed her forehead, her temples. "But it's not a wound, Annie. Your naked little sex is God's door. I know, I've seen it tonight. Don't let them tell you it's a wound. Don't let yourself be made love to by those who fill wounds." He stroked her with great care, tucked the sheets around her. "You're shivering. Are you cold?"

"No." Annie was crying. Bora worried that she might be in pain; he was about to pull away, but her voice held him back. "But it's true, Martin. Even healthy women carry a wound between their legs, and men have the cure. They taught it to me since I was small. God gives us the wound, and we carry it with us hoping that a man will heal it. If he is unable to heal us, then there needs be another, or another. Sometimes none of them can heal us."

"What nonsense. For God's sake, how can you believe such tales? Men are not even able to heal themselves." Her wet face met his lips. Bora tasted her tears and was ashamed.

GARDONE RIVIERA, 9:30 P.M.

"He doesn't talk." Mengs was dark in the face. Since Kappler had been unresponsive, he'd invited Sutor to dine with him at the Spielcasino. Now he pulled bits of candied citrus from the spongy crumb of the cake on his plate. "Fifteen hours Bora sits across from me and doesn't talk."

Sutor enviously put away the voluminous transcript. "It seems to me that he talks quite a bit."

"He doesn't betray himself."

"But is he afraid?"

"Yes." After disposing of the candied citrus, Mengs began to pull raisins out of the cake. "But it's sterile fear if it brings no results. I'm starting to believe that he spoke of nothing but music to his Russian counterpart in Brest-Litovsk."

Sutor followed the operation on Mengs's plate. Unlike him, he had an eager flush on his face. "You know, that's the traditional holiday treat here. It's much better with the fruit in it."

"I don't like complications. I agree it is imperative to keep track of whom Bora meets these days, but he's no fool."

"Frightened men do stupid things."

"The Reds took him prisoner and broke his arm, and he still got away from them and their dogs." Mengs took a bite of his ravaged piece of cake. "A week behind the Russian lines, bleeding, disarmed. I'm sure he was frightened then, too. Stupid? No. I should be so lucky."

"You have enough here to hang his ass, Jacob!"

"No. I don't know about Berlin, yet. I'm missing two pieces of evidence. And I want Colonel Martin-Heinz Douglas, Freiherr von Bora, bearer of the Knight's Cross and German Cross in gold, to supply them to me."

"Let me open it tonight." Bora coaxed her with every part of him, but Annie withdrew slowly. The room, the billowing sheet intervened when the little bedside light flickered on. Bora thought himself rejected until he saw the expectant perfection of her shoulders and hips, spared by the steel that had gutted her. Annie knelt on the bed like snow on snow, set amid blue shadows.

This could be the last time, Martin. Think of Jacob and the Angel in the tapestry at her father's house; bodies in the wind-filled forest, grappling until dawn. He knelt behind her as he'd knelt, many times in the snow. The ancient embrace around the woman's shoulders to subdue her had come naturally to him back then, pulling her to himself and going in – the ritual Dikta favoured and then reacted hungrily to, to the point of hurting him. But in Annie's case, it was a meek surrender, so full of want and grace that he had to keep himself from weeping.

And so it was that she unsealed for him her womanhood, deep, as if stealthy death had climbed onto the bed and opened a motherly womb to take him back where he'd first belonged. Bora broke into her through a lengthy, exquisite groove between lacy fringes of pain, tearing them irresistibly, and he would not be folded out, expelled, would take no fear from her, seeking the perfect privilege. And, when he could no longer tell himself apart from her, when tension and one-ness exasperated his need into precarious urgency, the release of tension was like a blackout, where he had no idea of who or what he was.

Afterwards, Bora did not pull away, grateful that she did not refuse him as Dikta had done when they were through. Moist, awed and defenceless, he needed that small security.

Annie looked at him from the wave of her pillow. "How do you do so well what you did?"

"I don't really know. A woman taught me."

"Your wife?"

"Before her, in Spain. She was beautiful, yes. Young, yes."

"Were you fond of her?"

"I'll think of her when I die."

"Will you?" And because she unexpectedly climbed on him, hugging the trim sides of his body, Bora simpered. "I'm not used to this."

"Why aren't you? You seem used to everything else."

"I don't like doing it, I suppose." Already her touch ran shivers like pinpricks on him, hardening his nipples, and Bora had feared it might be so good, so unforgivably comforting to allow himself to lie there and be made love to. He wanted to say that he was self-conscious and had never liked making love this way, but his shoulders were stiffening with pleasure. And when Annie crouched on his belly, his head dug into the pillow as when the surgeon pulled out bloody shrapnel from his groin, and the erection was shameful and full of pain. Tonight there was no pain, whether death lay in wait outside or not. Bora began unwittingly to respond and push back. Annie bent over him. "Do you like it, then?"

"Yes, but I shouldn't. I have no control."

"You don't need control now." Her hands mapped him, fingers trailing down his left side. "I love your scars. The little ones on your neck, this one and this one. And on your hip, your belly, all these. May I count them?"

"It'll do me no good to know how many I have."

Against his resistance, she took his left arm into her lap, stroking the muscular end of it. Down her shoulders, her dark hair flowed, rippling where the tips of her breast were imagined, not seen: a swan or a mermaid, white and wet on his stretched-out body. "I like your arm. It's hard and blond-haired and like a wounded cat's. Put it around my waist."

Bora would not. Careful not to separate from her, he nimbly turned her to one side and then under himself.

"Do you know why Kappler is going to Milan?" Sutor asked Mengs, as if the latter should care. "Mussolini is calling a meeting of his ministers tomorrow. He might be transferring the entire administrative circus to the city."

"Well, what other entertainment is there in Milan? They'll be just as ready to string him up next week."

"Week after next, maybe. He plans to sneak away from the lake and give a speech there at the Lirico Theatre around mid-month. It could be an immense success, or it could draw a lynch mob."

Mengs picked up flakes of cake crust from his plate. "Speaking of Milan, I will need interrogation facilities there at some undisturbed place."

2:00 A.M.

"Who took your virginity, Martin?"

Bora kissed her opulent, undone braid of hair. "A friend of my godmother's in Rome, when I was fifteen." When he started to kiss her neck, she freed herself of the sheets and lay on them.

"I was fifteen also. My uncle did."

Bora's kissing stopped, then began again, but more thoughtful, more deliberate, around the curve of her breasts and down the admirable, scented hollow of her armpits. "Did he take you?"

"No. I gave it to him. We were lovers for a year."

Propped on his elbow next to her, Bora felt every part of him again tight with want. "I wish we could be." In front of him, Annie rested perfectly still, perfectly made. Compared to her, how flitting and short-lived grief and pain seemed, impending yet endurable. "I wish you loved me, Annie."

"There's no time. Promise me you will tell no one you've been with me. Promise you won't tell my father, or my uncle."

"I wouldn't dream of it. Of course, I promise."

"Don't even tell yourself."

For a time, they remained in silence. Bora sat up with his shoulders to the back of the bed, eyes closed, so that her voice reached him through that self-made darkness.

"I can't believe your wife tired of you."

"I can. Sometimes I am tired of myself, too. I've made terrible choices in my life." He withdrew into the obstinate, restive pain of men. She continued to caress him, and although he hardened under her fingers, the response was at first only physical. His skin crawled warm, blood flowed to the flesh in small spasms. "Annie, why was the house unlocked tonight?"

"Because he has the key to it."

"*Who* does?"

"Death."

Hadn't he been thinking the same? The coincidence alarmed him. "Don't say that."

"He's out there for all of us." She spoke from under his fingers, resting on her lips. "A figure of speech, Martin." She made him slide down, submit to her touch, embrace her face to face. "If I could, I'd give you a son."

And suddenly those words, the luminous firmness of her body, severed by the scar into polished halves, so resembled her to the yielding Venus that Bora felt as if he could tumble outside of time, into a strange place that could deliver him from the useless trammels of existence. The urge to hasten the fall took him – to make himself a key to timelessness by kissing the lock to it. He shivered with his mouth on her white body.

Not even when his wife had come to Rome nearly a year before, and he was so desperate to keep her, had he done this with as much desire. In Spain, the image of the Holy Ghost had taken flight from its painted wall when he'd lain on Remedios in an abandoned chapel; but even Remedios had a veil of fleece, fiery red, to guard her glory. Between Annie and Martin Bora, nothing lay but the purity of naked, gentle womanliness, to which her martyred flesh led down like a Milky Way.

SATURDAY, 9 DECEMBER 1944, 6:32 A.M.

Mengs left for Milan in a lead-grey twilight. Sutor preceded him and, after leaving Kappler at the Ausserkommando, would meet with him again at nearby Cordusio Square. Twirling a cough drop with the tip of his tongue over the floor of his mouth, Mengs sat slumped in the back seat.

MESPILAI, 6:33 A.M.

In the sadness of the hour, after showering, Bora lay on his stomach at the edge of the bed, staring at the dark heap of his uniform as if it didn't belong to him. Annie sat beside him already dressed, her hair tightly knotted. Chin in the hollow of his folded arm, he hid his face from her. "How can you tell me not to come back to see you? I cannot live here and not come back to see you."

"You know as I do that there is no point."

"Not for me!"

"It is useless and dangerous, for you and for me. For me, if not for you."

She was right, of course. Bora rushed from the bed and began to put his clothes on. The cloth would not slip over his wet skin, so he jerked it and struggled with it. Annie said something; "I understand," he interrupted her, refusing to hear the rest.

Annie took him by the shoulder, turned him around. She began to button his shirt. "If you understood, you would not be angry."

"I don't need help." Still, Bora didn't move away. For the first time since they had undressed, he was ashamed of his mutilation, but Annie did not allow this either. "Give me your arm," she said. "Not the right one, the other. Give me your wounded cat's hand. It's the only part of you I haven't kissed."

"It is not a part of me."

"And neither am I. Come, Liese will be here soon."

Bora finished preparing. Gradually, the uniform made him anonymous, alien to the room. He was ready to go when she joined him in the vestibule and saw him look down at a wrinkle in the rug, troubled and unsmiling. Soon composure returned to his face like a severe, habitual disguise, an accessory to the uniform, like a belt or medals.

"Do not think I'm not grateful, Signora Tedesco. I'm more grateful to you than I can express. *Ich danke Ihnen, gnädige Frau.*"

Annie opened the door. "I'm grateful to you too, Colonel von Bora."

Outside it was raining.

VILLA MALONA, 7:00 A.M.

With no appreciable change in his expression, Pozzi balanced his cheque-book at the breakfast table. Only his voice grew hostile. "That's what I mean. I didn't have to walk in to know. It's been sprinkling overnight, and it was dry under Bora's car. If he hasn't slept with her, then he just left his car parked there all night."

Vittori drank a glass of water. "I knew this would come, right from the start."

"Well, it's *come* for sure now! It probably wasn't even the first time. With the Germans losing another swatch of Italy every hour, she sets herself up for this kind of trouble. No, I'm *not* fucking telling her anything! You recall what she tried to do when I told her to quit the Jew."

"But she didn't succeed. She was not serious about it."

Pozzi had the jaundiced voice of a merchant discussing a financial tort. "If it's the last thing you do, Walter, you have to convince her to move in with you. She won't stay here, but your place has been struck already, and lightning doesn't hit the same spot twice."

Down the road at Sohl's residence, where admittedly Bora arrived late for a man of his punctuality, the big news was about the fireplace. The general said it had cracked beyond repair overnight and would have to stay unlit from now on. "So much for the vaunted Renaissance craftsmanship. There's really no fixing it. But it isn't all bad news." He placed a typed report under Bora's nose. "See here? The Republican Guard and the Italian SS, in the wake of Xavier's last stand, 'stumbled across an enormous cache of weapons in a tunnel above the Great War trench road'. They were following your indications, Colonel. Along with the truce with the royalists and Xavier's elimination, even the plenipotentiary calls it an early gift for the holiday season."

Bora knew better. He stood reading, briefcase resting between his ankles, like a rushed passenger at the station. Which was the closest comparison he could find for himself at this time. "I do need to see you about the Venus, Herr Generalleutnant."

Without the roaring fireplace behind him, Sohl's puff of cheroot smoke was like the last breath of a defeated dragon. Was he relieved or troubled? Did he expect it, or had he hoped that Bora would admit failure? "You did the best you could, I'm sure," he said after hearing him out. "Under the circumstances, and given the times … I never really hoped we would get the Venus back."

"She is lost to us. And although it does change matters, to set the record straight, there was more than theft; tantamount to murder, too. I mean Conforti's death."

"What, the little Jew? He died of a heart attack, Bora!"

"He was ill, yes. A push was all it took." *Now he'll either ask for details, or he won't. If he doesn't …* Bora clicked his heels when no question followed. "Thank you for accepting my limited report in good part, Herr Generalleutnant." *Banality, banality. Banality will have us all.* "Please convey my respects to Frau Sohl, whose conversation in Milan I truly enjoyed."

A doubtful pause followed, before Sohl took up, in a friendly voice, "Thank you for the respects. You're looking better than you have in some time yourself. Sit down a moment; relax. Don't you want to hear what *your* Christmas gift is?"

9:37 A.M.

The Metropoli was crowded with Germans. The sprinkle had changed to rain, and, even with the lights on, the dining hall was as dim as an aquarium. Nearly as quiet, too, since the Germans breakfasted without a word.

"We knew it would happen." Vittori peeled an orange in slow circles with the dull restaurant knife, revealing the white layer under the rind. "What now?"

All in pearl grey, Annie shielded her temple with her gloved hand, so as not to see the officers sitting at the next table. "I don't know."

Since daybreak, army vehicles had been travelling the Garda road, lifting high sprays of rainwater. Trucks and staff cars were on the move, bound for the next operation, or God knows what. Patiently, Vittori parted the orange, segment by segment. He took one and handed it to her.

"I can tell he's been very good to you. Colonel von Bora is the best I can wish for you. But there's no starting love affairs with Germans now." He proffered the moist wedge to her between his fingers. "He makes you feel whole, doesn't he? He has the *cure.*"

"He's leaving."

"When?"

"In ten days. He found out this morning."

"Well, in ten days anything can happen, Annie." When she did not remove her glove, nor receive the piece of fruit from him, Vittori rested it on her plate.

"We won't see each other again," she said.

"Why? As long as you're not in love with him …"

She started to weep. The officers at the next table did not notice, or had enough tact not to show they did. They were older men, with brows marked by anxiety, facing their sixth Christmas at war. They drank their coffee and smoked in silence, keeping their eyes low.

10:04 A.M.

Saturday was the day Passaggeri had decided to leave work before noon, to nurse his lingering cold in bed. Hearing Bora's voice outside his office, he reversed his plans and took the stoical high road.

"My apologies for missing our Tuesday meeting," was the first thing Bora said, "and for not returning your calls in days past."

"Excuse *me* if I don't shake your hand, I don't want to give you my cold." His eye, accustomed to gauging covert emotions, caught an odd mix of stress and release in the German, and left it at that. "You might be glad to hear that, since we last spoke, I provisionally arrested our former inmate, the red-headed handyman. Among the private homes where he did yard work, there's Vittori's villa; he was in the crew that did some planting for him as late as two weeks ago."

"Yes, I remember seeing a red-head among the workers when I went to visit him in October."

"Well, he denies cutting Vittori's phone wire, and his alibi stands in reference to the latest murder. By all accounts, he didn't know any of the victims personally, and – whether or not he's guilty of the nineteen twenty-three killings – he is not the type who resorts to mises-en-scène. But I clapped him in jail, and there he stays until I have something better." Passaggeri sneezed and blew his nose fiercely. "On a more speculative note, Colonel, I've been trying to make sense of the order in which the murders took place. Ten days separate the first crime from the second, on the fifteenth and twenty-fifth of October, and a similar lapse of time runs between Romanò's death on the twenty-first of November and the attempted break-in at Signora Tedesco's."

Bora's heart leaped at the mention of Annie's name. "That was on the first of December." He flipped through his agenda, as if he didn't remember.

"Right," Passaggeri observed. "And the second and third murder were committed more or less a week before a full moon."

Bora made a mental note. *How many crimes take place on a full moon? Why, the Allies attacked Normandy on such a date. This is not the farmer's almanac.* "The attempt on Vittori's life, on the second of December, is entirely out of sequence."

"Yes. We're at sea." Passaggeri cracked his knuckles, a habit that surfaced again whenever he was frustrated. "The Brixia grenade used on Vittori's house was similar to the one thrown to create confusion when the Venus was stolen. On the first of December, Vittori's phone wire is cut. He makes no calls that day, so he does not notice. The next day, there's the attempted break-in, and only because he's at his brother-in-law's does Vittori receive his niece's distress call. What do we have here? I'm trying to create a calendar, but even if we find the mysterious Romanò husband on our doorstep, we'd have to link him to the first two murders to have a matching game. The three murders may not be related at all. Or only the first two are. Signora Tedesco doubts that her intruder is the killer. Maybe so. None of the other homes were broken into."

"Can you exclude the handyman?"

"Well, he *did* prune the hedge at the lady's property earlier in the fall, but he spent the night of the break-in at a charitable shelter, care of the Church." Passaggeri snorted. "Since then, and until she moves in with her uncle tonight, I have had a couple of men keeping an eye on Signora Tedesco's house."

Bora blushed uncontrollably. "I see." The wrinkle in the rug of the vestibule this morning, as if someone had stumbled on it in the dark … He saw the pointlessness of trying to protect Annie's reputation. The idea that she could have left her door open because she knew of police protection came and went through him too quickly to register. "You understand it is an entirely private matter between the lady and myself?"

Was it? Even after a night such as theirs, when he'd begged, "Let me think that you love me, because I don't have anyone else," and she'd said, "No. You're in love with the Venus – she loves *you*. You are safe with her, as you can never be safe with anyone else. I understand you, Martin, but understanding is not enough. I, your wife, the other women, we're all copies of the woman you love, who is not of this world. It's an unfair competition."

Passaggeri looked away a moment, surely not because he was himself embarrassed, but in order to give the German pause. "Please, take a look," he said holding up a photograph. "It shows Vittori's conservatory. Whoever tossed this grenade wanted to kill. Did the attacker also cut the wires, so that, had the victim survived the blast, he could not get prompt help? And if it's the same man, why didn't he cut Signora Tedesco's wire?"

Images of explosions, more than a year after his injury, were still painful for Bora to face. He forced himself to view the shattered Bauhaus furniture and what remained of the gramophone and the records. Only the back wall of the room had been spared.

"Is everything all right, Colonel?"

Bora sat back, nodding. In truth, he felt as he had when he'd leaned on the sink to vomit Jacob Mengs's coffee. Staring at the photograph, he took in this and that detail as if he should care – his habit of searching, searching, and trying to understand. When Passaggeri stretched the pack of cheap cigarettes across his desk, he took one gratefully. Tobacco held down nausea, as both men knew from their battle days; the stronger and cheaper, the better.

Just before dawn, Annie had said, "The woman you killed, Martin: did you know her well?" The question had made him cringe, because he did not expect her to remember, or ask.

"I did not know her at all. It had to be done."

Annie had drawn him to herself, and kissed him. "Martin, you should think that perhaps she *wanted* to die."

What a strange thing to say. It'd prompted him to speak up, pulling away a little. "Did you ever, Annie?"

"... I did. And you?"

"Yes. But religion and duty kept me from it. My men needed me more than I needed myself."

10:18 A.M.

Pozzi could not come to the phone when Bora called: "On account," as the maid put it, "of his expecting Signor Bossaglia

327

any time," and could he please call later. In fact, forgetting the seance for the time being, Pozzi grabbed the phone from the girl.

"No, Anna Maria isn't here, Colonel! She's 'not at home', either? Well, what do you want me to do? Seems to me you're better at keeping track of her than I am. Her uncle is I don't know where, buying himself another tree. Why do you ask about *him*? Now, if you only were so mindful when it comes to my Venus ..."

Bora sent him to hell.

10:23 A.M.

When Bora shifted gears to negotiate Vittori's private drive, the rain had ceased altogether, and a bright yellow ribbon of sky ran over Mount Baldo across the lake.

In his gardening overalls, Vittori came to the gate to meet him. "Well, Colonel! You bring the good weather. Ah, yes ... You heard what happened here. Is there anything I can help you with?"

"There is."

"Why, I'm flattered." The workmen in the garden briefly lifted their heads from the turf at the sight of the German uniform. "See my consolation prize, a pair of arborvitaes. We have been in and out of the garage because of the rain." Pointing to the demolished lakefront, Vittori sighed. "The conservatory's gone, along with the music room. Would you say the grenade was tossed from ... about here?"

Bora looked. "I cannot tell. No, not necessarily. I'm actually here in regard to your niece."

"I thought you might be."

"Do you mind if we go inside?"

"On the contrary. The workmen don't need supervision. I've made a reading room out of the basement lately – makeshift, but we can go and sit there."

Bora did not remove his cap upon entering, a sign that, despite appearances, this was not a personal call. Plaster, bricks, burned paint, the odour of explosive: each surface and element in the devastated room gave out its smell. A crude voice in him said, *Why do you do this? What do you care? You have your transfer. You fucked all night. You might make it out of here yet. Passaggeri and Lipsky can take care of the rest.*

"Tell me, what are we to discuss about Annie?" Still agreeably, but with a slight edge to his voice, Vittori led him to the undamaged back of the house. Bora followed, aware of that edge, himself on edge. When he met the staring eyes of the painted Ethiopian saints, Victor and Macarius, safe inside their unbroken frame on a different wall, he paused and stared back.

"It is evident that you are partial to her." Vittori was conceding. "And reciprocated, I believe. But we *know* about Annie."

Bora looked away from the painting. He let the implication of the words go past him because of that edge, but Vittori wouldn't let him. Glancing back apprehensively, or with concern, or something else, he suddenly sounded shrill. "She hasn't *tried* anything ..."

"No."

Narrow stairs, neatly carpeted, led down to a twilit space. Vittori sought and found a light switch. "I wish you'd tell me what troubles you about Annie, Colonel von Bora."

"I don't want her to die."

"*Die?*" Vittori gasped. There was no power, and flipping the light switch did nothing. "What are you saying?" He turned to search Bora's expression on the shadowy flight of steps. "Because of what she tried in the past?"

"Because someone attempted to enter her house."

"The police are keeping watch."

"Until she moves in with you, the inspector says."

"Yes, I *know* that!" Having groped his way to the bottom of the stairs, Vittori fumbled with matches and a candle. His voice was all edge, now. "I don't see how I can possibly assist you."

Blocking the stairway with his tall frame, Bora sternly addressed the edge. "By letting me look into your garden."

"Look into *my garden*?"

"You know why."

Vittori's reaction was nothing like Bora expected. Having lit the candle, he contemplated it for what seemed like a long time, although it was probably seconds. "Ah, well." The edge was sharp, fully perceivable. "Won't you take a seat?"

"No."

"*The saints Victor and Macarius, much venerated in Ethiopia … the only painting I would not part from.* I can't believe it's because I took down my dear Ethiopian saints before tossing the grenade."

The detail that struck him in Passaggeri's office as he reviewed images of the blast was so irrelevant now that Bora felt insulted by the very mention of it. "I don't care about that. It's the coincidence between your brand of charity – the soup kitchen, the charity sales, the shoulder to cry on – and what happened to three grieving women."

"Grieving women!" They glared at each other in the semi-dark. "As if you understood human grief. Do you call grief losing a hand in a war you helped cause? That's vulgar pain. Losing a wife who probably never loved you? That doesn't come close to grief." Vittori spat out the words with contempt. "Grief is made of different stuff, Colonel, introjected until the world itself becomes the burden and you are crushed under it. Life is the slip of paper that buys your way out of insufferable agony."

Bora's long-controlled anger was close to brimming over. "I forfeited that slip of paper long ago. And, Signor Vittori,

I wager that in your garden, for every tree planted in the last two months, there is evidence of a murder. The missing key to Bianca Spagnoli's flat, the box of cartridges to arm Fiorina Gariboldi's pistol, the clothes you wore when Miriam Romanò showed herself not so *crushed* as to let herself be talked into asking for your help. Or am I wrong?"

"Oh, no. No." Next to a finely designed metal chair, Vittori seesawed on the toes of his rubber boots. "No. I admit, it was only so credible that I should be in my brother-in-law's house during the break-in while my wires were cut, and the timing was tight. Being the victim of a grenade attack, too ... But *you* fell for it, like everyone else. Of course, all along you wanted what you wanted, and any excuse would do." The edge in his voice was all out, like an exposed blade. "I could smell your rut, Colonel, as you stood before her. I could smell hers." When Bora unlatched his holster, Vittori made a dismissive gesture of the right hand. "How predictable. Calling the scars in her cunt 'God's little door'! What won't men do to —"

Bora fired. The fraction of a second sufficed Vittori to pinch the flame between his fingers and charge with the metal chair held forward. He managed to strike Bora squarely, unbalancing him enough to go past him, up the stairs and through the door, which he slammed but could not lock, as Bora was hard behind him and shouldered it open. From the corridor, more stairs led up to a glass-paned door at the top. Bora shattered the glass with the grip of the gun. The sash would not give way under a kick of his riding boot, so he lost time holstering the weapon to open the lock from the inside and keep on.

Another hallway, empty. Offering no clue. Three doors per side, one in the end wall. One after the other, Bora kicked the doors in. The last one was locked, so he fired into the keyhole, kicked it in and stepped into a bedroom, shuttered and dark. A closet or door to another room, locked. Bora had to hold the gun between his left arm and chest to grasp the doorknob with the right hand. Beyond it, steep wooden stairs climbing, a glimmer of daylight from above. Two steps at a time, he climbed. Something from above came crashing down near him, a vase or other heavy breakable object, and then he was near the top.

Vittori flew at him with unsuspected strength. Bora swung around. He struck with the cut of his artificial hand. Pain travelled up his arm from it, but there was no time to gauge pain. They stumbled and lumbered down the tight stairwell. Bedroom, hallway, shattered glass door, stairs. The main floor. The P38 was nothing but an encumbrance at this point. Bora drove it into its holster, following Vittori down another flight of stairs, darker, uncarpeted, leading to a second basement or a garage.

Vittori was grabbing from the wall a long-handled pitchfork when Bora lunged from the last steps on him, tackling him with all his weight to the floor. The sharp, hefty tines rose up and missed him in the near dark.

They struggled, but not much, because Bora was heavier and stronger. Soon, he was forcing Vittori against the wall, grinding his face against the board hung with garden tools. The P38 sought the hollow at the back of his neck and drove up the man's nape. Vittori breathed hard with the struggle and Bora breathed hard too, but in anger. "Turn around."

A sliver of green light, Bora saw now, came through plants growing against a transom-like window, near the ceiling. He could see his hand holding the gun, Vittori's greying hair around the muzzle. "Turn around."

Vittori did not move.

"*Turn around!*"

Vittori had only obeyed halfway when Bora struck him with his armed hand, drawing blood. "For the first woman you killed." Vittori locked his knees to stand, and a second blow reached him, followed by a third, which collapsed him. Bora knelt on him, gun driven against his gullet. "And this is for what you did to Annie when she was a child."

The light went on.

"*Wait!*"

Power had returned, and a naked bulb overhead was nearly blinding. Passaggeri did not leave the step at mid-flight, eyes locked on the gun in Bora's hand. "Don't do it, Colonel. Wait."

Bora did not respond or change position. Voices came from upstairs, the pacing of several men. "They're below," someone said, and someone else unlocked a door from the outside. Moist greenness flooded the dark. The sound of rain on the garden trees seemed louder than any shouted words, and much wiser.

Passaggeri exhaled when Bora rose from Vittori's chest. His booted right foot stayed on the lying man. The gun still aimed at his head, but the contraction of muscles had left the German's neck.

Two policemen were clambering down the steps. Bora watched them manacle Vittori's wrists. Only then did he remove his foot. He crossed the basement to the door and walked out.

"*Cristo santo*, Colonel."

"You should have let me." Bora trembled with rage, and Passaggeri talked to calm him down. They stood smoking bad Italian cigarettes, while around them, in the drizzle, the calls of searching policemen and workmen rose from the garden.

"The connection through the charity works was a slim one, you must admit. Even the planting of Pozzi's calling card, to get him in a fix …"

"Maybe." Little by little, Bora put his anger down, but not so well that he could look at the policeman. "But he did choose to commit murder when his brother-in-law was away, making him into a credible suspect. Take the night of the break-in: at first, he didn't hear his niece's phone call for help, not because he was asleep at Pozzi's house, but because he wanted time in her garden. He knew damn well that no woman alone will open up to see who is prowling around her house. He just wanted us to *think* there was someone who stalked women."

Passaggeri shook his shaggy head. "There goes your distinguished and charitable vegetarian, ready to listen to women's troubles … At this point, I wonder if he had a hand in his sister's suicide back in Rhodes, or Signora Tedesco's attempt when her marriage was opposed." He realized too late that he'd told Bora something he did not know. He wheeled around when one of his men announced the recovery of a double-edged blade from the soil. "Well, damn you, keep looking!"

The policemen were rummaging through the wet dirt in the spot where Vittori asked Bora if the grenade had been thrown from there. Bora had answered that he could not tell, when he rather thought that it'd been tossed into the conservatory from the relative safety of a back room, after removing the prized African souvenir from the wall. "Today if not before," he said, "Vittori understood I suspected him, notwithstanding my regard for Signora Tedesco. He even favoured us, in a way." It was all he would say about that. He would never admit to others that, despite Passaggeri's stakeout, the killer had secretly heard or perhaps even watched them overnight.

It was the moment after a rain when clouds begin to lift, but there is no brightness. A cold breeze wafted from the lake. Bora put on the cap he'd lost in the scuffle. Outside the garden gate, Passaggeri sneezed and blew his nose. "Your orderly called on your behalf summoning us here, but we barely made it in time before things got out of hand. Why didn't you inform me in advance that you were coming? Damn it, there were moments when I even thought —"

"That I could be behind the crimes? God …" Bora opened and got into his car. He was suddenly very tired; even thinking cost him an effort.

"Wait. While we're on the subject … Do you see a connection between the murders and the theft?"

Bora wanted to leave, but politely listened. "No. I think there is one between the murders and the Venus." *Between the Venus and Annie*, he was thinking. Annie, who reminded Vittori of the painting. Beauty and its ephemeral lifespan; beauty and pain. Or grief, which, contrary to what Vittori said, Bora knew all too well. "I'll admit that it was only thanks to you, Commissario, that we have a solution."

"You flatter me!"

"On the contrary." Bora started the engine. "Your outline of the apparent sequence of the murders was crucial. Had Vittori not planted trees so regularly around the deaths …"

"Do you mean my calendar built around the full moon?"

"Precisely. After leaving your office, when I heard from Pozzi that another tree planting was due, I anticipated another murder. And I couldn't let Signora Tedesco move in with her uncle."

Standing between the open door and the car, so that Bora could not close it, Passaggeri insisted, "The photos of the women, the folder … What about that?"

Bora began slowly to reverse the car, forcing the inspector to step away. "You'll have to ask Vittori, but I doubt they had a role. After all, Conforti loved beauty more than the rest of us. Let's say it was a happenstance that became a clue, when Conforti photographed two of the beautiful victims." *If you do not find her, it will be your fault*, Conforti had told him. Was it the Venus that he meant? Weariness was turning to anger again, and Bora was trying to resist both. "Please, let me go. I'll explain tomorrow."

14

Lipsky, who'd flown a Fieseler Storch to Ghedi, saw at once that it was not the time for bantering with Bora about Annie Tedesco – or anything else. Wearing sunglasses in the glare of winter sun, he sat across from him in the small coffee shop at Treponti, where they'd chosen to meet in private. "*East Prussia*," he said. "That's a mouthful."

Bora finished his surrogate coffee. He placed the spoon on the saucer, adjusting its angle so that it sat perpendicular to the handle of the demitasse. How difficult it was to convey the ache of renewed hope. "The assignment is an opportunity."

"To get killed?" Habermehl had lately told him more about Bora than he should. Now Lipsky sat with the uncomfortable feeling that things with Bora had gone from bad to worse; how much worse, he couldn't tell.

Bora, in turn, would not open up. Seeing his diary in Mengs's hands, never mind how many pages he'd himself disposed of, made him feel naked, as if in the last seven years the occasional, faithful outpouring of his feelings had been perverted to witness against him. He tried to dignify his reserve by pretending it was meant to keep Lipsky out of trouble.

"It took me a few days, but I can confirm the suitcase is at the Untermais train depot," the major said. "I am not sure why the Sohls haven't yet shipped it to Germany."

"Hmm. Perhaps the Venus only needs to sit there."

"I don't understand."

"We must remove the painting from the depot, Lipsky."

"Jesus, Colonel! The implications ..."

"The implications are the least of our problems. I have much to do between now and Tuesday, Major. If you find a way to take care of this errand for me, I'll be grateful."

Lipsky was glad the sunglasses concealed the alarm in his eyes. "You call it 'an *errand*'? Yes, I know what's at stake, but that's an egregious request!"

"They know I'm looking for it: that's why I can't do it in person."

With a double knock on the table, Lipsky summoned the waiter. "What drinks have you got?" Having heard, "Monopol," as an answer, he mumbled, "Fucking Italian swill," but ordered a double. He replied nothing before downing the liquor. "I know I'll regret this, but if it must be done, I'll do it ... Did you tell *her* you're going?" he added, feeling that he deserved a small, spiteful reprieve.

"Yes."

"How did she take it?"

"Not well."

"Understandably." Lipsky breathed in, stretching with his muscular neck the collar of his grey shirt. "If I succeed, I'll deposit the Venus in a safe location and meet you in Brescia next Sunday."

"I hope so."

When Bora took the Garda road to the lake, black ice coated the shady side of the road. Events were accelerating beyond control. He was to spend the week before his departure in Brescia with his regiment; by 23 December at the latest, they would reach their new post east of Königsberg in a last-ditch effort to dam the Red Army flood. Chances of survival: next to nil. He had two days left in Salò to wrap up his business with reports to Plenipotentiary Wolff and Marshal Graziani, see Passaggeri one more time, perhaps Pozzi, and Annie, if she was willing to meet him after her uncle's arrest.

On a curve, the tyres hit an invisible ice patch, and Bora's car went careening across the road before he was able to regain control. A less than metaphorical close call, he thought, so near the final act.

And yet: "The love you give others," Dollmann had reminded him back in Rome, "is all you have in the end." Bora hadn't felt as much love on his wedding night as when Annie slowly let herself go under him. "I wish I could die now," he'd told her, meaning it.

They could never do that again, never like that again. Afterwards, moist to his touch under the sheets, she'd asked, "Martin, how long before it's over?"

"The war? I don't know. I don't think about it. I'm trying to keep myself from thinking about anything but the next hours, the things to do during the hours to come."

"Only the poor live that way."

"And soldiers. Timewise, they're the poorest of all."

Back in Salò, he sorted through his office papers, including the notes about the murders, which he would hand-carry to the police. The Venus material, he kept in his briefcase for now. Against hope, he tried Annie's telephone number, which rang out, as did her father's. When he drove past both villas, they stood shuttered and locked.

Passaggeri was easier to find. "Up to his ears with the Vittori case", as he said. Having with utmost brevity announced his reassignment, Bora asked for an update.

"Oh, it all fits but the German shirt at Romanò's place. Was it a friend's, a client's? No matter, since Vittori confessed. He acts as if we ought to thank him instead of jailing him. Some philosophy. I asked what made him think he could decide when people would be better off dead, and he seems convinced that, directly or indirectly, the victims themselves suggested a suicide."

"Nonsense."

"Agreed. Even if the process begun with Spagnoli had the pretence of a mercy killing, it all became quickly twisted. I wouldn't tell Signora Tedesco, but to you, man to man, I will say that the feelings you and the lady have for each other probably played a morbid role in the other two murders. He admitted spying on his niece, on account of you." Passaggeri did not look up from his papers. "Pozzi flew into a murderous rage when he learned of the charges against his brother-in-law. It's a good thing we took the pistol from him when we did. He asked that we let him inform his daughter, and I said yes. Frankly, Colonel, come the trial, I don't know how much of this muck I'll be able to keep from your fiancée."

The use of the word – so sensitive, coming from a gruff man – moved Bora deeply. "Do what you can."

Sunday evening, Bora called at the Japanese legation, where he took leave of Ambassador Hidaka, then to the Republican National Guard and to Borghese's Salò headquarters. By phone, he spoke to Zachariae at Mussolini's Villa Feltrinelli.

MONDAY, 11 DECEMBER 1944, 7:30 A.M.

"I don't want to see you leave," Annie had told him over the telephone on Saturday morning. "I'll call you before you go."

On Monday, Bora did not even try not to be disappointed when the call came from Pozzi instead. "Anna Maria is out of town," he cut matters short. "She wants to be on her own. Have you recovered my Venus, Colonel?"

"No."

Today he opened the mail with small, attentive gestures, as if the mail were important. Two envelopes contained cards inviting him to galas, one at the Metropoli, the other at the Spielcasino. He courteously sent his regrets to both.

He was putting on his greatcoat when Hager looked in. "Herr Oberst, there's a reporter from *Signal* below. Said the magazine's to do a write-up on you." (Better late than never: it concerned the brilliant mountain warfare in the summer.) "Should I let him in?"

"I have an appointment at the Ministry of the Armed Forces. Here, hand him the report on Mount Cassio."

In Soiano, Marshal Graziani took Bora's final report but would not shake his hand. "I can't say I regret to see you go. You've been a difficult charge."

The reporter from *Signal* had gone by the time Bora returned to Salò. He stayed at the office until late, long after having disposed of residual paperwork. The building grew quiet around him; only the radiator in the hallway made a low noise at times, like a breathing creature. When he left, it was humid more than cold, and no call had come from Annie Tedesco.

At the same time, back from a snow-capped Milan after a convulsed day, Mengs granted himself the leisure of taking no work home that night. Sutor had given him a bottle of champagne, and he popped it open, poured himself a sparkling glassful and gulped it down. He was no connoisseur, so it was just a dry, pleasant wash of carbonated alcohol in his mouth. Lying on the bed, he toasted himself, and the green light he had received from Kaltenbrunner's office. Held together by a rubber band, Bora's photographs from the Russian days had already begun to yellow and looked remote. The people in them, dead or soon to die. There were few blank pages left at the end of the diary.

TUESDAY, 12 DECEMBER 1944, 9:00 A.M.

Sohl was not yet in when Bora closed the door of the office behind him for the last time. He'd taken official leave of the general the evening before, as superficial a farewell as he'd ever experienced. He left the keys on his desk. The Moloch fireplace, unlit, dark as the mouth of a forsaken hell, gaped as if it'd swallow the wall.

Alongside the pavement waited his car. But, true to his habit of saving fuel while in town, Bora took a last walk along the lakefront. The frost on the roofs was melting in the sun, running down in lively chains of droplets, and a light steam sweated up from gutters and tiles. Shadows stretched out – crisp, blue like lengths of cloth under people and things. Across the lake, Torri and the spur of St Vigilio trembled over the water.

Try as he might, Bora noticed he was unable to think past today. Past today, nothing came to mind, as if he'd forgotten the incumbencies for tomorrow and the days after, not to speak of months to come. It had nothing to do with wisdom: it was a barrier in his perception, ominous or merciful or both. He had never met it before, which made him uneasy. He wondered what it meant, because it did not in fact hurt at all.

"Do you mind if I walk with you?" Pozzi was standing right beside him, and Bora had not heard him approach.

"I don't mind."

For nearly five minutes they walked, Pozzi with hands clasped behind his back and Bora looking away, at the villages on the opposite shore.

"You're limping." Pozzi said the words is if he were inform-ing him rather than asking about it. He cleared his throat, pausing to tie his scarf around his neck. "Anna Maria wanted me to see you."

Bora blinked but did not stop walking.

"You think I'm vulgar, Colonel, don't you?"

"What difference does it make?"

"I am vulgar, but I'm not stupid. And I am not such a bad man."

Bora looked up at a cloud that was obscuring the sun with a great sweeping tail. "I should have killed him."

Pozzi's golden teeth showed in a grimace. "*I* should have killed him thirteen years ago."

"How could you let him get close to your daughter?" Bora bit his lip to keep from crying out the words. "Didn't you *know?*"

"I knew nothing, that's what I knew! I was working too hard to think he'd pick up with her where he left off with his sister. *My wife.* The wife I loved more than myself. You think you know the world, Colonel. Am I crazy, talking to mediums and such? I'm aware that they flock around me because I have money, and that they tell me what I want to hear. What I want to hear is what they tell me: that Diamantina is somewhere; that she's safe forever, and that she loves me. I buy myself the afterlife I want my dead wife to have. That's the truth, Colonel von Bora. It isn't painted pictures on the wall, or the nice things we all aspire to be! He didn't like my nudes, the sanctimonious swine. I paid for mine, the framed ones and the live ones!" Pozzi adjusted the expensive coat on his shoulders. "Well, that's that. I'm not lifting a finger to help him. And anyway, apart from failing me regarding the Venus, you ought to be proud of yourself."

"I'm not proud of myself."

Out of the cloud's reach, the sun was once more bright on the shingle. Pieces of quartz glittered like stars in it. Pozzi squinted in the light. "Do you love her?"

Bora felt the question cut through the unprepared, thin layer of his pretence. "Yes."

For the rest of the walk, they said nothing else. Eventually they came in sight of the car parked at the verge of the road. Bora said, "Goodbye." Without turning, he walked back to the road and was soon driving away.

Pozzi stood behind a minute longer. At least Bora had not asked him why Annie sent him. Heavy-footed on the gravel, he retraced his steps in the opposite direction, to the place where the quartz shone.

Before noon, Bora left Salò.

Twenty kilometres out, past Gavardo and the turn-off to Nuvolento, the Garda road ran along the Chiese River towards Brescia. Bora was reading his orders when he felt the car reduce speed, not so sharply as to make him glance up. He knew they were coming to Treponti, where he'd met Lipsky; there, by a right-hand turn-off, they would leave the Garda road for State Route 11.

"Roadblock ahead, Colonel."

Bora looked. Parked across the grey stretch of the road, just before the junction, a truck and staff car were visible in the distance. Nothing unusual, although Bora did not recall seeing a roadblock here when he'd driven by two days earlier. The army driver was experienced; Bora knew him from his Polish days. He continued to slow down by degrees. "It's all right, Hannes. Stop."

It was an SS truck. There were armed men in it. The BMW car parked a few paces ahead, unmarked, had a plate Bora did not recognize. Straddling the space between vehicles, two

SS men with submachine guns slung across their stomachs signalled to halt. One of them walked to the passenger's side of the car. Bora rolled down the window. He noticed the SS did not salute.

"Get out."

Bora met his driver's nervous eyes in the rear-view mirror. It was pointless to ask the reason. Without raising his voice, Bora said, "How do you *dare*, soldier?"

In a prompting gesture, the SS man waved the weapon. Bora left his seat, with an undetected sweep of the hand unlatching his holster. He saw at the same time Mengs's silhouette surge from the unmarked car, and anger raced up to meet fear in him. Mengs stepped over, hands in the slash pockets of his leather coat. His dead eyes rested on him only the time it took to shift over to the SS men. "Disarm him."

They restrained Bora before he could pull away. The P38 was pulled out of his holster. "What is this, Mengs? *What are you doing?*"

"You're coming with us."

There was no hope. No hope, yet Bora tried to keep calm. "I'm ordered to the front. You cannot separate me from the regiment."

"Come now, Colonel. You're under arrest."

"On what charges?"

"Traitors don't need to be reminded of their charges."

Bora reacted to the outrageous words so vehemently that the SS men had to lock him in a wrestling hold. Whatever he shouted at Mengs, no one paid attention to Bora's driver, who stepped out of the car and came around it with his ordinance pistol in hand. "Let go of the commander!"

"No, Hannes, no!"

One of the SS half-turned and fired a burst on him. Hannes dropped back, blood exploding from his chest. Bora reacted.

He struck the barrel even as it swung against him, as if to wrench his shoulder off. The road reeled and came up, tilting red under the shock of gun-stocks.

At the Ausserkommando in Milan, Kappler looked up from the newspaper when Sutor's voice came high-pitched from his place by the phone. "Son of a bitch, we got Martin Bora!"

Johannesquade was not alone in wondering why the colonel did not show up in Brescia at the appointed time. Vice-Commander Major Lübbe-Braun placed urgent calls to Soiano, Salò and Gardone. He spoke to Sohl, who said that Colonel von Bora had left by motorcar three hours earlier.

It took another hour for news of his abandoned vehicle and dead driver to reach the regimental staff. Immediate speculation about a partisan attack was quashed at a quarter to two, when a dry communiqué was rung in from the Hotel Regina Ausserkommando. Other anxious calls followed, but it took the officers until late in the afternoon to secure a reliable contact in Milan.

In Milan, Mengs sat back in his chair.

"Well then, Bora. You see that all your cleverness and philosophy didn't do a bit of good: you've fallen like all people who think themselves above the law. An investigator, no less. That you should have the gall of exposing a murderer when you're no better yourself! You're too brazen and indiscreet and rely too much on your ability to turn a phrase. To me, you may be a Jew-lover, a saboteur guilty of criminal negligence and anti-German activities, and a friend to traitors. To Sutor, you're nothing but upwards of six feet of arrogant half-English flesh, and your mind doesn't mean a goddamn thing."

Bora looked away. He sat in the drab office of a Milan building: he had no idea where; it didn't make a difference at this point. He was numb with the trip and Mengs's continuous questioning in the car.

"Don't trust yourself, either." Mengs pursed his lips, a strange motion in his fat face. "Like all systems, we have a knack for grinding meat finely. This isn't the time for your speculative moods: do yourself and your mother a favour and tell the truth. It'll be much quicker and more dignified than having to get it out of you with methods you found fit to criticize in the East. As for your strolls in Berlin last July, or the killing in Rome, I promise you'll get a clean exit by firing squad if you just give us the name of your principal. This, I promise you."

Bora kept his eyes low, which seemed to Mengs a sign of weariness rather than fear.

"How could you think you'd get away with it? Kappler gave you the benefit of the doubt, I don't know why. Sutor will humiliate you, because he knows that everyone has a decency inside: you probably more than most. How I've seen that *stripped* from people! You may keep quiet now, but there's hardship ahead. Think of all the theorizing while you pursued your investigation. We did the same with you. We *caught* you. So, whatever is intimate or shames you when exposed, save it while you can."

Bora slowly returned his eyes to him. "I'm a product of the same system. You know I can't."

Lübbe-Braun moved the receiver from one ear to the other, impatiently. "Where is he being held?"

"In town, it's unclear where. Probably one of the 'house prisons'."

"May I see him?"

"Not likely. They've started interrogating him."

*

There was a smell of vomit in the room. It had been Bora's first impression, but pain blotted it out of his mind when they pulled back his shoulder to strap him down. Arm, head and chest ached. Lights burst before his eyes and left green spots behind. Sutor asked something to which he said, "No one."

He expected to be struck, but the blow came before he could cringe. His head hit the table in front of him. Light, dark, cold, a lash of reverberating pain at the nape of his neck. Blood spurted from his nostrils. When he tried to pull back, Sutor's hand kept him down.

"Who else is there, Bora?"

He strained to lift his face to speak. Blood filled his nose, and he was breathing it back, swallowing it, slick and sweet and like iron in his mouth. Mengs's voice said, "Let him talk." The pressure on his neck relented, and Bora sat upright. "Nobody else." Next, his cheekbone met the table in a shock of wood and bone. "There's no one else."

"Where did you get the informant's file?"

"There was no file."

His head was hit again, was lifted, and hit again. Sutor held him down. Bora gulped bloody air through his mouth. Strangely, the small wrestling figures of Jacob and the Angel in Pozzi's house floated before him. It was a brief image like an exposed film fading in his head, unrelated, disconnected, lost at once.

"Who gave you the informant's file?"

"No one."

His forehead crashed against the table. Had he been closer to the edge, it would have smashed the bridge of his nose. Bora glimpsed his lap briefly in an explosion of bright light. "Who gave you the file? Who gave you the file? Who gave you the file?" And at each question his head hit the table, until he said, "I don't know," and he knew it was an admission of some kind.

There was a minuscule green dot at the end of his mind, dazzling in the dark, whirling slowly. Bora spat fresh blood.

"It was Dollmann, wasn't it?"

Mention of the name rallied the defences within him. "No one gave me the file."

Sutor loosed Bora's arms from the chair, but not from each other. "Was it Dollmann?"

"No one gave me the file. I had no file."

The chair was kicked from under him. Flat on his back, Bora saw Mengs put a cough drop in his mouth. Sutor straddled him with a PPK gun in his hand. "Tell me it was Dollmann."

The gun was thick-barrelled, small and ugly. A pull on the trigger cocked and released the hammer with a click. Bora flinched. So, this was how it had been for Vittori. Fear of death raced through him, and he fought it without closing his eyes. "It was not Dollmann."

From the floor, livid with anger and spite, Sutor's face seemed too small for his body, distant and hazy behind the muzzle of the gun. Mengs stretched his hand over Bora's head and took the gun from Sutor's hand.

"Kick it out of him."

The thud of army boots was breaking through Bora's hunching body when Mengs left the room. He heard the chair clatter, the scrape of the table being pushed aside. Sutor yelled, "Get down, down, get his fucking rocks!"

Slowly Mengs struck a match on the box, lit a cigarette and started pacing.

When he returned, Bora was huddled with his head against the wall, and the guards were dragging him back towards Sutor. His face was bloody, and saliva welled out of his mouth in a drivel now clear and now stringy with bright red.

Mengs drove a cigarette into his mouth and lit it. Bora let it fall from his lips and Mengs put it back. "Who was it, Bora?"

"No one."

"Well, then. Let's start all over again, before you tell us about Berlin."

WEDNESDAY, 13 DECEMBER 1944

In Venice, Lipsky received a call from Sohl, who wanted him to vouch for his orthodoxy in case of a political probe, "since Bora nominally worked for me".

The major said that he would, of course, et cetera, but his mind was going full speed in another direction. Did this mean the general would hasten to ship off the Venus? Going to Meran became a priority. He flipped through his notebook for the number of the barracks where Bora's staff was housed in Brescia and immediately dialled Lübbe-Braun.

Bora was trembling violently. He could hardly stand. Before he knew it, his face was against the grimy latrine wall and his knees were giving way. He propped himself against the corner with his hand and kept himself from falling. He desperately needed to void his bladder and was unable to gather the strength to stand and unbutton his breeches over the hole. He stood against the corner of the wall, shaking, trying to lock his knees enough to continue standing.

As in dreams, he thought he'd turned and undone his clothes and was able to relieve himself. He let go, and with help-less dread, he felt warmth ooze between his legs, going down his knees, painful, painful and unstoppable. He groaned at the thought of urinating on himself, shamed into a strained effort to turn and try frantically to unbutton his breeches. He saw he hadn't urinated. It was blood. His shorts were soaked with it, and it didn't smell like urine: it smelled like blood. Shakily, he was able to void his bladder then, propping his stump against the wall. Such burning pain came with the passage of warm liquid out of his body that he cried tears with it.

After doing up his clothes again, he stood there, shivering with his back to the door. Mengs came to open it, causing him to stumble backwards.

"Out, Bora. Let's start again."

SALÒ, THURSDAY, 14 DECEMBER 1944

General Sohl was too agitated to wonder about Lipsky's presence in Salò.

"I should have known when the Security Service came probing back in October. Still, I thought it was minor matters. He's charged with killing a Gestapo informant in Rome, in the public square!"

Lipsky would have preferred not to think over the last few hours, what with the difficulty of securing a Fieseler Storch to fly there and landing while Graziani was away on the strip at Soiano. "It could be a misunderstanding." He faked optimism. "How can I see him?"

"Don't ask *me*. You're the lawyer. They transferred him to the city prison, San Vittore."

"Which ward, do you know?"

"The Fifth. Jews and Jew-lovers section." (*Jesus*, Lipsky groaned). "See what you can do." Sohl's jovial face grew hard. "And, in case you're here for the Venus, Bora confirmed that she is gone for good. If the Reich Marshal insists, bring him the Jew's copy. Bora gave it to the Tedesco girl."

Clever bastard. And how's your loving wife? Lipsky wanted to throw at him. "The Reich Marshal does not deal in copies."

"Then accept it, as I did."

In two relentless hours, all Bora was sure of was not admitting he'd been ordered to Abruzzi after leaving Rome on 5 June. Sutor himself had struck him with his bare fists and was heaving with anger when Mengs told him to stand aside. Promoted long since from the use of brute force, he directed a guard to fill a syringe and inject a liquid into Bora's arm.

"Now you'll tell us where you vanished for five days on the way to Bolsena and whom you met in Berlin," he began to say. Then he perceived the rustle of a body that falls upon itself. He turned quickly, but not enough to keep Bora from collapsing at his feet.

"Get up, Bora."

A guard leaned over, turned him around. "He's out."

"Fucking wake him up!" Sutor shoved the guard aside. "Toss water on him, get him up!"

"He's out cold."

Lipsky had to go begging the Italians for fuel, and only by handing out money here and there was he able to get what he wanted. Weather permitting, the flight to Bolzano, the closest airport to Meran, was under an hour and a half away. The weather forecast predicted strong winds and an ice storm on the Zillertal Alps, followed by an improvement. The sky was clear over the lake, and he was tempted to skip over to see Annie. His sense of duty prevailed, but he still had to sit tight for close to an hour before he heard that the storm had abated.

He took off, buffeted by residual squalls, only to be warned minutes later by radio that a large formation of Allied bombers was approaching from the south-east and might cross paths with him over the Trento area. His old fighting spirit flared and fizzled, in view of his chances and what was at stake. He glumly headed back for Soiano with a tail wind, and there he sat, because even travelling by car would take him in the direction of the air raids.

Someone was driving a needle into his right arm and Bora recoiled. He tried to speak, and the words came out indistinct. "What is it? What are you giving me?"

The hand belonged to Zachariae. Bora wondered how Il Duce's physician could be here, and why he spoke Italian as he knelt by him. *He* was lying on the floor, and there was too much light, too much light. His mind opened and closed like a camera shutter, blinding him and sinking him in the dark.

"Ephedrine."

Bora closed his eyes. The light bulb above him was an unbearable, inescapable sun reaching into his brain. Closing his eyes did not help.

The physician extracted the needle and rubbed cotton on his flesh. Bora felt the touch, but his flesh seemed miles away, as if his body lay disjointed. With the rush of ephedrine, consciousness came back dully, in flashes. He asked, in Italian, "Do I have my tunic on?"

"No. You're in your shirt."

The answer, for no reason he could fathom, made him feel like weeping, miserable and naked. "How long was I out?"

"I have no idea. I was just called in."

"It cannot have been pain. I cannot have passed out because of pain." Even Zachariae was so distant, his face like a small almond dipped in milk. And it was not Zachariae at all, but a civilian doctor or medic. "Is my tunic here?"

"It isn't."

When he tried to rise, everything went speckled and black again. The man held his head up. "Give the drug time."

There was a pause, and Bora did not know whether the physician was silent or he could not hear him. Bora pulled up his knees, and the cluster of his groin seemed to explode with pain; he was awake and struggling not to cry out.

"I don't know who you are, but you're in trouble."

Bora heaved with the growing pain. Consciousness came and went, it curdled at the edge of his mind until he was able to make sense again. He was lying in the middle of a small cell, where the man next to him held his pulse between his fingers, an eye on his watch. The other hand felt his belly.

Bora cried out. Still the other kept probing. "Tell them what they want to hear. Have mercy on yourself."

But, once outside the cell: "Your *truth serum* ..." the physician told Mengs with a twitch of the mouth. "He's obviously allergic to barbiturates. Give him scopolamine, and he'll pass out on you each time. Or, if you must, give him a good dose and kill him outright."

Dusk beat Lipsky to San Giacomo's airport north of Bolzano. From the lone non-com who spoke to him, he learned that rail junctions and marshalling yards had been battered all day. Despite his flyer's nonchalance regarding such news, Lipsky cringed. "Meran, too?" "No, Herr Major, not Meran." Tired, cold from flying in the unheated aircraft and plainly sore from sitting, he stopped for the night at the closest inn, where in lieu of dinner he downed a couple of schnapps.

In a troubled slumber, he heard or imagined aeroplanes heading north all night. To Austria, to Germany – who could say? By comparison, having to explain this unconventional leave of absence from Venice ranked low. If he only took his mind off the Venus and the need to recover her, Lipsky would become so galled at Bora that he could forget where Peter's brother was now, and what they were likely doing to him.

FRIDAY, 15 DECEMBER 1944

Bora found that if he concentrated he could slow down the nosebleed and swallow most of it back. He had to keep himself from thinking. This was the morning to give up thinking in order to function. He had to make his mind dark and small and unable to think ahead, because he was afraid. Not even the Venus could help him out of fear. White and tender as she was, she receded into her murky landscape, and Annie's red heels, red nails, red mouth were like bloody cuts in the dark. It was fear of giving out Dollmann's name or admitting his mission to Abruzzi on the Abwehr's behalf, fear of breaking down, fear for his family – the thought of his mother panicked him so that blood gushed and he couldn't control it. He staggered when he tried to leave his cot. So he sat, wondering what made him suppose it was morning, because there was no practical way of knowing. The small window was blocked, the light still on, and no noises came through the door.

When a well-rested Mengs walked in with a guard, Bora read 7:05 on his wristwatch. It was morning after all.

"You need to shave," Mengs said. "You smell of sweat and blood. You need to wash."

They led him to a row of shower stalls. He was told to strip naked and walk into the stall. Mengs handed him a safety razor. The water was icy. Bora braced under it. The shock of cold took his breath away as he began to slide the blade down his cheeks and chin; the skin above his upper lip was difficult to shave, because he shivered and his hand was unsteady. He cut himself under the jetting water, and already Mengs solicited the razor back. Bora wearily rubbed himself, trying to keep his attention from the bruises and crusted blood. He splashed water in his mouth to rinse the blood, anxious to be done with it and get out. His shirt and underwear were thrown at him to wash.

Mengs looked over the stall, careful not to get himself wet. He could hear Bora's teeth chattering. "All right, all right, enough cleaning. Let's go."

"Like this? Without even my shorts on?"

"Let's go."

It was just over thirty kilometres from Bolzano to Meran, a state route that in other days, for other reasons, Lipsky had travelled with a light heart. After a clear night, clouds were again rolling in from the north and would likely delay his return flight. Behind the wheel of the rattling wreck he'd borrowed from an officer in Bolzano, claiming extreme urgency, he had a window of two hours before returning it. He left the river Adige at Sinigo to enter the flat land south of Meran, and at once he began to worry. What he'd taken at first for drifting fog and low clouds were the signs of an overnight air raid. He could not judge from the car what section of town had been struck, but, driving down Reichstrasse to Untermais, Lipsky's heart sank.

Near the old Untermais cemetery, a team of civilian workers trudged in the rain with shovels and pickaxes on their shoulders. Nearly everyone spoke German in the town, which made his questioning easier.

The man he queried shook his head. "The Untermais train depot? I don't know it'll do you any good to go there, Herr Major. We're heading there to dig it up."

Bora only knew he had fallen because he felt his knees strike the floor. His face hit next, and it was as if part of him simply slipped out of his body.

Sutor drove his foot into the space between his jaw and shoulder and turned him around. "On your feet, and let's talk some more about Berlin."

Bora tried to rise but could not. He had *not* talked. Would not talk. He crawled, and not even having the barrel of a rifle pushed hard against his side gave him the strength to get up. He trembled with the need to moan.

"Give him his shorts."

At the other side of the room, Mengs meticulously folded the newspaper he'd been reading and walked out. Bora was unable to put his shorts back on. Sutor kicked him in his belly. "So, you'll learn to lay the woman of a Jew."

The mountain weather could turn foul in the blink of an eye. Lipsky drove the last stretch under a lashing rain that froze on the windshield. The windshield wiper did not work at all, so he drove, sticking his head out of the window, at a snail's pace on the road littered with shrapnel. He could hardly see, and when he halted to scrape the ice off the glass, the wiper came off.

Rain kept the smoke down. At the end of the boulevard leading to the depot and the river, Lipsky did not realize how fast he'd been going until he tried to brake and skidded into a half-turn before coming to rest on the shoulder. He turned the engine off and stepped out of the car.

Icy rain pelted him. A monstrous plough seemed to have scooped out the rail junction. At one end, a cargo car lay on its side, cases and materiel fallen out of it; burned stumps of walls rose above a tangle of train tracks, like arching serpents frozen in time. Among craters and heaps of dirt, workers soaked to the skin moved like ghosts. A string of profanities went through Lipsky's mind as he stumbled into the devastated, bombed-out jumble that had been the Untermais depot.

Kappler came to see Bora on Saturday morning. A guard handed him a clipboard before closing the door, and he flipped through the notes.

"I understand you're not eating. That won't do. You need to keep your strength up."

Bora sat on his cot, his back against the wall, and Kappler grinned at his unwillingness to look at him. "I see they had you up a couple of nights, and such. But look at this: you were 'very uncooperative'. You haven't said ten useful words since coming here. What a disappointment! I still think it's a shame and a waste, and you know it." He saw Bora wet his lips and expected him to say something, but he didn't. Kappler unbuttoned his greatcoat even though the cell was frigid and his breath clouded as he spoke. "But you killed our informant, no doubt about it. I have to hand it to you for cold blood: in the Lateran Square, with my men all around … You commit crimes nearly as well as you solve them. I hope, however, you don't think I disregarded the interrogation. I was here yesterday, actually, and heard you cry out during a session. You cried out quite a bit, but then it's a painful method, and those are sensitive body parts. On the other hand, if it's properly applied, there are no consequences: it just hurts like hell. But electrodes are better than glass rods. Those shatter the urethra right off."

Bora's stared at the floor, lips tight.

"As for the rest, your immediate future consists of stripping of rank and expulsion from the German army the moment you enter German territory." It was the first mention of a transfer Bora heard, and he did look up this time. Kappler was grinning. "I arranged for you to have a change of clothes for the trip. Now, you may ask me one question and one favour. What is the question?"

"I'd like to know if I'm to be shot or hanged."

"You're going to the People's Court. Surely Judge Freisler will make you hang." Bora's mouth contracted, Kappler saw it well. "If Mengs or Sutor had their way, you'd be dead already.

This way, you can prepare yourself. I know you're a *spiritual* man. Now the favour: what is it?"

"For the trip, I wish to have my prosthesis back, and my best uniform."

"The one tailored in Rome, eh? A bit sentimental, but why not." Kappler searched his breast pocket. "This came in with the mail this morning. You should take a look."

It was a black-edged newspaper clipping, an obituary. Bora had to rest it on his knee to read it, because his hand was trembling.

Dr Franz Augustus, Freiherr von Bora, beloved father, grandfather and great-grandfather, on Wednesday, 13 December.

"Bad news travels fast, Bora. I know what you're thinking, but we had nothing to do with it. It was probably the disgrace you brought on your grandfather and the family." Smugly, Kappler knocked on the door to be let out. A minute later, for the first time in nearly a week, the light in the cell was turned off.

With a harrowing flight behind him, about which it'd take years before he would brag to anyone, Lipsky made it to Milan on Saturday afternoon and secured a talk with Herbert Kappler. The SS commander heard him out in a tolerant silence.

"So, he has one friend in the world. Oh, I see: a *colleague*, not a friend. Well, Major, make sure you're at the station early tomorrow morning. I'll ask Herr Mengs to give you ten minutes: you lawyers can say a lot in a short time."

SUNDAY, 17 DECEMBER 1944, 7:52 A.M.

Run by straight, long clouds, the eastern sky had a rosy tinge, which would turn red at sunrise over the ruins of the latest air raid. Lipsky saw ice on the rails like crusted salt. It was very cold. Two guards rubbed their hands on the platform. On the farthest track, a locomotive was backing into a dead-end with the slick sounds of metal parts.

Bora had bruises and cuts on his face. A thin blue line across his jaw pointed to a crack in the bone, although, in view of a public trial, the evidence of manhandling was no doubt confined under his clothing. From the uniform, worn without a greatcoat, all insignia had been removed, including the facings on his collar. Lipsky blushed for him, more uneasy with the encounter than Bora seemed to be. Bora said he was glad to see him.

"You must be freezing, Colonel."

"I *am* freezing, but the rank no longer applies."

Wasting no time, Lipsky told his story, keeping an eye on Mengs, who sucked on a cough drop a few steps away. "… and when I reached the depot, a bomb had fallen through the roof. I clambered in and saw right away that hardly anything was left of the material stored in heavy boxes, not to speak of a suitcase. But I knew where it was and tried to gather what remained of it. Gutted and black, the rain was falling on it. Of the canvas rolled up inside, nothing but burned rags were left. The Venus crumbled in my hands. I'm not ashamed to tell you that I sat there and wept." Lipsky felt guilty for reporting the news, which Bora heard with a tense cast on his face. "I missed her by one night! One night! Now she's *really* gone, Colonel. How can I live with myself?"

Bora looked at the locomotive edging back on the tracks towards the man signalling to it. His train was due soon, on track number seven. *Seven*, Remedios had said seven years ago, meaning his death. For a moment, although Lipsky expected a different reaction, he only stared at the receding locomotive.

"Well, at least you'll get to live with yourself." He found the spirit to joke. "I do thank you for trying, Major." But stealthily, extracting a slip of paper from his cuff, he added, "Take this, quickly, while Mengs isn't looking. I sewed it up in this tunic. Thank God they let me wear it this morning. It is all written there."

Lipsky tucked the slip out of sight. "What do you mean?"

"Listen. Sohl had nothing to do with the theft. But his wife does, in as far as she was convinced by her lover to store and carry valuables across the border. Do you understand?"

"Wolff?" Alarmed, Lipsky only mouthed the name. "Is that why you are ..."

"I wish. At this point I doubt even *he* knows how much I know. But the theft wasn't Wolff's idea, either. When I last saw Standartenführer Dollmann, I penned a name and showed it to him, and he nearly fell off his chair. Do you remember A.L. Broeck?"

"Broeck ..." Racking his brain, Lipsky nodded. "The Swiss? One of those who bid on the Venus four years ago?"

"A.L. Broeck, from Lugano. Art collector and retired diplomat, presently assisting Reichsführer Himmler in his dealings with the Allies in Switzerland, Dollmann interpreting."

"Jesus, Colonel." Lipsky dropped his fair jaw. "Wolff stole the Venus for *Himmler*?"

"It's the only possibility: exchange goods with the Allies to save his skin and gain a future. He meant to take the Venus to the negotiating table with the Anglo-Americans, and Wolff promptly followed suit." Bora was tempted – it was a time for admissions – to tell Lipsky that he finally understood why Conforti had told him: if you do not find her, it will be your fault. All he said, was, "Do what you can with it, when the war is over and crimes can be exposed."

Lipsky made a face. "Your train is coming," he warned, looking over Bora's shoulder.

"Thank you." Bora shook his hand. He half-smiled, quelling the urge to speak of the night when he'd gone to the Rosenhof hospital for X-rays, but it was the Venus, not his hand, that had been radiographed in Zachariae's presence.

"Get on with it, Major!" Mengs called rudely from where he stood.

Lipsky turned. "I'm coming! Well, Bora. At least Annie has a copy of it."

Their hands were still clasped. Bora was on the brink, on the very brink of revealing that the real Venus had been for weeks at Annie's house. That she'd never left Salò, because Conforti, the magician from Prague, had switched the canvases, in view of German occupation. The reframing, the cleaning just before Sohl moved in … only excuses to *save her.*

If you do not find her …

"For what it's worth, tell Annie …"

"I will." Lipsky stood there, burdened with the moment and his sense of failure; he would never know he'd been asked to remove the painting from the depot only so that Broeck would not realize he had been delivered a copy.

From the end of the tracks, a train was entering the station. "I can forgive Frau Sohl everything, Lipsky, except saying yes to Wolff when he told her to call Conforti. But, of course, killing a Jew is no crime." Bora heard the engine come to a wheezing halt behind him. Skinny pigeons flew over the tracks in the red sky.

Mengs waved to Lipsky to hurry. Lipsky had been on the point of asking whether Bora knew what the *secret* of the Venus was, but the summons intervened. "All right, we're done! Anything else, Colonel von Bora?"

Bora nodded. "You took Peter's belongings to my parents. Do the same for me. It'll be time soon enough."

Lipsky was straight-faced but moved. Bora grinned. "Don't think I do not hate to die."

The train had travelled as far as one of the little solitary, battered stations to the north-east of Milan, when it slowed down to a stop. Mengs, who had been reading a newspaper across from Bora, folded it and put it in his coat pocket. Bora glanced at the guards at the end of the carriage and could not tell by their reaction whether the halt was planned. He sensed something like a shrill, discordant note when, in order to see, Mengs drew the shade and lowered the window. Outside, the sky opened above the haze and the long, straight clouds. Huge vistas of blue yawned to the east. But there was more rain from the bruise-dark mountains ahead. Bora listened to the thin calls of birds in distant trees, determined not to let pointless melancholy through. Regret and loneliness came from those acute clipped sounds in the countryside. Mengs's interest focused below, where a car idled on a country lane by the tracks.

"Sicherheitsdienst officers, Herr Mengs," said one of the guards.

Bora kept looking outside, where misty fields ran in parallel lines to the horizon. Mengs rubbed his knees as he stood and gestured for the guards to precede him outside. "We might after all take care of things right here."

The words dropped a veil from the day. With extraordinary, painful clarity, all the details of it stood out. The white gash on the side of a distant hill, landslide or exposed rock, etched itself into Bora's view, as if the presence of the rock at this time and place had meaning only in relation to him. Being manacled was suddenly outrageous; he had a momentary wild urge to start, to get away and run. The jolt went through his mind but did not reach the rest of the body. Neither battered bones nor muscles were listening.

At the foot of the escarpment, a field lay narrow and over-grown by grass sick with winter, a mangy carpet balding here and there. There was frost on the lane, where pebbles gathered as rain and snow had placed them. The lane curved ahead, where clumps of trees hid what lay behind the curve.

Many times, Bora had wondered how this moment would be and what he would think of. His mind, however, had no appreciable power of choice over thoughts. It was an empty inner place for thoughts to run unbidden, disconnected, like gusts of wind sweeping through. Beyond the field, not far, a farmhouse with a long blind wall – a firing squad wall, Bora knew from experience – and men armed with machine guns. *Pray for us sinners*, he thought. The rest of the prayer would not come. He simply wanted to get it over with. Without a priest, without Remedios, just *over with*. His heart, from the bottom of where it lay, rapped faster and faster. The muscle was excited; it pumped in jerks.

Seeing Dollmann enter the carriage, accompanied by SS men, made him suddenly weary. Dollmann wore his usual unruffled expression, as if he were not the one whose name Bora had never mentioned in days past. "We have just under nine minutes," he said petulantly.

It was an understatement at least. Bora watched Mengs talking to the SD officers below, next to the rain-shiny car in which they had arrived. He watched the brick wall beyond.

"I had to do somersaults to get here." Dollmann removed his gloves. "The plenipotentiary is justly *provoked*. What trouble you are, Bora. Had you simply left the diary in the safe, for us to take rather than the Gestapo. Had you understood that we put you in Salò in the first place, to keep an eye on your heedlessness. The next time a reporter comes to do a write-up about you, see the advantages of being in the news. And who do you think pushed your reassignment through, against Kaltenbrunner's insistence that you be shot on the spot in Milan?"

"Well, do it now, Standartenführer. It'll be a relief."

"Oh, shut up." With a flick of the glove, Dollmann ordered one of his men to unlock Bora's manacles. "Come on." By the elbow – Bora flinched, as it had been beaten raw – he led him to the end of the carriage and into the next compartment. "There's a medic to take a look at you." And, when Bora was made to strip to the waist, he stood with his back turned but spying on him over his shoulder. "They'll give you a couple of shots, some pills to keep you going. No, don't wear your tunic yet." From a brief-case held by an SS man, a small box appeared in Dollmann's hands. "Put your ribbons and medals back on." And, because Bora had difficulty doing it with one hand, Dollmann helped out. For two minutes or so, they stood together, pinning cam-paign ribbons and badges, snapping epaulettes and insignia, "I can't believe I am doing this," being Dollmann's only words. "This has nothing to do with you, you understand."

Bora was so removed from hope that he had no desire to reach for it. But he did say, "The plenipotentiary wants to save his hide afterwards."

"Well, I did tell him in all honesty I don't think you'd give testimony in his favour *afterwards*. But he gives you the benefit of the doubt."

Bora stared at him. Wolff probably did not know of the depot's destruction. "Where am I going?"

"You'll join your regiment in East Prussia. Things will be such up there that no one will mind you. Just see that you survive the war."

Hope was like a stab, unbearably painful. "My parents?"

"Screw your parents. I'll talk to them when I can."

"Three minutes left, Standartenführer," the SS man reminded him.

Through the window, Bora saw Mengs reading through paperwork. Surely, in his dull attention to detail, he wanted to study every line before signing off. But already another car came screeching, squirting icy mud. Hauptsturmführer Sutor must have followed the train, because there he was, alighting in a fury. Whatever the SD told him did not stop him. He tramped towards the train, unlatching his holster; within moments, his angry face showed at the carriage door.

Dollmann never lost his cool as he turned to him. "Sutor, you *annoy* me," was all he said, in a voice no different from what he had used with Bora. But to Sutor, he did point a silencer pistol in his chest and fired point-blank. "*Kaltenbrunner toady.* Come, Bora, we're on the left side of the train."

Stepping over the body, they reached the footboard. Near the track, invisible from the other side, a field-grey car was joining Dollmann's in the grass at the foot of the escarpment. "Army driver and plate. Your greatcoat, watch, pistol and holster are in the back seat," he said, then added meaningfully: "Your girl, the red-heeled beauty, wasn't the only one pining over your arrest."

"I don't think she loves me."

Dollmann shoved him down. "What do you know about unrequited love!"

"Eight minutes, Standartenführer," the SS man called behind him.

Bora clasped the collar of his tunic – a small, precise gesture. Above him, the sky was completely clear.